PRAISE FOR
COST OF ARROGANCE

"A complex courtroom drama, anchored by sharply drawn characters. In Caldwell's legal thriller, a law professor decides to represent an inmate on death row and finds it to be a daunting case. Caldwell's work shines in his ability to make the intricacies of the law accessible to laypeople while still satisfying those with legal experience."
— *Kirkus Reviews*

"This book is a must-read for any fan of courtroom thrillers. There is no stone left unturned when Jake Clearwater takes on a case. Author Caldwell certainly knows his subject matter and I look forward to reading more courtroom fiction by this author."
— Kristi Elizabeth, *San Francisco Book Review*

"A gripping novel about a former top prosecutor turned esteemed law professor who takes on a case to challenge the death sentence for a vicious, confessed, and convicted murderer. The trial details are accurate and dramatic reflecting the author's real-life experience as a prosecutor who now teaches law. I lost a night's sleep—I couldn't put it down."
—John Sharer, trial lawyer, Gibson Dunn & Crutcher, member of the American Board of Trial Advocates

"Law professor Caldwell knows whereof he writes and it blazes through every page. He does so in this novel with pinpoint legal prose, a razor-sharp wit and perceptive asides that turn humdrum courtroom battles into edge of the seat drama."

— Ivor Davis, Author of *Manson Exposed: A Reporter's 50-Year Journey into Madness and Murder*

COST OF ARROGANCE

TITLES BY H. MITCHELL CALDWELL

With Michael Lief and Ben Bycel
Ladies and Gentlemen of the Jury
Ten Greatest Closing Arguments in Modern Law

With Michael Lief
The Devil's Advocates
And the Walls Came Tumbling Down

With Tim Perrin and Carol Chase
The Art and Science of Trial Advocacy

With Terry Adamson
Criminal Pretrial Advocacy

With Gary Nichols and Sue Steding
California Ciminal Trialbook

With love to Kay and Joyce

COST OF ARROGANCE

A JAKE CLEARWATER LEGAL THRILLER

H. MITCHELL CALDWELL

COST OF ARROGANCE
Published by Nine Innings Press
First Edition 2021

Cover design: Jana Rade

ISBN: 978-1-7375123-2-5 Paperback Edition
         978-1-7375123-1-8 Hardcover Edition
         978-1-7375123-0-1 Digital Edition

Library of Congress Control Number: 2021913579

Author services by Pedernales Publishing, LLC
www.pedernalespublishing.com

10 9 8 7 6 5 4 3 2 1

Printed in the United States of America

xx-v11

CHAPTER 1

ELEVEN YEARS LATER

The large amphitheater-style classroom, with its ten rows gradually ascending away from the lectern, housed seventy-five third-year law students. The back rows were thinly populated, but the density of students gradually increased as it reached the front, as if closer proximity to the teacher would make the material more comprehensible. Those students who elected back-row status invariably reveled in their anonymity. The further away, their thinking went, the less likely to be called on. As I approached the front of the class, the murmuring silenced. Without any throat clearing, I called on a student in the third row. "Ms. Barnett, take this hypothetical." The game was afoot.

The seventy-four other third-year law students in Lecture Hall C visibly relaxed. Heather Barnett, a likeable, fresh-scrubbed twenty-something of USC vintage, tensed and listened to my hypo.

"A police officer on vehicle patrol at 2:15 a.m. sees a man dressed in dark clothing, wearing a bulky jacket, leaning against the wall of a twenty-four-hour convenience store. Upon noticing the officer, the man begins to walk away from the store and away from the officer. The officer gets out of his car and commands the man to stop. The man complies; the officer approaches and asks for identification." I watched her eyes, gauging her grasp of my hypo. She was right with me. "As the man reaches into his jacket, the officer grabs him, pushes him against the wall, and frisks him. The frisk reveals a packet of cocaine in the man's breast pocket." I paused. "Ms. Barnett, is the cocaine admissible?"

In a voice edged in anxiety, she began. "It seems as if the officer had just cause, so I guess he could arrest the man, making the cocaine admissible."

Poor start. My disappointment with her answer must have shown in my face, as her head tilted down and she peered over her stylish rimmed glasses, perhaps looking for an answer on her open laptop. "Let's back up," I said, as I moved up the side of the classroom toward her. She hesitated, apparently not clear on how to proceed. "Was this man seized?" I gently prodded. I had gone over how to approach this scenario in the previous class. *Come on, Heather, get it together.*

"Yes," she said tentatively.

"How do you know that?" Maintaining patience.

"Because of the officer's actions," her voice firming as comprehension dawned, "the man would not feel free to turn and walk away or even to ignore the officer's presence."

Better. Stay with her. "And how do we know that?" I moved closer to her.

Warming to the task, she answered, "Several things. The request for identification, the physical contact as the officer grabbed him, and then the frisk. The average reasonable person would surely feel intimidated and not free to walk away by such police action." *Not bad.*

I gave her a nod and began retracing my steps back down the aisle. "Since we have a seizure and therefore are required to undertake a Fourth Amendment analysis, what's our next step?"

She was ready. "We've got to know if the officer had reasonable suspicion for stopping the man." *Excellent.*

"Did he?" I rolled my hand encouraging her along.

"Well, it's a close call, but I think he did." Confidence had supplanted anxiety. "First of all, it's two fifteen in the morning, the guy is hanging out without any legitimate purpose, and it's at a typical robbery target. When the guy sees the officer, he takes off. It seems to me we've got enough objective facts to believe this suspect is engaged in criminal activity."

I nodded and looked at the class. "Anybody disagree?"

A flurry of hands went up. *It was easier being a volunteer than a draftee.* I called on Carlo Spigano. Spigano was one of the shadowy rebels who sat in the back row. Unlike his anonymous back-row mates who preferred anonymity, he enjoyed swooping down on a classmate with comments designed to humiliate and at the same time make himself look like he had some special insight. Law students have a term for students like Spigano; he was known as a gunner. "Go ahead, Mr. Spigano, make the defense case."

Spigano stood, a gesture not required. He turned from me and stared at Heather. "What if all this guy is doing is waiting for his buddy to get off work, or waiting for a lift home? There is nothing incriminating about hanging out at a convenience store at 2:00 a.m. If that were the case, I'd be in real trouble." Spigano's last comment elicited mild laughter, primarily from the denizens of the back rows.

Heather responded but directed her comments to me, ignoring Spigano's aggression. "What about his actions in taking off when the police arrived? Besides that, we're only talking about reasonable suspicion here. As the Supreme Court pointed out in *Terry v. Ohio*, the threshold for reasonable suspicion is much lower than required for probable cause." *Good for you, Heather.*

I stepped in. "Mr. Spigano, your suspect lifestyle aside, Ms.

Barnett is right. Reasonable suspicion isn't a difficult burden. And incidentally, if that was you outside the store, I hope you thought to bring your toothbrush; you'll need it in lockup." Mild laughter. Spigano was not well liked, and any rebuke of him was generally appreciated. I gave him a raised eyebrow, inviting him to respond. He looked away.

We went on for an hour, although it seemed half that. Class over, students began packing up their laptops, notebooks, and textbooks. I enjoyed the lively debate, the give and take. I had found my voice in the classroom and it was not to be that of a Kingsfield, that fictional law-professor–assassin depicted in print and on film. I had experienced several "Kingsfields" in law school and despised their peculiar brand of terror. While a pedagogic style that utilized intimidation and occasionally humiliation was the preferred method for some, I had detested it as a student and would never resort to it as a teacher. I was not above an occasional well-placed jab for the unprepared or mean spirited, but I never went for the jugular. *Not even with the Carlo Spiganos.*

It had been four years since I had joined the law faculty at Pacifico. My five-year stint as a trial prosecutor in San Arcadia, a midsized county two hours north of Los Angeles, had honed my abilities in the courtroom. During that time, I had evolved into a trial lawyer instead of person trying cases. I'm not saying that I was a Clarence Darrow or a Gerry Spence, but I did okay in the courtroom. Four years ago, Alvin Chauncey, the dean of Pacifico Law School, called and invited me to lunch to discuss an opening on the law faculty. As it turned out, that was pretty unusual. The typical hiring process involves candidates being subjected to a rigorous screening and then a "job talk" before the faculty. But because there was a very specific need for someone with a trial background, I got the first call. It probably didn't hurt that when I was a Pacifico student, I had

been Dean Chauncey's research assistant. We had stayed in touch, and I wasn't terribly surprised when he called. We agreed I would think it over.

In discussions with a couple of my prosecutor buddies, their various comments encouraged me to pursue the job. "For God's sake, Jake, people would kill for this opportunity. A law prof! It doesn't get much better than that. You'd be nuts to turn it down." They did not mention the Tice factor. Yeah, John Tice, the San Arcadia DA, my former boss, was an asshole. An asshole who had it in for me.

The Tice factor was the kicker. Tice had started as a prosecutor years before I joined the San Arcadia District Attorney's office. He had established himself as a solid trial prosecutor. He was a brilliant technician. His speeches—that is, his opening statements and closing arguments—were not great oratory but competently covered all the essentials, as did his direct exams. His cross-examinations, on the other hand, were brilliant. He could spot a weakness in a witness and would rip it open. And if a defendant dared testify on their own behalf, which didn't happen often in Tice prosecutions, only body parts would be left. If there was any criticism of Tice, and that was very muted, it was that he lacked charm. He did not develop a "relationship" with his jurors. He was cool and detached. Some lawyers, like the aforementioned Spence or Johnnie Cochran, had an ability to bond with their jurors almost as if their jurors were part of their extended family. Tice was aloof, but to his credit, his ability to milk the facts and effectively incorporate them into his examinations put him well ahead of most trial prosecutors.

By the time I joined the office, Tice was the go-to deputy DA. He was assigned the big cases, and he relished his role as the big dog. As a rookie prosecutor, I started where all rookies started, with drunk driving cases, petty theft cases, and an occasional minor drug case. They were the cases that constituted the learning ground. That's where mistakes could be made without substantial consequence. *And mistakes, I made.* But I learned from my mistakes and improved. Within two years, I had graduated to felonies. Along in about my third year, the supervising deputy district attorney was assigning me some of the more important cases, which, unbeknownst to me, had apparently generated Tice's ire. Tice accused me of politicking for the cases he figured were his due. It wasn't true, and I tried to explain that to him. He was unconvinced. This was the genesis of the ill will in our relationship. Office politics can be a nasty business, even if you keep your head low.

During what would turn out to be my final year in the office, the district attorney retired, and Tice ran for the job. He ran unopposed, and the day he was sworn in, I knew my career in the San Arcadia DA's office was headed for the ragged shoals. It was about that time that Dean Chauncey called.

CHAPTER 2

_____

THE CHALLENGE

I was humming an old Bob Dylan song as I made my way back to my office after class. That's right, Bob Dylan. I'm thirty-three years old and I'm humming an old Bob Dylan song. "Forever Young." That was my dad's favorite song. Says something about my dad, doesn't it? Says something about the relationship my dad and I had. *Damn, I miss him.*

Life as a prosecutor had been a series of mountains and valleys, crisis often piled on crisis, while my life as an academic allowed more personal freedom, more time to read, more time to write. But I had to admit, if only to myself, teaching was becoming a bit routine. God, I know it sounds unbelievable, but I guess I missed the stress of trials. It was strange, though, how even after four years of teaching, I still thought of myself as a trial lawyer. I stayed in touch with people I had worked with in the district attorney's office and vicariously reveled in their triumphs, at times longing for that rush that came with a jury trial. The lure of the courtroom was palpable. I suppose I was restless.

It was 5:35 that afternoon. The people from the Death Penalty Project were late. Since I had been contacted two weeks ago about representing a death-row inmate in appealing his conviction and death sentence, a whole range of thoughts had occurred to me. First off, am I nuts? A death penalty appeal? On a more rational level, I didn't think appellate work would fill the adrenaline gaps, but it would present intellectual and emotional challenges not present in academia. Unfortunately, it would also involve mean, grisly facts and a mean, grisly client. After all, we are talking about cases that merited the death penalty. At least as a prosecutor I was on the side of the angels. In retrospect, I was irritated with myself for agreeing to such a meeting. In a weak moment, I had agreed to meet with these people, and while I figured I would most likely not take on a death-penalty appeal, I would have to be polite before I could refuse.

A minute later, they were in my open doorway. One was a short blond woman in that vague thirty-five to forty-five age range, wearing a full, flowered dress in what appeared to be an attempt to disguise what looked to be a pear-shaped figure. The other was a young husky man. He was immaculately attired in a dark-gray three-piece suit with a red-and-black-striped tie. I uncrossed my feet from my desk, stood, and motioned them in.

The woman extended her hand. "Professor Clearwater?"

"The name's Jake."

"Charlotte Knight," she said, shaking my hand, "and this is Barry Sato." We shook hands around and I motioned them to sit. Knight arranged herself and her huge purse/briefcase and tucked several rolled-up charts next to her. Sato immediately went to the large window and gazed at the panorama of Malibu and the wave-swept Pacific.

"Beautiful campus. How do you ever get anything done up here?" Sato said.

"It's tough, but we manage," I replied good-naturedly. "I explained to your director that you were probably wasting your time flying down to see me." *Maybe a preemptive strike would get this thing over quickly.* "I've never done appellate work, and I've never tried a death-penalty case." I shrugged, looking only slightly apologetic. "I don't think I'm the person you're looking for."

"Professor Clearwater, just hear us out," said Knight. *My preemptive strike and my attempt to move to first names had both failed.* "Give us thirty minutes, and if you aren't interested, we're gone." I nodded without enthusiasm.

Sato picked up one of the charts and rolled it out on my desk. He said, "Twenty years ago, there were 325 people on California's death row, and everyone on the row had a lawyer for their appeal within one year of conviction. Ten years ago, there were 523 on the row, and only about 60 percent were represented within three years of conviction. Five years ago, there were 714 on the row, and only half had been appointed appellate counsel within five years of conviction." Sato referred to the chart that clearly depicted the information he relayed. *The chart wasn't necessary, but dammit, they had lugged it all the way from San Francisco, and he was going to use it.* "As of last week, we have 781 men and eight women on death row, and two-thirds of them are not represented." He again jabbed the chart to emphasize the import of his words. "Professor Clearwater, justice can't work like this. Justice delayed . . ." He trailed off. *Spare me from the zealots.*

"Death-penalty work sounds like a real growth industry," I said, in a flippant tone I regretted as soon as the words left my mouth. *Don't be a jerk, Clearwater.*

Sato looked perplexed by my insensitive comment, but Knight acted as if she had not even noticed. She picked up where Sato had left off. "Frankly, there just aren't enough qualified lawyers to represent everyone on death row. We've got plenty of lawyers who want the work, since it is compensated, but very few are qualified."

She paused as if inviting a comment. I didn't bite. "You are one of the qualified ones. There aren't many lawyers with your extensive felony experience, and now, as a law professor, you are unaffiliated and perhaps have the time and inclination."

"Well, it's nice to see that you've noticed that we law profs have time to burn, what with our cushy schedules." I teased her and smiled. *The reality, of course, was that I did have the time, if this happened to be where I wanted to use it.*

"I didn't mean that as a put-down," Knight said defensively. "The issue is one of commitment to a process, to the system."

"I know that wasn't a put-down, but let's get back to more practical considerations. Since my experience is as a trial lawyer, I'm not sure I'm qualified to represent someone appealing their death sentence."

Sato said, "There aren't many pure appellate lawyers, and the ones who work criminal cases have already been contacted. Some that were qualified came aboard and some didn't, but that still leaves us with a significant shortfall. We are now contacting people with extensive felony-trial experience who are no longer working in public law offices, to help fill that gap."

"There have got to be a lot of ex-prosecutors and ex-public defenders out there."

"There aren't as many ex-DDAs and ex-DPDs as there used to be, as I'm certain you know. So many government lawyers are now making it a career. It's not like it was even fifteen or twenty years ago," Sato countered. *Good point.*

I gave him a questioning look. "What makes you think I can do appellate work? I'm a trial lawyer."

He was ready for me. "Two things. First, it takes specialized knowledge of criminal trials to find and to recognize issues that develop at trial. Second, we've read your law-review articles. You write well and you have a balanced perspective." *I had been vetted and now I was being ego-stroked.*

As Knight and Sato played through their best hand, I remained skeptical; the nays resonating in my head continued to be in the strong majority.

It was Knight's turn again. In addition to being ego-stroked, I was being double-teamed. "We have a recording that we want you to see. This was filmed during a trial several years ago in San Arcadia, your former county. This took place before you started as a DDA there. It involved the death-penalty trial of Duane Durgeon. I'm sure you heard about it. *Of course I had. It was a notorious case and had generated enormous local press.*

"You want me to deal with a case from my former office?" I said, my antennae suddenly extended.

She nodded. "Just hear me out. This was recorded during the penalty phase. Durgeon, of course, had already been convicted of the double murders of a young couple. You are about to watch him testifying before the jury who would be deciding if he was to be executed or sentenced to life without the possibility of parole. Durgeon, against the advice of his lawyers, demanded that he be allowed to testify. His lawyers vehemently opposed his taking the stand, and if he did, they would refuse to participate and therefore wouldn't ask any questions. What you are about to see is a man talking directly to the jurors at the death-penalty phase of his trial without benefit of counsel. And, I add, urging the jurors to put him on death row."

"He was asking for the death penalty?" I was incredulous.

"That's right."

"While I had heard about the trial, I was unaware of the specifics. Other than that Tice had been the prosecutor." If it was a death-penalty case in San Arcadia, then Tice was the prosecutor.

"It's all on video. Can I play it for you?" Knight asked.

"You've got a recording? They don't let cameras in the courtroom in San Arcadia."

"It's a bootleg. Some guy surreptitiously recorded it on his cell phone."

Sato opened his laptop and set it in front of me. There was a head obscuring the right side and the picture wobbled from side to side. The shot opened on an empty witness chair next to an empty judge's bench. I recognized the courtroom. I had worked that courtroom. I flashed back to my first felony trial, a rape case. It had been in that courtroom. It had been part of my home turf. Indistinct, whispering voices were audible on the tape.

The shot panned right. There were two men sitting at the defense counsel table. One man had a head of perfectly white and beautifully groomed hair surrounding pink ears. The other head was golden brown and bald. I didn't recognize either head. The view pulled back to the right, showing the other counsel table. There sat Tice. Even from the back, there was no mistaking him. I could feel my pulse quicken. John Tice. The man who had put eight murderers on death row. He was sparse and thin with a fringe of black hair ringing an otherwise pale bald head. He wore a black suit. Black was his trial color.

Moments later, two uniformed bailiffs ushered in the main attraction. Durgeon was a big man, white, over six feet and easily 240 pounds, most of it on his shoulders and chest. He would probably have been considered good-looking during the Elvis era of the late '50s. His brown hair featured a pompadour with sideburns. His mustache was longer than the once-stylish mustaches favored by the *Sgt. Pepper*-era Beatles. He was the product of a different era. Dressed in dark slacks and a white long-sleeved dress shirt buttoned to the neck, he wore no coat or tie. He stopped as he entered the courtroom and stared menacingly at the two lawyers at the defense table. One of the bailiffs opened the gate to the witness stand and held it as Durgeon stepped in and sat. *He was a mean-looking sonofabitch.*

The judge entered and took her place of authority atop the bench. Judge Alise Harbarger. I had tried cases in front of her. She was no-nonsense, by the book. Ninety degrees was ninety degrees. Exactly.

With one whack of the gavel, Harbarger announced, "We are back on the record in People v. Duane Durgeon. The record will reflect that the jury is not present. Mr. Durgeon, his counsel, and the prosecutor are all present." Turning to Durgeon, the judge continued, "Mr. Durgeon, I have been in chambers with your lawyers and Mr. Tice. Your lawyers informed me that just before we took our last recess, you threatened to kill one of them."

Whoa, what a hard-ass.

Durgeon was staring down and did not react. "They further informed me that they feel they can no longer represent you and have asked to be relieved."

Durgeon raised his head and fixed his eyes on his lawyers. He started to speak, only to be cut off by the judge. "Sir, I don't want you to talk. I'll do the talking." She stared Durgeon down. "I think this is a ploy on your part to throw a monkey wrench into this trial. It's not going to work. You've got the only lawyers you are going to get. I will not declare a mistrial, I will not appoint new lawyers, and I strongly advise against any further threats or dilatory tactics."

Durgeon stared stoically at the judge, seemingly not the least chagrined by the dressing down. Harbarger went on, "Sir, your lawyers have informed me that you wish to take the witness stand and testify, is that correct?"

"Yeah." Durgeon's voice rumbled from deep in his chest.

"Your lawyers have informed me that they urged you not to testify and that you are doing so against their advice, is that correct?"

"Yeah."

"They have also informed me that, should you persist in this course of action, they will not participate." The judge waited. There was no response from Durgeon. "I'm going to allow you to make your statement without questions from your lawyers. Do you understand?"

"The less they *par-ti-ci-pate*"—Durgeon drew out the word in his deep baritone, looking scornfully at the defense lawyers—"the better off I'll be."

"You understand that once you have your say, Mr. Tice can cross-examine you?"

A slight smile wrinkled Durgeon's face as he looked at the prosecutor. "If Tice wants a piece of me, bring it on."

"One thing more before I bring back the jurors," Harbarger said. "Whatever threats you may or may not have made are for another hearing on another day. However, let me make it very clear that I will not tolerate any further disruptive behavior in my courtroom. Is that clear, Mr. Durgeon?"

"It's your courtroom, judge."

The judge nodded to a bailiff. "Bring in the jurors." The jurors filed in, most avoiding eye contact with Durgeon. One juror, however, an elderly Black man, looked directly at Durgeon as he took his seat in the jury box. Durgeon picked up the man's stare and held it. The juror finally broke off eye contact. Durgeon continued to stare at the man as if to make a point. The judge patiently waited for the four-man, eight-woman jury to get situated. "The record will reflect that we are back on the record, and that the jury has rejoined us. This is your opportunity to make your statement, Mr. Durgeon. Is it your desire to proceed?"

"Damn straight." *My interest was piqued.*

The clerk asked Durgeon to raise his right hand and swear to tell the truth. Durgeon with an ironic grin, "Nothing but the truth." He repositioned himself to make maximum eye contact with the jury, cleared his throat, and in his low gravelly voice, began. "I ain't much of a speaker, but there comes a time when the bullshit gotta stop."

I felt the hairs prickle on the back of my neck. *It was either a premonition of what was to come or a psychic chill emanating from Durgeon.*

"It's time to get things straight. You all know I am a badass sonofabitch. Those two assholes they call my lawyers don't know a goddamned thing about me or what I did or didn't do." Turning to Tice, "Hell, that shitty little ferret-faced prosecutor don't even know what happened. Shit, that prick couldn't find his ass with both hands."

Judge Harbarger, almost standing in her seat, shouted at Durgeon. "I will not have this profanity in my courtroom!"

Durgeon stood, returning ire with ire, his body arching toward the judge, his face a contorted mask. "Fuck you, judge. What are you going to do, kill me?" Bailiffs stepped to within arms' reach of Durgeon. The battle of wills between the judge and Durgeon cast a surrealistic pall over the courtroom.

With an obvious effort to control herself, the judge gritted, "One more display like that, and I put a gag in your mouth. I'm very serious. If you want to testify, you will do it civilly. Otherwise, I will cut you off right now. Is that understood?"

Durgeon broke eye contact and very deliberately brushed imaginary debris from the rail as he resumed his seat and began rocking his head and shoulders forward and back. He turned to the jury without acknowledging the judge. Carefully enunciating every word, he continued. "I ain't here because my conscience is bothering me, or because I can't live with my past. I don't give a—" Durgeon paused and grunted, "I don't care 'bout that. I've lived a mean life and enjoyed it. Hell, that rap sheet they read ain't the half of it. Got away with most of the shit I pulled. Been getting away with shit all my life. I know the jig's up, and I ain't talking about putting a nigger on the moon." The Black juror, who had had the silent encounter just moments before, pursed his lips. I'm thirty-six years old, and I ain't sorry for a goddamn thing." Durgeon's eyes flashed to the judge. "You have to excuse my language, judge. I only talk the way I know."

In a barely audible voice, Harbarger said, "Just get it over with."

Durgeon took another swipe at the rail, and turning back to the jury, continued. "I did my first killing when I was twenty-one. A man dissed me, so I killed him." He looked challengingly at the jurors to watch their reaction. "A year later, I hired out to kill some sorry sonofabitch. Shot him three times. Didn't feel nothin'. Made two thousand dollars for that. I spent the money on women and drugs, just pissed it away." The courtroom was absolutely silent.

"The third time, a guy walked in on me when I was robbin' his house, and I shot him. He twitched for a long time. Looked like a chicken after his head been cut off, not knowing he was already dead." Durgeon shifted in his chair, rubbing his chin as if to think what else he could lay on the jury. "Yesterday you heard from that boot-licker from that shithole of a prison in Utah where I did five years, that I was co-oper-a-tive about how I started that art school and how it was such good shit. I wasn't doin' that for nobody but me, that was how I got drugs in the joint. I squeezed the system. I used them fools. Hell, I didn't just use the system, I beat it like a drum. There wasn't one day went by in that shithole that I didn't have whatever drug I wanted. You heard I saved a guy's life while I was there? That's bullshit. It was me that stabbed him. There wasn't no way out, so I acted like I was helping him. I stabbed that poor fu—sucker, and he was too scared to say anything." He chuckled. *Good memories.*

Durgeon leaned back in his chair and began unbuttoning his shirt. The bailiffs nearest him tensed but did not move. He removed his shirt, revealing a sleeveless beater undershirt. His arms, shoulders, and neck were completely covered with tattoos. Durgeon pointed to his right forearm, turning his seat to bring his arm in view of the jurors, and pointed. "See that knife? I got that one when I stabbed a man to death. He was a faggot. I don't like faggots. I kill queers just because it's the right thing to do. I guess I'm not politically correct." He pointed to his left shoulder. "See this gravestone? It says R.I.P.N. You know what that stands for? Rest in peace nigger." He stretched "nigger" out, staring at the stoic Black Juror as he slowly and deliberately put his shirt back on and buttoned each button carefully.

"Hell, I ain't never going to spend any more time in prison, because you folks know you got to give me the death penalty because you don't like what I am." He gave a low laugh, a private insight. He motioned at his lawyers. "Them two assholes are trying to tell you I ain't had no upbringing, and I'm all screwed up because of drugs. That's crap. I am who I am because that's who I want to be. I beat the shit out of people just for the hell of it. I shoot people just for the hell of it. I do dope because I want to do dope. Ain't nobody caused me to be like this. I want to be like this."

Durgeon looked briefly at the ceiling before bending forward and refixing his eyes on the jurors. "You heard about mitigating circumstances." He gave a brief smile at such a weasel phrase. "That's bullshit; there ain't nothing mitigating about me. I'm tired of assholes telling me what I gotta do. I'm tired of nitpickers, fruit pickers, and dick lickers."

He paused and worked his eyes over the jurors. I felt a cold tickle down my back. "You send me to prison, I'll beat the system." He motioned at Tice. "He don't know nothing about this case. All he knows is that them people are dead. He thinks he knows what went down that night. He don't." His sudden turn on Tice didn't follow any logical path I could see. With a mean grin, Durgeon half rose out of his chair and yelled at the prosecutor. "I'd love to get my hands around your scrawny chicken neck! I'd wring you good."

Judge Harbarger exploded. "That's it. We are in recess! Get the jurors out of here now!"

Two bailiffs jumped to the jury box and hustled them off. Once they were removed, Harbarger turned on Durgeon.

"You are deliberately trying to create a mistrial by your threats and your language. But I'm not going to let you get away with it. Do you understand me?"

"Fuck you," Durgeon said, as spittle sprayed from his mouth.

The screen went blank.

We sat in silence. Finally, Sato spoke. "The person recording told me he got so unnerved, he hit the Stop button without realizing it. At any rate, that was the end. The judge had had it."

I leaned back in my chair. No one spoke.

I finally broke the silence. "How does Durgeon feel about things now? Has he changed his mind about wanting to be executed?" *For someone not interested, you're asking a lot of questions. Careful, Jake.*

"I don't know," Sato answered. "To my knowledge, no one at Death Penalty Project has talked to Durgeon. Even so, in looking at the bigger picture, his feelings concerning his own execution don't really matter. Somebody has got to represent him in his appeal."

I slowly shook my head and said, "Fascinating, isn't it? We have really concocted one hell of a system of justice. This guy is going to have an appeal, whether he wants one or not. And further, somebody is going to fight his conviction and sentence, whether he wants it or not."

"Professor Clearwater, we don't pick 'em," Knight said. "You know how it is. We just do the best we can, oftentimes under difficult circumstances."

I knew how it was. A death-penalty conviction is automatically appealed directly to the California Supreme Court. There is no discretion, and even under such rare and bizarre circumstances as when the condemned does not want to appeal his death sentence, it will happen anyway.

Again, I shook my head. "Even if I were inclined to accept a case, why wouldn't you bring me a person wrongly accused? Someone who is fighting their conviction with every breath, not some hard-ass who demands his own execution?" They looked at me without speaking. "And why," I wondered aloud, "a case from my old county?"

"To answer the last first, since this is an appeal rather than a trial, we didn't feel it would make any difference. And as to the other, Durgeon's been on death row without being represented longer than any other person. We can't get anybody to take him." *Big surprise that.*

I walked to the window and watched the late-afternoon wind whip the tops of swells into foam wash. A lone tanker was barely discernible on the horizon. I mused loud enough to be heard, "I wish I could feel the passion you feel in fighting these cases. I know that you're sometimes villainized for what you do, defending the worst our society can conjure up. Hell, some of these guys could have been scripted by Stephen King or Dean Koontz. To represent a Charlie Manson, a Ted Bundy, a David Berkowitz, or this guy"—I vaguely motioned at the laptop—"is about as difficult a job as I can imagine." I paused and shook my head, a little surprised at the depth of my feelings. "I admire that, but I'm not one of you."

I returned to my chair. When I was a prosecutor, I wanted to prosecute the "big" cases; you know, the career-builders. Toward the tail end of my career as a prosecutor, Tice in a very surprising move assigned me to prosecute a man who was accused of killing a grandmother and her granddaughter. For reasons none of my colleagues understood, Tice was passing on a capital case. I was initially flattered. I was just where I wanted to be: the apex of my career as a prosecutor, a high-stakes case, everything I thought I wanted as a big-time trial lawyer. Later on, I begged off that case. Some of that decision had to do with the death penalty. I didn't and still don't really know how I feel about it. The thought of a civilized society engaged in the business of execution is repulsive. But then the heinous nature of some of the crimes scream for revenge.

Knight began to speak, but I raised my hand to cut her off. "I'm sorry. I need a little time. Let me think about it." I surprised myself. Surprised that I had not refused flat out.

Knight and Sato looked at each other, packed up, shook my hand, and left. I sat alone in my fancy professor office, with my fancy professor view now dissolving into dusk.

CHAPTER 3

PUT UP OR SHUT UP

"Let's pick up our discussion of seizure," as the last students found their seats and the murmur quieted. It was a week after my meeting with the Death Penalty Project folks. I was leaning to a no but for some reason couldn't or wouldn't make the call.

"Mr. Reyes, help me out with this problem." Richard Reyes, an enthusiastic front-row student, immediately straightened in his seat. "Lacking probable cause and with only reasonable suspicion that the accused committed murder, two uniformed cops approach the accused and ask him to accompany them to the station house. The detainee reluctantly agrees and while at the station house blurts out an incriminatory remark. Over strenuous objection, the statement is introduced at trial. The accused is convicted and now appeals. As appellate counsel for the accused, frame your argument for excluding the statement."

Reyes nodded his head and began. "I would attack the confession on *Miranda* grounds. Since he was not given his rights, his statement was inadmissible."

I looked at him questioningly. "When must a suspect be

advised of their *Miranda* rights?" My follow-up question had shaken his initial self-assuredness.

"Any time a suspect is in custody?" His voice was halting, unsure . . .

Hands popped up around the room. "Ms. Caruso, help him out." Mavis Caruso was a gorgeous young woman from somewhere in the Midwest who spent too much time coming to my office. It is the Mavis Carusos of the world who can get guys like me in trouble. In my view, the students were hands off. *Not all my colleagues shared that view.*

"For *Miranda* to apply," she answered, "not only must the suspect be in custody, but the police must be questioning him. And since in your hypo the suspect blurted or volunteered the statement as opposed to responding to a question, the statement was not in violation of *Miranda*."

"You are right so far, so now let's go back to my initial inquiry. Frame the issue."

She thought for a moment. "The statement was the product of an unreasonable seizure and therefore inadmissible as fruit of the poisoned tree?"

"Okay, let's start there." *Not only beautiful, but she gets it.* "The police did have reasonable suspicion, so what's the problem with the seizure?"

Without hesitation, she answered, "Reasonable suspicion only allows the police to briefly detain someone to further their investigation. Here the guy was taken to the police headquarters. The police went beyond that brief detention. This was a full-blown arrest, and an arrest without probable cause is no good." *Right on the screws.*

Reyes, trying to regroup, jumped back in without being invited. "The suspect wasn't arrested; he voluntarily accompanied the police." With a note of satisfaction, he concluded, "No arrest, no problem, everything is admissible."

I gave him a shrug. "The only thing worse than an uninvited volunteer is an uninvited volunteer who's wrong." Reyes deflated; the class laughed. I gave Reyes a half smile; he knew it was not a malicious jab. "But since we're there, let's deal with Mr. Reyes's conclusion." Hands were up throughout the room, but I went back to Mavis. "Go ahead."

"A man reluctantly goes with the police to the station house, and you're saying he's not in custody?" She turned to Reyes. "A person can be under arrest without being in handcuffs or in a cell. This guy is entitled to the protection of *Miranda*. The statement is out." Her last sentence was uttered with the fervor of a closing argument.

"Opinions and speculations won't carry the day. I need some authority."

"*Oregon v. Mathieson*," she said, without missing a beat. "There, the police suspected Mathieson of burglary but lacked proof. One of the detectives called him and asked him to come to the station and clear up a few things. Mathieson drove to the station and was met by the detective. After they shook hands, the detective told him that his fingerprints were found inside the burgled home. Mathieson eventually owned up to the crime. The Supreme Court held the confession admissible because Mathieson was not in custody."

I kept pushing. "*Mathieson* doesn't seem to support your position."

"As you yourself have said, professor, *Mathieson* is a stretch. It is the outer limit of police conduct not found to constitute custody. And it seems to me, in your hypo, you have pushed beyond *Mathieson* to a custodial situation."

"How?"

"I think the key factor distinguishing *Mathieson* from your hypo is that Mathieson voluntarily drove himself to the station. I know the distinction is subtle, but the latter situation seems more coercive, a more pervasive sense of police heavy-handedness." *This woman was on fire.*

"Good, often the subtle nuances are the difference between admission and exclusion and ultimately between conviction and acquittal." I paused. "Incidentally, going back to *Mathieson*, the police told Mathieson that his fingerprints were found inside the burgled home. Were they?"

"No, they lied," answered Mavis.

"Was that proper?" I said, throwing the question to the entire class. There were no takers. So, I came back to Richard Reyes. I wanted to give him an opportunity to redeem himself. "Does the fact that the cop lied bear on our custody analysis or on our *Miranda* analysis?"

"I don't know. It doesn't seem right that the officer lied, but I don't see what bearing his lie has on either custody or *Miranda*."

"Your instincts are right," I said, nodding my head encouragingly. *I needed to throw him a bone.* "The police can lie with impunity, and it has no bearing whatsoever. Now, let's get back to our hypo. Let's assume Ms. Caruso is right and the confession is inadmissible. And further, that without the confession, the prosecution cannot proceed. Where do we go? Is this suspect bulletproof on the murder?"

Not a hand went up. In fact, most of the class was trying to look invisible. None dared make eye contact for fear I would call on them. *I remember that feeling when I was a student. Practiced anonymity.* I let the silence loom just beyond uncomfortable and then called on my best student. Most every class, thank God, has a go-to student, a person who invariably has a reasonable response, even if not always the correct response. And when the class is dead in the water, this is the person to get things moving again. Suzelle Frost was my go-to. "Ms. Frost, help us out. Where do we go from here?" She smiled shyly, and her face flushed a little.

Suzelle Frost was in her early twenties. Her grades placed her near the top of her class. She didn't wear her grades like an Olympic medal; she was gracious and well-liked by her peers. Her in-class analytical ability was as good as I'd seen. She leaned back in her chair and blew out some air. "I think the prosecution has a real problem. Could the police re-*Mirandize* the suspect and get him to confess a second time?"

"Let's go with that," I said.

"Well, I guess the argument would be that the second confession was the product of the first confession and would be the fruit of the poisoned tree and still inadmissible."

"If the second confession is the fruit of the first, inadmissible confession, is there any way to get a usable confession?" I asked. She was right on the edge of the solution.

"I don't think so. Whatever directly flows from the officer's error is inadmissible. It seems that the only way to get a subsequent confession is to somehow establish that it is completely independent of the officer's misconduct." *She was picking up momentum.*

"How can we establish that independence?" I asked.

"The passage of time might help to attenuate the taint," she offered.

"Perhaps. What else? How about the rest of you? Give Ms. Frost some help. Can you think of any other way we can attenuate the taint and allow in a second confession?"

Joshua Black, a young man who had not spoken all semester, tentatively and surprisingly raised his hand. "What if the officer told the suspect that the first confession was inadmissible, and the suspect, with full knowledge of his rights, confessed again?" he offered, in a very low, unsteady voice.

"You bet, that would be a strong factor in helping to purge the taint. Good job, Mr. Black. Now, how about the re-*Mirandization* of the suspect? The language in the warning itself informs that anything you say 'can and will be used.' The question of attenuation is going to be answered by reviewing all these circumstances: the passage of time, re-*Mirandization*, and even an explicit explanation that the first confession cannot be used."

I scanned the faces. Light was dawning. It was time to reverse the field. "Okay, let's go back and assume the confession is inadmissible, and that without the confession, the prosecution cannot proceed. Have we reached the difficult place where a confessed killer cannot be successfully prosecuted for the murder he committed?"

Reyes, undaunted by his previous failures, once again ventured into the fray. *His dogged determination, if not his analytic abilities, had to be admired.* "A system that would allow such an unjust result is flawed. We know this man's confession is truthful, the police didn't beat it out of him, and yet we can't use it? This is allowing a technicality to subvert justice."

This is exactly the place where I wanted to be. Now we would see what this group was made of. "That technicality you are referring to is the Fifth Amendment to the United States Constitution. But aside from that, if you were this man's lawyer, would you even hesitate to employ the full measure of the law to exclude that confession?"

"I would never be in that position," Reyes answered, with self-righteous indignation. "I would never represent someone who I knew had committed a murder."

"That begs my question. Would you hesitate to use the tools afforded those accused of crimes on behalf of your client?" I moved toward him. He wasn't going to get off that easy.

"I did answer your question." He met my eyes defiantly. "I would never be in the position where I had to make that decision. I just couldn't do it." *Had to admire his toughness in not backing down.*

I held his look as I stepped back. Continuing to hold his gaze, I opened my arms to the whole class. "How about the rest of you? How does the criminal defense attorney go about their job?" I began walking back to the front of the class. No response. "Hell, how does the criminal defense lawyer even sleep at night? How could Johnnie Cochran represent O. J.? When he took the case, he was confronted with overwhelming evidence of guilt. He knew O. J. slaughtered those two people. Yet he never faltered, never hesitated." *It was okay to refer to the Simpson trial. Even though some of the class was born after the trial, they all seemed conversant with the facts.* My voice was up; I was in closing argument mode. "In fact, he took the offensive and attacked the prosecution, attacked the police, attacked the victims. How can he take the money and prostitute himself and fight like hell for someone he knows viciously hacked two people to death?" The class pulled back; my fervor seemed to have intimidated them.

A back-row student, whose name I'd forgotten, had the nerve to speak up. "He was just a hired gun. Lawyers like Johnnie Cochran aren't concerned with truth and justice. I doubt if he lost one night's sleep over that verdict."

Mavis Caruso, without being called on, was nodding in agreement and said, "Professor, it offended me that Cochran picked a predominantly African American jury. To me, by playing such a blatant race card, he was subverting the whole criminal justice system."

"Is that right?" I answered. "There must be something wrong with a system that rewards people for raising roadblocks? Roadblocks that obstruct justice? Is that how you feel? Do you folks resent what Cochran did for O.J.?"

Stan Nelson, a clean-cut but otherwise indistinguishable student, spoke up. "I understand your point, Professor, about systems and all. But I'm not afraid to admit that I resented Cochran. He worked the system to an injustice."

I nodded my head, acknowledging their comments. I waited for more. When it was clear the class was spent, I said, "Do you people, you soon-to-be lawyers, have the luxury of these kinds of opinions? Lawyers have to accept the constitutional system that includes the Bill of Rights, and in particular the Fourth, Fifth, and Sixth Amendments. Those amendments contemplated an adversarial process in which the state would bring charges that must withstand rigorous scrutiny before someone could be convicted. That rigorous scrutiny demands that a lawyer put the state's case to battle, to prod it, push it, and even punch it. Is there no one to defend the right— no, the obligation—of a lawyer to use every ethical tool at their disposal in fighting for their client?"

An uncomfortable silence followed. Finally, John Pastor, an African American in his late twenties, raised his hand. I acknowledged him. Pastor had long since earned the respect of his peers. He did not speak often, but when he did, he had something worthwhile to contribute. *That alone stood him apart from half the class.* He stood and slowly looked around the room. "Is justice solely to be decided by the police, by the prosecutors, by public opinion? We know he's guilty, screw the proof. Why bother giving him a lawyer or a trial? It's the old lynch-law mentality. Why bother with all that constitutional crap?" He looked around at the faces that avoided his eyes. "You people make me sick."

You could almost hear people rethinking their positions on one of the fundamental questions confronting all law students, and ultimately, all lawyers.

In the heavy silence, John Pastor folded his laptop, gathered his books, stood, and walked from the room. The sound of the softly closing door punctuated his exit.

"Duane Durgeon," I said into the silence. "The State of California is set to execute a man named Duane Durgeon. He has been convicted of murdering two people. He appears to lack any redeeming qualities. But before California can execute him, they need to find him a lawyer for his appeal. Over the past couple of days, I've been thinking about his case and whether I should represent him. And I struggled with my decision. Frankly, I have come to miss the battle of the courtroom. I know it wouldn't be a trial, but it would be a battle. But what has taken place here today has made me realize how trivial and misguided my thinking was. Representing someone like Duane Durgeon is about a lot more than a law professor trying to inject adrenaline into his life. It's about why I became a lawyer. And why I think being a lawyer can, and should, be noble." Perhaps a quaint notion about lawyers. I followed John Pastor from the room. *The class be damned.*

～～～

Ten minutes later, I felt a presence in my office doorway and looked up to see Suzelle Frost, her face lined with worry. "Do you have time for me?" I motioned her to a chair. "I feel badly about what I didn't say in class. I really do believe what you and John were saying. I should have said something, I should have stood up."

"Join the club," I said. "Until today, I had pretty much decided to pass on this death-penalty thing. But today was 'put up or shut up' time for me. It's one thing to talk, and another to do." I looked at that honest, sweet, intelligent face and made a decision that would affect the rest of my life. "Our client was convicted of executing a young man and his wife. The facts are horrific. Make no mistake, he is an awful guy."

Suzelle flashed a puzzled look. "*Our* client?"

"He's been on death row for years. I saw a recording of his testimony at trial, and he looks and talks even worse than you can imagine, exactly like a man who should be on death row." Her eyes were open wide, her lips slightly apart as she listened. "I need a law clerk."

Her open mouth instantly became a dazzling grin. "I'm in."

CHAPTER 4

THE CLIENT

One week later, I landed in Oakland at about 10:00 a.m. It was an overcast October day. I rented a midsize Chevy that drove like a compact and went northeast on Interstate 880 through Oakland toward the Richmond Bridge and San Quentin State Prison. As I left downtown Oakland, I began working through what I intended to accomplish with Durgeon at this first meeting. How would he react to a former prosecutor? How would he react to anyone appointed to represent him? He had demanded his own execution. But that was years ago. Had he mellowed? Not likely. Gotten meaner? Possibly . . . probably.

At the Richmond Bridge, I paid the toll and, at the crest of the bridge, got my first view of San Quentin. This odd structure did not look like one of the most foreboding and infamous prisons in the country. Sitting next to the San Francisco Bay, it looked like it had been built simultaneously by four different contractors. The compound was painted a faded mustard color broken by sections of army green, which gave way at random places to faded brick. *Government issue, through and through.*

At the base of the bridge at the turnoff to the prison was a cluster of family homes that could have been from any small town in America. It struck me as odd that folks would choose to live in the shadow of such a place. I had learned from a google search that this little burg was originally built for the guards and support staff that served the prison but was now home to the retired, lured by the depressed housing costs courtesy of a prison-dampened housing market. Houses in San Quentin Village are not a hot item; the address frightens off potential buyers. I had learned that unlike the rest of Marin County, which had been transformed from rural enclave to strings of prosperous and high-priced suburbs, little had changed over the years in San Quentin Village.

I followed the sign to the visitor's parking lot. As I parked, a woman carrying an infant and leading a toddler by the hand was walking toward a low, narrow building near the prison gates. I followed. Inside, a ragged line of women, infants, and small children extended down the long corridor. They eyed me as I entered. *Do I stand in line with everyone else? Do I get special treatment because I am a lawyer?* I opted to stand behind the woman I had followed in. After a while she turned to me. "Lawyers don't wait; you go on up there," motioning to the front of the line. *I had always hoped I didn't look like a lawyer. But I was the only person in a suit.*

Through the glass doors, I could see two guards talking. I tapped on the window. They looked up briefly and indifferently resumed their conversation. *Maybe I didn't look like a lawyer after all. Or maybe I did and that explained the complete indifference.* I stood at the door, trying not to look self-conscious, and waited. It was a bit awkward. But in a matter of minutes, whatever interest I had generated among the visitors had already begun to ebb, as their good-natured chatter once again resumed. It seemed as if they all knew one another. The good spirits of the women, especially when you considered that their men were incarcerated in one of the toughest prisons in America, was surprising. But then again, what should they have been doing? Tearing their clothes and rolling in ashes? It was as if church had just let out, and they had gathered for a Sunday afternoon picnic.

The door buzzed. I entered, was asked for identification, filled out a visitor's request, and stood with my arms out as a wand was passed over my body. I was processed through a heavy metal-and-glass door that ushered me into the prison yard, and as instructed, I followed a yellow line to a small outbuilding a couple of football fields away. I felt like Alice falling down the rabbit hole, or more likely, Dorothy being whisked away to the witch's castle.

On reaching the outbuilding located at the base of an imposing twenty-five-foot chain-link fence topped with curls of razor ribbons, a guard checked my ID again. I was passed through another gate and directed to a red door another football field away. There, I entered a reinforced Plexiglas cage where, after the door had closed behind me, another Plexiglas door slid back, allowing me to pass through. I again showed my ID and was directed to cubicle number one. The hallway was lined with affixed metal stools stationed at small, round windows. Several of the windows were filled with the faces of inmates across from their visitors. There was no privacy. The visitors and the visited were talking on phones that hung next to the portholes. No one paid me any attention.

I was ushered past the stools into a small cubicle. Apparently, attorney-client visits get the cubicles. A chair had squeezed into the visitor's side. The wall separating lawyer from client had a three-by-four-foot reinforced window. The phone on my side dangled from its line. Ten minutes passed before the door on the other side of the glass opened and I had my first in-person look at my client. His appearance was radically different from what I had viewed on the recording. His unkempt hair fell to his shoulders, and he had grown a full, gray-streaked beard. Was this the real Durgeon? Had he just slicked up for his trial? Hard to figure. Did it matter? He was heavier and taller than I recalled from the recording. *Weren't you supposed to lose weight in prison? I made a mental note to check his mug shot and other intake info.*

He remained standing with his arms behind his back as the guard removed his handcuffs. He rubbed his wrists as he studied my face and then stepped into the cubicle and sat. The door behind him closed. Our faces, separated by glass, were no more than three feet apart.

I picked up the phone and held it until he picked up. "My name's Clearwater, and I've been appointed by the court to represent you."

He grunted and said, "I figured you're my new suit." His voice was deep, bored, and indifferent. *This was just another of life's little annoyances. Yesterday your shoelace broke, this morning you meet your death-penalty lawyer, tomorrow your goddamned soup is cold.*

Abruptly, he became agitated. "Ever been on the row before?"

The sudden shift was disconcerting. "No."

"Let me tell you what a fucking joyride the last forty minutes been. Your visit takes a piece out of me. They take me from my house, they cuff my wrists and my ankles. They shake me down. Do you know what that is?"

"I've got a fair idea."

"Well let me give you the San Quentin Death Row version." He leaned forward, his face about two inches from the glass. "You're stripped, your clothes are searched, and they body cavity you. Damn if that ain't a hoot." He stared at me. "All that to see some fucking goddamned lawyer."

I paused briefly and responded in kind. "And a fine fucking goddamned lawyer I am." *Fuck this asshole.* I forced a grin and met his stare.

It seemed as if our ninety-second-long relationship was at a critical stage. He would either blow me off like he had done with the judge and jurors at his trial (my money was here) or he would loosen up (the long shot). His face provided no early insight. His mouth was a straight line. His eyes looked as if they were trying to probe my head for signs of life. Then the line of his mouth and the corners of his eyes creased ever so slightly. The trace of a smile that I suspected was long dormant percolated up through years of hard-boiled attitude, and he said, "I like a man with balls."

Some of the tension left our small space. He gave it a moment and then said, "Yeah, well, things ain't changed. I still want 'em to pull the plug. To drain me. What's it going to take for the bastards to do me?" I took the last as a rhetorical question and didn't answer. He wiped imaginary stuff from the small shelf beneath the window and looked off to one side, rocking back and forth slightly. It was the same habit I had noticed on the recording. "Just do your thing and let me be. My life is my house, my TV, and my jerk-off magazines. I don't need no suit to hold my hand. I hate my time getting fucked up."

He turned part-way around and thumped the door twice with his elbow. "I'm through here." The door opened. He stood and put his hands behind him. He was cuffed and led away. *A brilliant start indeed.*

అలలల

I sat at my desk on a cloudy Wednesday afternoon, trying to focus on the law-review article I was writing. The working title was "Primary, Regency, Ethos, and Pathos: Incorporating Communication Technique into Direct Examination." I'd learned to have fun with the pomposity of titles of law-review articles. They were usually the only part of the article that got read. Now that I'd agreed to take on

Durgeon's appeal, my motivation to finish the article had waned. The view from my office offered a spectacular view of the ocean and hills.

I felt someone in the open door and looked up at Howard. He walked in and stretched out on my office couch. *I guess we were going to visit now.*

I leaned back and plopped my feet on my desk. Soon it was the NBA, the backstory about the newest visiting professor, and who we thought might be "interested" in Vera, one of the new administrative staff members. Vera had beautiful olive skin, black hair, and seductive flair. As if on cue, the object of our discussion walked past the open door, and talk ceased as we admired the bounce of her white crossover blouse and the flash of leg under a short skirt. Under lowered lashes, she slid a sideways look at us, and a half smile curled her lips.

Howard Alexander had a pale wide face and low forehead. He wore green contact lenses, checkered sports coats, and horrible op-art ties. I had never seen ties like his for sale anywhere. He was a bit arrogant and sometimes argumentative, with a razor-sharp mind. He was also as loyal a friend as I'd ever had.

As Howard resumed the couch, Tony Martin strolled into the office and sat on the edge of my desk with a distracted smile on his face that let us know he had passed the charming Vera in the hall. Tony was tall, good-looking, tan, in his mid forties, and always dressed sharp. He favored custom-tailored suits and bowties. Tony, my Mensa–Harvard friend, was my sounding board. I valued his opinion. Unlike me, he never acted without careful deliberation. While at times his style was a bit much, I appreciated his thoughtful advice. That doesn't mean I always followed his advice, but I did appreciate it. Tony was also my landlord. He was born into money and he and his wife, Eve, lived in a three-story beachfront in Malibu. They leased the third story to yours truly.

Tony's hair, usually immaculately coiffed, had been buzzed. It gave him a whole new look. His face looked leaner, almost hawk-like, and his nose and ears had suddenly become more prominent.

"Had your nose enlarged over the weekend, I see," Howard said snidely. *Howard left nothing unsaid.*

"Go to hell," Tony replied mildly.

"Eve likes your new nose—uh, haircut?" Howard was relentless. Tony didn't bite. I was disappointed. When so inclined, Tony could more than hold his own with Howard. Howard sighed. He was disappointed too. Howard sat up and picked through the fruit bowl I always kept on my side table, like a squirrel digging for nuts. "Where're the grapes? Last time you had grapes." He settled for the last apple.

Tony took a chair and was about to say something when Howard interrupted. "Have you two heard the latest Renick story?" He immediately had our attention. Helen Renick, a lifelong friend of Dean Chauncey's wife, had been forced to climb back into the professional world when she and her husband parted after thirty-five years of disappointment. As one of the dean's administrative assistants, she was living proof of the Peter Principle; she had somehow been promoted to a job completely beyond her level of competence. Her numerous gaffes became the stuff of instant legend, from keeping the chief justice of the United States Supreme Court on hold for ten minutes to scheduling not one, not two, but three classes to meet in the same classroom at the same time. Perhaps Helen had transcended the Peter Principle to an even loftier plane: the Renick Principle. If you are going to screw up, do it in a memorable way. Yet despite her frequent setbacks, Helen Renick was cheerful, fearless, and completely unaware of her remarkable failures. *Ignorance is bliss, right?*

"Okay," Howard said, hunching over in his eagerness to tell the story. "Remember the faculty meeting when we reviewed petitions for readmissions for students whose grades fell below the requirement?" We nodded. Every year the students whose grade point average dropped to a C- were academically dismissed. However, they had the right to appeal to the faculty to get reinstated. "Well, one of the students we denied was John Riles. You remember Riles? Rowdy, bit of a wild man, likeable guy. But it was a unanimous denial; his grades were south of Chile." We nodded, we were with him. "Renick, bless her heart, sent him the wrong letter. Not the 'you are out of here' letter, but the 'you are back in school but on probation' letter."

Tony and I groaned. "What a terrible mess for someone to have to clean up," I said.

Tony quickly added, "'Sorry, John old pal, we were just kidding. Actually, you're out of here. Don't let the door hit you in the ass.'"

"It's hard to believe nobody caught it," I added.

"Not until now, which I point out is months post decision," Howard said.

"What did the dean do when he found out?" I asked.

"Nothing," Howard smirked. "When Chauncey found out, it had been so long, he didn't have the heart to tell Riles."

"He just let it go?" Tony asked in amazement.

"That's right," Howard said, pleased that his story had gotten the proper response. He added, "And from his grades this semester, it looks like he's going to make it."

We all laughed, shaking our heads. "And so the Renick legend grows," Tony said.

Howard wasn't quite through. "Riles is now being affectionately referred to as 'The Renick Scholar.'" *Watch this guy go forth and set the world on fire as a lawyer.*

We were still laughing when Suzelle Frost appeared at my door, loaded with transcripts. She staggered with her load to my desk and, apparently oblivious to Professors Alexander and Martin, let everything slide onto the desk. Her blond hair was pulled back into a ponytail, making her ears stick out slightly. She was as slim as a teenaged boy. I sighed and looked at a long evening in the making.

"I take it that you and Ms. Frost are underway on your appeal," Tony observed.

"Indeed we are. Any volunteers?"

The room quickly cleared of all idlers.

CHAPTER 5

THE INVESTIGATION

Appeals from death-penalty convictions in California are heard by the state's top court, the California Supreme Court, bypassing the intermediate court of appeals. The court has been very tough on death-penalty appeals. Over the preceding five years, only one conviction had been reversed for a new trial, and that was on an ineffective-assistance-of-counsel claim. In that case, the lawyer had slept through big chunks of trial. Yeah, that's right, the guy had actually fallen asleep during testimony. *Tough to make objections when you're asleep.* In several other cases, the court had upheld the conviction but struck down the death sentence. In those cases, the penalty phase had to be retried. Realistically, even before I began reviewing the trial transcripts, I knew the chances of winning Durgeon's appeal and earning him a new trial, were, at best, remote. The reality was that, for the most part, his appeal was a mere formality on his way to execution. It could be said that I was just a necessary cog on the wheel that would grind him toward his death, which apparently was Durgeon's desire.

The transcripts for Durgeon's trial consisted of 6,652 pages of testimony, 3,306 pages of clerk's transcripts, and another three boxes filled with police reports, various witness accounts, and assorted materials, as well as newspaper accounts of his trial. As Suzelle and I read and organized, we took copious notes. It was the hope that, through careful reading, we would not have to go back and reread material once we turned to the actual drafting of the brief.

With the boxes came a letter from the court informing that the opening brief must be filed ninety days from receipt of the transcripts. I called Charlotte Knight from the Death Penalty Project. She told me that was, of course, unrealistic, and everybody, including the court, knew it. Nonetheless, the court had decided that the pressures of deadlines would spur advocates to quicker action. She explained that 180 days was the real drop-dead date. *The wonders of bureaucracy.*

Suzelle and I developed a routine in which we arrived at my office on Mondays, Wednesdays, and Fridays at 6:00 a.m., and we would work on the case until my criminal procedure class at 9:40. Tuesdays, Thursdays, and Saturdays were my swim mornings. The first couple of days, I brought in large coffees for us; but somewhere in the second week, Suzelle started bringing in some juiced concoction she made. I was hesitant at first, but it tasted better than the individual ingredients she used. *I could do healthy.*

Within four weeks, we had finished reading the transcripts and had developed an issues list. In doing so, several points about the trial stood out. First, this was the most sensational and grisly murder case to ever hit the greater San Arcadia area. I was already aware of that from the talk around the DA's office when I first started. An entire box of newspaper clippings, most from the front pages of the local papers, detailed the murders, the investigations, and finally the arrest, trial, and conviction of Durgeon. Second, Durgeon, as I already surmised, was a terrible man. That diatribe I had watched, in which he had delivered to the jury the details of his criminal career, was accurate. His entire life had been devoted to the pursuit of drugs and the infliction of harm on other human beings. Third, Durgeon's attorneys—especially his lead counsel, Dick Rosenblatt, though he hadn't slept through testimony—had done a poor job. Fourth, the prosecution's case against Durgeon consisted of the testimony of Durgeon's ex-girlfriend, a partial fingerprint identified as Durgeon's found on a piece of duct tape used to bind one of the victims, and the probable murder weapon, which Durgeon had access to. And not to be overlooked, was most likely Durgeon's sparkling presence, sitting day after day in front of the jurors. *Hell, that might have been the most compelling factor.*

As I read the police reports, the picture surrounding the murders of Doree and Robert Blanco and the subsequent investigation unfolded. In response to a 911 call, the first officer arrived at 5:00 a.m. and found Doree's naked body wrapped around six-day-old Jessica. The babe was unharmed. Doree had died from two gunshot wounds to the head. Inside the Blanco apartment, Robert's body, also naked, lay in a lake of blood and tissue. His muscled, conditioned body was at grotesque angles, with his head, nearly decapitated, bent over his left shoulder. Robert's hands and ankles were bound with electrical wire, which had eaten into the flesh.

The day following the murders, the police arrested a man named Anthony Graves, a convicted rapist who lived in a dilapidated trailer a block or so from the site of the murders. One of the Blanco neighbors told police that she had seen Graves at the front of the apartments where the Blancos lived about 8:00 a.m. the day before the murders. That fact, coupled with a very generalized eyewitness description of the shooter, led police to question Graves. Graves was a big man with shoulder-length hair and a full beard.

Ron Evans, the witness to the execution of Doree, had made the 911 call and had described the shooter as big, over six-foot, with shoulder-length hair and a full beard. Evans was uncertain from looking at a mug shot of Graves whether he was the shooter. However, the day after the murders, when Evans was ushered into Graves's interrogation room, Evans identified Graves as the shooter.

Following Graves's arrest, the police interviewed his live-in, who claimed that she and Graves had spent the entire night and following morning in their double-wide. Apart from Evans's identification, no other evidence was developed implicating Graves. After three weeks in custody, Graves's lawyer insisted that charges be filed or that his client be released. Reluctantly, Graves was released. The investigation continued, but no other evidence implicating Graves surfaced.

As I compared the police report of Evans's identification of Graves as the shooter with the trial transcripts, I was surprised that Durgeon's lawyers had not called Evans to testify to his ID of Graves. From what I could ascertain, this appeared to be a powerful piece of evidence pointing to somebody other than Durgeon. *Reasonable doubt is the defense lawyer's best friend.* Yet the jury never heard about the Evans ID. Why? What reason could there have been for Rosenblatt not to use the evidence?

A week after the murders and on a completely unrelated matter, the police, armed with search and arrest warrants, kicked in the door to Christina Atwell's house, looking for narcotics. The ensuing search uncovered a methamphetamine lab in one of the bedrooms. Arrested in the house with Christina were Durgeon and her son, Danny. When the police broke down the bathroom door, Durgeon and Danny were flushing gallon containers of meth precursors. Durgeon had been living with Christina since his release from a Utah prison months earlier.

The police turned Christina's house upside down. Included with the drug contraband were two rifles and three revolvers. One of the revolvers was a .22 caliber. All the weapons were tagged and placed in evidence bags. However, in one of those quirky circumstances that so often color big cases, the .22 caliber revolver—the one the police would eventually conclude was the weapon used to murder Doree—was inadvertently left behind, sitting on the kitchen counter in a police evidence bag.

Following her arrest, Christina, flush with money from her lucrative dope sales, made bail for her and Danny. Curiously, she did not post bail for Durgeon. Durgeon, as it developed, was never to be free from custody again. When Christina returned home, she found the revolver the police had left. Thinking the police might discover their mistake and return to retrieve the gun, she wrapped it in a plastic sheet and hid it under some bricks in a tool shed in her backyard. She hid the gun, she would later testify, because it was unregistered.

Meanwhile, the investigation of the Blanco murders was at a standstill. Other than Graves, no suspect had been developed. One witness had come forward and told the investigators that he had seen Robert talking with some men—he wasn't certain if it was two or three—outside the Blanco apartment at about 10:30 p.m. on the night of the murders. His view was from across the street, and he was unable to provide any other description of the men, nor could he supply any detail beyond that it appeared they were talking.

During the home invasion leading to the murders, the Blanco apartment had been torn apart. Drawers were dumped, mattresses and pillows had been cut open. Clothes, towels, diapers, and kitchen utensils were strewn about. Packing boxes had been ripped open.

Two months following Durgeon's arrest in the dope raid at Christina Atwell's house and with Durgeon still in custody, Christina called the San Arcadia Police and asked to speak with a detective

H. MITCHELL CALDWELL | 47

handling the Blanco homicides. That afternoon, Detective Harley Manlow, a twenty-two-year veteran of the department, met with Christina. With her permission, he recorded their conversation:

> Manlow: This is Detective Manlow of the San Arcadia Police Department. I am recording my interview with Christina Atwell. Ms. Atwell came forward on this date, claiming to have information concerning the Blanco homicides. Go ahead, Ms. Atwell.
>
> Atwell: I think I know who killed them people.
>
> Manlow: You are referring to Doree and Robert Blanco?
>
> Atwell: That's right.
>
> Manlow: Go on.
>
> Atwell: I'm pretty sure it's a guy used to live with me. He was staying with me when we got busted for meth.
>
> Manlow: I know about the bust.
>
> Atwell: Well, then you know who I'm talking about, don't you?
>
> Manlow: Duane Durgeon.
>
> Atwell: That's him.
>
> Manlow: Why don't you tell me what you know?
>
> Atwell: Not yet. I've got my ass and my son's ass to worry about first.
>
> Manlow: You're referring to the meth charges pending against you and your son?
>
> Atwell: Of course I am.
>
> Manlow: If you got something worthwhile for me, we can work something out.
>
> Atwell: This ain't my first rodeo, detective, and your word alone ain't getting it done.
>
> Manlow: How do you want to do this?
>
> Atwell: I want my lawyer in on it and I want it in writing.

In return for her cooperation, Christina and Dan Atwell's felony charges would be referred to the drug diversion unit of the probation department, and after twelve months of clean living, the charges would be dropped. The deal was contingent on Christina's cooperation leading to Durgeon's arrest for the murders.

Following up on Christina's disclosure, Manlow learned that Durgeon had been released from a Utah prison ten months prior to the murders. Durgeon had done five years for kidnapping and robbery. On his release, he had received permission from his probation officer to locate in San Arcadia and report to the local probation office. Durgeon moved in with Christina and had not surfaced on any police radar screens until the meth arrest at Atwell's.

Manlow, of course, also taped the second interview with Christina after the deal had been struck:

Manlow: This is the second interview with Christina Atwell concerning the Blanco murders. What do you have for me?

Atwell: Just before them folks was killed, me and Duane had seen them.

Manlow: Are you talking about Doree and Robert Blanco?

Atwell: Let me back up. We weren't getting along so good. I told Duane he had to move out.

Manlow: How'd that go?

Atwell: You don't want to know. I threatened to call his probation officer if he wouldn't get out. Anyways, I told him I would help him find some place. I knew the rent was cheap out at that converted motel, so I drove him out there. He didn't have a car.

Manlow: Go on.

Atwell: It was that couple who got killed that were the

managers. They were nice folks. They invited us in to look over the apartment, said that all the units were the same. We talked about the rent. They were packing up, said they were moving out, but they would still be the managers.

Manlow: And that was when?

Atwell: Two days before the murders.

Manlow: Go on.

Atwell: The night of the murders, he got all slicked up and took off with Dan and one of his friends.

Manlow: I take it you didn't go with them?

Atwell: No, it was boys' night out. At least that's what he told me.

Manlow: Where was he going?

Atwell: I didn't ask. All that would've got me was a backhand.

Manlow: What time did he leave?

Atwell: Eight, eight thirty.

Manlow: What did you do once he left?

Atwell: Hung out, watched TV, smoked a little shit.

Manlow: When did you see him again?

Atwell: He came home around six thirty or so the next morning. He looked like he just took a shower. His hair was wet and slicked down.

Manlow: Did he say where he had been?

Atwell: No, and I wasn't about to ask.

Manlow: Who does he usually hang with?

Atwell: When he's out catting around, he's usually with Todd Rode.

Manlow: Where can I find Rode?

Atwell: Last I heard, he was living out by the university. I don't have no address.

Manlow: How about your son, Dan? Do they ever hang together?

Atwell: Dammit, Danny's not part of this. Danny worked with me a little, you know, with the meth and all, but he wasn't any part of Duane's shit.

Manlow: All right, let's talk particulars. What do you know that links Durgeon to the murders?

Atwell: The gun started me thinking.

Manlow: What are you talking about?

Atwell: When the three of us got busted, they found my guns. But when I made bail and got home, the .22 was in the kitchen in a police bag. It looked like one of your guys bagged it and forgot to take it.

Manlow: An evidence bag?

Atwell: That's what I said.

Manlow: What did you do with it?

Atwell: I buried it under some bricks in the shed out back.

Manlow: Why?

Atwell: It wasn't registered. I don't need no more trouble.

Manlow: Still there?

Atwell: Nope, I threw it over the cliff at Ragged Point. Let me explain. The same day I got released and found the gun in the kitchen, I went to the jail to see Duane. When I told him about the gun, he freaked.

Manlow: About the gun?

Atwell: Yeah. I asked him, "What's it to you?" He looked around to see if anybody was paying attention and whispered, "Lose that fuckin' gun." I asked him what he was talking about and he said, "It's about them people that got killed." Right away I knew he was talking about that couple. I asked him what he knew about it, but he wouldn't say nothing. I went home, dug out the gun, and drove to Ragged Point and threw it as far as I could.

Manlow: What happened next?

Atwell: I went back to see Duane the next day. He didn't ask how I was doing or nothing, he just wanted to know about the gun. When I told him what I did, he said, "That's good."

Manlow: No more discussion about the gun?

Atwell: Nope.

Manlow: That was a while back. Do you still visit him?

Atwell: Some, but mostly we talk on the phone.

Manlow: What do you talk about?

Atwell: Just personal stuff. He's still kinda pissed that I didn't bail him out. But I told him I was tapped.

Manlow: You didn't bring up anything about the murders?

Atwell: You never met Duane. He's a scary dude if he feels like someone is screwing with him. I just wanted to leave things be. He wasn't going to be in jail forever, and I didn't want him looking for me.

Manlow: You got anything else that ties Durgeon to the Blancos?

Atwell: Just that sick feeling in my stomach.

Manlow: That's not enough to charge him. We need more. Let me talk to the DA, maybe we have you wear a wire and get him to talk.

Atwell: I told you. He won't talk about it. I can't get nothing out of him.

Manlow: Listen, we have a deal, and as part of that deal, you've got to fully cooperate. You back out now, and those felony charges against you and Dan are back.

Manlow ordered county search and rescue to join him at Ragged Point, where they searched the tide pools at the base of the point. At low tide, they found a .22 caliber revolver. It was badly corroded by the two-month exposure to the ravages of the Pacific. However, the DOJ analyst was able to determine that the bullets recovered from Doree's body were "consistent" with bullets that could be fired from that gun. He could not make a definitive finding that the fatal bullets had been fired from that gun.

Three days later, Manlow instructed Christina on the use of the wire that had been strapped to her chest for the jailhouse visit. The following is the Atwell–Durgeon exchange.

Durgeon: Hi babe. It's been a while.

Atwell: Yeah, I know. How they treating you?

Durgeon: Like shit. My food's cold. I'm in my cell twenty-three hours a day. Something's in the wind, though. You didn't hear nothing?

Atwell: No babe. It's probably just about your parole from Utah.

Durgeon: I don't know. Ain't anybody come back to your place looking for the gun?

Atwell: No. I don't think they even remembered about it.

Durgeon: You did right, getting rid of it.

Atwell: You told me it was important, so I tossed it.

Durgeon: Fuckin' right it's important.

Atwell: I know babe, you told me. How come it's a problem?

Durgeon: You don't need to know that. That's enough about that.

Atwell: Okay, I'm cool.

She then moved the conversation to safe ground. They visited another half an hour until the guard cut them off.

With new momentum, Manlow and his team went back and reanalyzed everything from the Blanco apartment. Nothing new developed. However, a partial fingerprint found on a piece of tape dangling from Doree's wrist, which the analyst had initially been unable to account for, had several points of commonality to Durgeon's right little finger.

That partial fingerprint was damning. Rosenblatt had done little at trial to attempt to minimize its impact. He did engage in an unenthusiastic cross-exam of the prosecutor's print analyst, but with little success. The fingerprint evidence was virtually uncontested. It was a festering, if not fatal, wound on the hide of the defense case. At first, I resigned myself to the fact that it was a piece of evidence without a plausible defense alternative. It was only later, while reading Christina's testimony, that I learned that Christina and Durgeon had been to the Blancos' apartment prior to the murders. And better yet, the Blancos had been packing for their move. *A plausible alternative explanation?*

The following day, Durgeon was charged with the murders of Doree and Robert Blanco.

CHAPTER 6

DURGEON'S EPIPHANY

Los Angeles Times, December 8, 2015
MORRIS EXECUTED

SAN QUENTIN (AP) — *After an extraordinary bicoastal duel between the US Supreme Court and the Ninth Circuit Court of Appeals kept his fate in doubt through the night, Nathan Morris died on San Quentin's death gurney at sunrise Thursday, becoming the thirteenth person to be executed in California since the death penalty had been reinstituted in 1978 and the first person to be executed since 1998.*

Morris, 49, was pronounced dead at 4:37 a.m., just forty-six minutes after the US Supreme Court overturned the last of four overnight reprieves that delayed his execution by more than six hours.

Early Thursday, Morris came within seconds of death but was rescued by a federal judge, who halted the execution even as Morris had been strapped to the gurney on which he was to die.

The final stay was quickly tossed out by the US

Supreme Court. In an unprecedented ruling that capped a night of coast-to-coast faxes and deliberations, the justices voted 6–3 to forbid the federal court from further delays in the execution.

Moments later, a solemn Morris was led a second time through the door of the mint-green chamber and strapped without resistance onto his metal deathbed.

Scanning the faces of thirty-seven witnesses peering through windows just steps away, Morris saw Steve Cooper, father of one of the teenaged murder victims. Morris, his voice inaudible through the thick walls, slowly mouthed the words, "I'm sorry." Cooper, a San Francisco firefighter, nodded in return.

Morris's relatives and friends embraced and turned away as he fell unconscious. Sharon Mason, the mother of another of his victims, smiled broadly. Her daughter, Linda, wept.

While Morris's appeals ping-ponged between the courts, the balding, mustached convict came to personify the wrenching battle over capital punishment.

As Morris's life ended, dawn was breaking in Marin County, where the aging San Quentin prison sits on the northeastern shore of San Francisco Bay.

Outside the prison gates, the dozens of death-penalty foes that had kept a nightlong vigil formed a circle and joined in a mass hug when news of the execution reached them.

જે જે જે

Three days later, I received a handwritten note:

Come see me, we got things to talk about.

Durgeon

༉ ༉ ༉

It was late afternoon when I seated myself in the same small cubicle. No other visitors were present. They had been cleared out at three thirty. It was already three forty-five, and I was told I had until four. My protest was met with absolute indifference—I would be out by four. The doors opened and Durgeon stepped into his side of the cubicle. The guard uncuffed him and closed the door. Durgeon sat and said without preamble, "What do you need from me?"

I shook my head. "Nice to see you too."

His face flushed with anger and he leaned close to the glass. "Listen, I ain't looking for no friends. I ain't looking for no social relationship. They did Morris, man."

Had he pushed for a death sentence because time on death row was easier than life-sentence time? Death row was single cell, everywhere else wasn't. The reality that California had actually executed someone, after years of mere threats, must have shaken him. *This wasn't the time to check motivations.*

"Okay." I paused briefly, thinking what I needed to know. "Let's cut right to the heart of things. Why didn't Rosenblatt call Evans, the guy who identified Graves, as a witness?"

Without hesitation: "Because that prick Manlow got to Evans and scared him shitless."

"You're telling me that the lead detective intimidated Evans out of testifying?"

"If you don't think that shit happens . . ." *Of course that shit happens.*

"How do you know Manlow got to him?"

"I'm not a fucking idiot. One day Evans is all over Graves as the shooter, next time he says I'm the shooter. Only thing changes is that Manlow went to Ohio and had a real heart to heart with Evans."

"How do you know that?"

"About a month before trial, Rosenblatt goes to Ohio, sees Evans, and everything is all set. Time for trial, we bring Evans out, and he goes sideways and tells Rosenblatt it wasn't Graves and that if Rosenblatt forces him to testify, he'll finger me." Durgeon leaned back. "Manlow's dirty. He got to Evans."

"I'll look into it." Then I ventured into the danger zone. "What can you tell me about the night of the murders?"

"I didn't tell Rosenblatt nothin' about that night and I ain't tellin' you. Let's just say I'm no virgin, but I can't talk about my friends."

"That's it?" I shrugged. "You get me up here and tell me Manlow is dirty, Evans is scared, and you're not going to share any details?"

"You can ask me other shit, but not about my friends. I can't abide snitches." He leaned in close to the glass, his voice barely audible over the phone. "I didn't kill 'em." *Yeah, of course you didn't, and Charlie Manson was just a wannabe singer.*

A guard knocked loudly on the door, and without waiting for a response, pulled open the door at Durgeon's back.

"Oh, before I forget, I got a letter from your mother," I told him quickly. "She got my name and address from the Project and says she hasn't heard from you and she's worried."

Durgeon, now standing with his hands behind his back, shrugged his big shoulders. The guard finished handcuffing him but waited for him to respond. *Maybe he wanted to hear what Durgeon had to say to mom.* Durgeon took a deep breath, and for an instant I saw the man behind the hard-ass. A man with a mother. "Tell her I got caught with a joint and they took away my writing stuff." He hesitated, aware of the guard at his back. "Tell her I'm okay and I'll write her when I can." Still facing me, he shrugged again, and they walked off.

I flew back to LAX, replaying the conversation. He had implied plenty and answered little. He referred to "friends," plural. Should I take that literally? Were there at least two others involved? What about the "I'm no virgin" remark?' Was he referring to the Blanco murders or just to his life in general? And then the big one, "I didn't kill 'em." Was that to be believed?

The next day, I called Mrs. Durgeon at her home in Mesquite, Texas.

"Hello, Mrs. Durgeon. My name is Jake Clearwater. I'm Duane's lawyer."

"Are you out there in California?"

"Yes ma'am, I am."

"I been worried about Duane. I keep sending him letters, but I don't hear nothing back. Y'all talk to him?"

"I talked to him yesterday, and he's fine. He wanted me to tell you he had a little trouble, and they took away his writing materials. He told me to tell you that he is okay and that he'll write as soon as he can."

"What kind of trouble?"

"They found a marijuana cigarette in his cell."

There was a short silence. "I told that boy and I told that boy that if he don't keep his nose clean, he's gonna get in serious trouble." *No question about it, that demon marijuana might really cook his ass.*

"Sounds like good advice, ma'am."

CHAPTER 7

THE DIVERSION

The late afternoon was dark and moody. The January ocean was alive with rain squalls and whitecaps. I was in my office working on the appeal, but the energy on the Pacific was mesmerizing, and I was having trouble concentrating.

"Professor Clearwater, excuse me, may I talk with you?" It was Suzelle in my doorway.

"Sure, come in. I was working on the brief." I motioned her to one of the two chairs facing my desk. "Everything okay? You look upset."

"My dad's in trouble," she blurted out, and her eyes began tearing.

"Come on in and sit down." Once she was settled, I said, "I'm sorry to hear that, anything I can do?" She picked at some tissues in her purse, dabbed her eyes, and made an effort to pull herself together.

"I'm sorry, I'm not usually like this, but I'm really scared. My whole family is scared. The police say my dad hit a police officer. But that didn't happen. The whole thing got so mixed up and confused, it's hard to know where to start. His lawyer says it looks like he's got to go to jail."

"Wait a minute, back up. When did this happen?"

"About six weeks ago."

"And I'm just hearing about it now?" We had been working shoulder to shoulder for weeks.

"I thought it was taken care of and . . ." She paused. "I didn't want anyone to know."

"So I take it that criminal charges have been filed?"

"Yes, I have the papers right here." She dug through her purse and handed me a two-page document. The complaint charged Brian Frost with misdemeanor battery on a police officer.

"So what's this about jail?"

"His lawyer talked to the DA and made a deal." She teared up again.

"Okay, let's start from the top. Tell me everything." She laid it out. Brian and Marilyn Frost own and operate the only hardware store in Mandrake, a small farming community situated inland from San Arcadia. A fact of the Frosts' professional life was the constant menace of shoplifting. On several occasions over the past couple of years, they caught shoplifters and held them until the police arrived. According to Suzelle, the police response times were very slow and that made things awkward, since they were holding the suspected shoplifter. On one occasion, a particular cop, Officer Herrera of the Mandrake Police Department, arrived forty-five minutes after they called, and when she finally arrived, Mr. Frost lectured her about the late response. Suzelle explained that the officer resented the attitude, and the seeds of animosity between the Frost family and the department, and particularly Officer Herrera, were planted. Since that time, ill will had continued to develop. Herrera had been the responding officer on two additional calls, and both times, she was late in arriving.

In late November, things boiled over. Marilyn Frost had been harassed and cursed by three teenage boys in the parking lot of their store. The boys refused to leave, and they threatened her. She ran into the store, told Brian, and then called the police. Meanwhile, Brian confronted the boys, who were now across the street. He waved a baseball bat at them. Herrera was the responding officer, and when she didn't take any action against the teenagers, she and Brian Frost had a heated exchange.

In telling her story, Suzelle's voice had gone up several pitches and her words began to come out in torrents. Then just as suddenly, she slumped back in her chair and pulled at her ponytail. She took a deep breath and continued. The exchange escalated to the point that Herrera attempted to take Frost into custody. Frost refused to be handcuffed, and he was tackled and choked unconscious. Suzelle teared up again and began admonishing herself. "I just stood there; I didn't do anything. I didn't try to help, and I didn't try to reason with them. I just stood there while they choked my dad out. I wasn't even sure if he was still alive."

"Suzelle, don't beat yourself up over something like this. Most people don't know how to deal with sudden violence. You could not have helped him."

"Yeah, but it was my dad. They were beating him up." Then, almost in a whisper, she said, "It was my dad." Her face collapsed.

I came around and sat in the chair next to her. "How is your dad now? Any aftereffects?"

"We took him to a clinic. He had a bruised trachea. But he's okay now."

"How long did he spend in jail?"

"We got him out that night around ten. So about six hours."

"I can't believe you haven't said anything about this."

"You've got so much going on, especially with the brief. I didn't want to bother you."

With the wave of my hand, I dismissed her concern. "I take it from your earlier comment that the lawyer your dad hired has talked to the prosecutor?"

"Dad talked to a Mr. Harp, a lawyer in Mandrake. We paid him $3,000, and now he's telling us we can't win, and that dad should just plead guilty and take ten days in jail. He told dad that he's talked to the prosecutor and that it was no use." She blew out her breath. "But I think he's afraid of going to trial and he's just trying to get dad to plead guilty so he won't have to go."

I offered a bark of laughter, shaking my head. "I don't know Mr. Harp or anything about his experience or trial abilities, but I do know there are plenty of lawyers who will take the fee with promises of an aggressive defense and then fold up when the case can't be favorably settled before trial." Maybe not. "I assume the case is set in San Arcadia?"

"Yes."

"When is it set for trial?"

"January 15."

"Day after tomorrow?" I sat up straight. "And I'm just now hearing about it? Brief or no brief, friends have each other's backs."

I picked up a pen from my desk and began fingering it. My first thought was to refer the case to any number of qualified criminal defense lawyers in San Arcadia, and I in good grace and in good conscience could bow out. But asking someone to come in on two days' notice was not practical. I looked at Suzelle slumped in her chair and not making any eye contact with me. She had practically become family. What choice did I have? And perhaps something short of going to trial in two days could be worked out. Maybe a continuance?

"How come your dad's not here talking to me?"

"He's disgusted with Harp, and he wants to fight the charges, but he wouldn't see another lawyer because he can't afford to." She rushed her words as if to keep me from commenting. "We can pay you, but we can't get it all to you now. I'm hoping we can work out a payment plan for the rest." She placed a neatly drawn check for $500 on my desk. *Ah, the riches to be garnered from criminal-defense work.*

"Can you get your dad here tomorrow afternoon?"

"Oh yes!" She gave me a big-eyed, hero-worshiping look and smiled. "What time do you want him here?"

"Four o'clock." I picked up the check and handed it to her. "Don't get the impression I'm doing this gratis; there is a lot of work left on Durgeon."

She got up and gave me a quick hug. Then she was gone, and I remained a goddamned white knight. *Perhaps a stupid goddamned white knight.*

CHAPTER 8

PAPA FROST

The next morning, I called the San Arcadia County District Attorney's office, and after three transfers, ascertained that DDA Joe Marsh had been assigned the Frost case. I didn't know him. He had obviously joined the office after I left. He was not in. I left a voicemail identifying the case and asking him to call.

He got back to me at two that afternoon. "Joe"—I hoped first names would smooth my path—"up until four years ago, I was in the office." That elicited no response. "I'm going to substitute in on Frost; it's set for tomorrow in Department 8 before Judge Slaughter."

"Hold on," he said. I could hear papers being shuffled. "Let's see, I've had a discussion with Dick Harp, and he told me Frost was going to plead."

"Well, things didn't work out with Mr. Harp, and I'm afraid you've been left with the wrong impression." I let that sink in. "Joe, this doesn't feel like a cop-battery case, and I would like to get your read on things."

Marsh, voice piqued with irritation, replied, "Since Harp told me this was going to be a plea, I called off my witnesses."

It was best to work with opposing counsel and reach a

settlement. Jurors were unpredictable creatures. Once you went to trial, you lost your leverage and most of your ability to control events. I always tried, as a prosecutor, to work out a compromise that both sides could live with. If that was impossible, then, and only then, I'd roll the dice at trial.

"I'm sorry for the trouble. Of course I'd be willing to agree to a continuance. In fact, since I'm just coming in, I could use a continuance." *If I could get a continuance, maybe I could hand this off.* I hoped my conciliatory attitude would be reciprocated. That notion was quickly dispelled.

Marsh would have no part of what I was selling. He carried the pomp of his office like a flag. He was acting the role of the stern, vigilant, take-no-prisoners prosecutor. *That would impress his higher-ups. Especially Tice.* Under that mindset, defendants had two choices: plead to the charge, or go to trial. Never mind all that high-minded pap about working toward justice and the special role the prosecutor played on the vast landscape of the American criminal justice system. That was for the academics, not the real world. In the real world, Marsh's boss, John Tice, wanted a tough, no-compromise prosecutor, and dammit, Joe Marsh was going to give him what he wanted. I knew that road, but I had managed to resist it as a prosecutor. In my view as a prosecutor, you always listened and considered the other side before committing to trial. Trial was the last option.

"Mr. Frost pleads straight up, or we put on our track shoes and run the race. No continuances. No deals." *What an ass.*

I kept my irritation in check and tried one last time. "Have you had a chance to talk to any of the witnesses to get a real feel for this case, or are you relying only on the police reports?" *It was my last volley. I sent it back across the net with little conviction and even less hope.*

Marsh replied in a firm tone with just a trace of sarcasm and just on the edge of anger, "Counsel, you've got your job and I've got mine. You don't tell me how to do my job and I'll reciprocate. I'll get my witnesses, and I trust you won't be asking for a continuance."

"I will be seeking a continuance. But either way, Frost isn't pleading." I guess I would find out if this guy could back up his hard-ass attitude. *Even though I hadn't tried a case in better than four years and had never tried a case from the defense side, I believed I could hold my own.*

"Like I said, I'm going to oppose any continuance."

"I would expect nothing less of you. See you in court."

❧ ❧ ❧

That afternoon, Brian Frost showed up in my office ten minutes early. He was alone. Short and beefy, he was carrying an extra thirty or forty pounds and had what looked like a perpetually flushed face and unusually squinty eyes, as if he were always looking into the sun. He was dressed in brown pants with a white Ralph Lauren shirt stretched over his belly.

He shook my hand warily. *Got to be careful of lawyers. Might steal your watch.*

"Have a seat, Mr. Frost. I'm glad to meet you. Your daughter is a remarkable young woman."

"She's always been a good girl." His face was stern; there would be no small talk. "She said you wouldn't take my money." It was an accusation.

"Mr. Frost, we don't have a lot of time here. As you know, the trial is set for tomorrow. What if we agree to work out the money afterward?"

"I'm gonna pay you."

"Fair enough," I said.

He handed me his file containing the police report. As we discussed events, he worked to stay calm. It was apparent he was still angry about the treatment he had received at the hands of the police. *And for that matter, he didn't appear to be real comfortable in my office.* It was clear that he was humiliated by the whole affair and wanted an opportunity to vindicate himself. I asked him to tell me what happened, and his version was fairly consistent with Suzelle's account. He didn't sugarcoat his animus toward the arresting cop, and unlike most people accused of a crime, didn't paint himself a saint. When he finished, I asked a few follow-up questions, explained what would take place the next morning, and asked if he had any questions.

One of his biggest concerns, other than staying out of jail, was confronting Dick Harp, his soon-to-be-former lawyer. I tried to assure him that I would handle Harp and that Harp would take his dismissal like a professional. Frost was unconvinced. Finally, I closed the matter by telling him that frankly, Harp's reaction was of no significance, and as the client, Frost had the power to hire and fire him, and if Harp didn't like it, so what.

I asked Frost for Harp's business card, and I called. Harp was not in. I left a message that I would be substituting in on the Frost case tomorrow morning.

Frost still appeared nervous and distracted, and he kept looking over his shoulder at the closed door. *It was as if he had snuck down to the box seats at Dodger Stadium and was waiting for an usher to kick him back to the cheap seats.*

When he left, I set to work. Although I hoped it wouldn't come to it, I had to be prepared to go to trial in the morning. *Imagine that. No trial work for years and then one on no notice.* Marsh was probably right about the judge not giving me a continuance. From the police report Frost had supplied and from what I had pieced together from my discussion with Suzelle and her dad, I put together a semblance of a game plan. I finally got to bed about midnight, fairly comfortable with my feel for the case. *At least as comfortable as one can feel when events are happening too quickly to catch up.* I was in no way properly prepared, but I was sure I could get through the early phases and buy a little time. I set the alarm for 5:00 a.m. That left enough time for my swim and the two-hour drive to San Arcadia.

CHAPTER 9

FAILED NEGOTIATION

I sat with three other lawyers, none of whom I knew, on chairs provided for our exclusive use just inside the three-foot mahogany rail of the courtroom. We were separated from about thirty-five people who were spread out in the public area. *God forbid we lawyers should have to mix with the rabble.* Suzelle and both her parents sat in the back row, stiff-backed, eyes forward. It was 8:55 a.m., and there were just now signs of life emanating from the court attaches. The court reporter was setting up her equipment, the bailiff had emerged from a doorway behind the judge's bench, and the clerk had assumed her position at a large desk to the left of the judge's bench. It looked as if our "8:30" appearance was about to get underway.

My attention was drawn behind me to the back of the courtroom. A man was gesturing to Brian Frost, who had remained seated. The man, in slacks and a houndstooth jacket, again motioned for Frost to get up and join him. Frost shook his head no and looked at me. I was up and moving. I brushed by the man who had to have been Harp and leaned over toward Frost. "Is there a problem?"

"That's Mr. Harp. I don't want to talk to him," Frost responded.

I turned to Harp. "Join me outside." He hesitated, gave Frost a withering look, and led the way out.

"Good morning. Jake Clearwater," I said, as I stuck out my hand.

Harp ignored my hand and said in a belligerent voice, "In my experience, lawyers don't take other lawyer's clients."

I had not expected attitude. *Well, maybe a bit. Either way, here it was, front and center.* "In my experience, it's the client's decision who to hire and who to fire, and you sir, have been fired." Despite my words, I kept my tone conversational.

"I already had a deal worked out with the DA."

"Mr. Frost wasn't impressed with your deal involving jail. That's why I'm here."

Harp grunted. "What are you going to do, take this dog to trial?"

"If that's my client's wish."

"Good luck with a cop-battery case in this redneck county." He dug through his briefcase and handed me a very thin file. "Tell your client I'm keeping his retainer."

"I'm sure he won't be surprised."

I weighed the file in my hand and briefly thumbed through it—nothing but the police report, the complaint, and a page documenting two calls to the DA's office. "I see you've been hard at it."

"Screw you and screw Frost," he shot back, as he turned and walked away. *I always love it when professionals can deal professionally. Maybe we can have a drink later on.*

Harp's sole work had been to belly Frost up to the DA and pack him off to jail. I walked back into the courtroom and knelt next to Frost. "He's gone, everything is alright." Just then, a smartly dressed and well-coiffed man breezed into the courtroom, confidently striding through the public area toward the front of the courtroom. He was tall, maybe six feet five, dressed in a perfectly fitted light-gray suit with subdued pinstripes. His dark hair, striking against his pale complexion, was parted on the left side and had a trace of premature gray at his fashionably cut sideburns. He had an intense face, his eyebrows arching at severe angles almost pointing at his nose.

The bailiff quickly jumped to his feet and held open the short swinging door that separated the assembled masses from the inner sanctum. The bailiff said, "Good morning, Mr. Marsh." *Of course it was Marsh.* Marsh managed only a sideways glance at the bailiff, hardly acknowledging the courtesy extended. Without breaking stride, he continued toward a door behind the judge's bench and disappeared. My initial impression that this guy was an ass, based on our phone conversation, had taken on a new dimension. He was not just an ass but a pompous ass.

Within moments, the door behind the judge's bench cracked and a woman whispered to the clerk, who then looked at me and said, "The judge will see you now, Mr. Clearwater." *Game time.* I could feel my pulse quicken. The door led to a hallway where another bailiff motioned me to Judge Slaughter's office. The door was open, and Marsh was sitting across from Slaughter.

Judge Slaughter saw me and smiled warmly. "Doggone it, Jake, this is sure a surprise. I haven't seen you since you fled to academia. Don't tell me you're back here as a defense lawyer." He came around his desk and stuck out his hand.

"Judge, it's awfully good to see you," as we shook hands.

"Do you know Joe Marsh?" Slaughter asked.

Marsh remained seated and said, "We spoke yesterday." His tone cold and dismissive.

Slaughter ignored Marsh's attitude. "It's been years since you broke in, right here in my courtroom."

"I learned more about trying cases from your postmortem of my first trial than from all the rest of my legal training."

He laughed as he returned to his chair. "Hell Jake, you were a rookie. I was just trying to show you the ropes." Slaughter had been the county DA before being appointed to the bench. "How are things at Pacifico? Was it a good move for you?"

"Things are good. Teaching and all the rest of it. But I've got to tell you, sometimes I really miss the DA's office. The sense of team, us against the bad guys. And the damn trials. I really miss the trials. Felonies, misdemeanors, whatever, I miss them."

"Well, it looks like you found yourself one," Slaughter said, as he leafed through the Frost file on his desk. He paused and said, "Looks like Dick Harp has been representing Mr. Frost."

"That's right, Judge. But I'm going to be substituting in this morning."

"Jake, you remember my long-standing policy has always been not to grant continuances on the day of trial. Absent some compelling reason, I'm not inclined." His tone pleasant but firm. *Old friendships only go so far. Business is business.*

"I appreciate your policy. I just got involved two days ago, and I could really use a few days to get ready."

Slaughter shrugged apologetically, and Marsh jumped in. "Judge, I told him yesterday there would be no continuance. In fact, it was my understanding from Dick Harp that Frost was going to plead out."

I ignored Marsh and spoke directly to the judge. "I explained to Mr. Marsh yesterday that I was coming into the case and that Mr. Frost was willing to consider any reasonable settlement offer."

Slaughter leaned back in his chair. "Alright, guys, let's save it for the jury. Jake, I can't give you a continuance. If this case cannot be settled, we start picking a jury right away." He offered me a smile. "You still remember how to do that, don't you?"

Before I could answer, Marsh said, "If Frost pleads, we'll recommend thirty days county jail and the usual terms and conditions of probation."

Slaughter nodded and looked at me expectantly.

"Judge, this just isn't a battery-on-an-officer case. There is considerable history—"

Marsh interrupted me. "Judge, we've had this discussion. I'm not reducing the charges."

I waited for Marsh to finish, and with exaggerated civility, began again. "Your Honor, as I was saying, this case does not have the feel of a cop battery. And as Mr. Frost feels he is guilty of bad judgment and poor timing, he is willing to plead to disturbing the peace if there is no jail time involved." I paused before continuing. "There's a history between Mr. Frost and the officer involved. This whole incident can be traced to their previous problems. I believe when this isolated incident is looked at in the context of their relationship, it becomes easier to understand what took place."

Slaughter looked from me to Marsh. "Joe, sounds like there may be some underlying currents here. I've never known Jake to BS." He paused. "What do you say?"

Marsh's answer was immediate. "We hear this stuff from defense lawyers every day. I don't care about any previous history; all I care about is that he hit a cop. Case closed. No deals."

"Joe, Jake is not just another defense lawyer, he was one of your own and, I might add, he is very good. You might want to take another look at your case. Maybe a disturbing the peace . . ." His voice trailed off.

"Judge, I understand you two know each other, but I really resent your heavy-handed tactics. It's my decision to make, and I've made it."

Slaughter turned back to me and shrugged. "Jake, I've done what I can. If your client chooses to go to trial and is unsuccessful, he may well do six months instead of thirty days. I trust you will so inform him. We'll wait for you." He nodded his head, dismissing us. The judge's leap from Marsh's thirty days to six months was grossly unfair but not unexpected. I couldn't take it personally; it was the price of exercising one's constitutional right to a trial. *There are times when the criminal justice system lacks justice.*

I reentered the courtroom and motioned Frost, his wife, and Suzelle outside into the corridor. They all looked at me expectantly. "Brian, the damn DA wants you to go to jail for thirty days."

"Thirty days in jail?" Frost slumped against the wall. "Harp only talked about ten days."

"He should have warned you that it might be more, but I'm not surprised. But here we are, and here are our options. Option one, plead guilty and do thirty days, not the option of choice. Option two, go to trial, win, and walk away. Option three, go to trial, lose, and take your chances with the judge." I paused before I went on. "I've got to tell you, the judge is talking tough, and he wants you to know if you go to trial and lose, he could sentence you to six months."

Marilyn Frost broke into tears. Suzelle stepped to her and held her. Both sets of eyes were red, cheeks glistening.

"Come on, now," I said, trying to calm them. "Let's not forget that we are on the right side of this, and we will have twelve jurors who will listen to what we have to say."

"But what if we lose, Professor Clearwater?" moaned Mrs. Frost.

Startling everybody, Brian wrapped his arms around his wife and daughter, and looking at them, said, "To hell with them. I haven't done anything to be ashamed of. Let's go to trial." He stepped over to me and clapped me on the shoulder. "Everything will be fine."

At that moment, the surreal reality that I was actually going to trial was outweighed by the acute responsibility of being this man's lawyer, the family's protector. *How in the hell had I gotten here?*

CHAPTER 10

INTO THE BREACH

Twenty minutes later, we were picking a jury. It was hard to believe I was in trial just forty-eight hours after Suzelle had alerted me to her little family problem. Usually it takes months, or at least weeks, before a case goes to trial. But here I was, and for all the suddenness of the thing, the rush felt good.

Jury selection used to take a lot longer, but the ever-informed California electorate, through the initiative process via significant lobbying from the state's prosecutors, had pretty much gutted lawyers' participation in the questioning of prospective jurors. Consequently, the judge asked most of the questions, and Marsh and I were reduced to mere note takers in trying to fathom how each potential juror might play out. It has always struck me that the forces of law and order, in an effort to streamline trials, had greatly hurt the prosecution by the change. Since in criminal cases it takes unanimity to convict, prosecutors have lost their most powerful tool for identifying that odd juror that could hang the jury. In my years as a prosecutor, I always worried about a lone dissenter standing between me and a conviction. By largely removing the lawyers from questioning, the prosecutor's chance of ferreting out that one who could hang a jury with an 11 to 1 result was greatly reduced.

The jury commissioner had sent forty individuals to Slaughter's courtroom. Twelve of them were selected by lot to fill the jury box. Slaughter questioned them for forty minutes. Neither Marsh nor I had any cause challenges. However, Marsh did use a peremptory challenge on a community college student who gave some quirky answers to some of the judge's questions.

The clerk then pulled a chit from her box and called out prospective juror number 1107. Marsh and I both looked back to see who that was. It turned out to be a beautiful woman. A tall Latina with a face and a body that belonged on the cover of a beauty magazine. As she was making her way to the jury box, Marsh caught my eye and with the slightest move of his head shook no. I immediately understood. He was signaling me not to use a challenge on 1107. He needn't have bothered, but I wasn't going to let him know that. Would I be happy having a gorgeous woman on the jury? Of course. But I've dated gorgeous, and it turns out that gorgeous outside isn't always reflected on the inside. Still, I'd make Marsh sweat a bit. I glared at him. Then I nodded and sneered, giving him the impression that he'd blown it, that I was going to use my peremptory just to spite him, though I had no plan to, unless the judge uncovered something troublesome during the questioning.

After number 1107 settled into her seat, the judge asked her questions similar to those posed to the other potential jurors. Though we did not get actual names of the jurors for security reasons, through her answers we learned she was a school administrator. I looked at Marsh, pausing for effect, then stated I had no peremptory challenges. Marsh then accepted the jury quickly and I promptly followed suit. Number 1107 was in the front row, far left, and without question would serve as a distraction throughout. *Focus, Jake.*

Once the jury was sworn in, Marsh delivered his short opening statement from the lectern while referring to his notes. As expected, he did not bother with any of the events leading up to the confrontation between Frost and Officer Herrera. He focused on Frost's turning and walking away against the officer's command and then knocking her arm away. Technically, Marsh was correct. Frost, in knocking Herrera's arm away, had battered her. Marsh saw the case in simple black and white, and that's how he told it to the jury.

As I listened to Marsh's opening and his sanitized and certainly simplified version of events, I had to acknowledge that I had been guilty of the same tunnel vision in my early career as a prosecutor. I had often been caught up in my shortsighted, simplistic version of events. As I graduated from misdemeanors to felonies, I had begun to appreciate the bigger picture, the nuances, the reasons people act as they do. Maybe part of that was also the distance of more years under my belt. I had been twenty-five when I started as a prosecutor right out of law school. A bit of maturity, a bunch of trials, and a few more years on the planet helped my perspective. I can remember, as a young prosecutor, criticizing some defense lawyers for trying to introduce "irrelevant facts" into the trial. But now I realized that sometimes it was the everyday stuff of our lives that determined the outcome.

As Marsh sat down, Slaughter looked at me and said, "Mr. Clearwater, would you care to make an opening statement on behalf of Mr. Frost?"

"Thank you, Your Honor." I stood and put my right hand on Frost's shoulder. "Good morning, ladies and gentlemen. I'm a little nervous as I stand here today. I haven't tried a case in a long time, and I've never been on this side of a criminal case before. It's an enormous responsibility. I represent an innocent man, and if I do my job right, you will see that he is innocent and let him go home with his family. If I don't do my job, you may find him guilty, and he and his family and I will have to live with that. You see, Brian Frost is not in this trial alone. His wife, Marilyn, and his daughter, Suzelle, are sitting right over there in the front row. They will be right here with us throughout the trial. They are Brian's comfort and foundation as he goes through this ordeal."

I moved around the prosecutor's table to the jury. When I reached the lectern, I picked it up and moved it aside. As I moved closer to the jurors, I said, "Brian Frost is fifty-three years old. He was born right here in San Arcadia County. Thirty-two years ago, he fell in love with Marilyn, and after a whirlwind courtship, they married." I was now in front of the jury box, where I stopped and looked at the twelve. Unhampered by notes, I was able to really take them in. "Twenty-three years ago, they were blessed with Suzelle." I motioned at her. She offered a small smile before looking down.

"And shortly after Suzelle was born, Marilyn and Brian were finally able to realize their lifetime dream, that of owning their own store. Mandrake Hardware had been the answer to their dream. Within the first year, they took that small break-even business, and through hard work, long hours, and fierce determination, they turned their store into a successful business. Marilyn can always be found at the checkout counter, while Brian takes care of inventory and stocking. When I was getting ready for this trial, I asked Brian how many hours a week they worked those first couple of years. He said if the store was open sixty hours a week, they worked at least ninety hours. They loved their business and they loved working together. Life was just about perfect."

"Objection, Your Honor. This simply is not relevant." Marsh, of course, was right, but I was working hard to personalize my client. *If they liked my client and identified with him, I hoped they would see events from our perspective.*

"Oh, that's okay, Mr. Marsh," Slaughter said while waving him down. "I'm sure Mr. Clearwater is going to turn the corner in just a minute." *I think the judge gave me the call for old times' sake.*

"Thank you, Your Honor," I said, nodding at him. Turning back to the jurors, I resumed. "Like I said, life was just about perfect. But then about two years ago, they noticed that incidents of shoplifting were increasing. The problem was becoming so great that the store had once again begun losing money. They consulted a security expert, and they installed one of those metal-detection devices at the door. And when a shoplifter was caught, they would call the Mandrake Police Department. Unfortunately, the police response was sometimes very slow. Brian and Marilyn noticed that one officer in particular was not only consistently late in arriving but also reluctant to take the shoplifter into custody. That officer was Teresa Herrera." I paused and softly repeated her name, "Teresa Herrera." I paused again to let that name crystallize.

"Finally, on one occasion about six months ago, things boiled over. The Frosts had caught a young man stealing, and it took the police forty-five minutes to respond. And sure enough, who was the officer?" I paused and softly said, "Teresa Herrera."

I put up my hands. "Let's stop right here for a moment and put this in perspective. Mandrake is a town of roughly 6,000 people. The main street, where the Frosts' hardware store is located, is only four blocks long. The whole city stretches about five miles, and yet it took Officer Herrera forty-five minutes to get there. When she arrived, Mr. Frost asked her why it took so long. She told him it was none of his concern. He pressed her, she told him to shut up. Shut up. Words were exchanged. The next day, Brian called the chief of police. The chief told Brian he would look into the problem and get back to him. He never did, and things just got worse."

I walked to the far left of the jury box with my head down.

I looked up into the eyes of number 1107 and began again. "The stage was set for November 27, 2015. Remember back a couple of months to late November? It was hot. It was one of those occasional winter heatwaves. The temperatures in the inland valleys were in the high nineties, and Mandrake was cooking. Just after lunch, Marilyn was walking to her car in the store's parking lot when she was almost knocked over by a teenage boy riding a skateboard. Startled, she asked the boy and his two companions to leave the store's parking lot. The boy who had nearly hit her rode up to her and said, 'Fuck off, you old broad.' She was stunned. She will tell you later on that no one had ever talked to her that way, let alone a boy. She felt threatened and hurriedly got in her car and drove off." I eased back to the right of the jury box. "But when she returned and parked, the same boy rode his skateboard up to her car and actually jumped with his board onto the hood of her car and rode across the hood and back off the other side. He turned and again cursed at her. She ran into the store, told Brian, and then called the police.

"Meanwhile, Brian, an angry husband, grabbed the first thing at hand, an aluminum baseball bat, and ran outside to the parking lot. The three boys saw Brian coming and retreated across the street, where they stood and cursed and taunted him. And this time almost immediately Officer Herrera pulled up, jumped out of her car, yelled at the boys to shut up, then went right up to Brian and demanded, 'What's the problem?'

"Brian, flushed with anger, pointed at the boys and said, 'Those punks threatened my wife, and I won't have it! I want them arrested!' The boys were still yelling and whistling at him, so Brian roared, 'You little shits,' and held the bat high in the air and shook it." I moved back to the left of the jury box, almost brushing the rail with my thighs. I was again right in front of number 1107. *My goodness, she was stunning.* Pulling away from her, I went on, "Officer Herrera grabbed at the bat, and Brian jerked it away from her grasp. She yelled at him to give her the bat. He refused and said, 'Don't worry about the bat. Why don't you just arrest them? That's what you were called here for.'

"Herrera said, 'I'll decide what happens here. Now give me the bat and shut up.' Brian dropped the bat. Herrera picked it up and tossed it into her car. A second officer arrived, they conferred, and Herrera went across the street. She briefly spoke with the boys and came back to Brian and the other officer.

"Brian asked, 'How come you're not arresting them?'

"Herrera got right up in Brian's face and said, 'I decide who gets arrested, you just shut up. I'm not going to take any more from you.'

"Brian threw up his hands and said, 'I should have figured as much.' Then he turned and began walking toward the entrance to his store.

"Now I want to slow the action a bit, almost like we're watching the events play out in slow motion. Brian, whose wife had made the call to the police, had broken off the discussion with Officer Herrera and was walking back to his store." I took my time and walked to the witness stand and patted it with the flat of my hand. "He is going to sit right up here and under oath tell you it was over. Over. But as far as Officer Herrera was concerned, it wasn't over, and as Brian was walking away, she yelled at him to stop, that she was 'investigating a police call,' and that he was to remain. Brian, with a dismissive wave of his hand, said, 'You're worthless, just get off my property,' and kept on walking. Officer Herrera strode after him and grabbed his right hand, trying to slap a handcuff on his wrist. Brian, surprised, instinctively jerked his hand back, pushing Herrera's hand away as she was trying to grab his arm. Brian started heading for the front door. Just then the second officer, a man, slammed into

Brian, knocking him down and cracking his head on the cement. Herrera jumped on Brian's back and locked her forearm across his neck. Suzelle," I nodded to her, "is going to tell you that she was no more than fifteen feet away and could hear choking noises coming from her dad, and then she will tell you her dad went limp and lost consciousness. He lay face down on the sidewalk. She is going to tell you that she didn't know if her father was even alive. Marilyn is going to tell you that it was the worst moment of her life." I looked right into number 1107's eyes; she had a pained expression. She was feeling their pain. "The two officers rolled Brian onto his back. The male officer felt for a pulse just as Brian coughed back into consciousness. They sat him up, handcuffed both wrists, pulled him to his feet, put him in Herrera's unit, and drove him to jail."

I slowly walked back to counsel table. I put my hands on Brian's shoulders and looked at Marsh. "I guess to some extent, the prosecutor is right. When Brian pushed Officer Herrera's hand away as she was trying to handcuff him, he did technically batter her. If that's all the trial's about—we're guilty. But what I'm hoping for, and what the Frost family is hoping for, is that you twelve folks will look at the whole picture of what happened that day and not just at the very limited and selected pieces of this ugly little incident the prosecutor told you about. Trials are not about technicalities. Trials are about people like you sitting in judgment of other people. Trials are about justice. Trials are about doing the right thing. And when the facts of this case are played out for you, the Frosts and I are confident you will do the right thing."

As I sat down, Judge Slaughter said, "Thank you, counsel."

Brian patted my arm and whispered, "Thanks, Mr. Clearwater."

I let out a long breath and whispered back, "The name's Jake. While we're sharing a foxhole, it's first names."

"Mr. Marsh, you may call your first witness." Usually there is a little breather after opening statements. Not today. Slaughter was pushing this case like he was double-parked.

Marsh was up. "Thank you, Your Honor. The People call Officer Teresa Herrera."

Here we go. I hoped she would display some of the same attitude she gave the Frosts. The bailiff walked to the back of the courtroom, cracked the door, and motioned. Officer Herrera entered and walked to the witness stand. She was about five foot six, dark-haired with an olive complexion, stocky but fit. She was dressed in her Mandrake Police Department uniform, replete with gun, nightstick, and a whole host of cop paraphernalia attached to her belt. She looked confident and in charge, every bit the law-enforcement professional.

She took the oath, and Marsh began. Behind the lectern and with benefit of notes from his legal pad, Marsh worked her through a very tight and focused version of events. As previewed in his opening statement, he hadn't bothered with any of the history or context of the Frost–Herrera relationship. *My opening statement hadn't moved him from his minimalist strategy.* As for Herrera, she came across as the consummate professional who regretfully had been forced to deal with a citizen who had just had a bad day. No grudges or hard feelings. Just a citizen who had lost it, and it was her job to deal with it.

As Marsh wrapped up, Judge Slaughter said, "Very well, it's time for the lunch recess. I must admonish you jurors not to discuss the case during the recess. We are now in recess until one thirty."

The Frosts wanted me to join them for lunch. I declined, explaining that I needed to get ready for my cross-exam of Herrera. I went to the courthouse cafeteria, got a large black coffee, found a table far away from everyone, and got out my legal pad. *Who needed weeks or months to prepare? I had the lunch break.*

CHAPTER 11

THE COST OF ARROGANCE

Cross-exam is the most misunderstood part of trial. There is the perception that the examining lawyer should rip into the witness and attempt to destroy them by virtue of the lawyer's superior intellect, aided by a rapier-like wit. Nothing short of a witness breaking down and admitting they are a liar or are themselves the culprit will do. Of course, better yet, a Perry Mason moment, with someone in the gallery jumping up and admitting that they are in fact the guilty party. The reality of cross-examination is far removed from the fantasy fueled by film and television. Cases are seldom won on cross but rather are more likely to suffer serious setbacks. Most seasoned trial lawyers will admit that a successful cross is one that did not assist the other side. A good cross, like a good plane landing, is one you can walk away from.

At one thirty, Judge Slaughter assumed the bench, nodded to the jurors, and said, "Officer Herrera, please step back to the witness stand." Herrera complied. "Officer, I remind you that you are still under oath." Turning to me, the judge said, "Mr. Clearwater, do you care to cross-examine?"

"Yes, Your Honor." I remained seated. "Good afternoon, Officer Herrera."

"Good afternoon, counselor."

"I was taking notes during your direct examination and I'm afraid I couldn't get everything down. Perhaps you could help me on a couple of points."

"I'd be happy to." Poised and confident. *Maybe even cocky.*

"Let's see. When you arrived at the hardware store, I believe you testified that you didn't know who had placed the call to the police, is that right?" I said, in a nonconfrontational manner; just a hardworking albeit slow-witted guy, trying to figure things out.

"That's right."

I picked up her report and asked, "Officer, you made a police report of this incident, didn't you?"

"Yes." Her voice held just the slightest hesitation. It seemed as if it had just dawned on her that she might have indicated in her report who made the call.

"You wrote your report on the same day of the incident, didn't you?" My tone was firm, no need to be deferential now; I had her on this point. She knew it, and I knew it. Now it was the jury's turn to know it. This wasn't a big point, but I started here to knock her confidence a bit. I wanted to establish that I was in charge.

"I believe I did." Her voice was flat, barely audible. Instead of admitting her mistake, which would have minimized her error, she went the other way, trying to squirm in order to create a little elbow room to avoid a direct impeaching hit. My job was to close down her options, to cut down her squirm room. *Bad move, sister.*

"I'm sorry officer, are you unclear as to the date you wrote your report?" My voice was conciliatory and helpful.

"I wrote it the same day."

"It's critical for you to be truthful in your report, isn't it?"

"Yes."

"Because police reports are the documents that are filed directly with the district attorney's office, aren't they?"

"Yes."

"And you are aware that those reports are used to determine what if any charges will be filed, correct?"

"That's right."

"So you strive to be as fair and accurate as you can when you prepare your reports, isn't that right?"

"That's right."

"Your Honor, leave to approach the witness with her report?"

"You may."

Standing at Herrera's left elbow and pointing to a specific part of her report, I continued. "Officer Herrera, please follow along with me. Didn't you write, 'I responded to a call initiated by Marilyn Frost'?" Herrera didn't answer right away. She appeared to be studying the report, perhaps hoping to find an out. It was such a small concession; she should have owned up to it. I didn't hurry her. The longer the pause, the greater the emphasis.

She finally nodded and said, "Yes."

"To be clear, you wrote that Marilyn Frost made the call, didn't you?"

"I write a lot of reports. I can't be expected to remember every word in every report." *A little snarky, that.*

"I fully appreciate that. Of course you are aware, as an experienced law-enforcement officer who has testified on numerous occasions, that if you don't remember something, it's perfectly okay to ask for your report to refresh your memory, isn't that true?"

She nodded but didn't answer.

"Is that a yes?" Force the adverse witness into an unequivocal response.

"Yes."

"Let's move on. After you placed Mr. Frost in custody, you didn't go back across the street and talk to the boys, did you?"

"No, there was no need to."

"Even though it was their conduct that initiated the call to the police."

"I had made my determination as to what had occurred."

"You didn't talk to any bystanders to see if they could shed a little light on the incident, correct?"

"I didn't see any need to."

"And you didn't talk with Mrs. Frost, the person who originally made the call, did you?"

"No."

"And you didn't talk to her daughter, who was right there?"

"No."

"You didn't arrest any of the teenaged boys, did you?"

"As far as I could tell, there was no reason to arrest them."

"Yet all the while, you were aware that Marilyn had made the call reporting those boys, isn't that correct?"

"Yes."

"You never undertook any follow-up on those boys, correct?"

"Again, I didn't see any reason to."

"Because you didn't do any follow-up, you were not aware that at least one of those boys threatened Mrs. Frost?"

"No, I was not."

"And because you did not do any follow-up, you were not aware that when one of the boys rode his skateboard across the hood of her car, there was over $500 worth of damage?"

"I was not aware of that."

"And because you did not do any follow-up, you were not aware that the boys cursed Mrs. Frost and refused to leave the store's parking lot, correct?"

"I was not aware of that."

I let that response rest with the jurors for a couple of beats before proceeding. "Now let's turn to a different matter. You choked Brian Frost unconscious, didn't you?"

"That was necessary under the circumstances." Some of the cockiness had fallen out of her responses.

"So that is a yes to my question, you choked fifty-three-year-old Brian Frost unconscious?"

"Yes."

"Correct me if I'm wrong, but the proper way to apply a choke hold is with your forearm across the subject's throat?"

Herrera paused ever so slightly. She sensed a trap and answered carefully, picking her words as if they might come back and bite her. "No, counselor, as I'm certain you are aware, the department-approved policy is to apply the choke hold with the crook of the elbow at the throat area."

"Why is that?" The rule is to never ask a question on cross, but from time to time, it could prove fruitful.

Herrera looked hard at me; she knew where I was going. She answered, "If the forearm is applied to the throat, the subject's windpipe could be damaged."

"And that could lead to serious injury or even death, couldn't it?"

"It could lead to injury."

"And even possibly to death?" I encouraged.

"Yeah."

"And, of course, you are certain that you used the department-approved hold on Mr. Frost?"

"That's what I always do."

"So, just so the record is clear, you are testifying that you did not use your forearm directly across Brian Frost's throat. Is that right?"

"That's correct."

"Your Honor, I have a medical report dated November 28, 2015, the day after the incident. May I have it marked as Defense B for identification?"

"So marked."

"I'm showing Defense B to Mr. Marsh."

Marsh looked at the report and objected on hearsay grounds.

I answered, "Judge, this isn't being offered for the truth of the matter but rather to impeach the witness." Stupid objection. I was using it to impeach Herrera and therefore the report works around the hearsay rule.

Slaughter ordered us to sidebar. "Let me see the report." After quickly scanning the report, Slaughter overruled the objection.

I carried the report up to Herrera and said, "You see the date of the report is November 28, the day after you applied your chokehold, isn't that right?"

"Yes."

"You see the diagnosis from the physician?" Herrera nodded. "You would agree it says that Mr. Frost was diagnosed with a severely bruised trachea?" I arched my eyebrows at Herrera. She did not respond. *Can't say I blamed her.* "Severely bruised trachea, officer?"

"That's what it says."

"Now that we have a much better picture of what took place that afternoon, let's move to your prior relationship with the Frosts."

Marsh jumped to his feet. "Beyond the scope of direct exam and irrelevant."

Slaughter waved him down. "The jurors have a right to hear about any prior relationship. Overruled." *Slaughter had warned Marsh to try to settle. Now it was time for Marsh to pay the price of arrogance.*

Without turning from Herrera, I asked, "You knew the Frosts before this incident, correct?"

"Yes, I had responded to their store on several occasions." Herrera then thought to add, "And every time, they gave me a hard time." *Again she sensed where I was going and was trying to get out front to blunt my attack.*

"Just to be clear, let me ask my question again. You knew the Frosts before this incident, correct?" *I wouldn't let her shift the focus. I was driving the bus, not her.*

"You know I did."

"It's important that the jurors know it. So that's a yes to my question?"

"Yes."

"When you had responded to their previous calls, it was typically because they had caught a shoplifter, true?"

"That's what they said."

"Well, in fact, every time you had responded, they were holding a shoplifter, correct?"

"I couldn't say."

"Would it be helpful if you had an opportunity to look at your previous police reports regarding calls to the Frosts' store?" I did not have any such reports because there had been no time, but Herrera didn't know I didn't have them. It was a calculated gamble, but since I had already impeached her earlier, I figured she would not risk yet another impeachment. I held my breath.

She blinked. "Yeah, that's probably true."

"Is that a yes?"

"Yes, that's a yes."

"So you knew that when the Frosts had called the police in the past, it was about legitimate police business?"

"To my knowledge, yes."

"On several occasions, you and Brian had some words, some disagreements, didn't you?"

"Yes." She didn't try to qualify her answer. She was much more compliant. *I had her; she was broken.*

"In fact, both Brian and Marilyn had voiced some concern that it had taken you a long time to respond, isn't that true?"

"Every time I responded, they complained." *Maybe there was still a little fight left.*

"So once again, that's a yes to my question?"

"Yes."

"And you were aware that on at least on one occasion they had called the police chief, your boss, and complained about your slow response time, correct?"

"Yes."

"And this all took place prior to November 27, the date of the incident, didn't it?"

"If you are trying to imply that I had hard feeling toward those people, I didn't." *Indeed, a little fight left.*

"Let me try my question again. All of this history took place before the incident, correct?" *My agenda, not hers.*

"Yes, it did."

"Thank you, officer. Now I want to move to our last point. You have discretion in certain situations to either make an arrest or cite and release, don't you?"

"On some offenses, that's right."

"And that decision to either arrest or cite and release is in part based on whether the subject is likely to flee the jurisdiction and never appear in court?"

"In part, yes."

"You arrested Mr. Frost for battery on a police officer?"

"I did."

"By arrest, I mean you actually handcuffed him, put him in your police unit, drove him to the station, and confined him in jail, correct?"

"That's right."

"Battery on an officer is the type of offense for which you have discretion to issue a citation for him to appear in court, isn't it?"

"It's also the type of offense where I can arrest him." Her voice had just a touch of mean. *That's what I wanted the jurors to hear.*

"Officer"—I dwelled on the word "officer" for just a moment— "Herrera. Battery on a police officer is the type of offense in which you have discretion to issue a citation, a simple ticket, isn't it?"

"Yes, it was my call and I believe I made the right call."

"In other words, you could have given Brian Frost a ticket and let him go on about his business?"

"I could have."

"Were you concerned that Mr. Frost would flee the jurisdiction?"

"No, I wasn't."

"Were you afraid that he would fail to appear in court if you simply issued him a ticket?"

"No."

"Just so we are clear. You could have just given him a ticket?"

"Yes."

I paused, nodded briefly at the jurors, then looked at the judge. "I have nothing further for this witness." As I walked back to counsel table, there was John Tice in the front row of the gallery, his legs crossed, his eyes on me. He gave me a brief nod; I didn't react. His presence made me feel uncomfortable. *How dare I be in one of "his" courtrooms representing a criminal defendant? It was as if I betrayed a solemn trust. After all, this was Tice country. I was a heretic in his cathedral.*

Marsh got up and went through the motions of trying to

clean up the damage on redirect. He went back and focused on Frost's refusal to halt when ordered and on his swiping Herrera's hand away. When Marsh finished, the judge dismissed the jurors for ten minutes and ordered Marsh and me back into his chambers. I glanced at number 1107 as she left the jury box; she was locked on me. *Whoa. I must have caught her attention.*

Slaughter waited for us to enter and then slammed the door. His face was flushed. "Marsh, you know how many cases I've got backed up for trial?" Without waiting for a response, he said, "Six. Six legitimate cases deserving of a jury trial. Unlike this piece of crap you've dumped in my courtroom." I was certain the judge's administrative assistant could clearly hear his comments through the closed door. Slaughter wasn't finished, and Marsh had the good sense to remain quiet. "Is there any screening going on in your office? Did anybody take any kind of a look at this case? My God, that cop was a mess. I don't know that I've ever seen such a pitiful job of policing or testifying." Slaughter took a breath; Marsh and I were still standing. "I saw your boss in the courtroom," he continued. "I'm going to call him and see what in the hell is going on. We just can't have this. Even if a case is mistakenly filed, it's the trial deputy's responsibility to feel it out, and if it's a dog, to deal with it pretrial. And Joe, this case has fleas." *I felt a huge wave of relief on behalf of the Frosts.*

Marsh had had enough. "Judge, you're not being fair. That cop wasn't my whole case. I've got her partner, and I think I can make my case." *After that dressing down, he still didn't get it?*

Slaughter cut him off. "Did you sleep through that cross? Your case is over. Those jurors saw what I saw, and what I saw was a petty, mean-spirited cop abusing her discretion. Hell Joe, all you are doing by bringing this to trial is setting up an even better civil case for this guy against that incompetent cop and her department." *I hadn't had time to even think about that. Not a bad idea.*

Judge Slaughter looked at me for the first time. "Jake, I don't know the full extent of the discussions that took place pretrial, but I guarantee they are going to be more fruitful in the next half hour. I'm going to extend the recess to a half hour." Then with a dismissive wave at Marsh, he said, "I want some results."

Marsh and I walked into the corridor separating the judge's chambers from the courtroom. Marsh said, in a barely controlled voice, "I'll reduce the charge to disturbing the peace. Frost does ten days."

I laughed at the absurdity of his offer. "Not a chance, Joe." *Oh how the pompous had fallen.*

Marsh got right up in my face. "Listen, I've taken all the goddamned abuse I'm gonna take."

"Afraid not." I shook my head at his pathetic ire. "Actually, Joe, you've only gotten what you deserve. I can see why you're still grinding out crap misdemeanor cases." Marsh's face reddened even further as I walked away.

CHAPTER 12

VINDICATION

I filled the Frosts in on the thrust of the judge's comments and also told them of Marsh's offer. Buoyed by the cross and the judge's take on events, they wanted no part of any compromise. *It was nice holding some cards.* We walked to the courtroom cafeteria to wait out developments. As we waited, I was once again struck with how engrossed I was when in trial. The rest of my life was suspended. There was nothing but the trial. It didn't matter whether it was a misdemeanor or a murder case; every trial demanded complete and total involvement.

We returned to the courtroom a half-hour later. Tice was nowhere to be seen. *I was hoping he might stick around and watch Judge Slaughter stick it to one of his guys.* Marsh was engaged in a whispered but animated conversation with Herrera and her partner in the back of the courtroom. From the body language, it was clear the two cops were furious. *Tough luck.* Their exchange broke off and the two cops slammed out of the courtroom. The jurors were ushered back into the courtroom, and the bailiff called court back in session as Slaughter emerged and took the bench.

"Mr. Marsh?" Slaughter inquired.

Marsh stood, and without looking at the jurors, said, "Your Honor, in the interest of justice, the people move to dismiss the charges." *I know it's not possible, but it felt like the air left the room for a moment.*

The judge nodded and said, "Very well, motion granted. Mr. Frost, you are free to go. And Mr. Frost, good luck to you and your family." He then turned to the jurors. "Members of the jury, the goal of the criminal justice system is just that: justice. Sometimes it takes a while to get there. I think what you have just witnessed is the system struggling through to a just conclusion. Thank you for your valued service. You are dismissed with my thanks."

Marsh was the first one out of the courtroom. The Frosts and I exchanged hugs, and as we left the courtroom, several jurors descended on us, wanting to know what had happened behind the scenes. Brian piped up, "The judge thought the woman cop was lying and made them dismiss the case." It was not completely accurate but close enough.

I looked for number 1107, but she was gone. *Dammit!*

I told the Frosts that we would talk later and left them with some of the jurors. As I walked down the corridor, I saw Marsh standing up against a wall, being lectured by Tice. As I got closer, Marsh saw me and gave me what I presume was his hard-guy stare. *It might have worked on some schoolyard years ago, but it was worthless here.* Tice dismissed Marsh and turned to face me. He extended his hand. The gesture appeared perfunctory, but I felt obliged to shake. "Jake, looks to me as if you still have it." He offered a mild grin. "It's been what, three or four years, and out of nowhere you pop up and kick my deputy's ass."

"It was a weak case. He should have looked at it before he tried it."

Tice ignored my comment, and turning the conversation on a dime, said, "I was surprised when I received notice that you were handling Durgeon's appeal." The change of subject was abrupt. "You never were a true believer, Jake. But taking on Durgeon is so over the top, even for you. How disappointing for one of my former deputies to debase himself by representing such a murdering lowlife."

Without rising to the bait, I said, "John, as long as I'm disappointing you, I must be doing something right."

"Like I said, Jake, I'm disappointed."

"John, I didn't take any crap from you when I was in the office, and I'm not going to take any now. As for Durgeon, I'm going to do everything in my power to get him a new trial, and as for you, go to hell." *I'd been wanting to say that to Tice for a long time. It almost felt as good as winning the Frost trial.*

As Tice was walking away, I added, "Good luck with Judge Slaughter. I think he wants a word with you." *Love getting in the last word.*

Suzelle had walked up behind me and, looking at Tice's retreating figure, she asked, "That was John Tice?" I nodded. "Does it have anything to do with dad's case?"

"No, that exchange was purely personal."

She cast another look at Tice's receding figure, and then turning back to me, asked, "My parents want to take you out to dinner. That alright?"

"No, I'm beat. You three go out and celebrate. I'm heading home. I've got class tomorrow."

She was disappointed. "Can I tell them we'll have dinner in the near future?"

"That works." I gave her a smile, and she walked off to join her folks.

ন্ত ন্ত ন্ত

I did make one stop before leaving. I vaguely knew the jury commissioner from my time in the office. I found her working through some files. "Ms. Machado, long time."

"Ah, Mr. Clearwater, I heard you had a very short trial." She was in her late seventies and sharp as a finish nail.

"I'll bet the jurors were pleased it was a one-dayer."

"Let me guess to what I owe this visit. It wouldn't have anything to do with one of your jurors now, would it?" *Sharp as a finish nail.*

"As a matter of fact . . ." I trailed off. "How'd you know?"

"With a woman who looks like she does, there are going to be men in the wings."

"And here I am."

"Mr. Clearwater, you know that information is confidential. I'll tell you the same thing I told Mr. Marsh: no way."

"Marsh was asking?"

"Indeed he was." *He must've quickly licked his wounds.*

"How about just a last name?"

"Sorry." *Damn.*

"Thanks anyway, Ms. Machado." *Who was I kidding? Somebody who looked like that had to be in a relationship. What was that old song? She must be somebody's baby.*

The exhilaration of the trial was only temporarily diminished by my run-in with Tice. Life was too short to suffer assholes. The trial had indeed been exhilarating. It had been about doing, not about the talking and the teaching, but about the doing. That said, it was a temporary aside in what would prove to be the long and winding road of Duane Durgeon.

CHAPTER 13

THE GENESIS OF DISDAIN

The next morning, I was fully awake at 6:00 a.m. Maybe an adrenaline hangover. There was a marine layer hanging over the beach. I slid on my Speedo. *I know they look silly, but heavy trunks and ocean swimming are a rough combination.* I worked my way down the outside staircase and eased into the fifty-six-degree surf. This was a major part of my everyday life. I didn't have a big life outside of school and my colleagues. I didn't date much and not seriously, and until I saw number 1107, I hadn't given it much thought.

My 9:40 criminal procedure class went fine. Afterward, I met Suzelle on the third floor of the library. There were pages of transcript strewn across the table. She popped up when she saw me coming, asked if she could hug me, and hugged me. "Thanks again. My parents are so relieved." And with a shy grin, she said, "You are my hero, Professor Clearwater." *For heaven's sake.*

"I'm your hero, huh? In that case, you ought to use my first name."

"Okay, Jake." Another nice smile.

I smacked my hand on a stack of transcripts. "Okay Suzelle,

I think it's time. We've spent a lot of time getting ready to start writing this thing. Let's do it."

Suzelle flashed a grin and propped her elbows on the table. "I was hoping you'd say that. I've read every case on ineffective assistance of counsel ever written." She pretended to collapse on a pile of books. *Funny stuff.*

I leaned back in my chair. "Let's sit back and think about Tice's case against Durgeon. What did he have?"

"Okay." She sat straight up and pushed up the sleeves of her sweater. "Number one, he had that darn fingerprint that puts Durgeon at the scene." *I doubt she had ever cussed in her entire life.* "Number two, the probable murder weapon Christina threw in the ocean; and three, the statements Durgeon made to Christina."

"That about sums up Tice's case." I shrugged.

"Seems like it didn't help Durgeon's cause that he was such an awful man. The jurors had to have hated him especially after his testimony during the sentencing phase," Suzelle added. *What's not to hate?*

"It's clearly not an overwhelming prosecution case," I said. "My hat's off to Tice; he tried the hell out of this case and steamrolled the defense."

"He must be really good. Did you work with him for a long time?"

"Actually, I worked *for* him. He was my boss for a while. He is a legend in prosecution circles. He's put more guys on death row than any other prosecutor in California."

She thought that over. "It seems strange that he is virtually unknown. I mean, I had never heard of him before I started working on this case."

What she said was true. Prosecutors are like offensive linemen. Nobody notices them unless their man sacks the quarterback, then everyone beats up on them. The glamour arena in trial work goes to the defense lawyers. With the exception of Bugliosi prosecuting Manson, or Clark and Darden screwing up O. J., nobody can name any prosecutors. And Bugliosi is only a name because the Manson case was so bizarre and frightening, and it didn't hurt that he wrote a book about it. I brought my thoughts back to Suzelle. "John Tice is like a force of nature. He wrings a case out for all it's worth."

Suzelle bit her bottom lip and drew little spirals on the paper in front of her, obviously uncertain of how her next comment would be received. "When I saw you with him yesterday, it did not look friendly."

I stood and walked to the window, looking north out to the hills, hands in pockets, mind in another time and place. It was my fifth year in the office, and as events would play out, my last year. Tice had just been elected DA. He surprised me by assigning me to prosecute Emile Peregrine. It was a capital case, and to this day I believe he pushed the case on me because he suspected I was conflicted on the death penalty. Otherwise, why assign me to a high-publicity trial? After all, he usually handled the high-profile cases himself. And beyond that, he had made it clear that he resented me.

A month earlier, a grandmother and her twenty-year-old granddaughter were found hanging from a citrus tree in Santa Paula, a small town about fifteen miles east of San Arcadia. Two days later, Peregrine was arrested. From the time of his arrest, his sanity was at issue. A psychiatrist often employed by the DA's office examined Peregrine. The psychiatrist was a man hard-pressed to believe anyone was insane, a viewpoint much admired within the office. However, this time he broke form and concluded that Peregrine did not understand the consequences of his actions and did not know right from wrong. The insane are bulletproof on charges and specifically protected from the death penalty.

I figured that was that. We would institute a sanity hearing and pack Peregrine off to a high-security mental hospital for as long as it would take for him to regain his sanity. And for Peregrine, that would be the rest of his life. I was wrong. Tice wouldn't accept the insanity finding and instructed me to find another psychiatrist. Reluctantly, I went to an out-of-county psychiatrist, and surprise, surprise, she also found him insane. That surely would be the end of things. Wrong again. When I reported back to Tice, he lost it. "I'm not going to have that sonofabitch lolling around in some fucking hospital," he screamed. "I want him executed. And you, Clearwater, are going to get it done."

Stupid me tried to tell him that the psychiatrists were right, but he wouldn't hear of it. He ordered me to scour the entire state until we found the "right" expert. I tried to reason through his rant. I told him that even if we could find someone with the right letters behind their name to prostitute themselves, Peregrine was insane and should be treated as any other insane person. "There is a basic question of right and wrong here." I maintained.

"Dammit, Clearwater! That creep had enough of a mind to kidnap two women, take them to a remote cabin, write a half-assed ransom note, and then tie a rope around their necks and hang them. I don't care what the shrinks say; he knew what he was doing, and he's going to die for it." Tice took a deep breath, trying to compose himself. "This district attorney's office is going to try Peregrine for those murders and pack him off to death row." He paused. "With or without you."

The challenge was full of enmity. I told him I wouldn't be any part of it. He turned away, dismissing me from his presence. My career as a deputy district attorney suddenly had a very short shelf life. Coincidently, just a couple of days later, Dean Chauncey called about the opening at Pacifico.

"Professor Clearwater? Jake?"

I turned from the window and gave Suzelle a brief, cleaned-up version of my break with Tice. She listened with rapt attention. "What finally happened?"

"Tice found his psychiatrist and Peregrine resides on San Quentin's death row with Mr. Durgeon."

Silence ensued. Then I clapped my hands. "That's enough history; let's get on with the new. First, ineffective assistance. Where did Rosenblatt screw up, and why were the screw-ups harmful? You've done the research, so you start there. I'll work on issues two and three, the statements Durgeon made to Christina and the fingerprint."

Suzelle looked puzzled. "What?" I asked.

"The other briefs I've read to get ready to work on ours bring up every conceivable issue, even the ones challenging the constitutionality of the death penalty. I guess I thought we'd do the same."

"Nope. We've got our three issues. We write them up and submit it. Raising long-shot issues just lets the real ones get lost in the shuffle and trivialized." I shook my head. "Hell, Suzelle, do you think the Cal Supremes are going to pick our case to throw out California's death penalty?"

She laughed. "I don't guess they will."

CHAPTER 14

JUROR NUMBER 1107

Malibu Road was a two-lane street that paralleled the ocean. When you turned onto the street, the first thing you saw on the left was the gilded, guarded gate to the exclusive Malibu Colony, enclave of the rich, famous, and reclusive. Just to the north were houses without the luxury of guarded gates. They were set close together on pilings just above the waterline, showing only their garages and their backsides to the world. The houses were not uniform. There were small, neat cottages; big, rambling, slightly shabby houses; and large, beautifully tasteful homes. The newer fancier places were rebuilt on the lots of the older teardowns.

I lived on the third level of one of the fancier houses. Tony and his wife, Eve, lived on levels one and two. Tony was rich. Family money. They rented me the top floor. I paid a modest rent, and in return, when they were out of town, which was more often than a law prof should have been, I watered their plants and generally watched over the place. It was beyond a sweet deal and even included garage space for my Jag.

It was late afternoon in late January, a couple of weeks after the

Frost trial. Tony and Eve invited me downstairs to a barbecue on their deck, sitting just above the mild surf. It was just the three of us with ribs, chicken, potato salad, and various spirits. The weather was perfect; it could have been August. There was a reason we lived in Southern California.

We were celebrating the end of the fall semester. I had just finished grading my exams; Tony hadn't started. Tony made Moscow Mules in those fancy copper cups, and they were delicious. I was on my second one when my phone chirped. I didn't recognize the number. "Hello."

"Is this Mr. Clearwater?" A woman's voice.

"Who's calling?"

"My name is Lisa St. Marie; I was on your jury." *Astonished. Number 1107?*

I quickly recovered. "You were number 1107?"

A brief laugh. "That's me, number 1107. I tried to talk to you in the hallway after the trial, but you were engaged."

My hosts were looking at me inquisitively. "Excuse me for a moment, Ms. St. Marie." I nodded to Tony and Eve and mouthed that I would be right back as I stepped from the deck, down the exterior steps, and onto the sand. *My God, number 1107.*

"Sorry for the interruption; I'm with some friends."

"I shouldn't have called on a Saturday night."

"You can call me anytime you want. I tried to get your contact information after the trial but struck out. I am so glad you called." Slight pause. "How did you get my number?"

"Didn't Suzelle, your student, tell you?"

"Suzelle? No."

"I was able to talk with her out in the hallway after the trial and I asked her about you. She told me that you were one of her law professors and she wrote down your cell for me."

"She never said a word." *That little sneak. I could hug her.*

Following a brief but awkward silence, Lisa said, "I know it's been a couple of weeks since the trial, but I wasn't sure if I should contact you. Maybe it's inappropriate." I started to speak but then she continued, "I thought you were fabulous during the trial, and I just wanted to tell you."

"Thank you. I was on the right side." *That was lame. You can do better than that. Think, Clearwater.*

"I've got to think Suzelle's parents were very pleased," she said.

"They were." A brief pause. "Suzelle didn't say a word to me about talking to you."

"I hope you're not upset with her."

"No, I'm going to owe her a thousand favors for giving you my number."

She laughed and said, "She thinks the world of you."

"She's pretty special. I was glad I could help out." *Now what was I doing, playing the modest hero. Come on, be bold. After all, she called you.* "I know this is kind of abrupt, but would it be possible to meet for coffee or lunch? We can discuss the trial," I managed. *Pretty bold.*

"I was hoping you would ask." She sounded like she was smiling. *Unbelievable.*

"Well," I said, with a huge grin on my own face, "let's figure out how to get together. Do you live right in San Arcadia?"

"I do."

I quickly thought through the options. "There's a Mexican restaurant called Raul's about ten minutes south of San Arcadia in Palms. They have outside seating with margaritas. They make a great salsa. How about meeting there?"

"I know the place."

"Would I be out of line suggesting we meet tomorrow?"

"Does noon work?" *This was a fantasy playing out.* "I'm looking forward to it, professor."

"None of that professor stuff. The name's Jake."

"Okay Jake, see you tomorrow."

As I climbed back up to the deck, I was having a hard time processing this. She was too gorgeous to want to go out with me. I wasn't being modest, just truthful. You just don't see someone like her hanging with mere mortals.

≈ ≈ ≈

I arrived fifteen minutes early. It was another beautiful January day, okay for outside seating. I took a table with an umbrella where I would be able to see her park and walk in. I was dressed in slacks, a polo shirt, and leather slip-ons.

A few minutes before noon she pulled in, driving a blue Prius, and parked next to my Jag. As she walked across the parking lot, I took her in. My goodness, what a dazzler. Short, dark hair framing that incredible face. She was wearing a floral sleeveless sundress that flattered her complexion. I realized it wasn't just her beauty but her elegance. She was almost unearthly.

I stood and pulled back a chair. She leaned in and gave me a brief hug.

"You beat me here, and I'm early," she said.

"You won't find any cool reserve with me. I have thought of nothing else since our call."

"I like direct; always this upfront?" she said with a smile.

"I try to be." My eyes were soaking her in. It wasn't just *my* eyes; the wait staff had virtually ground to a stop. She didn't seem to notice. Must come with the territory when you looked like she looked.

She said, "I haven't been here in years. It's nice that it hasn't changed much. I'm glad you suggested it."

"I did look for you after the trial. When I didn't see you, I went to the jurors' room and tried to wheedle your name from the jury commissioner. But she wasn't giving anything up."

"Good thing I had better luck with Suzelle,"—her eye contact was almost disconcerting—"who, incidentally, idolizes you. Must be tough, surrounded by adoring law students."

"Yeah, I've got to beat them off." I shrugged and then changed to a more neutral topic. "Your late entry onto the jury was a bit of a distraction for Joe Marsh and me." *Why did I mention Marsh? Wake up, Jake.*

She nodded slightly. "That sometimes happens."

"Is that the curse of the beautiful woman?" I smiled.

Our server arrived before she could respond. Lisa ordered a margarita, rocks, salt. I followed suit.

"Have you ever modeled?" *Of course she had modeled or been in a bunch of films.*

She was not surprised by my odd question. "In college, but not much. The money was good, but the work, boring."

"During jury selection, the judge didn't get much information from you other than you're in school administration. So tell me about that."

"I am a vice principal at a middle school." *Women who look like her weren't vice principals. Don't be a sexist pig, Jake.*

"Sixth, seventh, and eight graders just coming into their hormones," I observed. "That's a demanding job." I dipped a chip into chunky salsa. Great salsa. I hate watery salsa.

"Thanks for not minimizing my job. Usually when people find out what I do, I get some juvenile comment like 'I never had a vice principal who looked like you' or 'If my vice principal had looked like you, I would've gotten into more trouble.' I really don't appreciate those kinds of deprecating comments." *Yeah, it would take a real chauvinist ass to make a comment like that. First bullet dodged.*

"You're welcome. Which middle school? I'm familiar with San Arcadia."

"JFK, just off State Street on Breen."

"I know it. I once prosecuted a guy who stole an incredibly distinctive $300,000 custom Clenet roadster and then was clever enough to park it at the curb in front of his house near your school. Not a real bright guy. One of my easier convictions." She laughed, and it was fine.

"You did say during your opening statement that you were usually on the other side of criminal trials."

"Up until a couple of years ago, I was a deputy DA right here in San Arcadia."

"Was it difficult switching over to the defense?"

"It was odd, but since I believed I was on the right side with Brian's case, it came fairly natural. I like being on the right side, and as a prosecutor I usually was."

"I assume you got involved because Suzelle is your student." I nodded and took another chip. "Well, like I told you on the phone, you were compelling; it was easy to see the case from Mr. Frost's side of things."

"Thanks. I try to build a personal connection between my side and the jurors. If I do it well enough, they usually get it right." *Too much shop talk, Jake, move it along.*

Lisa wasn't ready to move on. "I see. Well, you did with me. I felt for the Frost family." After a thoughtful pause she said, "We heard from the bailiff that the judge was unhappy with the prosecutor."

"That he was." I grinned. "He should have done a better job

of screening his case. He should never have tried that case without thoroughly checking it out."

"Jake"—she touched my hand resting on the table—"I understand all that. But it wasn't just the facts. It was you. You were charming and compassionate. Everyone was on your side right away."

"Thank you. But enough shop talk. Let's talk about you." *This was going very well.*

The server reappeared with our margaritas. Lisa ordered two chicken tacos à la carte and I ordered a chicken tostada. The conversation flowed effortlessly. Following lunch and a second round of margaritas, we walked the two blocks to the beach. It was a bright, warm day. We sat on the sand and watched kids splashing in the calm surf, a toddler and her dad building a sandcastle, and some teenage boys throwing a football. Holding our shoes, we strolled along the edge of the wet sand. When we got back to Raul's, we'd earned another margarita.

"I don't want this lunch to end," I said.

"Me neither."

"There are only five working days and two hours of drive time separating us from next Saturday," I ventured. *Once again, pretty bold.*

She was on the same page. "Then we have a date. Say, 10:00 a.m. at my place. Come hungry, I'll make brunch. I'll have a surprise for you."

I walked her to her car, and she gave me a peck on the cheek. "See you Saturday. I'll text you my address."

"Wait, before you leave—did Joe Marsh try to get a hold of you? I'm just curious."

"He did. It was a short conversation." And with that she was off.

❧❧❧

That week couldn't have moved any slower. Yeah, Suzelle and I worked on the brief, I taught my classes, I played some three-on-three basketball with some students on the campus courts, and of course I took my swims, but my mind was on Lisa.

❧❧❧

Lisa's apartment was the left side of a restored grand old manse one block off San Arcadia's main drag. Watercolors hung on old-style plastered walls, creating a garden-like feel. The pictures were huge, with vibrant colors, and they exuded a cheery warmth. "I know virtually nothing about art, but I know what I like. And I like these."

She smiled and gave me a cheek kiss. "I'm glad you like my work."

I gave her a quizzical look. "I thought you were a vice principal."

"That's my job; this is my passion."

I took in the paintings with an intensified focus. Remember that movie a few years back about an artist who painted huge eyes on her subjects, that was her signature look? Lisa's signature look appeared to be vivid colors that practically jumped off the canvas. "Lisa, these are brilliant. They are so alive. They make me feel good just looking at them."

She beamed and hugged me.

Brunch was Eggs Benedict and Bloody Marys followed by strawberries and cream.

"And now for the surprise I promised. We're going to Musso's Gallery. I have a show this afternoon." And quite a show it was. I watched her interact with folks and I quickly realized she was a celebrity with the San Arcadia art crowd. Everybody wanted her attention. A jealous man might have been put off. I assured myself that wasn't me.

The show finished up around six o'clock. Her agent informed her that she had sold ten of the fourteen paintings and had potential buyers for the other four. Lisa was pleased but not excited. Interesting reaction, since the paintings were all listed north of $1,000.

She had made reservations at a bistro up in the hills over San Arcadia. The food was excellent, but the conversation had grown awkward. *Had I done something wrong, was the magic over?* When we got back to her apartment, she said, "Jake, I like you a lot, but I want to go real slow. I had a bad experience. I need to be very careful. Okay?"

"I'm glad you explained. I thought I had disappointed you. Time? I've got all the time in the world." She hugged me—I mean *really* hugged me. "So," I continued, "I propose next Saturday at my place? And we'll take it real slow."

Another week that crawled by. I did what I needed to do, but my thoughts were on number 1107.

❧ ❧ ❧

The following Saturday early evening, I surveyed my apartment. The entrance to the living room was directly off the staircase. You didn't really notice much about the room when you entered. You only saw the view, the light of the water, and the wide expanse of the sea. The far wall was completely covered with shelves of books and a well-used fireplace. Sliding glass doors opened onto a balcony which was just above Tony and Eve's second-floor deck. The balcony had two chaise lounges, perfect for afternoon naps, and two bistro chairs at a smallish table covered with a white tablecloth, matching napkins, white candles in crystal holders, and freshly polished silverware. That's right, polished silverware.

After showering from my swim, I donned a navy short-sleeved shirt, faded jeans, and white Nikes, and descended the three levels of stairs to await Lisa. She had just phoned and was only ten minutes away.

She rounded the corner and I waved her into my spot in the garage. Since parking was so tight along the curb, I had earlier moved my car to one of the rare open spots before they were taken. I opened her door and she gracefully stood and gave me a cheek kiss. She wore a pale-blue skirt that stopped above the knees and a butter-yellow sweater. *My God, she was beautiful. Once again, I had one of those moments—was I in the wrong movie?*

"Shall we ascend?" I motioned her toward the stairs. "The sunset awaits."

Lisa stepped through the living room and onto the balcony and opened her arms to breathe in the salty ocean smell. The air was still, and the waves were swirling around the pilings beneath us. She turned to the table, which I had to admit looked great.

"Professor, I am impressed."

"At your service, ma'am." I poured us each a glass of wine and we sank into the comfortable chairs facing the water to watch the show. The sky was streaked with the dazzling, unlikely color combinations that nature does so well—pink with orange, gold, purple, gray. We sipped wine in comfortable silence as the sun was slowly enveloped by the darkening ocean.

Show over, I refilled Lisa's glass and went to the kitchen to fetch dinner. We had chicken baked in wine sauce, mixed green salad, and crusty French bread—one of the few dinners I knew how to make.

"Do you entertain often? You make a great dinner, and you certainly have the right place for it."

"Often? No, only for special guests."

She ate a small bite of chicken. "This is very good."

I smiled my appreciation. "I only know a few dishes. Two more and my repertoire is exhausted."

That got a laugh.

"I enjoyed the exhibit. I'd like to attend the next one as well. How often do you show your work?"

"It'll be a while. That pretty much depleted my work over the past six months."

"How long have you been painting?"

"I cannot remember when I didn't paint. My life has always revolved around painting and shows."

"Shows? You had shows when you were a youngster?"

"My dad thought I was a prodigy, and he sponsored some shows."

"Yet you're also a vice principal? Seems an odd coupling."

"My father can be a little pushy. I push back. Don't get me wrong. I adore my dad and I also love painting, and as I told you last week, it is my passion. But I needed a path apart from dad."

"Sounds like you struck a fine compromise."

"For the most part, it has worked out. Dad is still a little pushy, but we've found our peace."

"Your paintings are just wonderful. He must be proud."

"He is. Let's talk about you. I know you teach law and sometimes try cases for families in distress," she said with a sideways flick of her eyes, "but I know little else about you."

I laughed at the quick deflection. "I teach criminal procedure and trial advocacy to second- and third-year law students."

"I guess we saw some of that trial advocacy at work during the trial." She cocked her head. "I understand you're also involved in a death-penalty case."

"Suzelle?"

"Suzelle."

"In a weak moment . . ."

"What did he do?"

"It was years ago, and he was convicted of murdering two people in San Arcadia." *Damn, nothing would turn off the makings of a great evening like talking about Durgeon.*

"Oh, was it the case where the husband and wife were killed, and they left behind their baby?"

"I'm afraid that's the one."

"I remember. It scared people." She seemed disconcerted. "What can you do for someone like that?"

I blew out some breath. "Review the trial to see if there were significant errors to warrant a new trial." *How could I move things along?*

She thought that over. "How do you feel about doing that?"

Apparently, we were going to stay here for a while longer. "Even guys like my client need a lawyer." *You're not answering the question, Jake.*

Her eyes were still studying my face. I don't think she was just making conversation. It almost felt like I was being tested. I continued. "I'm doing something that needs to be done. Ensuring that innocent people are not put to death or even that guilty people are not unjustly executed." I stirred uncomfortably in my chair. *What the hell, Clearwater? Sitting across from you is a world-class beauty and you talk about defending the world against injustice. It was hard to believe.*

"Which is it with your client, innocent or guilty?"

"I'm still working that out. But probably the latter."

I slipped off my shoes with my toes and stood. "Ready for that walk?" She smiled and unbuckled her sandals and stood. Our faces were very close and I wanted to kiss her, *remember go slow,* so instead

I motioned toward the balcony's stairs to the beach, and we walked down to the sand. The night was calm, with a slight breeze ruffling our hair. Our hands brushed, and I caught hers as we strolled in the soft light of the rising moon.

A wave, more aggressive than the others, surprised us and we dodged to higher ground. I looked at her laughing face, drew her into my arms, and kissed her. *Careful.* Her lips were full and warm and I kissed her again. We continued walking until a rocky promontory blocked our way. I lifted her onto a large rock and pulled up beside her.

She looked off. Was that a sign? Careful Jake, go slow.

Then apropos of nothing, she asked, "Did you always want to be a lawyer? Lawyers run in the family?"

Was she drawing me out or cooling me down? Maybe a bit of both. Maybe I needed cooling down. As for being drawn out, I usually resisted, but not with this woman. This was different. My usual relationships were transitory and initially exciting, and when over, bore only occasional regrets. I enjoyed life as it was with few complications. But when I looked at this woman, moonlight beaming on that lovely face, I had a feeling that life was already becoming complicated. I could be an open book.

"No lawyers in the family. My dad was a carpenter. He worked out of a garage in Ojai. He did all sorts of carpentry jobs. He was one of those guys who could do most anything with his hands. He was a great guy."

"Was?"

"He passed way too early, when I was in my third year of law school. My mom passed when I was just a kid. My dad and I were real close."

Lisa leaned over to watch the sea swirling around the bottom of our rock, and then out of the blue, "Ever been married?" *Again that sense of being tested. Was I being vetted to see if I was boyfriend worthy? If so, I hoped I was.*

"Right out of law school. Her name was Joanna. She was in my law-school class. We were young and thought what we had was love. It wasn't, and friendship wasn't enough. She lives in Las Vegas with her husband and two kids." I finished with a tone that I hoped would convey that was enough about that. I folded my arms behind my head and leaned back against the rock wall and asked, "How about you?

"It's a long story. I don't want to spoil the evening."

She suddenly shivered; it had grown chilly. Time to start back. I helped her down and we began walking, holding hands, arms swinging. I rambled on about Malibu, working to make her laugh, telling her about my neighbors who go skinny-dipping at midnight, the local surf scene.

We got back and climbed the steps. Lisa turned in the doorway and kissed me lightly, an *I had a really good time* kiss. I followed her to the balcony where we had left our shoes. I knelt and carefully lifted one foot and then the other, wiping the sand from her feet with one of the cloth napkins. She shivered as I held her ankle in my hand. I rose and looked into her large dark eyes. Her lips were slightly parted. The tight band I had felt around my stomach all evening tightened another notch. She slid into my arms, but then her hands were pushing back. She was breathing heavy, and her eyes were closed.

"Jake, it's been wonderful, but I've got to get going."

"I'm sorry, you warned me. I'm sorry." Then, we were briskly descending the stairs, walking to her car, and she was off. She had warned me, but all the signs were pointing green.

I lay in bed and went into autopsy mode. I kept replaying the evening. Had it ended so abruptly because I had pushed events?

That made the most sense. But the signals were so strong. I might not be the most attuned male on the planet, but I could have sworn I read her and the situation correctly. Maybe it wasn't me at all. Although that was a bit hard to imagine, given the intimacy in play. She had warned me. She clearly had something in her past. A recent breakup? When the topic of previous relationships had surfaced, she passed hers off as a long story. Had she suffered an abusive relationship? Had she been molested? It flashed on me that maybe she had psychological issues and I would be better off not getting involved. No! No, I wasn't better off. Beyond her physical beauty, we had, in a very short time, connected. I felt we were so connected, so in sync. I know that sounds like a lot of babble after only two dates, but I'm serious. There was something special going on.

The next morning, I called her cell. It rang four times and went to voicemail. I disconnected. She would see I called. The ball was in her court. Unfortunately, the ball just laid there and did not move. One day. Two days. Day three, I sucked up my pride and called again. No answer. I left a message. "Sorry I pushed too hard. I'd like to try again."

No return call.

CHAPTER 15

THE ORALS

It had been a month and a half since *the date*. Actually, forty-three days, but who's counting? Lisa had gone to ground, at least with me. What hadn't gone away was the Durgeon brief and the deadline. It was an exercise in patience, and after five drafts, it was ready. We filed in March, weeks inside our 180-day deadline.

Lisa called on April 28 at exactly 5:14 p.m. I recognized the number, took in a deep breath, and quickly calculated how I should react. I had played through several options over the months. Should I blow her off and not even take her call? Should I take the call and then blow her off? Should I take the call, shut up, and listen? Pride won out. I pocketed my phone. It rang four times. No voice message. I had a life, and I wasn't going to put it on hold. Even though, as Tony pointed out, I was a bit out of sorts.

๛ ๛ ๛

In June, three months after we filed, our opponent, the deputy attorney general, filed her response. Her brief was efficient but far from brilliant. Surprisingly, I found myself disappointed in the quality of her brief. I had pictured myself in a battle of wits with an able and aggressive adversary. Instead, it appeared I was dueling with a complacent opponent, perhaps her competitive edge dulled by years of success before a California Supreme Court singularly intent on upholding death-penalty convictions, oft-times despite significant errors committed by either the prosecutor or the trial judge. Given a reversal rate of two or three for every hundred death-penalty appeals, perhaps the AG's complacency was well founded. After all, she was on the side of the angels, while I represented Durgeon. The peach that he is.

I drafted the Durgeon reply brief. No Suzelle to help. She had graduated in May and was studying for the California bar exam. *I didn't envy her; what a miserable experience. The studying, and the test itself.* I filed my brief in August. And that was it until oral argument before the court. Meanwhile, life, as it tends to do, kept rolling along. Fall classes began. Three-on-three basketball was rough and fun and just as bad as ever, and the Malibu Pier seemed to have gotten a little longer. In November, Suzelle got word that she passed the bar. I joined her and her folks for a celebratory dinner.

Lisa was becoming a faded memory. It had now been about ten months since she had fled from my place. I'll admit I drove up to San Arcadia twice, and from my car parked across from Musso's Gallery, I saw in the window several brilliant paintings that had to be Lisa's. I drove by her house once but did not stop. *Was I moving into stalker turf?*

Just as I was convinced the court had forgotten about Durgeon and his appeal, I received a call from the court clerk that oral arguments were scheduled in three weeks, on January 9, 2017. My stomach lurched. It was one thing to view orals before California's highest court as something off in the indistinct future, something so far off it wouldn't actually come to pass. It was quite another when it was a stark reality looming in the immediate future.

I dug back into Durgeon, preparing my line of attack. I knew in which order I wanted to address the issues. But from what I'd been told, the justices usually had their own ideas about how matters would proceed. At any rate, I planned to be ready for whatever they threw at me.

When I told Tony and Howard that the orals had been scheduled, they organized a mock session with Howard playing Chief Justice Schmitt, and Tony and Dean Chauncey and four third-year students rounding out the seven justices of the mock supreme court. It was good practice, and frankly, a couple of the third years got the better of me. I would have to take my game up to avoid serious personal embarrassment, not to mention failing to adequately represent Durgeon's interests.

❧❧❧

Strong gusty winds woke me before sunup. Thank God the day was finally here. I had thought about little else for the past three weeks, my concerns rooted as much in the unknowns about the process as in the substance of my argument. I was a rookie at appellate argument, and yet here I was, having my first go at this appellate stuff, and hey, maybe I'd just start off with a death-penalty appeal before the state's highest court. *Whose idiot idea was this, anyway? Well, hell, one way or another, it would be over today.* With all that said, I admitted, if only to myself, the adrenaline buzz felt awesome. Suzelle, Howard, and Tony wanted to come watch, but for some reason, I wanted this to be just me. Maybe it was fear of failure. Maybe a fear of distraction. I didn't know.

I made coffee and climbed into the shower. Forty-five minutes later, dressed in lawyer dark blue, I set out for LAX. The Santa Ana winds buffeted my car as I drove PCH south, Sting's melodic voice easing the way. The flight to San Francisco was bumpy. I abstained on coffee, favoring unstained dark blue for my appearance before the court.

It was ten o'clock when I entered the cavernous courtroom in its mahogany splendor. My argument was set for eleven. The seven justices were situated in an arc facing the lectern, where a woman advocate stood, making her argument. I took a seat in the back. The advocate was undergoing tough questioning from several of the justices. Her voice had a slight tremble. My stomach tightened. Perhaps adrenaline was giving way to fear.

"Is it truly your position, Ms. Summers, that the insurance carrier is not responsible for picking up the tab?" thundered Chief Justice Schmitt. Schmitt was almost leaning over the bench, jabbing a finger at Summers.

She responded directly to Schmitt, not backing off. "As set forth in my brief, it is our position—"

"I read your brief, counsel, and as far as I could make out, it is loaded with verbiage and puffery. Let's cut through the weeds, Ms. Summers. The language in the contract drafted by your client would certainly seem to extend coverage. Tell me how it is that I am wrong." I, of course, knew nothing about the case, but it was my guess that Schmitt was not smitten with Ms. Summers's side of things. Mercifully, after another couple of minutes, her time was up, and she took her seat. The opposing advocate was now at the lectern, and Schmitt was immediately all over him. Chief Justice Schmitt appeared to be an equal-opportunity abuser. He seemed to have an even temperament: angry all the time. I'd heard this about him, and now I was getting an upfront view of his bombastic style.

Suddenly, a man was sitting in the seat next to me. "Clearwater."

It was Harley Manlow. I had not seen Manlow since I left the DA's office. He didn't offer a hand. I reciprocated.

"Harley," I said, without warmth.

"Keeping busy, counselor?"

"I figured once you got your guy on death row, you would lose interest and move on."

"Not hardly. Tice and I only lose interest when they take them to that little room and stick that black needle in their arm."

"Ah, pleasant thoughts, detective." I smiled. "What can I do for you?"

"Not a thing, Jake, just wanted to say hi."

"Trying to ice me, Harley?"

He gave me his hard-cop stare and leaned into me, his nose inches from mine. I held my ground. "Fuck you, and fuck your client," he said, just loud enough for only my benefit.

I smiled again. "Always pleasant visiting with you, Harley." Can't let the bastard see you sweat.

He sucked in his lower lip, got up, and walked over and took a seat next to John Tice. I hadn't noticed either one of them when I entered. Tice looked blankly at me and turned back to watch Schmitt and his cohorts grind down Ms. Summers's adversary. *What was that about? And why in the hell are these two here? Was I correct, was it to intimidate me?* Trial prosecutors never show up at the orals on appeals from their cases. The prevailing thought is that it's their job to convict and it's up to the AG's office to protect the conviction on appeal. I wondered if Tice had ever shown up at orals before. But I didn't have time to think about that now. It was just about time to be front and center.

The exchange with Manlow had revved the competitive juices. Any jitters I had were gone. The clerk stood and in a formal voice announced, "The State of California vs. Duane Durgeon." I hadn't noticed that Ms. Summers and her opponent had finished. I strode to the appellant's table, feeling the wonderful adrenaline rush I always experienced when I began a trial. I sat down and nodded to Ms. Woodruff, the assistant attorney general, who would be arguing on behalf of the state.

The chief justice looked at me. "Mr. Clearwater, you may approach."

I stepped to the lectern, which was equipped with a red light and a green light. The green light was lit. "May it please the court. I am here on behalf of Duane Durgeon. His trial was significantly compromised, denying him a fair trial, and I am here today asking for a new trial. Before I discuss the specific points of error, it would be helpful to view the overall case against Mr. Durgeon. It is—"

Schmitt interrupted, "We are familiar with the case, counsel. Perhaps your time would be better spent on the issues."

I nodded. "I appreciate the court's advice, and with all due deference, I believe my time is best spent in taking in the whole of the case." I paused and waited for Schmitt to rebuke me. In retrospect, challenging Schmitt right out of the chute probably was not the best way to begin my relationship with him, but strategically I needed to spin the facts to set up my argument.

"It's your limited time, counsel," he warned.

"Thank you, Your Honor. The prosecution's case was so thin that any error the trial court or defense counsel made was not harmless. I do not want this court to agree with me that there was error but then find the error was harmless when viewed in the context of the entire case." I again paused to see if Schmitt saw my logic and would let me proceed. He nodded for me to go on. He was being grudgingly accommodating. This cut against everything I had heard about him and certainly was nothing like what Ms. Summers had just experienced.

"The case against Mr. Durgeon was two-pronged. The first was the evidence offered by his ex-girlfriend who became a police informant. Even if this informant is to be believed, her testimony, while it may arguably have put Durgeon at the scene prior to the murders, was of little value beyond that. However, as I will discuss in a moment, the trial judge erred in allowing the informant's testimony to come before the jury. The second prong of the state's case was a partial fingerprint from a piece of packing tape. The partial print is the only incriminating evidence that did not come through the informant. The ex-girlfriend informant was the conduit for all other incriminating evidence."

I let the point settle for a moment, and Schmitt spoke before I could continue. "Mr. Clearwater, I read your brief and I'd like to ask you about the fingerprint." He looked down at his notes. "I believe it is your position that the fingerprint should not have come into evidence, is that correct?" So much for letting me play out my argument as I had planned.

"That's correct, Your Honor, may I explain?"

Schmitt raised his hand. "Hold on a minute, let me see if I understand your position." This was the Schmitt I expected. "It is your position that the state lab used a new scientific technique in finding the print on the tape, is that correct?"

"That is correct." I had not wanted to argue the fingerprint issue first. It was my weakest argument. I wanted to lead with an attack on the informant. Unfortunately, Chief Justice Schmitt had the power to control the agenda, and he appeared to be singularly intent on wielding that power. *Damn.*

"And since this was a new technique, it was, of course, not yet in common use. Am I on track so far?"

"Yes, Your Honor." I knew where this was going, and there was no way for me to defend against Schmitt's slow plod toward the Achilles' heel of my fingerprint argument.

Schmitt lumbered on. The other six justices seemed content to have Schmitt carry the discussion. "And since this technique was not in common usage, there is no way it could yet be generally accepted in the relevant scientific community?" He looked at me inquiringly.

"Absolutely." I hastened on to regain the initiative. "This court and the United States Supreme Court have always been vigilant in disallowing the results flowing from scientific procedures that have not been generally accepted in the relevant scientific community."

"Counsel, I am well aware of this court's position on new scientific tests and techniques."

I ventured forward in spite of his rebuke. "And as you are aware, this court has always been concerned with the taint of junk science in our courts. If a new or novel method has not been rigorously wrung out in the relevant community, its result has been excluded. This court, in particular, has always been the gatekeeper in preventing junk science from coming in."

"Counsel," Schmitt's voice had taken on a new firmness, "according to the attorney general's brief, the technique had been in use by the state lab about a year prior to its use here. Doesn't that qualify as a sufficient amount of time to see if the procedure works?"

I was ready for him. "This court's holding in *People v. Kelly* instructs that the burden is on the proponent of the new or novel technique to establish that the technique is generally accepted. In this case, the prosecutor produced no such evidence. All the trial judge knew was that this procedure had been in use in the state lab less than a year. Not one scientist was called to testify to its general acceptance." I paused, my point made. I hoped I had diverted Schmitt from going where I feared. "This court set the *Kelly* standard for sound reasons. Jurors are impressed with scientific evidence. They put tremendous stock in things scientific. Consequently, we have to guard against sham evidence being masqueraded as legitimate evidence. The generally accepted standard is in place, and it is workable."

I shifted my focus from Schmitt to the rest of the court. "The prosecutor, of course, knew of the *Kelly* standard, and yet he chose to ignore it. The standard has been in place for years. There was nothing new, there were no surprises. Yet, for whatever reason, he disregarded the clear directive of this court." *Take that Tice, you SOB.* "Without that partial print, Mr. Durgeon would not have been convicted. In fact, without that print, the case against Durgeon would not have even been filed."

Schmitt raised his hand. It was a directive to stop. I was surprised that he'd let me go on as long as he had. "Counsel, isn't it true that our concern over the use of novel scientific techniques is that they may be unreliable?" Schmitt had his teeth in the argument and would not let go. He was back on track, and I knew my *Kelly* argument was about to be flushed. All I had managed to do was briefly postpone the inevitable. I started to respond, but he cut me off. "And isn't it true that this technique found a fingerprint that matched the leading suspect, specifically your client?"

"Yes," I had to concede.

"Well, then it seemed to have worked pretty well in this case, didn't it?" Schmitt had finally gotten to where I feared. The logical consistency of his argument was irrefutable. New and untested or not, it revealed Durgeon's damn print. *Worked pretty good here, didn't it, counselor?* I was now reduced to arguing that the court should follow the rule simply because it was the rule. That was not a good place to be.

Nonetheless, I gave it my best shot. "Your Honor, this court in *Kelly* did not set forth a result-determinative test. This court correctly decided that new science should be vetted in the scientific community before we would allow it to be unleashed on our court system. That did not happen here."

"Mr. Clearwater"—it was Justice King this time—"are you suggesting that we exclude entirely reliable and extremely probative evidence in a double murder case?"

I could not answer that question that in any way advanced my argument. Instead, I had to recast the question. "Your Honor, I'm suggesting that this court should follow the rules you and your colleagues created to deal precisely with this situation." As soon as the words were out of my mouth, I regretted them. I had, in essence, called the court hypocritical.

Following an uncomfortable silence, Schmitt in a stern voice said, "Counsel, I strongly suggest that you move to your next argument." Not only had my fingerprint argument, which at best was tenuous, been crushed, but I feared my credibility might also be a casualty because I had chased the argument as far as I had. My argument, while legally sound, was logically flawed. Having completely lost momentum, I was forced to shrug it off and push on.

"Your Honors," I began again, "the testimony of Christina Atwell was prostituted and improperly considered." I knew this sounded forced, but I needed to generate some steam. "Ms. Atwell was Duane Durgeon's confidant, his lover, and his only friend at the time of his arrest. Nonetheless, following the arrest of Durgeon and Ms. Atwell on unrelated narcotics charges, she made bail, and while Durgeon languished in jail, she went to the police and told them of her suspicions of his involvement. Bear in mind, these were simply her suspicions. She did not have any direct evidence linking him to the murders." I paused again and directed my eye contact to the three justices to the left of Schmitt. "The police were frustrated. Their investigation had stalled. Atwell gave their investigation new life. It is critical to remember that Durgeon was in custody on felony drug charges and was represented by counsel. He had a lawyer and, knowing full well he was represented, the police taped a wire on Atwell and sent her in to interrogate Durgeon."

"Again, let me remind you, we have read the briefs and know the facts; get to your point." This time it was Justice Kirkpatrick, one of three women on the court.

"I am there, Justice Kirkpatrick. The police, through their agent Atwell, surreptitiously interrogated Mr. Durgeon, and in so doing, violated his Sixth Amendment right to counsel."

Justice Connelly broke in. "Mr. Clearwater, I understand from your brief that your claim is built on *Massiah*."

"In part, Your Honor."

"But *Massiah* involved decidedly different facts. Most importantly, the police interrogation of Mr. Massiah concerned the very matters for which he had been indicted. True?"

"Yes, however—"

"Yet here, your client was in custody and represented on the narcotics charges, not on the murder charges. I would agree with you if the police had sent the informant in on the drug charges. But Ms. Atwell was sent to your client to investigate completely different charges. Counsel, I read that as a significant departure."

"Respectfully, I do not think so. Sixth Amendment protection is vacuous if the police are allowed to circumvent the right to counsel through surreptitious measures. Once a person has a lawyer, the police must go through the lawyer to get a specific waiver of counsel from the accused."

"Counsel, I disagree with your conclusion." It was Schmitt again. "It's one thing to go around a lawyer and question a suspect on the very charge for which they have been indicted, as in *Massiah*. But it is another thing to say that once a person is represented on any charge, they are protected from police interrogation as to crimes other than those for which they are represented. That clearly is beyond the holding in *Massiah*."

"Of course you are correct as far as the facts of *Massiah* are concerned," I said, without missing a beat. "However, the right to counsel as set forth in the Sixth Amendment is the critical buffer between the police and the accused. Once the accused is represented, police efforts to obtain statements must cease. They knew he was represented, and they ignored that to facilitate their investigation."

Schmitt leaned over his bench to ask incredulously, "Counsel, if your view of *Massiah* is correct, once any accused has a lawyer, the police cannot question them with regard to any other crimes?" Schmitt was trying to draw me into a philosophical debate. My argument could not withstand that scrutiny. I needed the court to focus only on the facts of my case.

"My concern is Duane Durgeon and the particularly exploitive tactics used by the San Arcadia Police. Mr. Durgeon had been in custody for weeks, he had just recently been released from a five-year prison sentence, he had no family in the area, and he had only one friend. That 'friend' was sent by the police to prey on that relationship and induce incriminating statements."

Schmitt said, "Mr. Clearwater, I appreciate your fervor and I must admit you paint a compelling picture, yet however convincing your unfairness claim might be, the law is not with you. *Massiah*, as you are well aware, did not speak to the circumstances currently before this court. I challenge you to cite any authority in support of your position." He gave me a quizzical look, daring me to respond.

I was not going to fold my tent and leave the field. "While *Massiah*'s facts are different than the circumstances here, it does speak to the special role of counsel in the criminal justice system.

Once an accused, especially an accused in custody, is represented by counsel, they have the expectation of assistance from their lawyer. They have a legitimate belief that their lawyer is now in place to buffer, to protect them from questioning by the police. When that buffer is eliminated, and the police are free to use friends and lovers to lower the resistance of the jailed even further, basic fairness and due process are violated."

Dead silence. No one answered my challenge. My argument had failed to engage even one of the seven. The only chance this argument had of convincing this court to extend the *Massiah* rule to cover Durgeon's circumstances was to appeal to their sense of fairness. Their lack of response spoke volumes. Zero for two. First the fingerprint and now the statements. *You're throwing a shutout, Clearwater.* I had one pitch left.

"Your Honors, I would like to turn to my last point, ineffective assistance of counsel." I paused, allowing everyone to turn to the new topic. "Duane Durgeon's trial counsel's failure to call an eyewitness to the murders who identified someone other than Mr. Durgeon as the shooter constituted monumental ineffective assistance."

Justice O'Neil, one of the other two women, spoke for the first time. "As you know, counsel, trial counsel's error, if it is to be deemed harmful, must fall below the standard of care a reasonable criminal defense attorney would have rendered."

"Thank you, Justice O'Neil. Attorney Rosenblatt's performance did precisely that."

I spoke directly to O'Neil. Now using both my hands, I attempted to draw the whole court to me. I had resorted to my trial courtroom manner; I was talking to the justices as I spoke to jurors. I was completely at ease, in my element. "There were numerous incidences of counsel's deficient efforts. But I want to speak to just one of those deficiencies, and as I lay out the facts, I invite this court to ask, was there a reasonable doubt as to the identity of the killer? Was there a reasonable doubt?

"Ron Evans witnessed the murder of Doree Blanco. From a distance of not more than fifty feet, he saw the man who shot her. He told the police that the shooter was large, had full facial hair, and had shoulder-length brown hair. Duane Durgeon fit that description. Your Honors, so did a man named Anthony Graves. On the morning of the murders, Mr. Graves lived in a trailer park next to the apartments where the murders took place. Mr. Graves was a twice-convicted rapist. Mr. Graves, shortly before the murders, told a friend that he thought Doree was 'hot.' Mr. Graves's only alibi was supplied by his live-in girlfriend." I stopped to assess how the justices were reacting to my soliloquy. They were ready for me to tie things up. "Graves was immediately arrested. The following day, Mr. Evans was brought into the interrogation room, and immediately on seeing Graves, said, 'That's him, get me the hell out of here.'"

Justice O'Neil asked, "I assume the police conducted a thorough investigation of Graves and determined he was not involved, is that correct?"

"There was an investigation of Graves. I am not certain how thorough it was, Your Honor, but that is not my point."

"What is your point?" Irritated tone.

"If Rosenblatt had put Evans on the stand and elicited from him the events I just described, Duane Durgeon's jury would have had a reasonable doubt." The justices by their facial expressions were not rejecting my argument out of hand. *I had some rope here. I had to be careful how I let it out: no tangles, no knots.*

Justice O'Neil, perhaps a bit irritated at my brusqueness, said, "Counsel, it has long been the law that appellate courts should be very circumspect in second-guessing the strategy of trial counsel. Are you asking this court to break from that precedent?"

"Not at all, Your Honor. If the decision not to call Ron Evans as a witness was a mere tactic or strategy, I would not have raised it. But here, that decision to not call Evans went well beyond tactics or strategy. This was a sketchy identification case, a whodunit. And in that kind of case, the powerful visceral reaction of the only eyewitness to someone other than the defendant goes to the very heart of the case. Evans's testimony would have been the difference in finding Mr. Durgeon guilty or not guilty."

"I'm sorry counsel, you are way ahead of me." Justice Schmitt had rejoined the fray. "I'm still stewing on the second-guessing of trial tactics. I assume the record is bare as to why trial counsel did not call this witness?"

"That is correct."

"Is it possible that the witness had disappeared and was therefore not available for trial? Is it possible the witness changed his mind about this Graves character being the shooter?"

"The record does not indicate one way or another."

"Is it possible that this witness had now come full circle and was prepared to identify your client as the murderer?"

"Again, the record is of no help."

"Counsel, it seems to me we have just done what all of our decisions in this area prohibit, and that is to engage in speculation. To second-guess why trial counsel, entrusted with the case, did what he did. We simply don't have the information he had at the time he made his decision. It is precisely for those reasons we cannot second-guess trial counsel." He looked at me as if things were settled.

Schmitt had walked into my trap. I had him. "The policy prohibiting second-guessing is sound, and I am not suggesting that this court should vary from its long-established policy."

"Mr. Clearwater." Schmitt smiled warily, his eyes peering over his glasses. "Are you conceding the point?"

I grinned and shook my head. "No, Your Honor, I am not."
I was careful to structure my argument precisely. "This court need
not engage in speculation to grant Mr. Durgeon a new trial. All this
court has to do is recognize that, regardless of whatever information
defense counsel had concerning Ron Evans, he had viable options
available to him to get Evans's powerful identification of someone
other than Durgeon before the jury."

"Go on," Schmitt said impatiently.

"If Evans was not available, trial counsel could have laid the
foundation for unavailability and had his statement come in.
If Evans was available but at the time denied he made the ID of
Graves, trial counsel could have impeached him with the prior
statement, and again the statement comes in. And I am certain this
court need not be reminded, but the statement comes in not just to
impeach but as substantive evidence the jury may consider on the
question of guilt or innocence. Or, if Evans was available, and at the
time of trial, maintained he was mistaken about Graves being the
shooter, and that it was Durgeon, again impeach him, and again the
statement comes in." I locked eyes with Schmitt. "However it plays
out, that powerful statement by the only witness identifying another
individual as the shooter comes before the jury. Sir, that's reasonable
doubt." I almost slapped the lectern but caught myself.

There was a long silence before Schmitt said, "Thank you
counsel, you are out of time." The red light was flashing. I thanked
the justices and sat down.

The AG picked up the ineffective-assistance argument and
reiterated that to second-guess trial counsel's tactics is to engage in
pointless speculation. However, to my surprise, Justices Schmitt and
O'Neil peppered her with questions. Schmitt, in particular, seemed
to agree with my view that Rosenblatt should have called Evans,
regardless of what Evans might have testified to. Schmitt could be

a powerful ally. *If, indeed, he was an ally.* Even though Schmitt and O'Neil seemed to be leaning in my direction, I had to temper my thoughts with the cold hard reality that this was a law-and-order court that went to great pains to uphold convictions, especially death-penalty convictions.

When the AG's time was up, I had time for a five-minute rebuttal, which I waived. Frankly, nothing Ms. Woodruff said needed rebutting.

Court adjourned, and the justices filed out. I walked over to Woodruff and we shook hands. She smiled ruefully. "You are one ballsy guy. You really went 'round with Schmitt. Their decision in this case should be interesting." She finished packing her briefcase and was off. She was not nearly as pumped as I was. Of course, she did this kind of thing all the time. I was the rookie. Maybe I was just feeling a rookie rush and had not really scored much with my last point. At any rate, Ms. Woodruff did not seem overly concerned. Tice and Manlow were gone. I savored my one dig at Tice.

On the flight back to LAX, I had a Coors Light, sat back in my window seat, and stared out at the remains of the day from 30,000 feet.

CHAPTER 16

JUROR NUMBER 1107 REDUX

It was raining. I was finished for the day and walking to my car when there she was, standing under an umbrella next to my car. "Hello, Jake." Her voice was tentative and cautious, her eyes studying mine.

"Lisa." My pulse and brain went into hyperdrive. Discordant thoughts flashed. Saying she had caught me off balance did not do justice to that phrase. I had envisioned maybe two- or three-thousand times what I would say to her if I ever saw her again, but now all my rehearsing was lost in the white noise of my brain. What do they say about the best-laid plans going to hell with the first shot? I'd been shot.

"I am sorry, Jake."

I stared. Her face gave me that *what are you going to do?* look. My first words were meaningless. "How long have you been out here?" *How's that for missing the point?*

"Since three." Brief pause. "Once I decided I needed to see you, I didn't want to miss you. I knew a call wouldn't work."

Needed to see me? I walked past her and opened my car door. "Thanks for the chat, but I've got to get going."

"Jake, please wait." I turned to face her. "Can we talk? There are some things I want to explain."

I let out my breath. "It has been months and now you show up out of the blue and want to explain. I don't need this."

"I don't blame you for being angry. Please hear me out. Then I'll go."

I took a long moment and relented. "There's a Starbucks down the hill. We can talk there."

"Why don't we go back to your place?"

My voice still neutral, I replied, "Starbucks will do." It made for a quick getaway. I did not know where this was going. Hell, it had been almost a year.

At Starbucks, I motioned her to a chair and then ordered two plain coffees. I placed the drinks on the table, sat, and looked at her.

"Thanks for hearing me out. I have some serious psychological problems." She let out some breath. "I've been struggling to work through them. My therapist thought it best to not contact you until I was stable." She was on the verge of tears.

"Stable? What do you mean?" My voice softened. She was clearly hurting and remorseful; my lingering anger was dissipating.

"Until you came along, I believed I could never again commit to anyone. I was psychologically beaten down. But then that trial. I saw this compassionate, charming man, and I dared to hope. I know it was presumptuous, I didn't know your situation, but you felt right. And in just the few times we were together, you brought me hope for a real relationship again." She blew out her breath. "I know it probably sounds crazy, but that hope was scary and dangerous. If things failed again, I worried I would never recover." Tears streamed down her face. She did not bother wiping at them. "I had a terrible and abusive marriage. It scared me and screwed me up so that I developed into a person thinking that I couldn't trust anyone, especially men. I thought when I was on that jury and saw and heard you, though, that maybe I could have a relationship." She wiped at her tears and blew her nose. "But when we were becoming intimate, everything came flooding back."

I didn't fully grasp all she was saying, but I was becoming a believer. "You warned me about going too fast. I didn't listen. That is on me. I am so sorry." Her cheeks had grown roses as she gave me a rueful smile.

"Thanks for understanding. Thanks for listening. It took almost a year of therapy to come and tell you what was going on with me."

We looked at each other for what seemed a long time. I broke the silence. "Let's take our coffees to my place and start phase two of the Lisa and Jake story."

༺ ༺ ༺

I poured wine in place of our coffees. Lisa sat on the sofa, I on the armchair near her end of the sofa. I was being very careful. We caught each other up on events. Things were okay at her school, although she did take two weeks off after the evening at my place. She had not painted much; she explained that painting took inspiration, and she had not been inspired. I told her about the Durgeon argument. She had lots of questions. We were both steering clear of her psychological concerns and her marriage.

The afternoon turned to evening. We could hear the waves crashing and rolling, and then she was talking about her marriage. Her voice was halting. I did not interrupt, even when I didn't understand something.

Brad had inherited money. Lisa was vague about what he did. He took over companies, invested in the stock market, played golf and tennis, and collected art. Lisa met him at one of her art shows.

When Brad walked into her life five years ago, Lisa was twenty-nine and he was thirty-five, handsome, and oozing Southern charm. He fixed his attention on her, and in her words, "bowled me over." They married, contrary to her father's advice, three months later. The first year was okay, then late one night after a party, he turned on her as soon as they were inside their elegant beachfront condo. He accused her of flirting with one of his colleagues. Indignant, she denied it. He hit her in the face, closed fist, knocking her to the floor. *That sonofabitch.* She lay dazed and bleeding as he paced back and forth, raging. He finally slammed out the door. She did not call the police, she didn't leave the house. She did not explain why.

The next morning, he returned home and, kneeling next to her as she lay on the couch, gently brushed her hair from her face. As he looked at her swollen cheek, he cried. He cradled her in his arms, apologized, and swore it would never happen again. She lied to the outside world. She had fallen. She forgave the bastard. *Classic pattern of spousal abuse; I had prosecuted these cases.*

Months later, it happened again. The instant they got home from a late dinner, he turned a furious face to her. Did she think he wouldn't notice what she was doing? How long had this been going on? Did she think she could get away with it? She backed away, confused and afraid. He followed her retreat across the room, head pushed forward, disgust and hatred in his eyes. He hit the wall near her head and stood, fists clenched, calling her vile names and looking as if he meant to kill her. She struck out at him, hitting him in the face and screaming, "You hit me this time, you're going to jail!" She wept with relief when he turned and stalked out. Twenty minutes later, with hastily packed suitcases, she left. "He called, I don't know how many times. He sent flowers. He sent me a custom CD asking for forgiveness. I finally texted him and warned him to leave me alone or I would get a restraining order. He backed off after that."

Her story made my muscles tense. She fell silent, limp and exhausted. Then she patted the couch next to her. I joined her. She turned into my chest. I gently ran my hand up her arms to her face and brushed the tears away.

"Is your therapist okay with you being here?"

"Not really, but I needed to see you and explain what was going on with me. I needed to know if we could have a relationship." She gave me a tired smile. "Katherine is going to want all the details. She is concerned that I'm pushing things a little too quickly."

"Sounds like she has your best interests at heart. Tell her I promise to go very slowly and carefully."

"She would like you, Jake."

"One thing confuses me. When I watched you at the art show, you were so up and happy and conversant with everyone, and yet inside you were hurting. How does that happen?"

"Katherine and I have been working to figure that out. Best guess, I'm fine in social and professional relationships, but after the trauma with Brad, my psyche rebels at any sense of intimacy." She shrugged. "Jake, not to scare you off, but you may be the elixir to what ails me." *I've never been an elixir before.*

❧ ❧ ❧

We did start again, very slowly and very carefully. Physical intimacy was limited to hugs and kisses. We alternated weekends. I introduced her to Tony and Eve. The Tony, Eve, and Jake weekends now included Lisa. Lisa and Eve soon became as close as sisters. I invited her to take a day off and sit in on one of my classes. She was so focused, I even threw a question at her. She nailed it, and my class applauded. *Who needed years of law school?* In a brave move, we brought Howard into the mix. With Howard, you never quite knew what his reaction might be. But when introduced to Lisa, he swooned. That's a word I do not use often, but it was appropriate here. Howard treated her like royalty.

CHAPTER 17

THE DEAN'S BRUNCH

The Dean's Brunch, held the first Sunday in March, is a high-light in the social tapestry of the law school. It brings together select alumni, local celebrities, judges, and big-money donors to mingle with the faculty and congratulate each other on their own successes as well as those of the law school. Dean Chauncey's luxurious home rested high on a bluff behind the school and had a spectacular panoramic view of the coast. Beyond the bluff, rough hills led away from the plush beach town and continued all the way to Highway 101, about fifteen miles inland. The steep hills were unstable, and the thin winding road, with Falling Rock warning signs at every curve, got washed out most winters. Further back in the undeveloped hills, *M.A.S.H* was filmed. You can still find the site, marked by the hulls of rusty jeeps and other relics not worth hauling away.

Chauncey's Spanish-style home had five bedrooms, six bathrooms, and a forty-foot terrace on the ocean side. Just right for two people. Lisa and I walked through the wide, curved doors and stood in the entry, surveying the sunken living room. The walls were a smooth white, the better to display the impressive lithographs that lined the room. The pale-green brocade furniture was arranged in conversational groupings around beautiful Persian rugs.

Lisa wore a buff-colored jacquard skirt-suit, the skirt hem just below the knee. The room was crowded and buzzing with animated conversation. We joined Tony and Eve in the sun-brightened living room, with small plates of food and large mimosas in hand. We gazed upon a sea of tweed and tasseled loafers, bright dresses, bare arms, and high-heeled pumps. I smiled at Eve, who while not really pretty, had such a lively, vivacious face that people believed she was. From my lofty vantage point, she presented a lovely expanse of smooth skin and shadowy cleavage. In her dark-pink dress, she looked like a delicate rose from a perfect birthday cake. She gave me a peck on the cheek.

"You are looking especially fetching this late morning," I said to her.

"Thank you, Professor."

Tony scowled, making us laugh. A man would have to be dead not to respond to Eve, and Tony was well aware of it. He was not jealous—he was careful. He slid up behind Lisa. "Let's you and me dump these two and run off."

Lisa, conspiratorial: "Count me in."

I laughed and said, "Speaking of running off, a former student comped me at the MGM for next weekend. I'm trying to talk Lisa into going."

"We're still at the talking stage." Lisa gave me a look.

As we mingled, I scanned the room, marveling at the eclectic mix of people these occasions always elicited. There were the faculty, of course, smartly dressed as a whole but with several marvelous eccentricities in the way of ponytails, earrings in unusual places, and other less-compelling attention-seeking devices. Everyone was being clever and charming, putting forward their best persona as they hobnobbed with the rich and famous. I recognized most of the usual donors—the rich—who held court to a circle of admirers, some of whom undoubtedly hoped that proximity to money-making success would rub off on them. These same people were sneaking unobtrusive peeks at the actors—the *Game of Thrones*-level famous—and sport stars—third-base Dodgers—and enjoying an up close and personal look at those well-known faces.

As my gaze wandered appreciatively over the crowd on the long terrace that adjoined the living room, I saw Chief Justice Schmitt. Go figure. Lisa stopped midsentence as she saw my face and looked where I was looking. I nodded. "There's Schmitt from the court. Didn't expect to see him here."

Tony walked up when he saw me staring at Schmitt. "The dean has a broad expanse of friends."

Schmitt had not seen me. I excused us from Tony and hooked Lisa's arm as we worked our way to Schmitt. I had no idea what I was going to say, but I was intrigued to talk to him as an equal instead of dealing with him in his official capacity. As we approached, he saw me coming, and I could see a flicker of recognition, but I didn't think he had placed me as an advocate. "Justice Schmitt, Jake Clearwater. I argued a case before you several months ago."

With a relaxed smile, he said, "That's right. I recognized you but could not immediately place from where." We shook hands. "Professor Clearwater, let me introduce you to my wife Ellen." Ellen and I shook hands and I introduced them to Lisa. Schmitt took Lisa's hand and kissed it. *A bit weird.* He lingered on Lisa's face and the tops of her breasts. Then turning to me, "As I recall, you represented your client admirably."

"Thank you, Your Honor."

"Let me ask you this, Professor. In preparing myself for the orals in your case, I noted you were formerly a prosecutor in the county from which the case arose. Did that create any special problems?"

I could not be certain, but I think he was implying that, given my connection to San Arcadia, my involvement was somehow unprofessional. Maybe he was even implying that I had betrayed the trust of my old office. But then again, maybe I was just plain wrong.

"The way I see it, Judge," (note "Judge" instead of "Justice" or "Your Honor"—I was taking him down a notch or two) "is that a man was convicted and sentenced to death because the state afforded him a lawyer who wasn't up to the job. Seems to me, justice trumps geography."

He gave me a hard look, then pointedly focusing on Lisa, "Ms. St. Marie, it has been a pleasure to meet you. Good afternoon." And with not another word, he and his wife moved on.

Lisa looked at me. "Did you just insult the Chief Justice of the California Supreme Court?"

"I believe I did, and I am okay with that."

Lisa worked to suppress a laugh. "Jake, you are a piece of work."

The rest of the brunch was uneventful. I did make a point of introducing Lisa to Dean Chauncey and his wife. Chauncey lit up when I introduced Lisa. "Are you the Lisa St. Marie that does watercolors?"

"I do paint watercolors."

Chauncey took us to his den, where one of Lisa's watercolors hung. He gushed over Lisa's talents and made her promise to let him know when she would have another showing of her work.

CHAPTER 18

VIVA LAS VEGAS

I talked her into the Vegas weekend. If she wanted a separate room, I was okay with that. She did insist on separate beds, but same room. The suite was spacious and had a view of the Strip. We had driven over that Friday morning, had lunch, and took a nap. Same bed, no sex. As the sun was grudgingly giving way to the glitter of the Strip, we walked the pedestrian sky bridge to New York-New York. Lisa wore a cream-colored short-sleeved sweater, cut low. With her heels, she was nearly six feet. I had on fashionably worn blue jeans and a light blue pullover sweater. We had good seats for a Cirque du Soleil show. The energy of the performers and the bass beat of the music was exhilarating. We strolled back over to the MGM, then passed countless slot and video poker machines which opened up to the live gaming area.

"Ever play craps?" I asked.

"No. It always looked like fun, but too complicated."

"It can be. It's kind of like baseball. You can enjoy it on different levels. It doesn't have to be complicated." I steered her to an open corner of a twenty-five-dollar craps table. We drew every eye. The men stood a little straighter, tummies in, shoulders puffed.

Being with Lisa so much, I'd gotten used to the pretty-woman effect on men.

I pulled out two large and laid them on the table. They were snatched up and replaced with eight twenty-five-dollar chips. I placed two chips on the pass line in front of Lisa and two on the line for me.

"We want a seven or eleven, right?" she asked.

"That's right. We don't want a two, three, or twelve." I hugged her for luck.

Five dice were passed to an older gent with a white sweater over a dress shirt and sporting a bow tie. He picked out two dice and turned one so that a four showed and the other to a three. With his forefinger he tapped them several times, as if admonishing a potentially recalcitrant child. He scooped up the dice, and with a confident toss, propelled them across the table. Four and three—just like obedient children.

"Seven, seven!" called the stickman, and two twenty-five-dollar chips were placed next to each of our bets.

"Well, that wasn't too complicated," Lisa said, laughing, and she gave me a peck on the cheek. The bow-tie roller looked at Lisa as if he had done something heroic. I think he felt he deserved a kiss as well. I leaned over and picked up my winnings, leaving the other two on the pass line. Lisa watched and did the same.

Next toss was a four and a two. The stickman chimed, "Six is the point."

"Let's gamble," I said, placing my four twenty-five-dollar chips behind my pass-line bet. Lisa again followed my lead.

"What we need now is another six. Sevens are bad." The roller sent the dice across the table surface littered with chips. A two and a one.

"Craps," the stickman bellowed.

"We lost?" Lisa asked.

"We only lose on a seven." I kissed her. *How could I lose? I was the luckiest guy in the building.* I pulled out a twenty. "Give the lady the hard six." The stickman flicked his eyes at Lisa and put four five-dollar chips on the hard six. "We want a pair of threes."

Lisa leaned to me and whispered in my ear, "Feeling lucky tonight, big guy?" *How was I to take that? Would this be the night? Best to make light of it.* "I'm the luckiest guy in this entire outrageous city, and it has nothing to do with dice."

She put an arm around my waist as the dice sailed into the far wall of the table. A one and a four.

"This is exciting," she whispered.

Bow tie again laid the dice out so that threes were up. He tapped with his forefinger. He was serious. He had five hundred dollars on the pass line with a thousand backing it up.

As he flicked the dice he urged, "Thirty- three."

"Six, hard six," shouted the stickman, only to be drowned out by the shouts around the table. I got a full-mouth kiss. *Maybe it was going to be a lucky night.*

Both of our pass-line chips were matched, and four chips were placed next to our odds bet. "Hard six over here," the stickman said as he tapped his stick in front of Lisa, and eight five-dollar chips were stacked in front of her.

"We may stay here all night," she said, gathering her chips.

I put fifty dollars on the pass line. Lisa put a hundred.

"Bold bet, darling."

"This is easy," she said, with all the confidence of the uninitiated. The dice banked and came up six again. I doubled back my bet.

Lisa asked, "What should I bet?"

"You can back up your pass-line bet with two hundred." She looked uneasy.

"Cold feet already? What happened to easy?"

"Three hundred dollars is three hundred dollars."

"True enough, you don't have to back it up." The bow-tie roller once again went into his routine. He laid out a three and a three and gave each a finger tap. As he picked up the dice, there was an almost palpable force emitting around the table, willing a six.

Four and a three. "Craps," said the stickman. Groans and mutters. And in a heartbeat, the felt was swept clean of all chips.

"Nuts!" said Lisa.

"Nuts?" I laughed.

"Yeah, nuts."

"Had enough?"

"I've got all of these left." She had at least a couple hundred in chips.

"There's no rule that says you can't just walk away."

The stickman pushed five dice toward Lisa. "Your turn," he said.

She quickly studied my face and smiled. "It's only money."

I took out two more large and they were converted.

I put fifty dollars on the pass line for each of us and flicked a twenty-five-dollar chip, instructing, "On the eleven for the lady."

"Come on, seven eleven," Lisa said; she was now a craps veteran. She shook the dice, and as they left her hand they flew into the face of the stickman. One hit him on the lens of his glasses and ricocheted back onto the table. The other struck a glancing blow off his scalp and sailed off beyond the table. There was a stunned silence before the table exploded in laughter. Lisa turned nine shades of red. I had never seen her embarrassed before. Things like this did not happen to the elegant people of the world. After the laughter subsided, she asked the stickman, who was examining his glasses for cracks, if he was alright. He assured her no harm was done. She again apologized, explaining, "I was a little nervous. I think the dice stuck to my hand."

Lisa pulled some tissues from her purse and carefully wiped her hands. By the time the table had recovered, five new dice were tentatively—the stickman was attempting to be cute—pushed toward Lisa. She hesitantly picked up two and carefully rolled them across the table. A five and a six.

"Yo, an eleven."

Lisa gave a little jump. Chips were passed around. The "yo" bet had generated a stack of chips. There was no stopping her now. Her next roll was five, and two rolls later she made the point. Two points later, we were playing with hundred-dollar chips, and we had ventured into the numbers. With each point Lisa threw, the crowd around our table grew deeper and deeper. People were three and four deep. And for a short while, we were the center of the Las Vegas Strip. When she hit a hard eight, the scream of jubilation was deafening. *The gorgeous woman with the hot hand.*

Twenty-five minutes later, she missed. Brief groans, but then the table applauded. Lisa gave a little bow and then grabbed my arm, and looking me square in the eye, said, "Let's go."

"Okay." I scooped up my chips and then hers. There were a number of thousand-dollar chips in the mix. "Let's go to the cashier's cage and cash them in."

"No," she said, and grasped my arm again. "We are going to the room, now."

Comprehension dawned on me. It was going to be the night. We walked briskly to the elevators and were fortunate enough to have one to ourselves. I backed her against a side, her arms around my neck, pulling me close. We kissed more passionately than we had ever done. I grasped her and pulled her even tighter to me. The door opened and we nearly stumbled as we uncoupled, leaving the elevator and managing to get to our room. I fumbled with the damn key card with Lisa urging me to get the door open. Once inside, we were frantic as we tore at clothes and tumbled onto the bed. She on top. I entered her and we rocked with abandon until we climaxed together. Lisa collapsed on my chest, heaving for breath with me still in her. As we lay there, she kissed my eyes while I stroked her body.

I think we dozed off for a while. Then she slid off me and I rolled onto her, kissing her breasts and taut nipples. My mouth on her nipples elicited moans and a thrusting of her pelvis. We made love again, this time slower, savoring the pleasure.

Some say the first time is the most memorable. I wouldn't disagree, but I was looking forward to the next time.

CHAPTER 19

UNEXPECTED NEWS

It was four months following oral argument. I entered my office, having just finished my last class of the spring semester. Life was good. Classes had been good. Lisa and I were particularly good. I had not heard from Durgeon since I wrote and reported on the oral argument. I swiveled in my chair to take in the glorious bright and crisp late morning. My cell chirped; it was a San Francisco area code. "Hello?"

"Jake Clearwater"—a woman's voice, high and breathless— "this is Charlotte Knight from the Death Penalty Project. I have incredible news." Instantly my heart rate accelerated. "We just got advance notice from the court. You won!" My brain went white. "The Project gets twenty-four-hour advance notice on all death-penalty decisions. Let me read you what we just received. 'State of California vs. Duane Durgeon. Appellant received ineffective assistance of counsel. The conviction is vacated, and a new trial is ordered.'" She was giddy. I was dumbfounded. You weren't supposed to win these cases. You were supposed to put forth a good effort, lose, and let the death-penalty mechanism grind forward.

"Wait. I need a moment." I heard what sounded like a giggle

from her end. She of all people knew the appeal was a long shot. And that long shots rarely break the tape. I was trying to bring it into focus. Since the orals, I had mentally worked my way to the point where we had no chance. I was prepared to lose. I was not prepared to win. I was trying to catch up with events. Shit, I won! "How will Durgeon hear about this?" I finally asked.

"Usually, the lawyer breaks the news. You better get up here and tell him." Her exuberance had not abated.

"I'll be there tonight," I said. "Charlotte, thanks for the call."

"My pleasure, Jake. It's a call I wish I could make more often." In a flash of irrelevance, it occurred to me that it was now first names. *Perhaps winning an appeal was the necessary icebreaker.*

I needed to share the news. There should always be someone special to share life's big moments. Lisa. I punched in her number, got her voicemail. Suzelle. Voicemail. Tony. Voicemail. Apparently, some moments are not to be shared.

৵৵৵

It was 5:45 p.m. I slouched into the same cramped booth that I had sat in nineteen months ago during that first meeting. I stared into the three-foot by four-foot Plexiglas window that would soon separate me from Durgeon. The visitors area was quiet but for an occasional indiscriminate metallic noise off in the distance. It was well beyond visiting hours; I had once again talked my way in.

The door opened and Durgeon stepped through. He stood and stared flatly at me. A guard stepped in behind him and took off his handcuffs. He sat and continued to stare.

"Hey," I finally said. "I got news on your appeal." I suppressed a grin. I wasn't going too far with this guy. God knows where his head was at any one time. My demeanor was that of a mere messenger, as neutral as pre-Hitler Switzerland. "The court granted you a new trial. They said your lawyer was ineffective."

Durgeon didn't say anything. I didn't either. He continued to stare and brushed at the narrow shelf at the base of the window. A mean straight grin took shape on his face. "In-e-ffec-tive. That fucker was fuckin' in-e-ffec-tive." *To be that articulate was indeed a thing of beauty.* "A new trial?" I saw full comprehension dawning.

"A new trial," I repeated.

He leaned forward. "When."

"I'm not sure, probably within months. It will most likely be back in San Arcadia again."

Durgeon slumped back in his chair. "A new trial. I fuckin' can't believe it. Hell, Clearwater, you can't do a shittier job than Rosenblatt." *As fine a compliment as a lawyer is likely to get.* He grinned at me. A genuine grin. "A new trial." He liked tasting that phrase. He leaned forward again, his face nearly pressing the glass. "When do we start getting ready?"

"Wait," I said as I caught up to his question. "I only did the appeal; now I step out of the picture. The court down in San Arcadia will appoint you a lawyer for the trial."

"Fuck that shit," Durgeon flashed. This was the Durgeon I had come to know. His voice was low, guttural. "I had their lawyers. I don't do that again."

"Listen"—it was my turn to lean into the glass—"I signed on for the appeal. That's as far as I go. I got you back to square one, before Rosenblatt screwed up the guilt phase."

"So now, just like that, you bail! Those fuckers in San Arcadia ain't gonna give me anybody worth spit. Be the same bullshit again, and I end up back in this shithole." He shook his head bitterly. "Thanks for nothing, counselor." His eyes fixed on mine as he leaned back and thumped the door twice with his elbow. He stood when the door opened and put his hands behind his back, his stare unabated. The handcuffs were fastened, and he turned and walked out.

How could this visit end so poorly? This was to be celebratory, joyful. Of course, I would not take on a new trial. I was a professor, not a death-penalty trial lawyer. *Although the idea of it was intriguing. Maybe even more than intriguing.*

Ah, to hell with him. And to hell with this damnable situation. I slammed out of the cubicle and stalked out of the prison. I sped down the interstate toward the airport. I was merciless on the little blue something-or-other rental. By the time I reached Oakland I had cooled; my anger had gradually slipped out the open window and blown away into the night. Damn Durgeon anyway. He had made me feel guilty, as if I was deserting him at a critical time. Instead of continuing through downtown Oakland and on to the airport, I jerked the car over to the right lane. It was the connector to the Oakland Bay Bridge heading to San Francisco and the Death Penalty Project office.

It didn't matter that it was after hours. I suspected the Project people were there well into the evening. Came with the job. Comes with having a passion instead of a mere job. It was seven thirty when I knocked on the door. After repeated knocking, someone opened the door, and I was escorted back to Charlotte Knight's office. Of course she was in. Charlotte looked up, surprised to see me. She was dressed in a floral shift, her hair down, disheveled and streaked with gray. She was Woodstock at fifty. I suspected this was the real Charlotte Knight, not the cleaned-up version who recruited me. She hugged me, her head against my chest.

"Jake," she gasped. "Congratulations, great job." I smiled, cheered by her enthusiasm. Her office was just what I expected, buried in files, papers, and books. She went to one of her guest chairs, picked up a stack of files, put them on the floor, and motioned me to sit. She cleared another chair for herself. She did not assume the power chair behind her desk.

"I'm glad I caught you. It's getting late for office hours. You sleep here?"

"Sometimes." She had a nice smile. "Tonight I'll be here all night, but I won't sleep. I've got a habeas petition that needs filing by 9:00 a.m." She waved that discussion off. "Jake, let's talk about you and Durgeon. I can't tell you how pleased I am. I read your brief, and I have to say, your ineffective-assistance argument was right on." *Right on! The sixties lingered.*

Instead of basking in the glow of her approval, I felt guilty, counterfeit. "I've just been to see Durgeon. When I told him the news, he expected me to try his case."

She gave me a disappointed look. "Oh, that's too bad." Her whole face collapsed inward, and a furrow ran from the bridge of her nose into the mass of her hair. "But it's not surprising, is it? Our clients see us as their lawyer; not as their appellate lawyer, but their lawyer across the board. I expect you explained the situation?"

"I tried. He was not having any of it."

"Well, I guess that's to be expected. Frankly, Jake, we don't have much experience in winning new trials on DP cases. So I'm not speaking from a position of great experience here."

I rubbed my finger across a cigarette burn on the arm of the chair. "Maybe he's right, maybe he shouldn't have to differentiate between his appellate lawyer and his trial lawyer," I said.

"Come on, Jake. You did a great job, but your work is finished. We would love it if you would take another appeal, but as for Durgeon, it's over."

In that moment, the certainty of what I had to do was overwhelmingly clear. I grinned and rose. "Charlotte, you have been a great help."

Surprised that I was leaving, she rose quickly to cut me off before I reached the door. "Jake, you are going to let this be, aren't you?"

"No," I said, and extended my hand. She took it and held it in both of hers.

"Jake, you teach. What about your job? Just getting ready for this kind of trial takes months, sometimes years."

I gave a shrug as I stepped around her. "That's what I hear."

"What makes you think the San Arcadia courts will even appoint you? You know that only level-five attorneys are qualified for capital cases."

"You're not really arguing that I'm not qualified, after all the flattery you spouted to get me to take the appeal?"

"This is a trial, not an appeal."

"And trials are where I play. The appeal was a sidelight." I again extended my hand. "I'll keep you posted."

She almost ran down the hall, keeping pace. "You are letting your emotions cloud your judgment. Jake, you are making a mistake."

"Probably."

"Why did you come here? You've ignored everything I've said."

"Maybe I just needed to be in the presence of a cause lawyer again." She stopped trailing me. I turned, gave her a nod, and walked off.

☙☙☙

Sometimes you go with your heart. There was no intellectual rationale for what I was about to do. My last impulsive act had been the Frost trial. Things had worked out there. But who was I trying to kid? That was a one-day misdemeanor trial. This was the World Series. The Super Bowl. Could I get a leave from Dean Chauncey? Would I be appointed? This would dominate my life for months. Here I was, determined to set forth on the most significant endeavor I had ever undertaken, and I wondered if I knew what I was doing.

As I waited for the last plane from Oakland to LAX, I called Lisa and then Suzelle. Suzelle had earned the call, Lisa just because.

From LAX, I drove up to my place about 11:30 p.m., and Suzelle sat cross-legged on a beach towel in front of my garage. As my headlights played over her, she held up a bottle of champagne. I left my car out of the garage and walked over to her, offering a hand. As I helped her up, she handed me the champagne and hugged me. "Congratulations!"

"And to you." I saluted her with the bottle. "I've been up north sharing the news with our client. Come on up and I'll fill you in." I motioned her to the deck while I retrieved champagne flutes. When I joined her, she was settled into a deck chair looking out at the black of the Pacific. It was a warm May night with a slight breeze coming in off the ocean. I popped the cork, poured, and we toasted to a successful venture. I settled into the other deck chair and filled her in on the visit to Durgeon and then on to Charlotte Knight.

"You're really going to try it?"

"Barring unforeseen circumstances."

"Durgeon couldn't get a better lawyer."

"I don't know about that, but thanks." I tipped my glass. I replayed the scenes with Durgeon and Charlotte under Suzelle's incessant questioning.

"It's almost one, I better get going. I've got work tomorrow."

"Thanks for the homecoming," I said.

I walked her to her car, went back upstairs, and lay awake most of the night, my mind working back and forth between Durgeon and Lisa, with an occasional sneak appearance by John Tice, who would be waiting for me.

CHAPTER 20

GETTING READY

Tony surprised me. I had expected him to rain on my parade, to tell me that I was a law prof, not a trial lawyer, and that trying a death-penalty case was ridiculous. And to point out, as Charlotte had, the months of preparation and the weeks of the actual trial. How could I get the time off? I had, of course, already considered the arguments, and despite the multitude of sound reasons screaming no, I heard yes. *Or maybe I just wanted to hear yes.*

Instead, from Tony I heard, "I think you ought to do it. You've been itching to get back in the courtroom." He fingered his pen around in slow circles as he sat behind his desk. "You need something with some heft, something to convince you that being a law professor is not such a bad gig. I know that battery case you tried a while back wasn't enough to satisfy the itch."

"Is it that obvious?"

"Your itch is safe with me. But I think you may be taking for granted your value as a teacher. I think you've forgotten why you left trial work in the first place, and I know it was more than just Tice."

"I never ran from trial practice," I answered defensively.

"I am not suggesting that. What I am saying is that you made a decision to leave the DA's office and come here. It was not a matter of running from, but rather choosing between attractive options. You made the right decision for you. But I do think you need an occasional foray back to the courtroom to confirm that you made the right call in coming to Pacifico."

"You're probably right, but it's not just that. Seems like the job I signed up for is not finished. At first it was just about an appeal, doing something new and worthwhile, but now I've come to think of myself as Durgeon's lawyer. When I told him he was getting a new trial, he seemed to come back to life. But when I told him I was out, he went right back into his funk." I made a dismissive gesture with my hand. "Hell, I don't know why. It's just right. I need to do it. This may be the most important thing I ever do. For better or worse, I am Duane Durgeon's lawyer."

"I get it. When do you think the trial will go? You're going to need a leave."

"I've got this summer to prep, and my best guess is I'll need the fall semester off."

"You want me to break ground with the dean for you?" Tony was tight with the dean. He rolled his pen between his palms. I gave him a *that would be nice* look.

All this, of course, was premature. Hopefully, I would be appointed. Nonetheless, I proceeded as if it was a go.

రా రా రా

I would need a second chair. Someone to help with the motions and to prepare the penalty phase if we lost the guilt phase. No one came to mind. I made a chain of paperclips as I ran prospects through my head. The chain was about three feet long when Suzelle knocked and walked into my office. "How come you're not at work?" I asked.

"I'm interviewing instead."

"Not happy with your job?"

"I'm interviewing with you."

"What do you mean?"

"You can't do a death case by yourself. You need someone to help out."

"What about your job with Big Law?"

"I hate it. I'm working stupid hours on cases I don't really care about." Then she added, "I can work cheap."

"You did great work on the brief, but this is going to be a trial, and a mean one at that. I was thinking about hiring someone with trial experience."

"Why? You're going to try the case; you're not going to turn any part of the trial over to someone else." She raised her eyebrows. "True?" She was right about that. She went on, "But you cannot do all the motion work and all the other prep. I know this case inside out. I am exactly the person you need."

I sat staring at her, thinking, looking at that very young, eager face. She did know the case, and she was extremely bright. Her eyes were riveted to my face, willing me to make the right decision. I rethought my need for a trial lawyer. A bright young lawyer to sit as my second chair was tempting. I moved around my desk, sat on the edge, and stuck out my hand. The team of Clearwater and Frost was primed to take on all comers. Somehow, I did not think Tice would be intimidated. "Don't quit your job just yet. Let's wait until I get appointed." I added, "If it happens, we'll work out the financial stuff once it's official."

ལལལ

I sent Durgeon the following handwritten note:

> I have reconsidered my position, and I would be pleased to represent you during your upcoming trial. I will see you in court and ask the judge to be appointed.

> Jake
> P.S. The courtesy of a reply is requested.

Seven days later, I received the following:

> Clearwater. Thanks. Durgeon.

ལལལ

Anticipation of the three-day Memorial Day weekend with Lisa propelled me through my swim. I had finished grading my spring finals. That meant the semester was really over. I was looking forward to a little R&R with Lisa before setting forth on the great Durgeon adventure. Suzelle and I had begun our prep. I hadn't been appointed yet, but I figured that was just a formality. After all, I had been a felony-trial prosecutor in that very county. Beyond that, who else would want the job? That last consideration probably would carry more weight than any other factor.

Dean Chauncey had been supportive. He would arrange for someone to cover my classes in the fall. It was, of course, an unpaid leave, but I would be compensated by the state once I was appointed. I sure hoped there would be no snag with that. *Talk about plans getting scrambled.*

I walked to Doogie's for breakfast. The threat of rain and the brisk breeze blowing from the ocean gave an unusual snap to the late-May weather. I nodded to the walkers and joggers on Malibu Road and, cutting through the strip mall, stopped at Starbucks to visit with some of my students and neighbors who were sitting and enjoying their concoctions. I was in no hurry. Lisa wouldn't be here until one o'clock.

Easing through the talkers blocking the door to Doogie's, I settled at a table in the back. Jesse, a law-school dropout who was waiting tables while she figured out what to do with her life, hurried past tables whose occupants had been waiting longer than me and greeted me with a delighted smile. She was a twenty-something hippie, a holdover from a time before she was born. Her face was bare of makeup, and her hair was in braids that bumped against her shoulders. Rubber bands were wrapped tightly on the ends of her hair, but little sprigs escaped the braids and stuck out unevenly. Her fingernails were blue.

"Hi, Professor Clearwater," she enthused. "How are you this morning?"

"Jesse, I'm doing well. How about you, any plans yet?"

"I'm thinking of becoming a paralegal." She then dropped her voice, "If I need a recommendation, could you do that?"

"In a heartbeat. Just give me the word."

"Thanks, I knew I could count on you." She gave me an extra-warm smile. "What can I get you?"

I ordered an omelet, which I ate with the *Times* propped in front of me. Only four more hours until Lisa.

She arrived right on time. We took off for Santa Monica and the Third Street Promenade. We drove down the coast, top down, heater on high. Lisa's hair whipped like a flag in the wind; her cheeks were flushed, her eyes shining.

We walked through a light rain to Jose's, a Mexican restaurant with a view of the beach and the Santa Monica Pier. As we sat, the rain picked up and was sliding in sheets off the large window. We were in a corner, our backs to the room, watching the storm. A sense of intimacy enveloped our small space in the noisy room. We held hands. Sometime into lunch, the topic turned to Durgeon and the hours that would be consumed by the trial, and of the pressure involved in defending him.

"You look tired already," she said, stroking my cheek. "I can tell you carry it with you even when you're doing other things."

"Anything in particular?"

She blushed. "Be serious, Jake."

I breathed out a long sigh, trying to catch at a nagging thought that dangled just out of reach. "I'm wondering if I missed something in my work on the brief that would help me at trial. Something that would allow me to get a grip on things. I couldn't quite seem to find a handle to build around."

Lisa shook her head. She had asked to read the newspaper accounts of the murders and the trial, and like everyone else, had an opinion. It didn't favor Durgeon. "Trying this case in San Arcadia is going to be a problem. He is already convicted in the minds of people who live there and remember the murders and trial."

I nodded. "I'll make a motion to get the trial moved to another county, but I don't have much hope of that happening."

"Will you and Suzelle be in danger?"

"Danger?" The question was a surprise. I had not even thought about that. "Of course not." I squeezed her hand, perversely pleased that she worried about me. "It's been a long time since those murders. Time dulls memories and takes the edge off. Besides, I am not the bad guy."

"From what I read and remember from the time, people were horribly repelled by the murders and by the person they thought did them. You are bringing back the nightmare."

I was suddenly exhausted by talk of the trial. I leaned into her. "I am a fool for talking about trials and bad guys when I am with the most exciting, desirable woman on the planet. No more talk of Durgeon for the entire weekend."

CHAPTER 21

AND SO IT BEGINS

A week later, I was walking with Suzelle to the courthouse in San Arcadia. There was a crowd mulling around the stairs leading to the courthouse entrance. A young woman wheeling a stroller carried a placard that read "Justice for Robert and Doree." Another sign read "Send Durgeon to hell where he belongs." So much for memories being dulled by time.

I was thankful the throng didn't know who I was or why I was there. *They would know soon enough.* As we walked up the steps to the first of what would be many appearances, I noted a camera crew from the local television station. The reporter recognized me from my DA days. She hustled to cut me off. "Mr. Clearwater, is it true you are going to represent Duane Durgeon in his retrial?"

"I hope to."

"I have some questions for you."

"I'll bet you have." I kept moving. I had yet to develop my television persona.

Department 3 was tense and expectant, every seat occupied. Tice was already seated at the prosecutor's table, Manlow beside him. They glanced up as I placed my briefcase on the counsel table, and Suzelle and I sat. Tice turned to Manlow and said something in a low voice. Manlow nodded. Tice returned to the file he was reading.

There were six bailiffs in the room, rather than the usual one. I recognized the face of one of the bailiffs, although I could not remember his name. I walked over to him and caught his name from his badge. "Sergeant Carillo. It's been a while."

"Mr. Clearwater." There was no warmth or any hint that we had once known each other.

Undaunted, I commented, "Pretty heavy security."

"Yeah."

"Are the families of the victims here?"

He nodded. "Right there in the front two rows."

The Blanco and Bennett families numbered in the twenties, and the hate they directed at me was palpable. Lisa's perception had been right. I had come into town wearing the black hat. Not only was I the guy who got Durgeon's conviction overturned, now I was asking to represent him at the retrial. As far as these people knew, Durgeon might soon be free to walk their streets again, to slaughter more of their loved ones, to rape their daughters and murder their sons, and I had put it all in motion.

I took my seat, and ten interminable minutes later, the judge appeared, ascended the bench, and stood next to her throne.

Sergeant Carillo: "All rise. Department Three of the San Arcadia Superior Court is now in session. The Honorable Alise Harbarger, judge, presiding." Harbarger sat. Carillo said, "Be seated."

Judge Harbarger nodded at Tice. "Mr. Tice, good morning."

"Good morning, Your Honor." Tice, as always, was perfectly groomed, wearing his trademark black suit, a tailored shirt with French cuffs, and a perfectly knotted tie. It felt odd sitting at the defense table opposite him.

Harbarger looked at me. "Mr. Clearwater, welcome back to San Arcadia."

"Thank you, Your Honor."

Harbarger turned to Carillo. "Is Mr. Durgeon with us?"

"Yes, Your Honor."

"Bring him in."

Carillo stepped to a side door, opened it, and two bailiffs ushered a shackled Durgeon into the courtroom. He was in a jail-issue orange jumpsuit. He looked straight ahead as he shuffled to the chair I held for him.

"Murderer!" someone yelled. There was an angry rumble of agreement throughout the room. "Satan!" called another, spurred on by the crowd's assent. Carillo, in a booming voice, demanded silence and threatened expulsion. Silence immediately descended—no one wanted to leave. This was the place to be.

"Morning," I said softly to Durgeon. To say we were the focus of attention was to understate things a hundredfold.

"Hey," he murmured.

Harbarger: "Mr. Durgeon, we are here this morning to appoint counsel to represent you at trial and to set a trial date." Durgeon did not react. "Do you understand me, Mr. Durgeon?"

"Yeah," he rumbled.

"Mr. Clearwater has filed papers requesting this court appoint him and Suzelle Frost to represent you at trial. Is that what you want?"

"Yeah."

"Mr. Tice, I assume you have no objection to Mr. Clearwater and Ms. Frost representing Mr. Durgeon?"

"No, Your Honor. It is my hope and the hope of the families of Doree and Robert Blanco that Mr. Clearwater will competently represent Durgeon so that he can once again be convicted and then promptly executed." As Tice spoke, he had turned and was looking directly at me. A clamor rose from the assembled masses, punctuated by several amens. *Whoa! That was way out of bounds.*

Harbarger raised her voice. "Mr. Tice, I'll admonish you now. This is a court of law, and I will not tolerate unprofessional conduct. That outburst, Mr. Tice, will cost you $500, payable by five o'clock this afternoon." *It was going to be Harbarger's courtroom, not Tice's. Excellent.*

"My apologies to the court and to Mr. Clearwater." He nodded insincerely at me. I did not nod back. *This was not just about convicting Durgeon this time. He wanted a piece of me as well.*

Harbarger: "Mr. Clearwater, given your extensive felony-trial experience and your familiarity with this case, I hereby appoint you to represent Mr. Durgeon. Counsel, waive reading of the charges and prepared to enter a plea?"

"Waive reading and enter a plea on behalf of Mr. Durgeon of not guilty and deny the special circumstances."

"So ordered." Looking at a calendar, she continued, "I'm looking at commencing jury selection on July 13."

I jumped to my feet. "Judge, you are giving me five weeks to prepare a death-penalty defense? I need at least three months."

Harbarger, maintaining a very neutral voice, said, "Mr. Clearwater, you represented Mr. Durgeon on his appeal, you wrote the briefs, you argued it before the California Supreme Court. You know the case, you understand its nuances and intricacies. Five weeks is more than adequate." She pounded her gavel. "We are in recess. I will see counsel in chambers."

As Tice, Suzelle, and I entered, Harbarger took off her robe, and while she was hanging it in a closet, motioned for us to sit. No one spoke until the judge was seated. Harbarger looked at Tice. "John, what the hell was that about?"

Tice answered, "I've put eight murderers on death row; this is the first one to come back. That a cold-blooded executioner like this monster is getting a second bite at the apple . . ." His voice trailed off. "It won't happen again."

"You're damn right it won't." Harbarger turned to me. "Mr. Clearwater," she said in a warmer tone. "I never expected to see you back in my courtroom. I thought you had taken a teaching job."

"I did, Your Honor, and frankly, I'm surprised to be back. It's been a few years."

Harbarger nodded. She was working to be civil, but I was the vehicle Durgeon had ridden back into her life. I could sense she virtually cringed at the thought of presiding over another Durgeon trial. And to mix my metaphor, I felt caught up in the ominous wake of dark vessel Durgeon.

"I would like you to reconsider the July 13 date; it's just not realistic," I said.

"I understand your position and even appreciate it, but jury selection will begin on July 13. That issue is closed." She stopped and shuffled through some papers on her desk. "Now let's turn to motions. John, do you anticipate any motions on behalf of the state?"

"No, Your Honor."

I noted the use of the first name with Tice and last name with me. This was, of course, Tice's home court. I was the out-of-towner. "Mr. Clearwater, how about you?"

"I'll have several motions."

"Why bother?" Tice interrupted. "The fingerprint issue and the *Massiah* issue have both been heard and rejected by the Supreme Court."

"Ah hell, John, I'm a slow learner."

"Okay." Harbarger waved away our mutual animus. "All

motions to be filed by June 13 and arguments on June 20. Now let's move forward. Is there any point talking some kind of settlement?" Harbarger was looking at Tice. Tice controlled the game board. The DA always controlled the board. All other actors on the criminal justice stage were pawns to the DA's queen. *I'm sure Tice would love that analogy.*

"No, this has always been a death-penalty case and it's always going to be one." Spoken with the cockiness of a young Muhammad Ali.

"I figured that would be your position." Harbarger turned to me. "Since you read the transcripts of the last trial, you are aware this was a most difficult case. I'll expect you to do everything in your power to keep Durgeon under control. If you can't or won't do it, I will."

I did not like that she and Tice were implying that this trial was a mere exercise in formality before Durgeon could be packed off for good to death row. "I'll try my case."

"What does that mean?" Tice again.

Ignoring Tice, I held Harbarger's look. Finally, she said in a dismissive tone, "That's all. Good morning."

I went to Judge Orloff's chambers and discussed financial arrangements. Orloff was the money judge. All monies had to be approved by him. We discussed a flat rate to defend Durgeon. I would be paid in three installments, the first paid immediately. He also approved my request that Suzelle be paid an hourly rate, and I was given permission to hire an investigator.

Suzelle drove as we headed back to Malibu. I jotted notes and began organizing what needed doing. She was a bit nervous driving the Jag but quickly got the hang of it, and at one point I asked her to keep it under eighty. She relinquished the car at her place. I stopped at the school and picked up the case files. I stopped again and picked up Chinese and then home.

I settled down with dinner and called Lisa.

"Hello sweetie, how did it go?" We had moved to affectionate names. I referred to her as "gorgeous."

"Even worse than expected. You were right; seems no one has forgotten round one. It will be a war." I filled her in, and we made plans for the weekend.

CHAPTER 22

COUNTDOWN

I began drafting my motions. I started with the no-brainers: attempting to suppress Durgeon's remarks and the fingerprint, which were guaranteed losers, but which had to be preserved for a possible appeal. *Never forget that if or when I lost, some appellate lawyer was going to scrutinize my performance.* I added a change of venue argument, which I held out little hope for, but I would at least run it up the pole for Tice to shoot at. *Hell, perhaps Harbarger was so weary of presiding over another Durgeon trial, she might grant it.*

Suzelle and I got everything drafted and filed by the June 13 deadline. Suzelle then moved on to preparing for the penalty phase. If we lost at the guilt phase—everybody's money was on that—then the trial would go directly to the penalty phase, when the jury would decide between life and death. For the penalty phase, Suzelle needed to contact Durgeon's parents, siblings, and any significant others he had acquired during his rare stints of freedom from prison and other lockups. She was looking for two things: first, proof that, by genetics and environment, Durgeon was preordained to a life of crime; and second, evidence mitigating his prior criminal acts. Again assuming we lost at guilt, Tice at the penalty phase would be allowed—within certain limits—to go into Durgeon's past criminal behavior. That included convictions as well as uncharged criminal acts. Rosenblatt had not done a thorough job in preparing for the penalty phase, even had Durgeon not torpedoed the effort.

I focused my attention on the guilt phase. I started where I always start, the jury instructions. It had always made good sense to me to build my case around the instructions, to incorporate concepts and phrases from the instructions to help the jurors see how the evidence tied into the law. If jurors failed to make the necessary connections, the evidence would drift without a mooring. The quaint notion that jurors suspend judgment until they receive the law at the end of trial is nonsense. Despite their oath, jurors do what comes naturally: they jump to conclusions. Studies, as well as my personal experiences as a trial lawyer, have established that most jurors have made up their minds as early as jury selection. That is, before hearing any facts, let alone any law, most of the good citizens we press into jury service have come to their verdict. *How unsettling is that?* Consequently, trial lawyers start "selling" their case from the get-go. Starting with jury selection and continuing throughout the trial, lawyers spin the facts and the law that favors their side and begin diffusing the facts and law that cut against them. Durgeon's side did not present a vast host of favorable facts. But, as always, the law is stacked to favor the defense. My greatest assets would be the requirement of a unanimous jury, and the prosecutor's burden of proof beyond a reasonable doubt. The reasonable-doubt instruction includes the wonderful phrase "abiding conviction," a phrase the jurors would definitely be hearing from me early and often.

A follow-up instruction to reasonable doubt relates to circumstantial evidence and instructs that if there are two reasonable interpretations of circumstantial evidence, one pointing to the defendant's guilt and the other pointing to the defendant's innocence, the jurors must adopt that interpretation that favors the defendant's innocence. Were there two "reasonable" interpretations of the evidence? Was my defense that the evidence could not establish that Durgeon was there—the unsuccessful Rosenblatt approach—or that he was there but not the shooter? If the latter, he would still go down as an accessory to the double murders but most likely be spared the death penalty, since most juries would only impose the ultimate penalty on the actual killer. I had to choose, otherwise I would go into the trial under the burden of a multiple-choice defense: they cannot put him at the scene, and even if they can, he wasn't the shooter. Such a defense is flawed, and a talented prosecutor would expose it for the fraud it is. And there was no doubt that I was facing a talented prosecutor. I had to pick my theory, but so far Durgeon had provided little help. Would he be more forthcoming with me now that we had a new trial?

Another instruction concerns witness credibility. Jurors are told that if they find that any witness was materially false in one portion of their testimony, jurors are free to disregard everything that witness has said. Christina Atwell, the former girlfriend, certainly came to mind. Regardless of my actual theory of the case, I knew that her credibility had to be hit, and hit hard. That instruction was a powerful tool.

☙☙☙

Tuesday morning, June 20, I arrived at the courthouse solo; I figured Suzelle's time was better spent on her prep. The crowd was not nearly as dense as before, though I took a couple of taunts as I walked up the steps. I held out little hope for Judge Harbarger to grant any of my motions. My skepticism was warranted. Of course, the motions dealing with Durgeon's statements and the fingerprint were peremptorily denied, but the venue motion which I had hoped might resonate, didn't. Harbarger was "convinced" we could find jurors who could sit fairly. *A truly absurd notion.*

Some intelligent soul threw an egg at me as I hustled to my car. The egg missed me and struck that same persistent television reporter I had stiffed the last go-round. The reporter not only got nothing from me again but egg yolk on her pretty blue shirt.

☙ ☙ ☙

Driving back to Malibu, I found Steve Duke's number on my phone and called him. Duke used to work as an investigator with the San Arcadia DA. He had retired from the office several years ago and had hung a private investigator shingle. When we were both in the office, we worked a couple of cases together. I liked him and trusted him. He was a first-rate investigator.

After greetings, he asked, "Still got that cushy job in Malibu?"

"Of course, what a ridiculous question," I laughed. "But I'm going to trial in a couple of weeks."

"Well, now I'm confused."

"I had a weak moment, and now I'm up to my neck in a death-penalty trial."

"I did not know you went in for that kinky stuff."

"Like I said, I had a weak moment."

Duke laughed. "What do you need, Jake?"

"I need a first-rate investigator."

"You got him. When?" No hesitation.

"Pretty much now. First, I need you to locate a guy named Ron Evans, and then I'll need you with me in San Arcadia."

"I've got some things to wrap up here." There was a pause and the ruffling of paper. "How about I get down there the first week of July, that would be Monday, July 3?"

"That works. Meanwhile, if you can squeeze it in, play with your computer. Last word I have is that Evans has family in Ohio, either the Columbus or Cincinnati area. He was a bus driver forever in San Arcadia. I don't know if he's working now. Probably in his early sixties."

"That's all you got on this guy?"

"Afraid so. Hell Duke, you got his name and a state. Should be a piece of cake."

"We will see what we see."

"Base camp for the duration will be the Ramada Inn in beautiful downtown San Arcadia. See you Monday."

☙☙☙

Monday, July 3, trial minus ten days.

Suzelle and I set up shop in the aforementioned Ramada. The two-hour commute from Malibu was too long. The hotel's primary redeeming quality was that it was only two miles from the courthouse. I rented a one-bedroom suite that would be our office. Suzelle had an adjoining room. Peach and green were the colors of choice. Everything from the sofa and chairs to the assembly-line wall hangings shared liberal doses of that combination.

While Suzelle continued her efforts to round up Durgeon relatives, I turned to the witness list Tice had turned over as part of discovery. There were no surprises. It listed exactly the same witnesses, even in the same order that he had called during the first trial. *Why not, it worked the first time.* I methodically went through the transcripts of Tice's direct examination and Rosenblatt's cross-examination of each witness, making notes. Rosenblatt's crosses were adequate, if not inspired, although on several exams he had missed points.

Late Monday afternoon, Duke knocked and pushed into the partially opened door of Suite C. I was seated at the table that now served as my desk. Suzelle was out at the library looking at newspaper coverage of Durgeon's arrest and trial.

"Use a little company?" he asked with a big grin.

"Absolutely." I grinned too, pleased to see him. I got up to shake his hand and retrieved two Coors from the suite's mini refrigerator. I flipped one to Duke, who tipped a chair against a wall and crossed his feet gingerly on the edge of a table. He was in his sixties and a little seedy looking. He wore a blue tieless dress shirt that stretched across his belly and opened little peepholes to his white undershirt. His brown cuffed trousers bagged at the knees, showing that he did a lot of detecting sitting down. Dark-brown Rockports worn with white socks completed the ensemble.

"It's been a while," I said.

"Almost like the old days. Except we're no longer on the side of truth, justice, and Tice."

"So you've figured out what we're into."

"Hard not to. It's big news in this small county."

"You will also not be surprised that we drew Tice himself for this little soiree." Duke, too, had crossed swords with Tice and was not a big fan.

"Alright Jake, fill me in."

I filled him in at length. "By the way," I said, "were you able to get a handle on Ron Evans?"

"Yeah, I got him. Living outside Cincinnati. From what I can tell, he's not doing so well. Looks like he's moved in with mom."

I nodded. "I think Durgeon was at the scene and maybe somehow involved in the murders. We need to find out who else might have been involved, and who was the actual killer."

"What do you have that makes you think there were others?"

"A witness from across the street puts the Blancos on their front porch about ten thirty the night of the murders. The Blancos were talking to two or three men."

"That's it?"

"Not quite." I cocked my head. "Durgeon told me he doesn't talk about his friends."

Duke snorted in derision. "How noble of him."

"It does imply that others were involved."

"Fair assumption," he said noncommittally. "Where do you want me to start?"

"The girlfriend, Christina Atwell, told Harley Manlow that Durgeon hung out with a guy named Todd Rode. She said Rode lived out by Cal State. She didn't have an address."

"Harley's working this case?"

"Yup. Good old Harley," I said, disgusted.

Always a quick study, Duke asked, "Harley being a pain in the ass?"

"Harley's always been a pain in the ass. Even when I was still in the office, he was a pain in the ass. He's taking this case personally. Showed up with Tice at the appellate argument and tried to rattle me."

"Harley's usually good but always classless." We stared into our beers for a while, thinking about the always classless Harley.

"Anyway, seems to me that Rode might shed a little light on things."

"Do you have anything else on Rode to help me run him down?"

"What, you slipping, Duke? You got his first and last name. And we know he lived near the university at the time of the shooting."

"Right." He gave me a mock salute.

Our discussion of his hourly fee took a minute and was firmed up with a handshake. "How about some dinner? I'm starved."

Duke, never one to miss a meal, looked pleased. "Lead on." We swung by the library and texted Suzelle to come out and join us. The three of us went to a mediocre steakhouse a block from the courthouse. I enjoyed watching my crew size each other up.

Duke's look: Jesus, where did he get this kid—junior high? Either she's brilliant or he's jumping her bones.

Suzelle eyes flashed to mine: My God, this relic must be a hundred and four! It's a wonder his brain hasn't calcified.

They smiled sweetly at each other.

After dinner, we walked Duke to his seen-better-days Dodge. He nodded at me, gave a curiously old-fashioned bow to Suzelle, and departed with the surprising growl of a powerful engine.

అావావా

Tuesday, July 4, trial minus nine days.

Duke called in. "A couple of months after the Blanco shootings, Rode got busted for dealing and was packed off to Folsom for double digits on a parole violation."

"You'll go see him?" I asked, and without waiting for an answer, "When?"

"I'm already on my way." We were in complete sync.

I hung up and turned back to my preparation. Once I thoroughly understood Tice's case and had formulated a cross-exam strategy for each of his witnesses, I was ready to shift my attention to the defense case. Of course, the primary problem hadn't gone away. In order to put on a case, you had to have one. During the first trial, the defense had put on no witnesses. Rosenblatt was working the same script I now held. At this point, with the exception of trying to get Ron Evans on the stand, my only "case" was calling into question the evidence Tice would produce. My job was to react and try to minimize his case. Precisely what Rosenblatt had unsuccessfully done. It was frequently the lot of the defense lawyer.

I called the jail and arranged for a Friday-afternoon visit with Durgeon. It was time to find out if I was going to pick up any cards. I was hoping to avoid aces and eights.

Lisa came to the Ramada and picked Suzelle and me up. We had dinner at a funky little seafood restaurant at Avila Beach near the university, then walked out on the pier and watched the fireworks. Back at the Ramada, Suzelle excused herself, and Lisa and I took our drinks back to the bedroom.

ฉะฉะฉะ

Wednesday, July 5, trial minus eight days.

Duke called with news that Rode had died in prison two years ago. *Damn, damn, damn.* Apparently, he had been trimming trees on a prison work detail, fell, and broke his neck. *How inconsiderate of him.* Duke, ever thorough, had reviewed Rode's visitor records and found out that only two people had visited him at Folsom: his wife and Dan Atwell.

"Dan Atwell?" I asked incredulously.

"That's right."

"The same Dan Atwell who is Christina's only child? The same Dan Atwell who was busted along with Christina and Durgeon in the dope raid on Christina's house just after the murders?"

"Apparently so. Any ideas why Atwell would be visiting Rode in prison?" Duke asked.

"No, but I think we have a new avenue of exploration."

"Does that take precedence over visiting Evans in Cincinnati?"

"Yeah, I think we need to find out what that's all about. I want you to take a hard look at Danny-boy."

"Okay, I'm on my way back."

৵৵৵

Thursday, July 6, trial minus seven days.

Suzelle and I were taking a break and were eating Double-Doubles and fries from In-N-Out. Suzelle ate cross-legged on the sofa, bent over to avoid drips. I was sitting back with a towel on my chest to save my shirt. Duke walked in the open door, grinned at the picture we made, and went to the fridge and helped himself to a Coors.

"Have you eaten? This stuff's pretty good," I said with my mouth full.

"I'm fine."

"Good hunting?" I asked.

He flopped down on a chair. "Whatever you are paying me, it's not enough. In fact, the services I provide are of inestimable value," he said with a smug grin.

"Lay it on us."

"Dan Atwell graduated from San Arcadia High in 2002." He lingered over his words, savoring the moment. "Robert Blanco also graduated in 2002. Doree Bennett graduated the following year."

I sat up in my chair and put down my Double-Double.

Duke went on. "Even in a city of modest size, such connections make one think. So I took things a step further. One hundred fifty kids graduated in 2002. When I got back yesterday, I started making calls and learned that Doree's best friend was Amy Arthur. Ms. Arthur is now a fifth-grade teacher at Golden Elementary School here in town. Teacher Arthur and I just shared a lunch. A lunch"–Duke smiled–"at your expense."

"Of course you did." I laughed. Duke's initiative was never a surprise.

"Ms. Arthur was at first reluctant to talk about Doree. She shares the feelings of pretty much everybody that Durgeon should already be rotting in hell. And, as she added, 'Hell is too good for him.' Be that as it may, I pointed out that the first trial left unanswered questions. One of the biggest was whether Durgeon acted alone. I reminded her that a witness had seen Doree and Robert talking to two or three men about ten thirty that night. She said she had often wondered whether anyone else might have been involved, that it had been bothering her ever since the trial. With a little coaxing and a thirty-eight-dollar bottle of California Merlot, Amy decided that discussing Doree with me wasn't necessarily helping Durgeon but was just trying to get to the truth."

"I'm surprised that one bottle was sufficient."

"It wasn't; the second was on me," said Duke with a straight face, "but we digress."

Suzelle laughed so hard she nearly choked on her hamburger.

Duke patted her on the back and then resumed his seat without missing a beat. "In Doree's junior year, she and Dan were an item, albeit, according to Teacher Amy, a mismatched item. Doree was a good girl. Conservative, no drugs, no drinking. A regular Sunday-go-to-meeting girl. Danny, on the other hand, was the proverbial high school bad boy. A classic case of opposites attracting. He was suspended a couple of times, got kicked off the football team his junior year. According to Amy, that was a big deal, because Danny was one of the stars on the team. He was a lineman, played both offense and defense."

I held up a hand to stop Duke. "I've never seen a photo of him. If he played line, he must have some size." The killer was big. Durgeon was big. Graves was big. And now, at this late date, I come to find that Dan Atwell was a big man. Why had that connection not occurred to me earlier?

"Kind of makes you think, doesn't it?" Duke observed.

"There's been no lack of thinking. Only a lack of quality

thinking." I shook my head, irritated at myself. "But before we begin running off into the land of great speculation, let's pull back and fill in a few holes. Let's circle back to Dan and Doree."

"It was short and ugly. According to Amy, Dan figured that if you were fortunate enough to be his girlfriend, then you should be his girlfriend in every way. Doree declined. Amy said Dan got real nasty and showed up at the Bennett family house one early a.m., pretty tanked up, pounding on the front door and yelling for Doree. By the time the dust settled, the juvenile court had slapped Dan with an assault conviction. He caught a two-week suspension from school and was kicked off the football team. And like I said before, it was the football that hurt most. Dan thought he had a chance to be recruited. He blamed that on Doree."

"The plot gets curiouser and curiouser," I muttered, mostly to myself. Duke had had the benefit of time to reflect; Suzelle and I were just catching up.

Suzelle asked Duke, "Did you ask her if she knows how Dan was wearing his hair at the time of the murders?"

"I did and she didn't know. She hadn't seen him since high school. But she said Dan had long hair and the beginnings of a beard in high school."

"Had Amy been contacted by anyone before you?" I asked.

"Nope. Neither side."

"Doesn't it strike you as coincidental that Dan's lovely mom will once again be the primary witness against Durgeon, while her own darling son keeps popping up around the fringes of the case?"

"I don't believe in coincidence," Duke offered.

"I would like for you to have a photo of Dan to show Evans. Further, I would like to interview Dan Atwell."

"That's what I figured as well," Duke said. "Any ideas where we might find him?"

"No. From what we've been able to piece together from studying Tice's discovery packet, Dan is not mentioned anywhere, and he was not called during the first trial." After a pause, I said, "Seems as if Dan Atwell is a forgotten character in this picture."

"Has Tice given us an address for Christina? If so, maybe we can track Dan through her," Duke said.

"He hasn't turned over Christina's whereabouts. He's only going to give us what he is absolutely required to turn over. We've got all her statements but no address. I would not be surprised if he has her somewhere out of the area and is only going to bring her back for trial."

Suzelle said, "I know it's been years since the first trial, but doesn't there have to be some footprint of her out there?"

"Probably," said Duke, "but since the new trial has cropped up, I agree with Jake and wouldn't be surprised if Tice has hidden her away. And if Tice and Manlow have hidden her—and perhaps Dan—away, it's going to be hell finding them." As an afterthought, Duke said, "I can use my contacts to get Dan's mug shot from the drug arrest to show Evans."

"Let's keep digging. We start picking a jury in a week. Duke, I need to know what's happening with Evans ASAP. Meanwhile, I'll call Tice and see if I can get Dan's rap sheet. It could prove interesting."

"I'm sure that will be a pleasant conversation," Suzelle observed.

I stood. "Speaking of pleasant, tomorrow morning I visit with everyone's favorite felon."

Duke shrugged off from the wall. "And I, my friends, am off to Cincinnati."

❧❧❧

Friday, July 7, trial minus six days.

Durgeon was being held in isolation at the San Arcadia jail. I was greeted by a small, wiry sergeant that I recognized from my DA days. "Mr. Clearwater," he said, "I heard you had gone over to the dark side."

I shook my head in resignation. "Yeah, I'm just another guy who's been seduced by the wealth and glory of defense work. I understand you've got Mr. Durgeon in the Plaza Suite. Would he be available for callers?"

My sarcasm was wasted on this dolt.

The dolt said, "I have to tell you, man, I was surprised when I found out you were representing someone like Durgeon. I guess I always thought of you as one of us." *Cops and DAs, cozy bedfellows.*

I didn't bother replying as he escorted me to a holding cell where Durgeon was waiting, his elbows propped on the metal table. He was animated and looked almost happy to see me. The change of environment from San Quentin's death row to county jail probably had that effect on everyone. "Jake, come in and sit down." Our relationship had moved to first names and full sentences. I handed him a can of Dr. Pepper I'd purchased from the vending machine.

"Duane." I nodded. First names it would be, at least as long as it lasted. "Good to see you," I lied, "especially several hundred miles from San Quentin."

Durgeon grinned. "Here's to never returning." He popped open the soda, saluted me, and took a long drink. He motioned me to the other metal chair.

"How are they treating you?"

"Same old shit," he shrugged. "But I don't give a damn. This time it's different, I can feel it."

"What do you mean?"

"Let's just say last time they were running me, but I ain't runnin' no more. And they're starting to figure it out. They can keep on with their stupid head games, but"—he tapped his head—"they're playing with theirselves. I'm outta here. Enough of that shit."

I was not sure what he meant and frankly didn't care. "Looks like Tice is going to try the second trial just like he did the first. But then, why not, he won."

"Well, fuck him," Durgeon said, almost amicably. "Not this time. This one's our dance."

I liked his confidence, but I was unsure whether it was well placed. "Let's not get too far ahead of ourselves. We are looking at exactly the same evidence that got you convicted last time. The fingerprint, the gun, Christina's testimony, all that's coming in again. The only thing that might change is Ron Evans."

"Hey man, you're going to kick his ass. And I got me a front-row seat to watch the action."

"Dammit, Duane, cut the crap." I shook my head. It was time for a dose of reality. "How am I going to kick anyone's ass when I don't know anything about what happened? We are a week away from a very nasty trial and I'm scraping bottom. I need help."

Durgeon took another long swallow of his Dr. Pepper, looking over the can at me. We sat in silence. He was better at it that I was. I finally caved and rolled the dice. "I believe Dan Atwell and Todd Rode were with you that night," I bluffed. I had little basis for the bluff, but maybe it would help shake something out.

Durgeon's face drained of its good will. Very deliberately putting down the can, he said, "I told you, counselor, I don't talk about my friends."

"I know that's what you said. And that's bullshit." I leaned forward and tapped the table with my finger. "Number one, Rode is dead. No one to protect there. Number two," I tapped again, "Atwell's mom put the nails in the prosecution's case. I can't imagine what you think you might owe her or her son." Durgeon was studying the Dr. Pepper can as if it had nude photos of Charlize Theron. No response.

"Let's talk about Dan Atwell." I rested my elbows on the table, cupping my chin in my hands. "Let me tell you what I know, then we can go from there. Dan knew Doree from high school and maybe had an unresolved problem with her. Maybe, and I am speculating here, Dan had somehow gotten the three of you there. But it is not clear to me why you and Rode would go along with him." I had made huge speculative leaps to get to the point where the three men on the Blanco porch the night before were Atwell, Rode, and Durgeon.

Durgeon broke his silence. "It don't matter who was there, your job is to show I wasn't one of them." I was swimming against a riptide.

"Wrong, I already know you were there. You left your fingerprint. What might work is to show that someone else was the shooter. If we can establish that, we can probably keep you off death row."

Durgeon crumpled his empty can in one hand. "Snitches die in the joint."

"I understand that, but Rode's dead and Dan's in the wind, as far as I can tell."

"You don't understand shit. I don't give a fuck about them two, but I do give a fuck about being a snitch. Word gets around any joint about that." He leaned to me in a low voice. "You starting to get the picture, counselor?"

"I get the point, but I also get the point that you are facing DP charges." I paused briefly. "I need to know why those people were killed and who killed them. I'd also like to know if Graves was involved before I put Evans on the stand to incriminate him." We sat in silence, our eyes locked. We had both shot from point-blank range and were now waiting for the smoke to clear to assess the damage.

I held out this time, and finally Durgeon spoke. "I ain't telling you jack."

I got up. I was drained as well as frustrated. "I've arranged for a haircut and clothes. You should have them by tomorrow. I'll come see you before we start." I knocked and was let out without looking back.

❧ ❧ ❧

Saturday, July 8, trial minus five days.

Duke called from Cincinnati. "Was our boy at mom's house?" I asked, after checking caller ID. I was having a late lunch at Lisa's.

"Close enough. Mom directed me to the neighborhood bar where Evans has pretty much taken up residence. He wasn't happy to see me. But I got him to look at a bunch of photos. He told me off the record that he's just not sure anymore who he saw. But if we drag him back to California, he says he's going to ID Durgeon."

"I was afraid of that. What an asshole this guy's got to be. Any reaction at all when you showed him the Dan Atwell photo or the Graves photo?"

"No, none that I picked up on."

"Did you lay a subpoena on him?"

"Yeah. And he was just tickled about that. I thought he was going to take a swing at me."

"I'll have Suzelle send him an airline ticket."

As I disconnected, Lisa asked, "Good news?"

"No, but not unexpected. Evans, the guy who originally ID'd

Graves, is uncooperative. He threatened to ID Durgeon if we put him on the stand."

"Are you still going to call him?"

"Got no choice, though I do have a fallback strategy if he tries to screw with me."

"It really is a game of chess, isn't it?"

"Fair analogy."

༉༉༉

Sunday, July 9, trial minus four days.

I called Tice's answering service and was eventually put through. He was detached and icily professional. "It's Sunday. What is it?"

"I need Dan Atwell's rap sheet."

"What for?"

"I think Dan was involved in the Blanco murders, and I want to see what kind of person we're dealing with."

"Is this a fishing expedition? Do you have anything that would lead you to believe that he was in any way involved?" Tice's voice was careful, neutral.

I told him what Duke had turned up. After a brief pause, "Sounds like a witch hunt to me. That is not enough for me to release Atwell's sheet."

"You know it's enough. If I have to go to Harbarger, I will. It is amazing your investigation didn't find a connection between Atwell and Doree Blanco. You know this is significant enough to be checked out."

"San Arcadia isn't Los Angeles. It is a relatively small community, and lots of people know lots of other people. This 'connection,' as you call it, is far from compelling. You sound just like any other desperate defense lawyer grabbing at straws." He stopped to see if I would react.

I didn't. "But I'll tell you what, Jake. I'll run the rap, and you can chase this angle as far as you can. There is nothing there." His voice was conciliatory. "You can pick it up tomorrow."

~~~

Monday, July 10, trial minus three days.

Dan Atwell's rap sheet showed two narcotics arrests, including the arrest with Christina and Durgeon days after the murders. It also showed an arrest for rape that was dismissed. Rape? I needed Duke to follow that up. From the autopsy, it was inconclusive whether Doree had been raped. Atwell's juvenile contacts were not included on the sheet.

One thing I always tried to do before starting trial when I was a prosecutor was go to the scene. I wanted to have a visual overview in which to fit events. Where was the Blanco unit vis-à-vis the courtyard where Doree was shot? How far was Ron Evans's unit from where she was shot? What kind of lighting, if any, illuminated the courtyard? I drove to the apartment complex and walked the grounds. The unit from which Evans had seen the shooting was vacant, and after explaining who I was, the manager let me inside. Using the police diagram, I was able to pinpoint where Doree was shot. True to his word, Evans did have an unobstructed view of where the shooting occurred. The diagram indicated that Evans's bedroom window was sixty-five feet from the site of the shooting.

Nothing particularly useful emerged from the visit except I now had a clearer visual of the scene. Never know what might prove useful.

కావాకా

Tuesday, July 11, trial minus two days.

Duke had not run down the woman who Dan Atwell allegedly raped. I had hoped he would have found her, and we could interview her and see if she would be a useful witness, in the off-chance we could involve Dan Atwell in the trial. So far, I had nothing concrete that would allow Harbarger to permit evidence about the "other guy did it" defense. I needed to provide something objective to move against Atwell.

I then mapped out my strategy for my direct exam of Ron Evans. If he persisted in going sideways on me, I would take him as a hostile witness. That would allow me to essentially cross-examine him. Using leading questions would permit me to more precisely bend his testimony my way, so the jurors could see him for the snake he was. Based on Duke's report, I was pretty confident that I would have to employ that strategy. I also carefully examined Rosenblatt's cross-exam of Tice's fingerprint expert. The cross was lackluster. Two years ago, I had done a law-review article on fingerprint examination; it was a topic I was well versed in. I could kick up some dust on Tice's expert.

Other than tying up some loose ends, I had exhausted all I could do.

కావాకా

Wednesday, July 12, trial minus one day.

It should have been time for nothing but Durgeon. But I felt ready and couldn't think of what else to do. So I sat around the Ramada being very unproductive. Suzelle, who was still working the phones for the penalty phase, said I was underfoot. She suggested that I go for a swim to get me out of the room. I took her "suggestion" and did precisely that. *Good idea.*

After the swim, Lisa invited me to her place for dinner. I arrived with flowers and wine. She prepared a chicken dish over brown rice while I sat on a kitchen chair and we chatted. We talked about everything but the elephant in the room. After dinner and wine and a bit more wine, we retired to her bedroom and her bed. Surprisingly, I was able to sleep.

When morning came, I awoke with her warm body nestled against me. I kissed her awake, and forty-five minutes later, we had coffee and orange juice. Over coffee she asked, "Do you want me at the trial?" She ran her hand through my hair. "I want to support you. God knows there are going to be plenty of people there against you."

"That's a sweet offer, but I don't want you anywhere near the courthouse. You have a life here and a great future here. I don't want you to be tarnished by the fallout from the trial."

"I understand your concern, but I want to be a support for you."

"You're a school administrator. There could be fallout." I leaned in and kissed her. "I know you're in my corner, but please stay away from the trial. I've got to go, lots of things to check on."

CHAPTER 23

ONE-ON-ONE WITH TICE

It was Friday late morning, and we were in the second day of jury selection. Even though the murders had been committed thirteen years ago, it was difficult finding San Arcadia jurors who were not conversant with the details of the Blanco murders and the circumstances of the first trial. By Friday afternoon, I was pleased to find a juror who claimed she could be impartial when asked about the murders. This was far from the impartial jury of one's peers the English Common Law envisioned. In the end, it was the best I could do. The jurors were sworn in midafternoon. We settled on seven women and five men. We then picked four alternates, just in case. *There were no last-minute Lisas on this jury.*

Tice, as was the prosecutor's due, was at the counsel table closest to the jury. Manlow, as the primary investigating officer, shared that table and sat at Tice's right. At our table, Durgeon sat to my left, furthest from the jury (*no happenstance that*), Suzelle to my right (*I didn't want her next to Durgeon*). Suzelle had two large Pendaflex file folders which held every report, every statement, and every photograph connected to the case. She transported them to and from the courtroom in an oversized rolling briefcase. It made it seem as if we had more of a case than we had.

Durgeon had not spoken a word since we started picking the jury. His communication was limited to an occasional grunt. The bonhomie I had witnessed at the jail was no longer evident.

Looking down from on high, Judge Harbarger nodded to Tice and said, "Mr. Tice, you may make your opening statement." I was a bit surprised that Harbarger had not recessed for the weekend.

Tice, ever ready, stood and nodded to the judge. "Thank you, Your Honor." He walked to the lectern and spread his notes. The capacity crowd was eagerly quiet. Looking up at the jury and then looking over at the families of Doree and Robert sitting in the first two rows, he began. "Members of the jury, on November 15, thirteen years ago, the defendant invaded the home of Robert Blanco, his wife Doree, and their five-day-old baby, Jessica. Hours later, after being stripped naked by the defendant, bound by the defendant, and tortured by the defendant, this young, decent, God-fearing couple was murdered by the defendant."

Tice stepped from the lectern to the jury rail, dropping his voice to a conversational tone. He knew additional drama was not needed, that the gruesome facts provided all the drama necessary. "As you know from jury selection, my name is John Tice, I am your district attorney. You good folks have elected me to prosecute criminals, and that is exactly what I am doing during this trial. This is going to be a mean and ugly trial. The facts are grisly and disgusting. But you have to stay with me, and together we will see this through."

Tice stepped back to the lectern, checked his notes, and continued. "The evidence will show that the defendant forced his way into the Blanco home about 10:30 at night, and from 10:30 on that terrible night until 4:57 the next morning, that little apartment was hell itself. We know Robert and Doree were both stripped. We know Doree was bound at the ankles with packing tape. We know that they were burned with cigarettes and both were beaten. We don't know if Doree was raped. She had given birth just six days earlier, so the doctors were not able to make that determination."

"Objection!" I was out of my chair, almost screaming my protest. Harbarger motioned us to sidebar.

"Counselor?" Harbarger said to me in a low voice as she cupped one hand over the microphone.

"There is no evidence of rape. Yet his last sentence implies that she could have been raped. It's offered solely to prejudice Mr. Durgeon."

Harbarger looked questioningly at Tice. Tice shrugged and said, "I'll withdraw the statement."

Harbarger motioned us away and said to the jury, "I'll sustain the objection. Jurors, you will disregard that last remark. Mr. Tice, you may continue." It was a small but hollow victory. Despite the judge's admonition, that bell couldn't be unrung. Tice's suggestion of rape would linger.

Unruffled, Tice continued. "Sometime just before 5:00 a.m., Doree somehow managed to break free of her bindings, grab her newborn, and run from the apartment. We know that at that time, the defendant had already cut Robert's throat from ear to ear, almost severing his head from his body. As Robert lay bleeding to death, the defendant ran after Doree, who had gotten only fifty feet or so into the courtyard of the apartments. He knocked her to the ground. She pleaded for her life while wrapping her body protectively around her baby. The defendant fired twice into Doree's head."

Tice dropped his eyes to the carpet in front of the jury rail and started again in a low voice. "I am sorry to have to be the teller of this awful story. It is a story that never should have been told. These are events that never should have happened." Tice walked back to counsel table, picked up a controller, and illuminated, on a large video screen between the witness and the jury box, a two-foot by three-foot PowerPoint photograph of Robert Blanco. The jurors solemnly looked at the young, clean-cut face of Robert. "Robert was a hardworking young man with a deep religious commitment. He was a lay minister for his church. He was friendly, outgoing, and deeply devoted to his wife and their new daughter."

Tice again activated his PowerPoint and a photograph of Doree Blanco appeared. "Doree Blanco." He took a deep breath. "Doree was nineteen. She played the organ and took care of the secretarial duties for the church and had now begun her life as a mother. Doree was quiet and pretty and very much in love with Robert. This is Doree's high school photograph.

"Their daughter, Jessica, is now twelve years old and lives with Doree's parents in Morro Bay. She, of course, has no memory of her parents and will only know them through what others tell her."

"Excuse me," I said as I rose to my feet. "Your Honor, there is no purpose for these comments other than their appeal to the passion and prejudice of the jurors."

Harbarger waved me down. "Overruled. Mr. Tice, you may continue."

"Fuckin' judge," muttered Durgeon under his breath. Suzelle shot a glance across me at Durgeon. Durgeon turned to her and she quickly turned away. *What a peach.*

Tice had not turned away from the jury. He acknowledged neither my objection nor the court's ruling. "That baby was the only survivor of the carnage wreaked by the defendant on November 15, 2004. This trial is about the night before and that early morning. This trial is about the cold-blooded execution murders of Robert and Doree Blanco."

Tice moved back to the lectern and shuffled several pages.

"The case against the defendant is built on compelling evidence. There is the testimony of Christina Atwell, a woman with a criminal past. She used to run with a dangerous crowd. She used to run with people like Duane Durgeon. People on the edge of society, bikers and dopers—"

"Objection!" I called and stood. "This is way out of line. The prosecutor is characterizing Mr. Durgeon in an inaccurate and negative light."

This time Tice turned to the judge. "Nothing I've said is inaccurate." Tice's voice was conversational, completely in control, the consummate trial lawyer. I realized it contrasted starkly to my agitated demeanor. Tice was the picture of the professional prosecutor going about his business without rancor or anger. In contrast, I looked like the "typical" criminal defense attorney, trying to sanitize the facts in order to prevent the jurors from seeing the true story. Tice was beating me up with his matter-of-fact recitation of his case. I needed to dispel the notion that I was on the defensive, that I was attempting to prevent the jurors from getting to the facts, that I was an obstructionist. *God, I hoped I wasn't.* I had to do better than this. I was all that stood between Durgeon and execution. *Yeah, he was an asshole, but he was the asshole I was defending.*

Judge Harbarger did not sustain my sustainable objection. Instead, she motioned to Tice and said with only the slightest admonition, "Move on, Mr. Tice." It was clear from that point that Harbarger was not going to keep Tice in check. Tice was the elected DA, while I was an out-of-town defense lawyer representing a despicable lowlife who should have never been released from his ten-by-twelve cell in San Quentin except to be executed. I would be fighting Harbarger as well as Tice. It was a reality I had already recognized on an intellectual level, but now it hit me on a more personal level. *Suck it up, Jake, and get tough.*

Meanwhile, Tice moved ahead like Schwarzkopf through Iraq, as he methodically laid out his case, damning Durgeon with every word, every gesture. When he told of Durgeon's paranoia about the gun, several jurors looked over at Durgeon. He didn't spare them a glance.

Twenty minutes later, he was wrapping up. "After I've proven everything I told you I would prove, it will be your duty to finish the job and convict this man," he pointed at Durgeon, "that murderer," he paused again, "that executioner."

Durgeon was rocking back and forth in his seat with his eyes fixed ahead. I reached under the table and put my hand out to stop him. The courtroom was pin-drop quiet.

Harbarger tapped her gavel twice lightly and, looking at the jury, said, "Ladies and gentlemen, we will adjourn for today and resume promptly at 9:00 a.m. Monday. You are admonished to not discuss the case with anyone. Have a pleasant weekend."

Damn, I was afraid of that. Tice's words would have all weekend to resonate with the jurors. *Bad timing.*

CHAPTER 24

TV CRITIQUE

That evening, Suzelle and I met Lisa at Guido's, an upscale Italian restaurant. My spirits were low, as were Suzelle's. Tice's opening statement had been compelling. It felt as if the war might well be over with the first battle. Lisa worked to buoy our spirits. "I saw your magical opening statement for Suzelle's dad; there is no reason you can't do it again."

"Magical?" I grunted. "I had something to work with there. Here, I don't. I just might have to reserve our opening until we hear Tice's entire case. Which, frankly, I do not expect to vary much from the first trial." Over a bottle of Chianti, we discussed the merits of reserving the opening. The obvious risk was that the jury would hear nothing from the defense until Tice had presented the entire prosecution case—and by that time, the jurors most likely will have solidified their impressions favoring the prosecution. The lone possible upside of reserving was that perhaps something might develop during the prosecution case that we could sink our teeth into. Perhaps a key witness couldn't be located—Christina Atwell, for instance—or some physical evidence was lost or mishandled. As I sat and pushed some very good rigatoni around my plate, it became clear that I had to give my opening on Monday. The overwhelming case Tice had painted of Durgeon's guilt had to be rebutted, at least to some extent, or the trial was effectively over. If nothing else, I had to let the jury know we were in the courtroom and not conceding.

≈≈≈

It was dark when we walked Lisa back to her car and Suzelle and I walked the four blocks to Chez Ramada. I settled in to work some more of my opening while Suzelle went to her room to review transcripts. At 11:00 p.m., she hurried into my room, and without speaking, flicked on the television. It was the local NBC affiliate. The anchor was talking. "District Attorney John Tice vowed to once again convict the man accused of killing Robert and Doree Blanco thirteen years ago. Many local residents will recall that Duane Durgeon was previously convicted of the execution-style double murder, but his conviction was overturned by the California Supreme Court. In one of the highest-profile trials in San Arcadia history, Tice made his opening statement this afternoon. I have with us well-known local attorney Taylor Hunt. Ms. Hunt, an accomplished trial lawyer in her own right, has agreed to provide commentary throughout the Durgeon trial." Turning to Hunt, the anchor asked, "Ms. Hunt, what was your take on the start of trial?"

Taylor Hunt was a beauty. She was not in Lisa's class, but not many are. Her hair was blond and shoulder length with a simple part. Her cheekbones were high and her eyes were unusually large and strikingly blue. "John Tice is a brilliant trial lawyer," she began. "Today we heard a first-rate opening statement setting forth the prosecution's case. Mr. Tice was focused, passionate, and did precisely what he needed to do. He gave the jury a powerful overview of his case. His manner and tone conveyed a compelling case against Duane Durgeon."

The camera shifted back to the anchor. "Monday the defense attorney, Jake Clearwater, is scheduled to make his opening statement. What do you expect?"

"As you know, Mr. Clearwater was formerly a prosecutor in the San Arcadia district attorney's office and, in fact, worked under John Tice. So we know he has some experience. However, he has been teaching law for the past few years instead of trying cases. It remains to be seen whether he can hold his own. Opposing John Tice on a case of this magnitude is going to be a formidable task." *No shit.*

"What will Mr. Clearwater need to do Monday?"

"I think it critical that he assert his presence. Tice filled the courtroom today with the seemingly airtight nature of his case. When he concluded, it must have seemed to the jurors that the case against Durgeon was overwhelming."

"Thank you, Taylor." The anchor turned back to the camera. "Taylor Hunt will be with us throughout the Durgeon trial to keep us posted on all the developments . . ."

Suzelle clicked off the television. "You know her?" she asked.

"No, never seen her before. She must have blown into town after I left."

"She's very pretty."

"I noticed."

"It looks like she's going to be critiquing your every move."

"You know what they say. 'Those who can't . . . go on television and tell the world how it should be done.'"

Suzelle retired back to her room and I got back to my opening statement. I got to sleep around 2:00 a.m. and slept in until 9:00 a.m. I headed down to the local beach and got in a cold, vigorous swim. I met Lisa for lunch, and as we spoke, it finally occurred to me why I was struggling with the opening statement. I knew what I needed; unfortunately, it required help from Durgeon. I phoned the jail and made an appointment for Sunday afternoon.

৵৵৵

Armed with a Dr. Pepper, I joined Durgeon. "Didn't expect to see you today," he said, as I handed him the drink.

"Duane"—I wondered if we were still on first names—"I need your help. I realize that you won't discuss any others that may have been involved, and I can respect that. But what I really need right now is for you to answer one question. Regardless of the answer, I am going to do my damnedest to defend you, but my approach depends on your answer to that single question. I know you told me once already, but now I need it straight. Did you kill those folks?"

"No." A flat unequivocal answer.

"That is all I need for now. Of course I would like to know more, but I'll settle for this." It didn't matter if I believed him; I could now ethically go forward with a factual-innocence theory. I had my hook for the opening statement.

৵৵৵

I relaxed during dinner that evening with Team Durgeon. Lisa invited us to barbecue at her house. Now that I had a handle on the opening, I relaxed and enjoyed my friends. We discussed pretty much everything but the trial. After we helped Lisa clean up, Duke said he would drive Suzelle back to the Ramada. As he was leaving, he told me he was going to continue his efforts to run down Dan Atwell's alleged rape victim. He had identified her as Carrie Thompson. I stayed with Lisa.

CHAPTER 25

OPENING STATEMENT

Monday morning. "Mr. Clearwater, does the defense care to make an opening statement?" Judge Harbarger asked. The courtroom was once again packed. I heard one bailiff tell another that people had started lining up at 6:00 a.m. to get one of the precious seats. The families of Robert and Doree were guaranteed the first two rows. Their constant presence and disdain for Durgeon and for me weighed heavily. I could not begrudge them that. I also noticed Taylor Hunt three rows back.

"Absolutely, Your Honor," I said, as I got to my feet. I slapped the counsel table with my open hand—the crack rebounded off the walls. Several of the jurors flinched. "Duane Durgeon did not kill Doree Blanco. Duane Durgeon did not kill Robert Blanco." I walked from behind the table to the lectern Tice had used, and set it aside. Turning to the jurors, speaking without notes, I continued. "Two young adults are dead, a baby was left an orphan. We are faced here with an overwhelming tragedy. When something like this happens, we are angry, we are frustrated, and we want to punish those responsible. And that's okay, that's part of what makes us human. But in our anger and frustration, we have to be careful that we don't compound the tragedy by seizing and punishing the first likely suspect, especially an unlikeable human being like Duane Durgeon." I paused and looked at Doree's parents in the front row. "I know it would provide some relief to lay those innocent bodies at his feet. Let's just do it and be done with this terrible business." I shook my head. "But what if we are wrong? What if he wasn't the killer? What then?"

"Objection, argumentative." Tice was up.

"Sustained," said the judge in a tone that broached no equivocation. Of course it was argumentative. My only surprise was that Tice let me go on as long as he had.

Without acknowledging either Tice's objection or Harbarger's ruling, I had kept my eyes on the jury and waited for them to finish before I continued. "You heard one account of what happened that day, but you didn't hear all the evidence that will be forthcoming during the trial. Let me fill in some of the gaps the prosecutor did not discuss. For instance, you are going to hear from a witness who lived in an apartment just across the courtyard from where the Blancos lived, who actually saw Doree being shot. He witnessed the shooting. He will tell you how, just one day following the murders, he identified another man—not Duane Durgeon—as the person who shot Doree. That other man was arrested and taken into police custody. That eyewitness was so sure this other man was the shooter that immediately on seeing him at the police station, he told the detective, 'That's him.'" I repeated slowly, "'That's him.'

"You are going to hear a lot of evidence about the man who the eyewitness identified. His name is Anthony Graves. You are going to hear how this Anthony Graves had a prior rape conviction, and how he told some friends just days before the murders that Doree Blanco was some hot chick. You will hear that Graves lived just down the street from the apartments where Robert and Doree lived, and how his only alibi was his girlfriend. Anthony Graves was then and is now a very strong suspect."

In my view, Tice had erred in not raising Graves's identification. Raising and then mitigating hurtful facts is called pricking the boil. The idea is to deal with bad facts and discount them before the other side could exploit them. I had just exploited them.

Tice was up again, and he was hot. "Objection! Judge, this is supposed to be an opening statement, not a closing argument."

Harbarger looked at me with an exasperated expression. "Mr. Clearwater?"

I held up a hand. "I'll submit, Your Honor."

"Move on, counsel," she ordered.

"The case against Mr. Durgeon consists of two things." I held up a finger. "First, that fingerprint the prosecutor discussed, and second," I held up two fingers, "the ambiguous comments Mr. Durgeon made to an undercover police informant. An informant who just happened to be Durgeon's disgruntled former girlfriend and who just happened to receive a sweetheart plea bargain from Mr. Tice." I shook my head at the ridiculousness of it.

"Let's talk a little about each one of these. What about that fingerprint? You are going to hear about a partial fingerprint that a state-paid technician said matched Durgeon's. You are going to learn that opinion was based on very scant evidence, and that there is a real question as to who left that print and when it was left. You are going to hear testimony that Mr. Durgeon and that disgruntled girlfriend visited the Blanco apartment just days before the murders. Durgeon was looking for an apartment, and the Blancos were moving out. Robert and Doree invited Durgeon and the girlfriend inside. Inside was messy because the Blancos were packing to move. There were boxes and packing supplies, including rolls of the same packing tape on which the partial fingerprint the prosecutor talked about was found. You are going to have to decide not only whose print that was, but when it was left there." I did not honestly believe the fingerprint wasn't Durgeon's, but at this early phase I was reluctant to quit on any possible angle. I might be criticized for setting up multiple defenses, a strategy I disdained, but given the limited number of options, I could not afford to dismiss any of them.

I shifted up close to the jury. "The second primary piece of evidence the prosecution is relying on is a conversation Mr. Durgeon had with that same girlfriend while he was in custody." I put my hand up to stop for a moment. "But before we talk about that, we need to back up a little bit. The girlfriend, as you heard from the prosecutor, is Christina Atwell. She is a woman who makes her living by selling cocaine, heroin, and methamphetamine. You are going to hear how, just days after the murders, the police raided her house and arrested her, along with Mr. Durgeon and her twenty-five-year-old son, Dan, and seized a cache of illegal substances. All three of them were charged with assorted and serious felony drug charges. While they were awaiting trial on those drug charges, Christina Atwell cut a deal with the DA." I motioned at Tice. "Your DA, John Tice, would reduce the serious felony narcotics charges against Christina and her son Dan if she agreed to set up Duane Durgeon. She did what a lot of people would have done; she protected her own."

"Objection, misstates the facts."

Harbarger looked at me expectantly. "Judge, Christina Atwell is going to testify that she would not talk to the police until there was an agreement on both her charges and her son's charges. That sounds very much like cutting a deal, and the deal was to set up Mr. Durgeon."

Harbarger nodded, "Overruled. You may proceed."

It was nice to get a call. I turned back to the jury. "Ms. Atwell and her son were facing serious charges and serious time. She knew the Blanco murders were a hot topic. She also knew her relationship with Durgeon, which had always been rocky, was over. It was save-your-butt time, and she knew it." I stepped back from the rail. I wanted to give the jurors time to absorb this last point. "When you listen to her testify, keep in mind the circumstances behind those statements."

"Objection. Argumentative."

"Sustained. You made your point, counselor, move on."

I walked back to counsel table, stood behind Durgeon, and rested my hand on his shoulder. "Duane Durgeon is not a nice man. He has lived a rough life. But I am convinced that once you hear all the facts, you will agree that he did not shoot Doree or kill Robert." I turned to face the grieving families. "I know you have been terribly hurt. I know you are in great pain. But let's make certain we punish the right man or men." Doree's mother turned away. Doree's father gave me a hard look, and without taking his eyes off me, put his arm around his wife.

I sat down. The jurors were looking intently at me. The battle had been joined. The good people of San Arcadia, and in particular, the twelve jurors, were on notice that we did not intend to slip quietly beneath the waves.

Judge Harbarger pounded her gavel and ordered a fifteen-minute recess.

Suzelle and I walked out of the courtroom. The hallway was jammed with people. We drew a lot of looks, but I sensed that perhaps the crowd was not quite as hostile as before. Maybe that was just what I wanted to feel. I could not be sure, and I couldn't let it matter. They were not the audience that mattered.

In a low voice, Suzelle said, "You took him on point by point. The jurors were focused, especially when you talked about Graves."

CHAPTER 26

FIRST COPS ON SCENE

Harbarger gaveled us back to order. "Mr. Tice, you may call your first witness."

Tice called Josh Call. Officer Call was the first officer on the scene of the murders. After establishing the preliminaries, Tice got to it. "Deputy Call, on November 15, 2004, did you respond to a call of a shooting at the Palms Apartments on Geary here in San Arcadia?"

"Yes. I arrived at the scene shortly after 5:00 a.m."

"Describe what you observed as to the overall condition of the complex." It was an odd question.

I stood. "Your Honor, I'm hard-pressed to see the relevance."

Harbarger nodded at me and said, "I tend to agree, Mr. Clearwater, but I am going to trust Mr. Tice to quickly tie this in."

Tice turned his attention back to his witness. "Go ahead, Officer."

"Those apartments were in pretty rough shape. I remember being on patrol with my partner before all this happened and joking that a strong wind might take out the whole thing. The roofs had shingles missing, some windows had been broken out and replaced with plywood, there was assorted junk and trash piled up. The central area, I guess you could call it the courtyard, was mostly dirt and weeds. In the back, a couple of cars had been up on blocks for as long as I can remember." Call raised his eyebrows to Tice as if to ask, "Was that sufficient?"

Apparently, it was. Tice asked his next question. "Have you ever responded to that location before that morning?"

"Yes sir."

"What kind of calls?"

"Objection, relevance?" I was on my feet. This time it was clear what Tice was after. He wanted this cop to characterize the Palms as the dope flea market of the greater San Arcadia area. Tice was attempting to plant dope as the underlying motive for Durgeon, a career doper, to be there. There had been vague references during the first trial that Durgeon believed the Blancos had narcotics in their apartment, hence some motive for Durgeon to be there.

"You may be heard, Mr. Clearwater."

"May we approach?" I asked. If we argued this in front of the jury, Tice's innuendo would be planted despite the judge sustaining my objection.

Harbarger motioned us up and looked at Tice. "John?"

"Judge, the jury has the right to be given a fair description of the scene. This testimony is offered for no other reason."

Harbarger nodded for me to respond.

"Despite Mr. Tice's innocent protestations, this is being offered to suggest that drugs might be a motive for whoever it was that entered the Blanco apartment. Its prejudicial impact far outweighs its probative value."

"I don't see it as particularly harmful. I think you're overreacting, Mr. Clearwater. I am going to overrule the objection." *Bad call.*

After we resumed our positions, Tice continued. "I'm sorry you were interrupted, Officer Call. Let me ask my question again. What kind of calls did you typically respond to at the Palms?"

"Narcotics calls. Everyone in the department knows that the Palms is a place where narcotics transactions take place." Call offered his answer while looking at me and waiting for an objection. There was no point in objecting. Even though his opinion as to what everyone in the department knew was objectionable, to object now would be to call even more attention to this harmful testimony. I had to let it pass. Tice won that skirmish.

"I want to turn your attention now to the early-morning hours of November 15. Describe what the day was like at the time you arrived."

"It was dark, there was patchy fog."

"How long after receiving the call that shots had been fired did you arrive?"

"Four, five minutes."

"Describe your action on your arrival."

"We pulled up and exited our unit twenty feet south of the entry to the apartments."

"That was you and Officer Perroni?"

"Yes, sir."

"Go on."

"We drew our weapons and moved to the side of the first unit on the south side. From that location, we could see what appeared to be a body in the center area of the apartments."

"Go on."

"I instructed Officer Perroni to maintain his position and radio for backup. I ran to the body. I felt like I needed to get there to render assistance."

"Were you concerned that the shooter was at large somewhere in the apartments?"

"Yes sir, but I needed to check on the condition of that person."

"And what was that condition?"

"It was immediately clear she was dead."

"Describe the body as you found it."

"It was a young Caucasian woman. She was unclothed except for a pair of slippers. Her body was curled in a fetal position. The left side of her head had been blown away." He paused, drew a deep breath, and continued. "I saw some movement under the body. I rolled her body slightly to one side and saw a baby."

"How did the baby appear?"

"The baby looked fine. There was some," he groped for a word, "tissue from the woman on the baby's pajamas. I brushed it off."

"What do you mean, 'tissue'?"

Call took a breath. "It looked like part of the woman's brain."

Tice let the point linger for a count before asking, "What happened next?"

"Backup arrived, and they secured the scene. Officers started going door to door."

"What did you do?"

"I took off my jacket and wrapped the baby."

"Were you involved any further in securing the scene or in any investigation arising from the murders?"

"No, I wasn't."

"Thank you very much, Officer." Then turning to the judge, Tice said, "I have nothing further for this witness."

"Alright, Mr. Tice." Harbarger turned to the jury. "It's eleven forty-five. We will adjourn for lunch and begin this afternoon at two o'clock."

❧ ❧ ❧

"Mr. Clearwater, your cross of Officer Call." We had all reassembled.

I stood and looked at the all-American, square-jawed face of John Call. "Your Honor, I have no questions of Deputy Call." Then looking at Call, I said, " Deputy, thank you for your courageous work on this difficult case." *Only attack when necessary, and always wear the white hat.*

Harbarger excused Call and instructed Tice to call his next witness. Tice called Tim McCoy.

After McCoy was sworn in, Tice began. "What is your rank, sir?"

"I am a lieutenant with the San Arcadia Police Department."

"And were you on duty during the early-morning hours of November 15, 2004?"

"Yes, I was."

"Directing your attention to approximately five fifteen that morning, did you respond to the Palms Apartments?"

"Yes, Deputy Perroni told me that we had a body of an adult male in an apartment and the body of an adult female in the courtyard. I ordered additional units to respond."

"Why more units?" Tice was seated so as to not draw attention away from his witness, and indeed all eyes were on McCoy.

"From what I had been able to ascertain, I had a double homicide that had happened a short time ago. The perpetrator might still have been in the area. I wanted as many police personnel in the vicinity as I could get."

"What did you do next?"

"I entered apartment 1 and saw the body of an adult male, later identified as Robert Blanco."

Tice, recognizing a poignant moment and wanting to draw it

out, pushed back in his chair and slowly stood. "Lieutenant, tell us about Robert's body."

I half stood. "Isn't this best left to the coroner?"

Harbarger looked at Tice. Tice, his demeanor unruffled at my interruption, responded, "I am asking Lieutenant McCoy to describe what he saw, nothing more."

"Overruled," Harbarger ruled, and then turned to McCoy. "Lieutenant, you may answer."

"His body was unclothed, his ankles were tied together with wire. His wrists were tied behind his back, also with wire. He was lying face down in a large pool of blood." McCoy's voice was that of an automaton—the facts, and nothing but the facts. He had found where he needed to be in relaying such a horrific sight.

"Describe, please, the inside of the apartment."

"It was torn apart. The sheets were ripped from the bed, the mattress was slit, the contents from the bureau drawers had been dumped on the floor. The kitchen cupboards were all open. There were a dozen or more packing boxes that had been ripped open and damaged. It looked like a cyclone had ripped through the apartment."

"After you surveyed the damage to the apartment," Tice asked, "what did you do next?"

"I ordered the scene secured for the forensics people. I then checked on the body of Mrs. Blanco and then assisted in interviewing the residents of the apartments."

"Before we discuss the interviews of the residents, did you find any money or drugs in the Blancos' apartment?"

"No."

"I understand there was one eyewitness." Tice leaned slightly toward the witness, adding weight to his question.

"That's correct."

"Before we turn to the eyewitness, did you and your people interview the residents of the apartments?"

"Yes. There are fourteen units, but at that time, only ten were occupied. We contacted everyone who was at home that morning. Several reported hearing the gunshots, but only one person said he saw the shots being fired."

"Other than the eyewitness, did any of the other residents report anything that aided your investigation?"

"There were no reports of a disturbance or unusual noise prior to the gunshots. However," McCoy examined a report he had with him, "one resident, a Peter Turner, said that he was across the street at the Circle K the evening before, about ten or ten thirty, and noticed two or three men, he was not certain of the number, talking to Robert Blanco. He did not recall any details about those men." McCoy's testimony relaying what Turner had said was hearsay. During the first trial, it was established that Turner was unavailable, and thus the statement was admissible. No point in objecting.

"Let's turn to the person who said he looked out into the courtyard and saw the shooting. Who was that?"

"Ron Evans. His apartment was on the south side of the units, opposite the Blancos' apartment. Based on our interview of Mr. Evans, we ascertained that he was the individual who had called in the shooting of Mrs. Blanco. He reported that he witnessed the shooting."

"Did he provide a description of the shooter?"

"He said the man was big, with long hair and a full beard."

"Did your investigation lead you to any particular individual?"

"Yes, initially we focused on Anthony Graves."

"What were the circumstances that led to Mr. Graves?"

"Several things. First, he lived in a trailer just down the street from the Palms. Second, an individual came forward right there at the scene that morning and said Graves on several occasions had expressed an unhealthy interest in Mrs. Blanco. Third, Graves matched Mr. Evans's description as a big man with long hair and a full beard. And finally, Graves had a history of violence, including sexual assault." Tice was now pricking this boil. It was surprising to me that he had not done so during his opening statement. But from his perspective, better late than never.

"Were there any other developments in your initial investigation of Graves?"

"Yes, the day after the murders, we arranged for the eyewitness, Mr. Evans, to see Mr. Graves."

"Was this done with a lineup involving other individuals bearing a general resemblance to Graves?"

"No, we had Mr. Evans enter an interrogation room where Graves was seated."

Tice spread his arms in a gesture of disbelief. "You mean Graves was the only suspect present?" Tice's mock surprise was theatrical. This was boil pricking 101.

"That's right." McCoy shifted in his seat.

Tice let out a breath and let his admonishment of McCoy hang in the air. He then asked, "Did you see Mr. Evans before he entered the interrogation room that contained Graves?"

"Yes."

"Describe how he appeared to you."

"He was very reluctant to enter the room. He appeared to be very nervous."

"And what happened when Evans entered the room?"

"Evans took one very brief look and quickly turned to leave. He said something like, 'Get me the hell out of here.'"

"How long would you say Evans looked at Graves?"

"It was very quick; I'd say two seconds."

"Lieutenant, how long have you been in law enforcement?"

"Twenty-two years."

"Have you seen a number of identifications?"

"I have."

"Did Mr. Evans's ID of Graves convince you that Graves was the killer?"

"Objection! He's asking for an improper opinion." I was on my feet.

Without waiting for the judge to make a ruling, Tice responded, "This man is a thirty-two-year veteran with extensive experience watching people make or attempting to make identifications. His opinion on this matter would be helpful to the jury."

Harbarger, ever the homecourt jurist, agreed. "Overruled. You may answer."

"He just wanted out of there. He would have identified Mother Teresa if she had been in that room."

Some of the jurors grinned. Tice waited a beat. "I assume your investigation of Graves continued." The boil had been thoroughly pricked. Evans's identification of Graves was still there, and it would still hurt the prosecution case, but much of its impact had been mitigated. My cross would not be as effective as it would have otherwise been.

"Yes, he told us he spent the entire night of November 14 and the morning of November 15 until about 10:00 a.m. with his girlfriend," McCoy replied.

"Was his story checked out?"

"Yes, I believe Investigator Manlow spoke with . . ." He paused and checked his report. "Deirdre Plumber on the sixteenth."

"She was the girlfriend?"

"Yes."

"Did she confirm his whereabouts during the time of the murders?"

"She did."

"Lieutenant, at the completion of the investigation of Graves, did you believe he was in any way involved in the murders of Robert and Doree Blanco?"

"Objection. Again, improper opinion." I was irritated that Tice would persist with this improper-opinion evidence. He knew it was clearly over the line.

This time Harbarger did what she should have done the last time and sustained my objection. "That is enough, Mr. Tice, move on."

Tice, unfazed, continued. "Lieutenant, were you satisfied with the way your department handled this investigation?" It was an odd question, but it was clear Tice was at the end of his examination and was simply looking for a graceful exit. *Never end an examination on a sustained objection. Looks weak.*

"There are a couple of things we could have done better, but overall, I felt we conducted a thorough investigation."

"Thank you, Lieutenant McCoy. I have no further questions."

꙳꙳꙳

Harbarger nodded to me. "Mr. Clearwater, you may inquire."

"Thank you, Judge." I stood and turned to the witness. "Lieutenant McCoy, we need to talk a little more about Anthony Graves."

"Yes sir." McCoy was respectful and had a professional, detached air.

"Your initial investigation revealed that Graves lived in a trailer just down from the Palms, correct?"

"Yes."

"And your investigation revealed that a person actually on the scene the morning of the murders told one of your officers that Graves knew Doree Blanco?"

"That's correct."

"And that same person reported that Graves was sexually interested in Mrs. Blanco?"

"Sexually interested may be too strong," McCoy said, shrugging.

"Didn't the informant report that Graves thought Doree was hot?"

"That's what he said."

"But you do not consider that sexually interested?"

"Not necessarily." Again, McCoy shrugged.

I paused. The jurors would have the final say on that point. "You were aware that Mr. Graves had previously been convicted of rape, weren't you?" I was being careful to elicit only one fact per question. It reduced the opportunity for the witness to be evasive and allowed me to maintain complete control of the exam. Furthermore, it allowed me to make it more painful for the witness. *The slow bleed.*

"I was aware of that, yes."

"Doree Blanco was found stripped naked, correct?"

"Yes, sir."

"Which might well indicate some manner of sexual assault upon her, correct?"

"Yes."

"You were also aware that Graves had only been out of prison on his rape conviction for six months at the time, weren't you?"

"That's correct."

"Lieutenant, Mr. Evans, the eyewitness, gave a description of the man who shot Doree, didn't he?"

"Yes, sir."

"He said the shooter was a big man, correct?"

"Yes, sir."

I went back to my table and Suzelle handed me McCoy's report. "I'm looking at your report. You wrote that Graves was six feet and approximately 240 pounds, didn't you?"

"That's right."

"The eyewitness said the shooter had long hair and a full beard, correct?"

"Yes."

"Graves had long hair?"

"He did."

"Anthony Graves had a full beard, correct?"

McCoy was too seasoned to bicker with me and agreed, "Yes, he did."

"Now, the identification that Mr. Evans made of Mr. Graves took place the day after the shooting, isn't that right?"

I walked behind Tice's table and stood at the jury rail. "When Mr. Evans first saw Graves in that interrogation room, his body immediately tensed up, didn't it?"

"Yes."

"And at that point—" I held up my finger indicating for him to hold on a minute and walked back to my counsel table and looked at my legal pad. I turned back to McCoy. "And at that point, Mr. Evans said, 'That's him. Get me the hell out of here.' Isn't that right?"

"That's what he said."

"I noticed on direct examination you told us that Evans said, 'Get me the hell out of here.' But you did not tell us that Evans said, 'That's him.' Why was that?"

I could afford to ask a "why" question because McCoy had nowhere to go.

"I was not trying to mislead; I just misstated."

"That concerns me, Lieutenant. It seems to me that when Evans said, 'That's him,' that was confirmation of his identification of Graves as the shooter."

"Counsel, again, I was not trying to mislead. I just misstated."

"Misstated," I said in a puzzled tone. "But you omitted the actual identification."

"I wasn't trying to mislead."

"I see." I nodded understandingly. "So we are all clear, when Evans said, 'That's him,' that was confirmation by the only eyewitness that Graves was the man who shot Doree Blanco, correct?"

"Yes."

"Lieutenant, following the Evans ID of Graves, you continued to hold Graves in custody for the murders of the Blancos, didn't you?"

"Our investigation was ongoing."

I paused. "Perhaps my question was not clear. Let me ask it again." I was the essence of patience. "Following the Evans ID of Graves, you continued to hold Graves in custody for the murders, correct?"

"Yes."

"Thank you, Lieutenant. I have nothing further."

On redirect, Tice briefly attempted to clean up the "misspeak." He also reminded the jury that Graves had an alibi.

Harbarger rapped her gavel. "Alright, ladies and gentlemen of the jury, I have some other matters to take up this afternoon, so we are to adjourn early today. I order everyone back at nine o'clock tomorrow morning. Again, you are admonished to not discuss this matter with anyone and to refrain from reading, watching, or hearing anything about this case. Dismissed."

Durgeon was led off without saying a word. *Perhaps my cross was not to his liking.* Suzelle lingered at our table, allowing the crowd to file out. The last thing I wanted was to brush shoulders with Blanco or Bennett family members.

"How do you think the jurors reacted to McCoy?" I asked Suzelle.

"They were put off by his poor handling of the identification." Suzelle was looking at the notes she had made during McCoy's testimony. It was apparent that she had questions.

I cocked my head and asked, "Was there something else you think I should have covered on cross?"

"I don't know," she said deferentially. "But maybe you let him off a little easy."

"Fair enough. What else should I have done?"

"It's not any one thing." She hesitated. "It's just that you were nice to him. I expected you to beat him up."

"You think clubbing around a police lieutenant was the way to go?"

"But you didn't go into his failure to conduct a real lineup involving Evans and Graves instead of just allowing Evans to see Graves alone."

"I considered that, but actually I didn't want to draw any more attention to the shaky show-up. Its suggestibility doesn't help us. We want the jurors to trust Evans's ID of Graves, right?"

"That makes sense," she said. "But I think I would have gone after him harder."

❧ ❧ ❧

That evening, Lisa, Suzelle, and I ordered in Chinese to the Ramada. Suzelle was anxious to catch the local news at six o'clock. "Let's see what Taylor Hunt has to say about today's action." Lisa had not seen Hunt's Friday "report," but Suzelle had filled her in. Sure enough, the trial was the second story. The anchor turned to Taylor Hunt. "Fill us in on the third day of the Durgeon trial."

"It was fascinating. Defense counsel Clearwater made a strong opening statement, countering DA Tice's earlier opening statement.

Mr. Clearwater did what I think was critical: He let the jurors know that he was going to put up a robust defense. He told the jurors that his client did not commit the murders and that he was set up by his former girlfriend. He caught everyone's attention with his statement."

The anchor asked, "Was there testimony today?"

"Yes, DA Tice called two of the first responders. First was the officer that found the Blanco's one-week-old baby wrapped in her mother's arms. Heartbreaking testimony. The DA then called the lieutenant who was in charge of the scene. His testimony primarily focused on an early suspect identified by one of the residents who claimed he saw the individual who shot Doree Blanco. DA Tice went to great pains to discount that witness's ID, whereas the defense emphasized the identification. The jurors witnessed two very good lawyers going head-to-head."

The anchor thanked Hunt and moved onto other matters.

Lisa's first comment: "Looks like you have another female fan, Jake. And a pretty one, at that." Suzelle laughed. I shrugged.

CHAPTER 27

THINGS TURN UGLY

Tuesday morning, Tice called the San Arcadia medical examiner to detail the various injuries suffered by the Blancos and to establish the cause of death. Before beginning the exam, I asked to approach. At the bench, I inquired whether Tice was going to use any photographs during the examiner's testimony.

"Of course I am," he said.

"Well, I'd like to look at them first and see if I have any objections. Given the short notice for trial, I haven't had time to see what Mr. Tice proposes to show the jury." I caught a sharp look from Harbarger. *My screwup; I should have checked earlier.*

"Defense counsel should have expressed his concerns pretrial," Tice said.

"I need to see what photos he intends to display. I am concerned that some may be used simply for their emotional impact."

Judge Harbarger leaned back and looked over us to the jurors. "Members of the jury, let's take a brief ten-minute recess. The lawyers and I have to discuss a few points in chambers." Harbarger was not pleased with me, and for good reason. I should have viewed the photos earlier and raised any objections then.

In chambers, Harbarger excluded some of the more horrific photographs. However, over my protest, she allowed Tice to use photographs of both Robert and Doree that in my opinion were unnecessarily prejudicial.

Back before the jury, Tice had the examiner stand at the PowerPoint screen and, using various slides, begin detailing Robert's injuries. The last photograph was obviously taken during the autopsy. It showed the examiner tilting Robert's head back, exposing the cut that had almost severed his head from his body.

Tice and the examiner then turned to Doree. The first three photographs showed her curled body as it lay in the courtyard. The body, the examiner explained, was not precisely as it had been found because the first officer had moved it to pull the baby from her. In looking at those photographs, Doree's body looked out of place. The courtyard was mostly bare ground. The back wheel of a bicycle was partially visible near her feet, which were covered in purple knit slippers. The medical examiner testified that Doree had died from two shots from a .22 caliber revolver, one entering the right temple, the other entering the back of her skull and lodging in her brain. The bullets were identified and moved into evidence.

Tice then moved onto the autopsy photographs of Doree's body lying naked on her back. Her body had been cleaned; the two blackened holes on her head were clearly defined. Tape had pulled off a two-inch strip of skin from one of her wrists. Four cigarette burns were on her stomach and there was a red welt across her right breast.

Tice's next photograph was the one I particularly had objected to. It depicted hands holding open Doree's vagina. Before Tice could display the photograph, I stood and again asked to approach. Harbarger motioned us up. "Judge, enough is enough," my voice an angry whisper. "I know you've already ruled, but you need to reconsider. What is the point of further degrading this poor woman and her family? What's the point?" I was furious. Tice was using this photograph to inflame. It served no purpose beyond that.

Tice was unperturbed. "Your Honor, you have already ruled on this. Since Mrs. Blanco had just given birth, the examiner could not ascertain if she had been raped, but she did suffer some trauma. I want the jury to see the trauma. They have a right to be fully apprised of the defendant's handiwork."

"This is wrong, and both of you know it's wrong." Futility mixed with rage in my voice.

Harbarger gave me a threatening look. "Watch it, counsel. The jury needs to see it all. Objection overruled." *You hometown jerk.*

As Tice put up the photograph, an inhuman shriek ripped the room from directly behind me, causing me to pull my head down for a heartbeat before I spun around to see what was happening. Doree's mother was standing stiffly in the first row, her hands drawn into claws, her features all but unrecognizable in her distorted face. She was screaming at Durgeon. "Damn you, you murderer! Damn you to bloody hell!" Spittle spattered her blouse. "You killed my Doree, you sonofabitch, and you sit there leering at the things you did to my baby! Damn you! Damn you!"

Harbarger hammered her gavel. "Order! Order! Bailiff!"

Mr. Bennett tried to put his arms around his wife. She threw them off and kept screaming. "If I had a gun, I would shoot you and let you die in the street like a rabid dog!" She continued to rage as bailiffs pushed through people who were standing in the way. She was still screaming as they hauled her from the courtroom, her distraught husband following helplessly.

Durgeon leaned to me and whispered, "Fuckin' glad she didn't have a gun. She would've taken all three of us out."

Judge Harbarger pounded aggressively, and the chatter stilled.

Abandoned seats were resumed. "There will be no more disturbances in my courtroom. None. Is that understood?" She glared over the room, bringing to her quelling look the full power of her office. Silence.

Tice slowly walked to counsel table and shuffled some notes. He wanted to draw out the unexpected outburst of emotion. *Given the circumstances, it was not that unexpected. I felt Mrs. Bennett's pain.* Tice calmly resumed his examination. "Other than the trauma you noted, was there any other evidence of rape?"

"No. We did not find any semen."

"Is it possible she could have been raped even though no semen was found?" *Tice wanted to park on the idea of rape for as long as possible.*

"Of course it is. The perpetrator could have used a condom or not have ejaculated."

Tice finished at eleven thirty. My cross was brief. There was nothing to contest. I was still seething. I confirmed that there was no definitive indication of rape and let it go.

Harbarger adjourned for the day. She had told us prior to trial that this was to be a half day. She had a scheduled medical procedure. At this pace, we would be here for months. It seemed that full trial days were a scarce commodity in Judge Harbarger's courtroom.

As we left the courtroom, Taylor Hunt was waiting. She stuck out her hand. "Taylor Hunt, I'm covering for KPET."

"We caught you last night," I said, and turning to Suzelle, "This is my colleague Suzelle Frost."

"Nice to meet you both. Mr. Clearwater, that was an impressive opening statement."

"Thanks."

Hunt stood expectantly, apparently ready for more of a reaction from me. Up close, she was even more beautiful than on television.

When I offered no more, she asked, "What did you make of the reaction of Mrs. Bennett?"

"Didn't seem terribly surprising. That autopsy photograph should have never come in."

"We on the record?" she asked.

"We are."

"How would you assess the trial so far?"

"The prosecutor is pretty much putting on the same case that resulted in conviction last time."

"Are you expecting any surprises?"

"Not from the prosecution."

"Does that mean we can expect some surprises from you?"

"We'll all have to be patient and see how things play out."

"Are you being coy, Mr. Clearwater?"

I offered a slight grin. "I don't know how to be coy, Ms. Hunt. But I do know it wouldn't be in the best interest of Mr. Durgeon to share our trial strategy with a television analyst."

She backed off a step. "Thank you, Mr. Clearwater. Perhaps we'll talk tomorrow."

"Perhaps."

ॐॐॐ

Back at the Ramada, Duke was sprawled across the lone upholstered chair, Heineken in hand. "Glad to see you hard at it," I said as I dropped my briefcase on the desk and took two beers from the mini. I opened them and gave one to Suzelle, who looked momentarily surprised, then shrugged and took it. *I wonder if she drank much before coming into my circle.*

"How did it go today?" Duke asked, slowly straightening in his chair.

"Just another half day in trial. Aside from the bailiffs carrying out the victim's mother screaming and cursing us to hell, there were no surprises. Tice is following the script to the letter from the first trial. So far, we're through the first two cops and the medical examiner." I took a long pull on the Heineken. "Any luck running down Carrie Thompson?"

"Not yet, but I'll find her," he said with absolute assurance.

"If we can get the judge to allow us to explore the Dan Atwell angle, we'll probably need her sometime next week." Shifting my attention to Suzelle, I remarked, "You look beat, and it's only noon." Her face was pale, her eyes huge with fatigue.

"I had no idea what a strain it was to be in trial. I'm not really doing anything, but the constant tension is overwhelming. Do you ever get used to that?"

"Yep," I lied, and saluted her with my beer.

"That's it? Yep?"

"Yep," I repeated, giving her a grin.

She shook her head and turned away. "I'm going to get back on the phone to Texas."

Duke asked, "Durgeon's people?"

She nodded. "The family's not very enthusiastic about flying out here and standing up for him. So far, I've only got mom."

"Penalty phase?" Duke asked.

"Correct," she answered as she rolled her briefcase toward the door.

"Just keep pounding away," I called after her. "We'll catch a few breaks before this thing is over."

"That's what I like about you, Jake," Duke offered. "The cavalry is always just about ready to crest the hill."

CHAPTER 28

UGLIER AND UGLIER

That evening, Lisa again joined us in our suite and the four of us ordered pizza. At eleven o'clock, Duke flicked on the television to the local news. After enduring some painful local commercials, the trial was the lead story.

"Oh good," was Suzelle's comment. "An assessment from your latest admirer." Suzelle filled Lisa and Duke in on our brief encounter with Taylor Hunt.

The news anchor turned to Hunt, poised in front of the camera for her summary of the day's proceedings. "Well, Taylor what happened in trial today?"

"The biggest news is what we've learned within the hour. Death threats have been made against Duane Durgeon, the man on trial for the 2004 double murder of Robert and Doree Blanco. A reliable source within the police department confirmed they have received death threats against both Durgeon and his lawyers."

The anchor: "This is startling; how will this affect the trial?"

"I don't know. I assume that the trial will proceed but under heightened security. I don't see any other options."

"And how about the trial itself?"

"It was a very emotional day at trial. Doree Blanco's mother screamed at Duane Durgeon and had to be removed from the courtroom. I've received word that after being taken home, she was later transported to St. John's Hospital with chest pains. We have no information on her condition at this time."

"Was she reacting to something specific?"

"DA Tice was questioning the medical examiner about whether Doree Blanco had been raped."

"I see." The anchor shook his head solemnly. "A most difficult day all around. Thank you, Taylor."

"Enough of that crap," Duke said as he turned off the television.

"Well, I guess we've got their attention now," I said, in a voice intending to make light of the report. *Death threats?*

"Shouldn't we be concerned?" Suzelle asked.

Lisa weighed in. "Jake, I thought this could get dangerous. I was living here at the time of the murders and trial. This really scared the whole city. I am not surprised at this kind of reaction."

"If we start thinking too much about everything else, it just gets that much harder to stay focused on the trial," I counseled. "It's probably some attention seeker looking to make some news. Let's stay focused."

Before anyone else could speak, the phone rang, and I picked it up. It was a police captain informing me that he was on his way to our room to discuss security. *So much for staying focused.*

When he arrived, he didn't go into specifics except to say an anonymous caller had made some threats, directed primarily at Durgeon and also a few at me. He did not seem overly concerned that a real problem existed. "Probably some crackpot blowing smoke." However, an officer would pick us up every morning for the duration of the trial and escort us to and from the courthouse.

I had received a couple of threats as a DDA, usually from the family or friends of someone I had convicted. I figured it came with the job. But never a death threat. Should I be concerned about the people in my circle? Suzelle would be with me under police protection. Duke was Duke, a former cop. But what about Lisa? If anyone had bothered monitoring us, it was clear we were involved. Would a threat extend that far? I had to think not. In the end, I decided to let it be.

CHAPTER 29

THE FINGERPRINT

When Suzelle and I stepped from the lobby Wednesday morning after coffee and bagels, we were met by a police officer who had been assigned to drive us to and from the courthouse. The officer was young with a fledgling mustache, and he most likely had drawn the duty because he had absolutely no seniority. Several print reporters and both local TV crews came toward us as we climbed out of the car at the courthouse. The officer who had driven us stepped in front of Suzelle and me, clearing a way into the building. Just when it looked as if we were going to be overwhelmed, Frank Bennett and several of his family rounded the corner. The media folks left us to intercept this more-newsworthy arrival. They swarmed him like crows to roadkill. I heard several questions concerning Bennett's wife. "She's in the hospital, you sorry sons-of-bitches," Bennett snarled, shoving a microphone out of his face. His eyes were haunted, his clothes were wrinkled, he hadn't shaved. It didn't look like he had been home. We, along with Bennett and his group, were hustled through the courthouse door, around the line of people waiting to pass through the metal detector and into the courtroom.

ৰ৵ ৰ৵ ৰ৵

The first witness for the prosecution that day was Jim McCorkle, the chief forensics analyst at the county crime laboratory. He had been called to the Blanco crime scene to collect and analyze the evidence found there. He was a longtime forensics expert with a great deal of experience in fingerprint analysis. When I was a DDA, he had been my witness on several occasions.

Tice's examination of McCorkle took the better part of two hours. McCorkle stated that he had exhaustively examined the Blanco apartment and contents for fingerprints. After excluding the nonsuspicious prints, no useful prints were found in the apartment. However, when he examined Doree Blanco's body after it was removed to the morgue, he found a partial print that matched Durgeon's right little finger. The print had been lifted from a crumpled piece of packing tape that was stuck on Doree's wrist. McCorkle had also examined the bullet retrieved from Doree's brain and compared it with a bullet test fired from the .22 caliber revolver retrieved from Ragged Point. He concluded that the bullet taken from Doree was consistent with the test-fired bullet. Consistent, but not conclusive. Because of the deteriorated condition of the gun, he could not testify to a conclusive match. *Consistent was damaging enough.*

On cross, I confirmed that the bullet was only consistent and not conclusive and that the bullet could have been fired from any number of .22 caliber revolvers. I also firmed up that the fingerprint on the piece of packing tape could have been left days or even weeks before the murders.

In preparing for this cross-exam, I had gone back to a law-review article I had written when I started at Pacifico, focusing on fingerprint analysis and the persistent problem of false positives. *Who knew that a law-review article would have some practical benefit?*

"Fingerprint examination and comparison is an exact science, isn't it?" I asked.

"Yes, it is."

"The found print either belongs to a particular individual or it doesn't. It's as clear-cut as that?"

"That is perhaps a bit simplistic, but in essence that's exactly right."

"When you determine that found prints match a particular individual, you are confident in your findings, aren't you?"

"I would not testify if I were not."

"Just to be clear, you are 100 percent certain of your findings?"

"Yes, I am."

"As a print examiner, you are familiar with the International Association for Identifications, the IAI, aren't you?"

"I am."

"That organization certifies print examiners, correct?"

"They have a certification process."

"Well, in fact, that is the most respected of the certification programs, isn't it?"

"I believe that's right."

"So that is a yes, it is the most respected of the certification programs?" Once again on cross, beat the witness down to a monosyllabic answer.

"Yes, it is."

"As a person who has been working in this area for a number of years, you understand that the IAI was created to address concerns of incompetence in latent fingerprint examinations, isn't that so?"

"As I understand it, that was one of the goals." *Good enough.*

"Mr. McCorkle, incompetence is a problem in the area of print examination, isn't it?"

"I don't know if that is true."

"Are you saying that incompetence in print examination is not a problem?"

"It can be a problem."

"Okay." I nodded my head, considering his answer. "You are familiar with the tests the IAI conducted in 2015, just a few years ago, correct?"

"I am aware of those tests."

"During those tests, thirty-four examiners—22 percent of the total—reported false positives, didn't they?"

"I do not recall the exact percentages."

"I have the exact results right here." I held up a document. "Would you like to take a look?"

"I will take your word on it."

"I appreciate that courtesy, Mr. McCorkle." I smiled at him. He knew precisely where I was going, and there wasn't a damn thing he could do about it. "A false positive? That's when an examiner made a determination that a found print matched a particular individual when in fact the found print did not come from that particular individual, did I get that right?"

"That is what a false positive is."

"So, just to be clear, more than one in five examiners incorrectly concluded that a suspect's prints found at a crime scene were in fact the suspect's prints?"

"According to that test."

"That's right, according to the test run by the international association created specifically to certify print examiners."

"Yes."

"You would agree that this organization is the preeminent organization in the field of fingerprint examination and comparison, wouldn't you?"

"It is a well-respected organization."

"Mr. McCorkle, it is the preeminent organization in the field, correct?"

"Yes."

"Mr. McCorkle, you are not certified as a fingerprint examiner by the International Association for Identification, are you?"

"It's not required by the state of California."

"Let me ask my question again," I said, ever so patiently. "You are not certified by the International Association for Identification, are you?"

"No, I'm not."

I walked back toward my table to give the jurors an opportunity to absorb. "Mr. McCorkle, let's turn to points of similarity. Isn't it true that there can be disagreement, even among experts, as to what constitutes a point of similarity?"

"I suppose that is possible."

"Well, in fact, that happens quite often, doesn't it?"

"It can happen. That is why we like to have a number of points of similarity."

"So you would agree that there can be disagreement, even among fingerprint experts?"

"Perhaps as to individual points, but not as to the overall opinion."

"You are familiar with the work of David Stoney, aren't you?"

"Yes, I am."

"He is a well-known forensic scientist, isn't he?"

"Yes."

"Would you agree with this statement he made as recently as last year?" I read from a paper Suzelle handed me. "The criteria for absolute identification in fingerprint work are subjective and ill-defined. They are the products of probabilistic intuitions widely shared among fingerprint examiners. Not of scientific research."

McCorkle shook his head. "I would disagree with that."

"I appreciate that; however, he is a well-known forensic scientist, correct?"

"He is. But that doesn't mean he has all the answers."

"Fair enough, but you would agree he is well published in this area?"

"That's true."

"You yourself have not written extensively in this area, isn't that true?"

"No, I haven't."

"In fact, you are not published in the area of forensic print identification at all, true?"

Indignantly, he replied, "No, I'm out in the field doing the work."

"I appreciate that, Mr. McCorkle, but it is important that the jurors understand the relative expertise of you and Dr. Stoney. So let me ask again, you are not published in the area of forensic print examination, are you?"

"No, I'm not."

"You don't personally require a fixed number of points of similarity before you confirm a match, do you?"

"No, I don't. Depending on the quality of the prints, I can sometimes confirm a match with fewer points of similarity than at other times."

"But you do feel more comfortable with more points of similarity."

"Of course."

"Mr. McCorkle, the British require sixteen points of similarity, don't they?"

"I believe that's correct."

"And, if they don't identify sixteen points, they won't confirm a match, will they?"

"That is my understanding."

"In fact, in this country, Mr. McCorkle, most print examiners will not confirm a match with anything fewer that eight points of similarity, isn't that right?"

"There is no requirement for eight."

"Mr. McCorkle," my voice still ever patient, "the generally accepted standard is eight, isn't it?"

"I expect that is true."

"In this case, you found five points of similarity, didn't you?"

"That was all I needed."

"So to clarify, you found five points of similarity, correct?"

"That's right."

"So the British require sixteen, most American courts require eight, and you in this case found five."

"That's right. Like I said, I felt that was all I needed."

"You didn't just stop once you reached five, did you?"

"I had exhausted the points of similarity."

"To be clear, you looked but could not find any more points of similarity, correct?"

"There were none."

I paused and then said, "Mr. McCorkle, I appreciate your candor. Thank you." Turning to the judge, I said, "Your Honor, I have no more questions for Mr. McCorkle."

It was twelve thirty, and Judge Harbarger adjourned for the day. She said she had an upset stomach. We would start again tomorrow morning.

By two that afternoon, I had thrown a few things in my duffel, crammed my briefcase, and was ready for the two-hour drive home to Malibu. I needed some space for at least a night. I invited Lisa, but she had school commitments, even though it was the middle of the summer. Suzelle and Duke had their assignments.

CHAPTER 30

THE BEATING

It was a relaxing afternoon and evening. I got in a late-afternoon swim. Tony and Eve barbecued, and I caught them up on the trial. I slept in my own bed. My cell alarm went off at five thirty. I showered and prepared a to-go coffee and made my way down to the garage. As I began to open the garage door, I caught a movement from the corner of my eye. Before I could straighten, a heavy fist hammered against the back of my neck and sent me headfirst into the partially opened door. Shock and panic coursed through my system. *What the hell?* As I pushed off the door, trying to stand, a boot landed on my left side hard enough to lift my 190 pounds off the ground and land me on my butt. Through shocked eyes, I peered up at my attacker. He was wearing a hood that covered the upper part of his face. He was big, with a mean grin on his wide mouth. He had very white teeth; I wondered fleetingly if they were false. Nothing else about him was false. His white tank undershirt showed a chest and arms that would have done Duane "The Rock" Johnson proud. He stood balanced on the balls on his feet, waiting for me to get up.

He gave me a "come" with both hands, impatient, wanting me

up so he could knock me down again. I slowly climbed to my feet and held my hands out defensively. I was dazed and disoriented. He slapped me, hard enough to bring tears. I staggered, and he motioned again, grinning. I had two options. Go after him and get beaten to a pulp, or stand there and get beaten to a pulp. Again I put up my hands, trying to stop the action for a moment. "Listen," I said, "I don't know what's going on. But you've got the wrong guy." I was stalling, of course, trying to clear my head, to get my breath back. It was obvious that I was the one he was after. He was at my house, my garage, and no one else was around. *Had the Durgeon case brought this goon to my door?* I tried to think of something else to say, waiting for some help to come, some neighbor to yell out.

Weaving as though blown by a strong wind, I pretended to be in worse shape than I was. *No mean feat, that.* I lashed out at his face with my left hand. He brushed my fist aside easily but carelessly as my following right caught him on the bridge of his nose. It hurt him. Blood spurted from his nose. *I had succeeded in really pissing him off.* Furious, he moved in, pounding my ribs unmercifully, moving around as if working the heavy bag in a gym, hitting me in the stomach, face, and kidneys. I tried fighting him off, but I was severely overmatched. I went down, caught a vicious kick in the stomach and curled into a ball, trying to protect myself. He went on kicking me. As through a mist, I heard him say, "Quit messin' where you shouldn't, fucker." He kicked me again. I thought I heard yells, then the beating stopped.

I knew I had been hurt badly, as I lay curled and dirty in the gravel of the driveway. My vision slowly narrowed to a small circle of light that abruptly went out.

I was lying on my back in the driveway, a rolled-up beach towel stuffed under my head. My eyeballs tried to center but they felt loose. I painfully rolled them to the side.

"Hey Jake, what happened?" My eyes focused to the voice of my neighbor's sixteen-year-old son Dex, and three of his friends, who were leaning over me. They're good kids that I surf with occasionally down at Surfrider. I weakly tried to sit up, but Dex easily pushed my shoulders down. "Relax, okay? We called 911."

I tried to speak, but everything moved out of focus as the drums in my head beat to the accompaniment of the wail of the approaching ambulance. My head was a fuzzy ball of unbelievable pain. I was occasionally aware of insistent voices trying to break through into the place where I lay, but it hurt too much to try to listen. It was much easier to fall back into the dark.

☙ ☙ ☙

When I finally became aware of movement, I realized that the pale shadows I sometimes saw were actually people. A steady metallic pinging drilled into my head. My teeth ached. My tongue felt like a piece of raw liver, and I had the coppery taste of blood in my mouth. My ribs ached with every breath.

"Waa . . ."

Immediately, one of the pale shadows was at my side. Through slitted eyes I tried to discern if it was male or female. It was the voice that gave her away. "Mr. Clearwater, I'm so glad you decided to join us at last. You want water?"

"Waa . . ." I agreed. She put a straw in my mouth, and I sucked greedily. Even that hurt. I thought about what I wanted to say.

"Wha . . ." I asked.

"You want to know what happened?" This time she didn't wait for an answer. "You were brought in by ambulance Thursday morning. I understand you were mugged. You are in intensive care and . . ." She faded out.

I awoke in the night, aware of pain that seemed to be everywhere, a raging headache, ribs constricting every breath, and grotesque dreams. Tony rose up in one episode, bald, eyebrows shaved, and demanded to know why Durgeon was living in my house. Before I could cope with that, Durgeon, with booted feet, stomped on my chest. I moaned, and Lisa, in nurse's white, gave me a pill, and I retreated again to the fuzzy place.

When I awoke again, late-afternoon sun was stretched across the foot of the bed, and Tony was standing there. He evidently read the confusion in my eyes. "You've been in and out of consciousness, buddy."

"Wha . . . ?"

"You have a severe concussion and a whole lot of other injuries including broken ribs and ruptured internal organs. But the docs say you're going to be alright." He smiled wryly. "Although it probably doesn't feel that way now. You got beaten on Thursday. This is Saturday."

Shock rolled through my system. *All that time lost to nothingness. Do you get that time back at the end of your life? Probably not.*

"Hoo di this?" I managed through swollen lips.

"They have no idea. The police are assuming it's related to the trial."

I shrugged in agreement. "Nuh suspect?" I winced.

"Nothing. At least nothing they are sharing."

A nurse came bustling in, all crisp white and efficient. "I see we are feeling much better, Mr. Clearwater," she said cheerfully. "Would you like some soup?"

We did not want soup. Soup would hurt. Breathing hurt. We did not want chirpy either, but we got it.

Tony squeezed my toe and said, "Good evening" to the nurse. Then to me, "Before I leave, I should tell you that Lisa's been here since soon after they brought you in. She just went to get some sleep at our place an hour ago."

The nurse brought me a mug of soup with a straw, and to my surprise, it tasted good, and it didn't hurt as much as I feared. She checked the machines monitoring me and gave me a pill to help me sleep. She smoothed back my hair and tucked me in. *No kiss goodnight.*

On Sunday afternoon, I was moved to a regular room and I was allowed, poor, pitiful creature that I was, to look into a mirror. A nightmare face. One eye was completely shut, and my mouth was a wreck. The left side of my face was grossly swollen, and my bottom lip was turned inside out. The tape around my ribs was pulling on my chest hairs and constricting my breathing. Lisa was dabbing a cool cloth on my face. A sheriff's detective had just left. I wasn't much help to him. Other than the man was big, muscular, white, and had white teeth, my description was pretty worthless. The detective said he would come back later when I was better able to talk.

That afternoon, as I was trying to make some kind of sense out of the beating I'd taken, and Lisa dozed in a chair pulled to my bed, Tony and Suzelle walked in. They tried to conceal their winces when they saw my face. *My Halloween-mask face had that effect.*

Suzelle squeezed my hand. "How are you doing, boss?" She whispered so as to not wake Lisa. Tony patted my foot.

Tony asked, "Want anything?"

"Ged ow heh?"

He thought that over. "You want out?"

I nodded.

"Fat chance, buddy. You have a severe concussion, a couple of broken ribs, a contused liver, and whiplash from a blow to the back of your head. And that's not counting the cuts and bruises across your body. And that's just the stuff I remember. They need to keep you under observation to make certain there's no further hemorrhaging. You can probably go home in a couple of days."

"Tony, you don't have to whisper, I'm awake," Lisa said.

"Durja?" I tried.

Suzelle brought me up to date. "I informed Judge Harbarger Thursday morning when I got the news. Everything is on hold for two weeks, until your condition can be assessed." She gave me a smile. "Don't worry, they can't do anything without you. The judge sends her best."

I am certain everyone up north was real pleased that everything was on ice. Especially Tice. To hell with them all, I thought bitterly. I looked at Suzelle and gripped her hand. "You otay?"

"I'm fine, Jake."

"Duke?"

"He's fine, too."

I was relieved that my circle was okay. My thoughts once again focused on why. Was this connected to the trial? What was the warning about? Was this a crude way of coercing me to quit the trial? Lawyers do not quit cases midtrial, everyone knew that, didn't they? What else? Was this to get me to quit a particular line of inquiry? Hell, I hadn't done anything that Rosenblatt hadn't already tried. My foray into Graves was a misdirect, he'd been thoroughly cleared.

Eventually, everyone cleared out save Lisa, who was still there as I dozed off into a troubled narcotic sleep.

❧❧❧

The next day passed slowly as I lay in my hospital bed. As for the trial itself, perhaps the extra two weeks would pay off if Duke could turn up anything. *The power of positive thinking.* I tried to nap but kept snapping back to why. Lunch was chicken noodle soup, Jell-O, and apple juice.

About two o'clock, Lisa came in, looking distraught. "I'm feeling better," I lied. Holding her body against mine—very, very carefully— would go a long way toward the healing process. Even as I lay in a hospital bed, thoughts of sex with her were never far away.

She held up a trembling hand. "I've been thinking . . ." She closed her eyes. "I didn't . . . you . . . he . . ." She continued to stare at my battered face. Her mouth worked to get the word out. "Brad." *Brad? My mind refused to track. Brad, the guy she had divorced? That Brad?* Lisa's face was drained of color, her eyes sick and guilty looking.

"Wha . . . ?"

"It happened before."

"Wha you mea?"

Her eyes picked a point on the bed between us. She took a trembling breath. "Two years after I left him, Brad showed up at my school. In my office, he warned me to stop dating a man I had only recently met. I told him we were divorced and that he had no say in my life. And then he said something that scares me even now. He told me I'd better remember that I belonged to him. That was all he said, and then he left. Two days later, William was in a hospital. A man had attacked him and nearly beaten him to death." She closed her eyes, unwilling to look at me. Her voice was barely audible. "Brad called me that night. He said I would always be his. I could forget about anyone else."

Bile rose in my throat. My mind ripped back to the attacker's words, "Quit messin' where you shouldn't." I couldn't speak. She knew all this and hadn't said anything? I stared at her in stunned silence. I felt numb, disconnected. I gave her a "What the hell?" look. She studied my face and slowly shook her head, tears slipping down her cheeks. She bent to kiss my mouth, but I pulled back. She closed her eyes, turned, and groped clumsily across the room. And then she was gone.

Comprehension of my reaction instantly descended like a stifling blanket. It was not her fault she had a psycho for an ex. I was such an ass. Yeah, she should have told me. But those events were several years back. She surely couldn't have foreseen this, could she?

I called her every half hour until midnight, until it was obvious she did not intend to take my calls.

The next morning, I passed on breakfast or whatever it was, and declined the scheduled physical therapy. The anxious feeling was still there when I dialed Lisa's cell. Again, no answer.

It took another couple of days to move from semi-ambulatory to ambulatory. On Wednesday, after nearly a week, I gathered the tatters of my pride around me like a shield to get on with what I used to think was a pretty good life. I was beaten both emotionally and physically. Eve and Tony took me to my house. It seemed like it took three days to negotiate the flights of stairs. Lisa had finally taken one of my calls. I apologized. Her tone had a forced quality. Distant. There was no intimacy. I told her I would be back in San Arcadia in a couple of days and maybe we could talk things out.

"Maybe," she said, and then added, "I'll never get over the look on your face. I really don't know if we can get past that."

"Let's try."

"Maybe." I took her "maybe" as a chance to heal.

CHAPTER 31

TRIAL, TAKE TWO

It was Sunday afternoon, two weeks and three days after getting my butt kicked. Suzelle, Duke, and I were back at the Ramada. Suzelle had taken a few days off to spend with her folks and then drove me back north to resume the trial. A court appearance had been scheduled with Judge Harbarger at nine in the morning the next day. I had reluctantly told Suzelle and Duke about Lisa's suspicion that my pounding was done on behalf of her ex. I wanted them to know that it might not have been provoked by the trial.

The three of us discussed possible suspects and motives behind the attack. The families of Robert and Doree had to be considered, but there was nothing concrete, despite Mrs. Bennett's threat to kill Durgeon. We discussed the Atwells, both Christina and Dan. While I had raised Dan as a person of interest with Tice, I didn't have anything of substance to label him a suspect. As far as I knew, my question about Dan Atwell never went beyond Tice. And, of course, Brad, Lisa's ex, had to be considered. But neither the LA County Sheriff's Department detectives nor the San Arcadia Police had been able to implicate Brad. Brad, we learned, was outraged to even be questioned.

Another puzzling question was how the attacker would have even known I was returning home that afternoon. It was a spontaneous decision on my part. Lots of questions, not any answers. The discussion wore me out. I was still stiff, sore, and prone to headaches, and had fallen into bed by eight thirty in spite of too many things undone. I had not seen Lisa since our falling out at the hospital. That hurt most of all.

When Suzelle and I emerged into the Ramada lobby Monday morning, we were met, not by our young officer, but by an older, grim-looking sergeant. Apparently, the heavy gun had been brought in. Sergeant Powell Booker appeared unhappy with his duty as bodyguard to the lawyers defending a scumbag. He did not deign to talk to us beyond the bare minimum. His communication primarily consisted of grunts and pointing. Booker's upper body evidenced much gym time; his chest and shoulders did not hang at his side but stood out from his body. His jaw jutted out aggressively, and his shave would never last the day. Suzelle's eyes rounded, and she darted a look at me as we took him in. I lifted my brows and shrugged. He wouldn't have been my choice either. *Although I bet he could beat the shit out of my attacker.*

While Suzelle and I ate breakfast in the hotel dining room, Booker, who had, not surprisingly, refused the offer to join us, sat stiffly in a chair by the door, arms folded, eyes focused on the far wall. I wondered if it was worth putting up with his presence to have his protection in the event of violence. At any rate, the choice was not mine. Reportedly, Booker, by order of Her Honor, Judge Harbarger, was ours for the duration.

As I limped toward the courtroom using a cane, I caught a glimpse of myself in the glass doors. Although the black and blue on my face and arms had begun to fade into green and yellow, my hair had not grown in where it had been shaved in order to get some stitches into my scalp. I wished I had at least gotten a haircut to minimize the gaps. The past two weeks had been a wasteland, a desert of bleak thoughts and self-recrimination. My sleep was disturbed by bizarre images of Lisa and Durgeon and Tice as they rolled across my unconscious mind.

But I was determined to put the past behind and give the defense of Durgeon my complete and undivided attention. There was nothing I could do about Lisa right now. Now had to be about the trial. Our case had yet to take on any shape. While rationalizing that we were at least holding the line with cross-exam, we had no real plan of our own. I had hoped that the Dan Atwell lead might develop, but so far, Duke hadn't turned up enough to sink our teeth into. He was still looking for the woman Dan reportedly raped.

When we entered the courtroom, I drew curious looks from the capacity crowd. Suzelle and I were ushered back to Harbarger's chambers. Harbarger rose from behind her desk, gave me a look of genuine concern and sympathy, and pointed to a chair. "Jake, I was so sorry to hear of your situation."

I offered a rueful grin. *Situation?* "Thanks, Judge."

Tice entered, looked with disinterest at my face, and said nothing. *Bloodless sonofabitch.*

Harbarger resumed her seat. "Well, gentlemen and Ms. Frost, we've lost two weeks; I suggest we get on with it." Then, leaning to me, she said, "Jake, if you wear out, let me know."

"Thank you, I appreciate that, Your Honor. Before trial resumes, can I have a few minutes with my client? I haven't had a chance to talk with him since I got back."

"Ten minutes," she said. "I have a jury waiting."

Suzelle and I made our way to Durgeon's holding cell. When he saw me, he said, "They weren't kidding when they said you got your ass whipped." *An honest reaction.*

Durgeon pulled one of the chairs out for me. I sat and we looked at each other. Suzelle assumed her usual spot at the wall furthest from Durgeon.

"You up for this?" he asked.

"Probably not. But if I delay this thing any further, the judge may appoint someone to replace me." I put up my hands in a resigned gesture.

"Who did ya?"

"No idea."

৵৵৵

When I reentered the courtroom and made my way slowly to counsel table, I wasn't sure where to put my cane. Finally, I decided to put it on the table. If I put it on the floor, it would mean bending over and picking it up later. Bending over hurt.

Harbarger called us to order, thanked the jurors for their understanding of the delay, and then looked at Tice.

"The People call Christina Atwell," Tice announced. Heads from the audience swiveled to the door at the back of the courtroom, wanting to catch the first sight of this woman who had disappeared from San Arcadia following the first trial. The door was pushed open by one of the bailiffs, and Christina Atwell stepped into the courtroom.

She was not what I had expected. My generalized vision was of a hard-bitten biker mama who had seen and done it all. Instead, I watched as a middle-aged woman, dressed in a black skirt that fell below her knees and a long-sleeved white brocade blouse, walked toward us. *Where were the tattoos, the nose rings, the missing teeth?* She had a full figure and an erect posture, and her hair was a sedate blond, cut short and stylish. As she passed me on her way to the witness stand, I could see the lines of a hard life about her mouth and around her eyes, which were fixed straight ahead, steering well clear of Durgeon. She approached the clerk, and her courtroom experience was evident as she placed her left hand on the Bible and raised her right hand without being told. Her "I do" was crisp. She took her seat and looked directly at Tice. Tice nodded at her, but she did not respond. *Perhaps there was trouble in the prosecution camp.* I could well imagine that she was not pleased at having to leave her life, whatever and wherever it was, to come back to San Arcadia and once again testify against her former live-in lover.

Judge Harbarger said, "Please state your full name and spell your last name."

"Christina Julia Atwell. A-T-W-E-L-L." She spoke slowly and clearly. She did not look at Harbarger but kept her eyes on Tice.

"Mr. Tice, you may proceed."

"Thank you, Your Honor." Tice remained seated. "Good morning, Ms. Atwell." She nodded but did not speak. "Ms. Atwell, you of course know the defendant?" Her eyes flicked to Durgeon. "How did you first meet him?"

"He answered one of my ads in a biker magazine." Her voice was low pitched, as deep as a man's.

"Please explain."

"I used to draw tattoo designs, and I had an ad in *American Motorcycle*. He wrote me."

"To your knowledge, where was the defendant living at that time?" I could feel Durgeon, to my left, intently studying her.

"He was in prison in Utah."

"Did you write him back?"

"Yeah." Atwell gave every impression that she was a reluctant witness. She was making it clear from the outset that she was testifying not out of some civic obligation but because she was being forced to. Apparently, she was going to make Tice work.

"Did the two of you establish a relationship?"

"You might call it that," she snapped.

Tice, with an edge, said, "Tell us how the relationship came to be."

With a fleeting shadow of satisfaction at tweaking Tice, she said, "We wrote each other for a year, and I picked him up when he got out."

"When was that?"

"April 2004."

"Did the two of you live together?"

"Yeah." Atwell poured herself a glass of water. Her hand quivered a bit.

Tice waited for her to take a drink. "How were you employed during that time?"

"I sold dope," Atwell answered, without any change in voice inflection.

"Ms. Atwell, you need to explain."

"I sold cocaine, heroin, and some meth." Tice took that in as a matter of course. *Some folks were secretaries, some were mechanics, and some sold dope.*

"What did the defendant do when he moved in with you?"

"Hung around, mostly. He slept late. Went to bars a lot. Sometimes he helped around the house. He knew how to cook meth, and he did some of that."

"He helped manufacture methamphetamine for sale?" Tice was like a dog seizing a table scrap.

"That's right."

"Ms. Atwell, now that we understand the origins of your relationship with the defendant, I want to turn to the early part of November 2004, a week or two before the Blanco murders. Did your relationship with the defendant change during that time?"

"Yeah."

"Tell us about that."

"I was tired of him catting around on me, so I told him to get out."

"Catting around?"

She gave an exasperated look. "Seeing other women."

"Fuckin' A," Durgeon muttered under his breath. I had to stifle a laugh. Unconsciously I put a hand on his arm. He saw me holding in a laugh and gave me a grin. A shared moment. *Damn women anyway.*

"Go on."

"I told him he had to move out." Tice looked for her to continue. She reluctantly did. "He didn't have a car, so I drove him around, looking for an apartment he could afford."

"During the apartment search, did the two of you visit the Blancos at the Palms?"

"Yeah, they let us come in and look."

"Was it clear to you that the Blancos were the managers?"

She nodded yes. "They was the ones showing us the apartment."

"So did you and the defendant go into the apartment?"

"Yeah."

"Tell us about the apartment."

"It was small and junky. They was moving out. A lot of stuff was in boxes."

"How long did this interaction with the Blancos last?"

"Ten, fifteen minutes, thereabouts."

"Ms. Atwell, let's move forward a week or so to the evening of November 14 and morning of November 15? Do you recall that night and the following morning?"

"Yeah, Duane went out that night around eight or so and didn't come back until the next morning. That was the only time he stayed out all night."

"How can you be certain of the date?"

"Because on the fifteenth, all the news talked about was them Blanco murders, and somehow that date just stuck in my head."

"On the morning of the fifteenth, what time did the defendant come home?"

"Objection. Foundation." I winced as I stood. It was a legitimate objection that was easily overcome. But I wanted to break up the flow.

"Sustained. Mr. Tice, rephrase."

"To your knowledge, what time did the defendant come home on the fifteenth of November?"

"Around seven thirty."

"Describe how he looked."

"He looked like he'd just taken a shower."

"How so?"

"His hair was wet and combed straight back."

"Did you ask him where he'd been?"

"Yeah!" She bit off the word with a bitter bark of a laugh.

"And?"

"Let's just say he told me to mind my own business."

"You let it go at that?"

"Yeah, I did. Duane never did abide anyone asking him questions." Atwell leaned back in her chair, then took a drink.

"Got that right, bitch," Durgeon said under his breath. Suzelle looked across me at Durgeon.

"And during the time the two of you lived together, that was the only time he stayed out all night?"

"Asked and answered." I only got about halfway up.

"Sustained. Move on, Mr. Tice." Harbarger looked at me. "Mr. Clearwater, you need not stand to make objections."

"Thank you, Your Honor," I said, nodding at the courtesy.

Tice walked back to counsel table from the lectern, picked up a legal pad, studied it, tossed it down, and began again. "Let's move forward to the day the police raided your house. When was that?"

"It was about a week later."

"Would that have been November 21?"

"If you say so."

"Ms. Atwell, it was the twenty-first. Now tell me what happened about ten o'clock that morning?"

"I was in the kitchen getting coffee when the front door slammed open. Before I knew what was going on, the police handcuffed me and was all over my house."

"Who else was in your house that morning?"

"Duane and my son Dan."

"How old was Dan at that time?"

"I don't know, twenty, twenty-one."

"Did Dan live at home with you?"

"No, he had his own apartment."

"Why was he at your place?"

"I don't remember."

"What happened next?"

"They put us in a van and took us to jail."

"You, Dan, and the defendant?" Tice clarified.

"Yeah."

"What happened while the three of you were in custody?"

"I bailed me and Dan out that evening."

"How about the defendant?"

"I didn't bail him out and he didn't have any money, so . . ." She shrugged.

"Bitch," Durgeon again under his breath, just a tad too loud. This time I gave him a quelling glance. He ignored me but lowered his muttering.

"Did you go home after you got out?"

"Yeah. Dan went to his place and I went home."

"Tell us what you found when you returned home."

"They had tossed my house. It was really messed up."

"They?"

She looked at Tice with annoyance. "The police."

"What about the gun?" Tice prompted.

"Leading." Again slowly coming to my feet. Old habits die hard. I wanted the witness to tell the story, not Tice.

Harbarger looked expectantly at Tice, who nodded and with a bit of irritation, rephrased. "What else did you notice when you returned home?"

"They left my .22 on the kitchen counter. It was in a plastic bag with yellow tape and marked 'police evidence.'"

Tice looked at Manlow, who handed him a revolver. "Your Honor, leave to approach the clerk and have this gun marked People's 14 for identification?"

"You may."

Tice presented the gun to the clerk, who marked it. He walked around counsel table to me. "May the record reflect that I am showing what has been marked People's 14 to opposing counsel?"

"So reflected."

Tice held the gun out to me. I waved him off. He then approached Atwell with the revolver lying flat on his hand, still inside the evidence bag. "Ms. Atwell, do you recognize this gun?"

She took the gun from his hand and turned it over. "That's my gun."

"How can you be certain?"

"The handle is chipped." She pointed to the grip of the gun.

"Move People's 14 into evidence."

"Mr. Clearwater?"

"No objection, Your Honor." I remained seated.

"It's received."

"Was this the gun that was on your kitchen counter that morning?" Tice asked.

"Yes."

"What did you do with the gun?"

"I went out back and hid it under some loose bricks on the patio."

"Why?"

"It wasn't registered. They coulda come back for it and throwed that charge at me on top of everything else."

"To your knowledge, did the defendant know you had a gun?" Tice asked.

"I had a couple of guns and yeah I showed them to him."

"That was before the Blanco murders?"

"That's right."

"So he knew where you kept them?"

"Objection." I half stood.

Harbarger to Atwell, "To your knowledge."

Atwell nodded. "I showed him where I kept them."

"Okay, let's change topics. After his arrest, when did you next see the defendant?"

"Two days later, I went to the jail and visited him."

"Tell us about that visit."

"He wasn't real happy to see me since I didn't bail him out," she said with an edgy chuckle while flashing a quick glance at Durgeon.

"What did you say to that?"

"I told him that after I got me and Dan out, I was tapped."

"What else did you talk about?"

"I told him the police left the .22 after they searched."

"How did the defendant react to that?"

"He got worked up and asked me what I did with the gun."

"Goddamned bitch, dumb as a rock," Durgeon muttered, as he shifted in his chair. I grabbed his arm and squeezed.

"I told him that I hid it, and he said that wasn't good enough. I asked him why, and he said, 'Never mind that, just lose that fucking gun.'"

"What did you take that to mean?"

"Objection," I said. "Calls for speculation."

Without giving Tice an opportunity to respond, Harbarger sustained my objection.

"What happened next?" Tice hadn't missed a beat.

"I said, 'What are you worried about? It's my gun.'"

"What did he say?"

"He gave me one of those looks, like I better not ask any more questions. Then he told me again to get rid of that gun."

"What happened then?"

"I asked him what I should do about it. He told me to take it to Ragged Point and throw it in the ocean."

"Where's Ragged Point?"

"Out by the university."

"What else happened during the conversation?"

"Nothing. He told me he missed me and we just talked about personal stuff."

"What did you do after you left the jail?"

"It was already dark. I got the gun and drove out to Ragged Point and threw it as far as I could."

Tice picked up the gun. "This gun."

"Yeah."

"When did you next see the defendant?" Throughout the trial, Tice had not once used Durgeon's name. Personalize your side and depersonalize the other side. "Defendant" was the ultimate depersonalizer.

"The next day."

"What happened?"

"I told him I got rid of the gun."

"What did he say to that?"

"That was good. He gave me a thumbs up."

"Lying bitch." Durgeon's commentary was low and mean. Again, I grabbed his arm.

"What did you take that to mean?"

"Objection, he's asking the witness to speculate again."

Harbarger looked at Tice. "Mr. Tice?"

"It's asking the witness to share her personal thoughts with us," Tice said, with just a hint of irritation.

Without waiting for Harbarger, I interjected, "He's asking her to speculate on what the speaker intended."

"I agree," ruled Harbarger. "Objection sustained."

Tice asked, "What did you say after he said that was good?" The old double direct: incorporate a memorable phrase from the previous answer into the next question for added emphasis.

"I said, 'What do you mean?'"

"And?"

"He didn't answer. Then we talked about other stuff."

"When did you next see the defendant?"

"It was a couple of weeks."

"Why such a long time?"

She blew out a breath and slowly shook her head. "I got a bad feeling about him, and I guess I started thinking about him and them people."

Tice asked, "Them people?"

"That couple that was killed."

Tice stepped back to his counsel table to consult his notes. "Ms. Atwell, I want to turn to your meeting with Investigator

Manlow a month or so later, in early January. How did that meeting come about?"

"Yeah, tell 'em about snitching on me, babe." This time Durgeon was too loud.

Harbarger threw him a look. Durgeon returned the look unapologetically.

Harbarger: "Mr. Durgeon, keep your thoughts to yourself." When she received no response from Durgeon, she nodded for Atwell to continue.

"I called the police department and asked for someone on the Blanco case."

"So the meeting was at your suggestion?"

"Yeah."

"What did you hope to get out of the meeting?" Tice was pricking another boil by establishing that Atwell benefited from her help with the investigation.

Atwell appeared taken aback by the question and, for the first time, hesitated before answering. "Them people were murdered," she said tentatively, as if knowing that was not really the answer.

"But that was not what motivated you to set up the meeting, was it?" Tice was not going to let her hedge.

"No, it wasn't," Atwell said defiantly.

"Why did you set it up?"

"Because Dan and me was looking at felony drug charges." She glared at Tice as if to say, "Are you satisfied now?"

"So you wanted to strike some kind of deal?"

"That's what I wanted," she snapped back.

"No shit," Durgeon said in a whisper.

Again, I squeezed his arm to shut up. *A futile effort.*

"Did you strike a deal?"

"It took a while, but yeah."

"What was the deal?"

"The charges against Dan dismissed, and probation for me with no jail time."

"In exchange for what?"

"I wear a wire when I visit him in jail and testify at his trial." Atwell hurried her words, trying to get off a sensitive point.

"What do you mean, wear a wire?"

"You know, a microphone for the cops to hear," she said, as though talking to a slow witted child.

"Did you in fact wear a wire and talk to the defendant?"

"Yeah."

"How many times?"

"Once."

"Tell us about the conversation between you and the defendant."

"I renew my objection, Your Honor. Sixth Amendment grounds." I had already lost that objection at pretrial and knew it was destined for the same fate here, but I wanted the jurors to perhaps sense that this was an underhanded police tactic.

"Overruled."

Without waiting, Atwell answered, "Duane was mad because I hadn't come to see him. I said I had been sick, and some stuff had come up with Dan. After a while, he loosened up. I asked him why the gun was a big deal. He gave me a look and said the gun coulda been a problem."

"And?"

"Well, I asked him what he meant, but he wouldn't talk about it."

"Was that the end of the conversation?"

"Yeah, it was just personal stuff after that, nothing about the gun."

Tice walked back to counsel table and picked up an audio disc. "Your Honor, may I have this marked as People's next in order?"

Harbarger nodded and said, "That would be People's 15."

Tice handed the disc to the clerk, who marked it. He offered it to me. I nodded for him to proceed. Tice looked at Harbarger. "Leave to play the disc?"

"Go ahead, Mr. Tice."

It was as Atwell had described.

After it had run, Tice asked Atwell, "Was that the conversation you had with the defendant?"

"Yeah."

Tice nodded at Atwell. "Thank you, Ms. Atwell. Your Honor, I have no further questions of this witness."

Atwell then pushed the microphone aside and stood as if to leave. Harbarger said, "Excuse me, Ms. Atwell, but I believe Mr. Clearwater may have some questions for you."

Atwell flushed and resumed her seat. *So much for being an experienced witness.*

Harbarger looked at the clock; it was 11:40 a.m. "On second thought, perhaps your instincts serve you well, Ms. Atwell. Why don't we take our lunch recess now and pick up again at 1:30 this afternoon." She graveled, rose, and left.

I noticed that Atwell made no effort to talk to Tice or he to her as they left the courtroom. Atwell did stop at the back of the courtroom to watch Durgeon as he was led, shuffling, out. I could not read her face.

CHAPTER 32

CROSSING MS. ATWELL

Sergeant Booker drove us a half block to a sandwich shop frequented by county employees. Suzelle and I ordered and found a small table near the back. Booker sat alone at a nearby table. "Well, what did you think of Christina?" I asked.

"She was not what I expected."

"Yeah, how 'bout that? What's your take on how the jurors reacted to her?"

"She seemed to be credible. The jurors were very focused." She blew out a little breath and shook her head. "She hurt us a lot." Lunch arrived. Suzelle had tuna on white, and I had turkey on rye. The sandwiches were huge. Suzelle cut her halves into halves. I loaded mine with Dijon. My appetite was coming back.

Between bites I said, "Like you, I assumed she would be tough and unlikeable. Then I could really go after her."

"But now the white hat?"

"I'll white-hat it all the way."

ஒஒஒ

At one thirty, all the players were back in place. As I worked slowly into my seat, I looked around and saw Lisa sitting in a back row. Lisa! Was I forgiven? She nodded that I noticed her. I nodded back. Reluctantly, I turned to the notes I had prepared for Atwell. Had to stay focused. Hopefully, she would stay, and we could talk. *Stay focused.*

Durgeon leaned to me and grabbed my arm. "Bust Tina in the chops, counselor."

"Appreciate the advice." I tried to shake off his hand. "Now let me do my job."

"I mean it." Still holding my arm.

"So do I." I shook off his hand.

Harbarger stepped to the bench. "We are back on the record in People v. Durgeon."

Atwell was already seated in the witness stand. "Ms. Atwell, you are still under oath." Harbarger turned to me. "Mr. Clearwater, you may inquire."

"Thank you, Your Honor." I remained seated—it was a lot easier on my body. "Good afternoon, Ms. Atwell." She gave me a perfunctory nod. "Let's talk about the deal." I began very conversationally, Mr. Nice Guy. "You made a deal with Detective Manlow and District Attorney Tice?"

She gave a cautious "Yeah."

"And that deal was for both you and your son, Dan, correct?"

She nodded.

"Is that a yes to my question that the deal was for both of you?"

"Yes, the answer to your question is yes." Again, somewhat tentative.

"You were concerned that you might go to prison, weren't you?"

"I don't know. I thought I might get some time," she replied, her voice still wary.

"So you were thinking that you would only get some local jail time?"

"Maybe."

"Maybe? Well let's talk about that. How long had you been selling dope before you were arrested on November 21?"

"Irrelevant," Tice objected. "What does that have to do with any possible sentence?"

I did not wait for Harbarger to rule. "Judge, this woman is a career dope dealer. Part of the cost of doing business, her business, is weighing the possibility of prison. I have a right to probe her knowledge of how severe the consequences of her behavior might be. This bears directly on her incentive to negotiate a deal in exchange for her testimony."

"I'm going to overrule the objection. I'll admonish both counsel about speaking objections." Both of us had been guilty of not just making objections but arguing them without leave from the court. Harbarger turned to Atwell. "Ms. Atwell, do you have the question in mind?" She looked confused. "Mr. Clearwater, please ask your question again."

"How long had you been selling dope prior to November 21?"

"A couple of years."

"Thank you," I said. "During those years, you had been arrested once for possession of heroin, isn't that right?"

"Yeah."

"And you did six months in the San Arcadia County jail for that, correct?"

"Yeah."

"Just to be clear, that was for simple possession, not possession for sale or actual sale, right?" My voice was measured and soft. White hat.

"Yeah."

I leafed through the police report of the November 21 drug bust. I reached down and picked up my cane and slowly stood. I moved to the jury rail with the report in my free hand. "When the police raided your home on November 21, they confiscated forty-six two-ounce bindles of heroin, didn't they?"

"I don't know how much." She knew where I was heading and was trying to put off a direct hit.

I waved the report and started toward her. "Would you like to see the police report to refresh your memory?"

"No, that's right." She wadded a tissue in her hand.

"The reason you packed the heroin in bindles was to sell them, isn't it?"

"Yes."

"Isn't it true, Ms. Atwell, that you are aware that possession for sale is punished more severely than simple possession?"

"Yeah."

"And isn't it true that you are aware that repeat offenders are punished more severely than first-time drug offenders?"

"Yeah."

"Ms. Atwell, if convicted on this November 21 charge, you were looking at a state prison sentence, weren't you?" She gave a begrudging shrug. "Ms. Atwell, is that a yes, that you were looking at a state prison sentence?" *I love repeating a damning question.*

"Yes." She straightened the tissue against her knee.

"And that sentence would involve years, not months, wouldn't it?"

"Yeah, I guess it would."

"So, let's go back to my original question. One of the reasons you struck that deal was to stay out of state prison, true?"

"Objection, asked and answered." Tice was hot.

"Sustained. Mr. Clearwater, you've made your point; move on." *Indeed I had.*

I slowly worked my way back to counsel table and rested the cane on the table. *Let that first volley rest with the jurors for a bit.* "Okay, let's turn to your son Dan. He was twenty at the time of the November drug bust, correct?"

"That seems right, but he doesn't have nothing to do with this trial."

"Ms. Atwell, Dan was twenty at that time?"

"Thereabouts."

"And before the drug bust, he had had some problems with the law, hadn't he?"

"He had some run-ins."

I picked up Dan's rap sheet. "Let's talk about some of those 'run-ins.' Prior to the bust we are discussing, Dan did ninety days for being under the influence of heroin, correct?"

She nodded but caught herself; "Yeah."

"And shortly after that, he was convicted of assault with a deadly weapon, right?"

"Yeah."

"And he did eight months on that assault conviction, didn't he?"

She nodded again and Harbarger asked her to answer aloud. She did.

I looked back at the rap sheet. "Dan was also arrested for rape—"

Tice: "Objection! Approach?"

Harbarger beckoned us to the bench. Tice was furious. With Harbarger's hand cupped over her microphone, Tice said, "That arrest was just that, an arrest. He was not convicted. However, my objection goes beyond that. Dan Atwell and his past are irrelevant to these proceedings."

Without waiting for Harbarger, I responded. "My questioning of this witness about her son goes to her motives in cutting a deal that included him."

Tice answered, "This attack is a misdirection by counsel. Under the guise of probing Ms. Atwell's motives, he is engaged in an effort to bring Dan Atwell into this trial as a suspect. This is trial by ambush. He is attempting to set up a straw man to misdirect the jury. First it was Graves, and now it's Dan Atwell. He is not acting in good faith."

"Your Honor, this line of questioning legitimately goes to Christina Atwell's motivation to lie, and I believe I have every right to probe her motives."

Harbarger looked at me. "I am going to sustain the objection." She then turned to Tice. "But only because it was an arrest, not a conviction. However, I do believe that defense counsel has the right to raise legitimate alternative scenarios. And I trust, as an officer of the court, Mr. Clearwater is acting in good faith." *I was in the ballpark of good faith.* Either way, I had lost the skirmish but won the more important battle. Danny-boy was fair game.

We stepped back. The courtroom had been conspicuously quiet. Everyone was hoping to catch some of our acrimonious sidebar discussion.

"The objection is sustained. Members of the jury, you are to disregard the last question concerning Dan Atwell's arrest." *Ah, but that bell had been rung.* "Mr. Clearwater, you may resume."

I turned back to Atwell. "Ms. Atwell, would it be fair to say that your son's welfare was a significant factor in negotiating your deal?"

"He's my son." Tentative was gone, replaced by defiance.

"I appreciate that, and given the amount of heroin and methamphetamine found, as well as Dan's previous criminal record, you were concerned that he would be sentenced to state prison, weren't you?"

"Yeah." She gave me a hard look, all the while carefully shredding the tissue.

"Thank you for that, Ms. Atwell," I said, with a courteous nod. "Let's turn to your relationship with Mr. Durgeon. From the time you picked him up from that prison in Utah until the day of the drug bust, you lived together, is that right?"

"Yeah, in my house."

"And you were lovers, correct?"

"That's right. What's your point?"

I grinned. "Well, let's get to the point. You were jealous when Duane showed interest in other women, correct?"

"I guess it was only natural of him, after getting out of prison."

"That is very understanding of you. You weren't the slightest bit upset when he didn't come home at all on the night of November 14?"

"No." She shrugged, no big deal.

I played along. "So, it is your testimony that when the man who you had been sharing your bed with didn't come home at all that night and offered no explanations, you were not jealous or angry?"

"He's a big boy."

"Isn't it true that your relationship with Duane was already strained before November 14?"

"We were having some problems."

"You wanted him out of your house, didn't you?"

"Yes."

"And you drove him around to look at apartments that he could rent?"

"I did."

"In fact, only a week before the murders, one of the apartments the two of you visited was the very apartment where the Blancos lived, true?"

"I've already said that."

"Bear with me, Ms. Atwell. The two of you were invited in by the Blancos?"

"We was just in for a minute to talk about the apartment. They was packing."

"That's right. Packing boxes, packing tape, things out of drawers?"

"Yeah, like I said, they was packing."

"So, just to be clear, the two of you were inside the Blanco apartment at the time they were packing to move?"

"Like I said, we were in there for a couple of minutes." I had all I needed on this point.

"I want to turn for a minute to the .22 caliber revolver. The gun was unregistered, wasn't it?"

"That's what I said." Defiance on the edge of anger.

I slowed down, my voice deferential. "You were concerned that you could have been charged with illegally possessing it, was that your testimony?"

She snapped out a bitter yes.

"And because Duane was living in the house where the gun was found, he could have also been charged with possession of an unregistered firearm?"

"Objection, calls for speculation."

"Submitted, Your Honor." Without turning from Atwell, I asked, "Duane was on felony parole, wasn't he?"

"Yeah."

"One of the terms was to violate no law?"

"Objection, foundation."

"Sustained."

I did not care about the ruling. The point was made. It was time to return to Dan. I worked my way around Tice's table and once again stood near the jury rail. *Damn, I was stiff and sore.* "Dan and Duane developed a relationship, didn't they?"

Atwell looked perplexed that we were back to Dan. By moving my questioning around seemingly at random, I hoped to keep her from settling into a comfortable rhythm. Her answer was halting. "Course they knew each other."

I worked my way back to counsel table and leafed through several pages of notes. After consulting them, I asked, "But they had even become friends, hadn't they?" I was fishing. It seemed like a logical jump.

She blinked. "They hung out some."

I shrugged and again moved back to the jury rail. "Went out for a beer, a hamburger, that sort of thing?"

"I guess." Her suspicions were again aroused.

"Going back to the night of November 14 and early morning of November 15, you did not see Dan that night or early morning, did you?"

"Dan don't live in my house. I don't know where he's at all the time."

"I appreciate that, Ms. Atwell. However, it is true that you did not see your son that evening or the next morning, correct?"

"There wasn't no reason to see him. He lived in his own place." Her face flushed at my insinuation that her son was somehow involved. *Tough shit, lady.*

I paused, wanting the jury to settle on the point. "Thank you, Ms. Atwell, you have been most helpful. Your Honor, I have no further questions of this witness."

As I hobbled back to my table, Manlow was staring intently at me; I suppose that was to intimidate me. I gave him a wink and half smile the jury could not see, since my back was to them, and completed my slow cane-assisted trek to my table. Durgeon squeezed my arm as I sat. "Good job, counselor." *To have Durgeon's approval meant absolutely nothing.*

Tice went back and cleaned up a couple of points. When he finished and Atwell was dismissed, he announced, "Your Honor and members of the jury, the People rest."

Harbarger: "All right, members of the jury, we will adjourn for the day. Mr. Clearwater, we will begin the defense case at nine in the morning."

CHAPTER 33

THE DEFENSE CASE

As we were packing up, I made my way to Tice. "You have a moment?"

"What's on your mind?" Anger in his voice, still smarting from my Dan Atwell gambit.

I handed him a list of names. "I am going to pursue the Dan Atwell angle. Here are the witness names I'm going to call and a summary of their testimony."

Tice sat his briefcase down and scanned the list. He started to speak, then thought better of it. Finally, "I'll see you in chambers tomorrow morning." He tossed the list in his briefcase, buttoned up, and joined Manlow, who had been waiting at the back of the courtroom. To Manlow's left stood Lisa.

I told Suzelle and the bailiff that I needed a moment, and then we would join Durgeon in the holding cell. I walked toward Lisa. She met me halfway, and with a slight smile, said, "You are such an ass, Jake. And if you ever question my love and devotion again, there will be no forgiveness." She put her arms around me gently and held me.

"Never again," I said, with moist eyes. "Never again." I kissed her softly. "I've got to talk with Durgeon. Please wait; I shouldn't be too long."

"Of course. I'll be on the steps in front." As I hobbled back to the holding cell, I thought I was the luckiest guy alive. *Not only forgiven but loved.*

One of the bailiffs ushered Suzelle and me back to the holding cell. I took the chair facing Durgeon. Suzelle again stood against the wall farthest from him. "Boy, was Tina pissed." He gave a deep chuckle.

"Pissed or not, her testimony was damaging as hell," I said.

Durgeon ignored me and turned to Suzelle. "He messed her up good, didn't he?"

"Jake got some valuable information from her," she non-answered, in a small voice.

"What's the matter here?" Durgeon asked, his voice piqued. "You thumped her ass. Can't I enjoy that for a minute?"

"A minute is all we've got," I said.

Durgeon, suddenly serious, asked, "Has Danny been around?"

That surprised me. "Not that I know of," I answered. "Tice has probably got him squirreled away somewhere. I'll be surprised if we ever see him in San Arcadia again." Durgeon nodded his head but did not respond. I looked him square in the face and asked, "How close are we getting?"

"What do you mean?" he asked, looking away with feigned indifference.

Ignoring his misdirection, I asked again. "How close are we getting?"

"What do you want me to say, huh? You saw Tina. You know you're close. But it was all you." He pointed a finger at me. "You did it on your own."

"Yeah," I said. We sat in silence until I finally said, "I'm going to push the 'some other guy or guys' angle." That elicited no response. "After that, I figure we rest. I think we all agree you don't testify." I was nonchalant but held my breath. This was an enormous hurdle. If Durgeon testified, the trial was effectively over. Tice would crucify him and all his prior felonies and other mean acts in all their glory would come in. Even though the jurors knew he had been in prison, they didn't know the particulars. The particulars were, well, particularly ugly.

Durgeon just nodded. Before he could change his mind, I turned and motioned for the bailiff to open up. *I think I got away with one.*

On the steps of the courthouse, Lisa and Taylor Hunt were talking. That was something I didn't expect. They noticed Suzelle and me approaching, and when we finally made our way to them, Lisa gave me a hug as if there had never been a problem. *Talk about things turning on a dime.* She said, "Taylor just reminded me that we've met before, at one of my shows."

Taylor jumped in. "I've been a fan of Lisa's talent for several years and have one of her brilliant pieces in my home."

Booker was at the curb, waiting with his car. I motioned for him to give us another moment.

"Mr. Clearwater, a couple of quick questions?" Taylor asked.

"Lisa, Suzelle, is that okay?" They nodded.

"First, I want to tell you how sorry I am that you were attacked. How are you feeling?"

"It's getting better every day. I'll be fine."

"It must be particularly difficult to conduct such a challenging trial under these circumstances."

"I've got help and support," I said, nodding to Suzelle and Lisa.

Taylor nodded appreciatively at the two women and then back to me. "Do you have any idea if the attack on you was in any way related to the trial?"

"I can't be sure. But I cannot imagine anything else in my life that would have led to the attack. The LA County Sheriff's Office is investigating as well as the San Arcadia Sheriff's Office, but as far as I know, nothing has developed."

"I appreciate that answer. As for the trial itself, I noticed you tacked away from Anthony Graves and toward Dan Atwell today."

"It seemed appropriate, given the witness."

"Can you comment on the evidence that might implicate Dan Atwell?"

"Of course not." I smiled. "Let's just say it's an ongoing investigation."

"Fair enough, Mr. Clearwater. Good luck tomorrow."

"Taylor, since it looks like we are going to be doing this for a while, how about we use first names?"

"That works for me. Goodnight all. And Lisa, let's get together and talk art."

Lisa: "I'll look forward to that."

❧❧❧

Lisa agreed to come to the Ramada later that evening. After Booker dropped Suzelle and me at the hotel, I went straight to my room and laid carefully on the bed. It was still hard to find a comfortable way to rest. Sitting hurt, and lying down was only marginally better. God, I was tired. My head pounded, my hip was killing me, and the tension of just one day back in trial was taking its toll on my already depleted resources. But despite it all, I was a happy man. Lisa was back. I lay there and thought about her. My life was only whole with her at the center. She had become my soulmate and my confidant as well as my lover. I could not imagine the rest of my life without her.

But even as such warm thoughts passed through my mind, concerns about the damn trial would not recede. I began to second-guess the decision to keep Durgeon from the stand. I had long believed that defense lawyers often erred in not allowing their clients to testify. The jurors want to hear from the mouth of the accused either that they didn't do it, or if they did do it, that there were mitigating circumstances. Despite the judge's admonition to the jury that they could not hold it against them, a defendant's failure to testify certainly implies an admission of guilt. From everything the jury had heard, Durgeon was the shooter—no alibi, his fingerprint, access to the gun, and his damn admissions to Christina. Durgeon presented the classic scenario for not testifying; he had prior criminal conduct, which Tice would use to impeach him. And he was the proverbial loose cannon. One had to only think back to that videotape of his testimony in the first trial. Yet the jurors had not heard anything from him about what had happened that night. If I were a juror, I wasn't sure I would have any reasonable doubt on the evidence at this point.

Hell, I didn't need to make the final decision whether to have him testify yet. I pushed the decision away and mercifully fell asleep for an hour or so. I then climbed painfully to my feet and hitched my body into the shower. Visions of a naked Lisa in my bed tonight helped drive the trial anxieties away.

Later that evening, Lisa, Suzelle, Duke, and I sat around the room sipping Scotch and waiting to hear Taylor Hunt's eleven o'clock take on today's events in court. Lisa was curled up next to me. I glanced over at Suzelle as she took a swallow of Scotch with every indication of enjoyment. A far cry from just weeks ago when she made terrible faces at the taste. *Hell of a role model, Jake.*

"Well, Taylor," the anchor said, "I understand the trial has resumed after what, a two-week break?"

"Indeed it has. Mr. Durgeon's lawyer returned today after being attacked two weeks ago. Mr. Clearwater's injuries are still apparent, and he's using a cane."

The anchor's perfect eyebrows rose for the camera. "Do the police think the attack was related to the trial?"

"Since the attack happened in Malibu outside Mr. Clearwater's home, it's a Los Angeles County Sheriff's case. As of now, they have no comment on their ongoing investigation."

The anchor shook his head in mock wonder. "This is a very interesting twist to this closely-watched drama. Meanwhile, let's get back to the courtroom."

"All right." Hunt obliged. "Today, Christina Atwell, Mr. Durgeon's former girlfriend, testified, and as anticipated, really bolstered the case against Durgeon. She offered important pieces of testimony. She testified that Durgeon's whereabouts were unaccounted for from eight o'clock the night before the murders until approximately seven thirty the next morning. She told the jury that Durgeon had ordered her to destroy a gun that was possibly the murder weapon. And finally, she testified that he made statements linking him to the murders. Ms. Atwell was a powerful witness for District Attorney John Tice.

"That said, I must point out that defense counsel Jake Clearwater did everything possible to call her testimony into question. Mr. Clearwater, during cross-examination, suggested that her testimony is tainted because of a favorable deal she got from the DA's office. Her testimony took some serious blows. But what I found most interesting today was Clearwater's questioning of Atwell concerning her son, Dan Atwell. Mr. Clearwater, through his questioning, implied that Dan Atwell might have somehow been involved in the murders. However, all in all, it was another strong day for John Tice and the prosecution."

"Now that the DA has rested, how would you assess the case against Mr. Durgeon?"

"John Tice has a strong case. And from what I understand, it is essentially the case he used to convict Mr. Durgeon during the first trial."

"What do you expect from the defense?"

"I'm not sure. Jake Clearwater has proven to be a resourceful and skilled advocate. His opening statement and his cross-examinations lead me to believe that there is much more to come. And as I said, I'm intrigued with the Dan Atwell reference. I'll be interested to see if it leads anywhere."

"Thanks Taylor, we'll look forward to your report tomorrow."

"Not much there," said Duke, as he shut off the TV and took a last swallow of his Scotch. "Wait until everyone hears what we have in store for tomorrow."

"Duke, I read your interview with Amy Arthur. Can we go over it tomorrow dark and early?" I asked.

"No problem, Jake, I'll be here at six thirty with coffee and bagels."

Suzelle and Duke got up and took off. Lisa helped me into bed and gently massaged my back until I fell asleep.

❧❧❧

I awoke sweaty, restless, and early—again. Lisa had slipped out sometime during the night. She had a showing in LA. I pulled on my brand-new red robe. While I had been hospitalized, Eve had replaced my ratty gray one. I went to the window and pinched the blinds. The early morning was dreary. The streetlights were ineffective in the pale light of dawn, and a few cars on the street lit only the small area in front of them. I stiffly made my way to the small kitchen area, turned on the Keurig, and made myself coffee. It tasted bitter, and I sat it down without finishing. I popped four Advil and leaned on the sink, feeling weak; my hip in particular was screaming. I needed to run or swim, some kind of exercise to return to normal. I could feel my body turning to mush.

Tomorrow, I told myself, I'd try some laps in the hotel pool. I returned to my room and pulled the blind up and stared out. I had a memory flash of naked Lisa standing by the window at my place, her body drenched in moonlight. "Come back to bed, babe," I'd said, getting up and gathering her to me. I kissed and caressed her until she melted in my arms, then I pulled her to bed and made love to her with the silver light streaming over us.

At six thirty as promised, Duke arrived with provisions. Suzelle joined us. Duke, bless his heart, had laid out the direct examination of Amy Arthur, Doree's high school friend.

We went over it a couple of times, then Duke left to go pick Arthur up.

ঌঌঌ

I was surprised that I wasn't summoned to chambers. I had expected to do battle over my mini-prosecution of Dan Atwell. Instead, Tice apparently had decided not to take it to the judge. He likely figured I had leaked enough Dan Atwell innuendo already, and that he could deal with it. *Given his track record, he probably could.*

We resumed promptly at nine o'clock, and it was time to put on our case. I called Amy Arthur. There were audible intakes of breath when that name registered with Doree's family, which once again included Doree's mother, Donna Bennett. Duke escorted Ms. Arthur into the courtroom. A young woman sitting next to Doree's mother leaned toward Arthur as she passed. "Oh Amy," she hissed, in an admonishing undertone. Ms. Arthur slowed, but Duke didn't let her stop, and he got her through the gate. She moved as if in a trance, took the oath, and sat rigidly in the witness chair, her eyes down. Duke stepped to me, touched my shoulder, and took a chair just behind me at counsel table.

Judge Harbarger tried to ease Arthur's obvious anxiety. "Ms. Arthur, please just relax. Would you care for some water before we begin?" Arthur looked at the judge and shook her head. Following the oath, Harbarger said, "Please tell us your full name and spell your last name."

Arthur took a deep breath, and in a shaky voice, said, "Amy Melissa Arthur, A-R-T-H-U-R."

"Thank you, Ms. Arthur. Mr. Clearwater, you may question."

"Good morning, Ms. Arthur," I said, giving her a warm smile as I worked my way to my feet.

"Good morning."

"You knew Doree in high school?"

She nodded and in a very soft voice said, "Since fifth grade. My family moved out from Boston when I was eleven, and Doree was the first person I met. We were best friends from then on."

"As best friends, I suppose you confided and shared most everything with one another?"

"Yes, we did," she said as her voice cracked. She dropped her head and held up one hand as if to say, "Give me a moment." When she looked up, it was right into the eyes of Donna Bennett. "Mrs. Bennett, you know I loved Doree and your whole family. I just want to make certain the right people are punished."

Tice erupted from his chair. "Objection!"

Harbarger leaned toward Arthur and said, "Not another word." Arthur nodded obediently. "We are in recess for ten minutes; counsel in chambers." Harbarger's face was flushed. In chambers, she remained standing behind her desk. "What was that?" she demanded of me.

"I don't know." Arthur's impromptu plea to Donna Bennett caught me off guard along with everyone else. However, there is a presumption that the lawyer who calls a witness has some control over that witness.

"Didn't you prepare her?" Tice piled on. I ignored him and waited for Harbarger.

Harbarger looked at me. "Answer the question."

"I resent the implication of that question," I bristled.

Tice stepped up to me and demanded, "Answer the question!" I stared at Tice and remained silent.

Harbarger sat and leaned back in her chair and let out her breath. "Gentlemen, the bell has been rung. Let's deal with it. What do you think, John?"

"I don't want this SOB of a trial to go by the boards this late in the game," he snapped. "I think you have to admonish the witness and instruct the jury to disregard and move on. Short of a mistrial and starting over, I can't see any options beyond that."

"I agree," said Harbarger. "Jake, we can't have this kind of conduct. Please control your witness."

"I'll do my best." Harbarger gave me a look, blew out her breath and said, "Okay, let's pick it up from there."

We reentered the courtroom, and Harbarger warned Arthur from offering any other unsolicited opinions. She then instructed the jurors to disregard the witness's remark and told them her opinion was just that, an opinion, and entitled to no weight. The judge then nodded for me to continue.

"So, Ms. Arthur, you and Doree were best friends from fifth grade on?"

"Yes, we were." She looked ready to cry.

"And that relationship continued into high school?"

"Yes." A tear slid down her cheek.

"Do you need a moment?"

"No. No. I'll be alright."

I nodded. "I would like to talk about the fall semester of your junior year in high school. That would have been in 2001 is that right?"

"Yes." Her voice low and shaky.

Working off Duke's script, I asked, "During the early part of that school year, did Doree have a boyfriend?"

She nodded. "She went out with Dan Atwell." That elicited some buzz from the folks in the gallery, which was quickly quelled by Judge Harbarger.

"Tell us what you know about that relationship."

"He was a football player. He was big and good-looking—at least that's what Doree thought."

"I take it you did not share Doree's feelings?"

"No, I didn't."

"To your knowledge, was it a serious relationship?"

"It didn't last more than four or five weeks."

"Do you know why it broke up?'

"He kept pestering Doree, you know . . ." She hesitated, her eyes down. "To have sex, but Doree didn't want to. She didn't think Dan was looking for a serious relationship."

"So what happened?"

"Doree broke it off."

"And then?"

"Objection, calls for the witness to speculate."

Harbarger leaned toward Arthur. "To your knowledge. Just tell us what you observed or what Doree told you."

She nodded at the judge and turned back to me. "One night

when I was sleeping over at Doree's, Dan showed up in the middle of the night, yelling and threatening her. When the police arrived, Dan had broken Doree's bedroom window and was trying to drag her out."

"I take it Dan Atwell was arrested?"

"Uh huh."

"Did you personally have any contact with Dan Atwell after that incident?"

"Yes, a couple of days later. It was all over school that Dan had been suspended and kicked off the football team. He came up to me when I was alone and said . . ." She paused and looked at Judge Harbarger. "Your Honor, I'm uncomfortable with repeating the language he used."

"I understand your concern, Ms. Arthur, but it is important that we hear the testimony."

She said, in a barely audible voice, "Dan said, 'Your fucking friend really screwed up my life.'"

"How would you describe his emotional state when he told you that Doree had really messed up his life?"

"Very angry. It felt to me that it took all of his self-control to keep from hitting me. Just because I was Doree's friend."

"Were you afraid of him?"

"Objection, irrelevant."

"Sustained, move on, Mr. Clearwater."

"To your knowledge, was Doree afraid of him?"

Tice again, "Irrelevant."

I looked at Harbarger. "May I be heard?"

"Go ahead."

"Threats and strong actions from a man directed at the deceased are very relevant. Atwell had access to his mother's house and presumably access to the gun linked to the murders. And now we learn that before the murders, he threatened one of the victims. Judge, these circumstances are difficult to simply brush aside, and I need the opportunity to explore them." *This was it. I had invited the judge to make the definitive call concerning Dan Atwell. I'd been nibbling at the edges for a while, but now I wanted to begin laying out my case against Atwell.*

"I am going to let you proceed, counsel."

"Judge, I'd like to be heard," Tice said, his voice strained.

"I've made my ruling, Mr. Tice." Tice remained on his feet, staring at Harbarger. Finally, Harbarger motioned him down. *Whoa, Harbarger and Tice were not seeing eye to eye. Harbarger was going to let me chase down the Atwell angle!*

"Thank you, Your Honor." I turned my attention back to Arthur. "To your knowledge, was Doree afraid of Dan Atwell?"

"She was very afraid of him. He blamed her for getting him kicked off the football team. That's what he was really angry about." Amy was getting stronger as we went.

"Not school?"

"No, it was football."

"Thank you for your courage in coming forth, Ms. Arthur. No further questions, Your Honor."

"Mr. Tice. Cross?"

"Ms. Arthur, I know this is difficult for you," Tice said in a gentle voice. He had switched gears in a hurry. "You have no special insight on the murders of Doree and Robert, do you?"

She shook her head no.

"And the relationship between Dan Atwell and Doree was three years before the murders, isn't that correct?"

"Yes."

"They were both in high school, weren't they?"

"Yes."

"And to your knowledge, there had been no contact between the two of them after the event you described, isn't that right?" Tice was taking a risk with that question. He had no idea whether or not there had been any further contact. However, since I had not gone any further about any recent contact, Tice had to think he could push the point without a concern.

"Not that I know of."

"And as far as you knew, both Dan Atwell and Doree continued to live in the San Arcadia area since high school?"

"I know Doree never left. I had no contact with Dan, so I don't know about him."

Tice looked up at Harbarger. "Judge, I have nothing further for Ms. Arthur. Thank you, Ms. Arthur." Tice was all charm, sending a message to the jurors that her testimony was not hurtful.

తతతత

Next, I called Frank Thomas, and once again used Duke's careful notes to guide me through the exam. Thomas was the San Arcadia High School vice principal who had suspended Dan Atwell and kicked him off the football team. He testified that Atwell's expulsion was the result of his conduct at the Bennett house.

Duke, who had driven Amy Arthur home, slipped up behind me during Tice's brief cross of Thomas and handed me a note that read, "Carrie Thompson just got back to me. She's willing to testify. But we need time to prep her."

I looked up at Duke, surprised. I hadn't held up much hope that Carrie Thompson would testify, even if Duke was able to track her down. *Duke was magic.*

It was eleven thirty in the morning. Harbarger looked at me expectantly. I asked to approach. "My investigator just informed me that he has located a witness. I have not had an opportunity to prepare her. May we have until tomorrow morning?"

Tice started to speak, but the judge waived him off. "Mr. Clearwater, I know you are in considerable discomfort and I admire you for getting back into this trial as quickly as you have. Losing an afternoon is not going to matter in the larger sense." Turning to the jury, Harbarger adjourned until tomorrow morning. *Thank you, Judge Harbarger.*

৵৵৵

We took the elevator to the second floor of the Ramada, where we all got off. Suzelle headed to her room to continue preparation for the penalty phase. *Hope for the best, prepare for the worst.* Duke and I made our way down the staircase to the first floor and out a side door. The stairs hurt. Even though it looked as if Booker had left, we didn't want to take the chance of having Tice tipped off as to the whereabouts of our witness. Booker was, after all, a cop. As we drove, Duke filled me in on Carrie Thompson, now Carrie Washburn. She and her husband lived in Avalon Beach, a small community north of San Arcadia.

She was in her midthirties, with beautiful white-blond hair pulled back into a ponytail. She had freckles on her roundish pale-pink baby-like face and on her exposed shoulders and arms. She was nondescript, except for that hair. Carrie Washburn and her husband had just moved back into the area from Las Vegas. Her husband, a server at a Morro Bay restaurant, was at work.

"Ms. Washburn, Duke filled you in on the trial we are involved in?"

"He told me that you think Dan Atwell might have been involved in the murder of that couple years ago."

"That's right. We're trying to find out everything we can about him. We know that Dan attacked you. We are hopeful you'll tell us about that, and that you would be willing to testify."

"Yes." Her firm conviction was surprising. "What he did to me and got away with has bothered me for a long time. I was just a kid then, and I was afraid of testifying against him. But I'm not a kid anymore. And I want that . . ." She stopped and gathered herself. "Where do you want me to start?"

CHAPTER 34

A MEAN WARNING

It was nearly 5:00 p.m. when we returned from interviewing Carrie Washburn. As we entered the suite, Suzelle was slumped against a wall, clothing disheveled, and she was sobbing. "I thought he was going to kill me," she said, between sobs. Shock shivered through my system as a flash of the hulk who had beaten me ripped through my brain. But that was about Lisa. Right? Who in bloody hell would harm Suzelle? Duke and I eased her to her feet and got her to the sofa. I crouched down in front of her and pushed her hair from her face, making soothing sounds, feeling helpless and angry. Her swimming eyes looked first at me and then at Duke.

"Ja . . . Jake. I was so scared."

"Did he hurt you?"

She shook her head no.

"What happened, honey?" I asked, as Duke eased a pillow behind her head. She took a breath and started to speak, but then her face deflated. She sobbed, mouth open, gulping for air, tears streaming down her face. Duke gently dabbed a damp face cloth over her cheeks and eyes. I could hardly contain my anger as she clutched my shirt and continued sobbing. For the first time in my life, I had the urge to kill. *But whom?*

When the sobs ran out and there were only occasional hiccups, we were able to piece together what had happened. Suzelle had been walking back to the Ramada with a Starbucks when a car jerked to a stop just ahead of her. Before she could react, the driver was at her. He slammed the coffee from her hands, grabbed her by the front of her blouse with both hands and pulled her to him.

"'I'm just going to say this one time, little chickie. You tell that asshole you work for to let sleeping dogs lie.' Then he slammed me against the building. And then said, 'Are you listening, chickie? Let sleeping dogs lie.' Then he held a knife to my face and said, 'You don't want me coming back.'"

"Sonofabitch," Duke grunted.

"I thought he was going to kill me."

"I'm so sorry, honey," I offered weakly. "This thing has gone off the rails." My brain was working so hard, it felt on fire. "It's Danny!" I nearly yelled. I suddenly knew with absolute certainty. "Duke, you got that mug shot of Atwell?"

Duke's brain was furiously chasing mine. He was already up before I asked. He pulled several folders from his briefcase, flicked through some pages, pulled out a sheet and brought it back to us.

Suzelle briefly glanced at the photo and said, "It could be him. Except he's bald now." She shuddered and turned away.

The mug shot taken after the drug bust of the Atwells and Durgeon had him with dark, shaggy hair and a beard.

Suzelle looked at the photo again. "I can't be certain, but I think so. I was so scared. I focused on the knife."

"How big was he?" I asked.

"Big—tall and broad."

I flashed to Lisa. It hadn't been her ex. She needed to know that.

Dan Atwell was no longer on the periphery of the trial or on the periphery of our lives. He had moved front and center. This character, if indeed he was Atwell, was motivated and dangerous. The fact that Atwell was no longer just a defense theory but perhaps was right here, very tuned to the trial, and willing to physically interject his will on the trial, was chilling. But for what reason? I couldn't make sense of it.

Duke screwed up his face and said, "Jake, it just now occurs to me that you were attacked after you asked Tice for Atwell's rap sheet."

I stood up at that realization. "You're right, Duke. There had been no indication we were thinking Atwell prior to that." I hesitated. "But how would that get back to Atwell?"

"Maybe Manlow? He had to have been in contact with Christina and maybe Danny."

"That's a stretch. He's an ass and he's taken a personal interest in this trial, but he's a cop, and this is a double murder case. Could he have really done that?"

"Like I said, maybe he didn't leak it to Dan himself, but just happens to mention it to Christina that we might be trying to connect her son. Perhaps as an additional inducement to amp up her testimony." Duke went on, "I can see a scenario where Mama Atwell informs Danny."

Duke called the police. Detectives arrived, interviews were conducted, reports written. Dan Atwell was now a person of interest. Sergeant Booker, along with two other officers, were now assigned to our protection around the clock, instead of simply as escorts. Dan Atwell was on everyone's radar.

I called Lisa and filled her in. She was relieved the attacker was not acting on behalf of her ex. "Thank God." She immediately came to the Ramada to comfort Suzelle. I insisted that Suzelle stay in my room going forward. She had the bedroom, I had the couch. Lisa and I would improvise.

ॐ ॐ ॐ

Later that evening, Suzelle came out of the bedroom wrapped in a white terry-cloth robe. She sat on a chair and curled her legs under her. "How are you feeling?" asked Lisa.

"Better."

Speaking to Suzelle, I said, "I'm glad you came out. We need to talk."

Lisa and Duke sensed the moment and offered their goodbyes and slipped out.

"Jake, I'm fine. I was rattled, but I'm fine now." Her eyes were intent on mine. "I know what you're going to say, but I'm not leaving."

I offered a soft grin. "You have to leave. It's become too crazy, too unpredictable, and frankly too dangerous. I should have had you leave after I was attacked. I admire your pluck, but I can't have anything else happen to you."

"Pluck? Did you say pluck? Dammit, Jake, I'm an adult. I don't need a man being condescending to me or ordering me around. You can fire me if I haven't done a competent job, but you can't just send me away when things get tough, and you think you've got to watch out for me."

I sighed and stared at the floor to get my arguments in order. "Dan Atwell very well might have executed Doree and Robert after he tortured them for hours. Dan Atwell raped Carrie Washburn. Dan Atwell is probably the man who nearly beat me to death, and he could have carried you off and done God knows what. This is a dangerous man who is right here and appears to have targeted us.

We need to do everything possible to protect ourselves, and that means we've got to get you out of Dodge."

"I'm not going." She was defiant. "I've got too much work to do getting the penalty phase ready, and there is no one else to do it." She held my look. "I am not leaving. I will be careful. I will not go anywhere without you or Duke or a cop, but I am not going home like some child who gets packed off when things get rough."

I sat and looked at her. She could tell I was wavering. With just a hint of a grin, she said, "Besides, he's not really after me. You're the one he's really after. I was just the conduit for the message. Notice how he just scared me; it was you he beat up."

I gave a resigned smile. "So you're saying everyone else is in the clear?"

"Right."

We sat some more. I finally said, "Nowhere, not even Starbucks, without a cop?"

She came to me and gave me a long hug. But instead of returning to bed, she pulled two beers from the mini, handed me one, popped hers, and resumed her chair. "What I can't figure is why Atwell is doing what he's doing. If anything, it draws attention to himself for a double murder. What's his game?"

"I've been working through that same question. By attacking us, is he trying to create a mistrial for Durgeon? If so, what's in it for him? Why would he try to help out Durgeon? And even if there was a mistrial, Tice would just crank it up again. But on the other hand, if he can induce us to just roll over in defending Durgeon and Durgeon is convicted again, maybe he figures he's in the clear on the murders."

Suzelle said, "Going back to your first what if. Maybe by showing he is a dangerous man, people will believe he's the murderer and create reasonable doubt as to Durgeon. If that's the case, it would be almost impossible for Tice to try Atwell for the murders after making the case against Durgeon."

It was my turn to speculate. "Even if that is his motive, Durgeon's jurors will never hear of the attacks on you or me. It's not admissible, and the jurors have been instructed to not read or listen to any trial-related news."

Suzelle nodded and then added, "I've got a wild idea. Maybe he is just really stupid, and he's angry with us for trying to implicate him. I don't know, we may not be dealing with a real rational actor with rational thought patterns."

We went round and round without resolution until we finally called it a night.

As I lay on the couch trying to get comfortable, I felt a growing sense that Duane Durgeon did not kill Doree and Robert. I might actually be representing an innocent man. It made my stomach churn. Being the barrier trying to prevent a possibly innocent man from being executed was exquisite pressure, so sharp and intense I couldn't sleep.

≈ ≈ ≈

The next morning in chambers, I informed Judge Harbarger of the attack on Suzelle. Tice, of course, had long ago been apprised of developments by his law-enforcement minions. Harbarger asked Suzelle if she was alright. She nodded her assurance that she was fine. I then tried to push things. "Based on the attacks on Ms. Frost and me, it is our intention to introduce these attacks and the statements of the attacker into evidence." I threw this out, knowing with absolute certainty I had no chance of success. Beyond that, I knew the next battle was going to be about whether Carrie Washburn would be allowed to testify. Once the judge ruled against me regarding the attacks, maybe she would be more inclined to give me the next call.

I made my pitch.

Tice shook his head. "For what purpose?" he asked. "What has any of this to do with Durgeon? There are no actions or statements linking this alleged conduct to the murders in this case. From what we heard, there is only counsel's wild imagination that links the conduct to Atwell."

"Alleged conduct? I've still got the bruises and cracked ribs; there is no alleged conduct." I looked at Tice. "I was beaten senseless and my associate accosted and threatened by a man we believe is the killer, and a man we have made every effort to implicate in this double murder. And you ask for what purpose? This is a man who had access to the alleged murder weapon and who knew and had motive to harm Doree Blanco." I shifted from Tice to Harbarger. "As this court is well aware, relevant evidence is that which has any tendency to make a fact of consequence more or less probable than it would be without that evidence. Atwell's actions, threats, and statements are an undeniable fact of consequence in this trial that someone other than Durgeon killed those two kids. That fact of consequence is made more probable by virtue of his attacks."

"Mr. Tice?" Harbarger looked at Tice. *I hadn't been shut down yet. Go figure.*

Tice calmly and precisely addressed my argument. "As this court well recognizes, there are several concerns with such testimony. For one thing, it would require defense counsel to testify. If he testifies, a new lawyer will need to be appointed, and in all likelihood, we would have to try this case again. Beyond that daunting consideration, the proposed evidence is vague and ambiguous. The alleged statements contain no specifics, and frankly there is nothing other than Atwell's relationship with his mother that connects any of his conduct to the central question in this trial. Counsel has no idea who the attacker is other than an uncertain identification by Ms. Frost. Furthermore, such testimony would have a substantial likelihood of confusing the jury and leading them into base speculations. The prejudice and harm that this testimony would wreak on this jury could not be undone. It simply cannot come in." *A brilliant argument on every point.*

I started to speak, but Harbarger cut me off. "While these events are unfortunate and regrettable, I am very concerned about how this testimony would be used by the jury. I deny the defense request."

I tried to speak, but Harbarger was not finished. "And further, counsel, I don't want this jury to hear any of this." She was looking at me. "I do not want anyone discussing this with the press. Even though the jurors have been instructed not to listen to, watch, or read anything about this trial, I do not want the temptation out there."

Tice: "Judge, I am concerned news of these alleged attacks will leak out, despite your admonishments to the contrary. I suggest that we sequester the jurors for the duration."

Harbarger looked at me. "Your Honor, I do not think it's necessary, but I suspect you've already made up your mind."

Harbarger looked at me with surprise. "I do not appreciate your attitude, counsel. We will not, however, sequester the jury at this time."

Now that I had lost round one and couldn't bring in evidence about the attacks, I launched into round two. I laid out my argument that Carrie Washburn be allowed to testify.

Tice's response took two tacks. First, that Washburn's testimony was irrelevant to the guilt or innocence of Durgeon. Harbarger had already made the decision to let me pursue the Atwell angle, so

I knew I was okay there. Tice's second tack concerned discovery. Since I had not provided notice of her testimony, and since he had been denied the opportunity to investigate her, he was unfairly disadvantaged.

I countered that I had only recently become aware of Ms. Washburn and her tragic encounter with Atwell.

Harbarger ruled in my favor and offered Tice a two-day continuance to investigate Washburn. Tice declined. His response was not surprising. I believed he was concerned that the longer the trial went, the greater the chance of further unforeseen events muddying it up.

Suzelle and I went back to fill Durgeon in on the attack on Suzelle as well as the court's ruling allowing Washburn to testify. He listened without interrupting, his eyes keenly focused, his mouth slightly open. By the time I finished, he had started that rocking motion again. He didn't speak. I broke the silence. "You got anything to say?"

"I'm glad he didn't hurt you," he said, looking at Suzelle.

"Thanks, Duane," Suzelle said.

"I don't think you killed them," I said. He nodded but did not speak. He dropped his head to his knees and slowly shook it. When he sat up again, his eyes were watering, and he brushed at his face with his sleeve. I suspect it had been a long time, perhaps forever, since someone said they believed him.

CHAPTER 35

CARRIE WASHBURN

Judge Harbarger banged her gavel. "Mr. Clearwater, you may call your next witness."

"Carrie Washburn," I said. After she was sworn in, I started. "Ms. Washburn, tell us a little about yourself."

In a confident, clear voice, she answered. "I grew up in Pismo Beach and went to high school there. I then went for one year of local community college before moving with my parents to Las Vegas. I lived in Las Vegas for the past ten years and just recently got married and moved back to California."

"I want to zero in on the time when you were going to community college right here in the area. When would that have been?"

"2004, thirteen years ago."

"Were you raped during that time?"

She did not hesitate. "I was raped by Dan Atwell on September 13, 2004." A collective expulsion of mutters followed.

"Let's back up a little bit, Ms. Washburn. How did you know Dan Atwell?"

"We were on our second date. We had gone to a movie, and

afterward, he took me back to his apartment to listen to music. When we got there, he made it pretty clear that he expected me to have sex with him." Her eyes brightened with moisture and then a trail of tears began to trickle down her face. But her determination to get through this was also evident on her face.

I did my best to convey to her my support and patience with my eyes and my tone. "Please go on when you're ready."

"I tried to leave, but he wouldn't let me. And then, when I wouldn't"—she sucked in her breath—"wouldn't . . . he just went off. He grabbed me and ripped off my shirt and my bra. He threw me on the couch and ripped off my pants. He kept slapping me and saying terrible things. I was bleeding from my mouth and one of my ears. He had some rope and tied my wrists behind my back. He told me that if I screamed, he would kill me. He made me have oral sex with him and then bent me over the back of a chair and raped me." There were no more tears, but the crystal-like tracks on her cheeks glistened in the light of the courtroom.

"Ms. Washburn, how long were you in his apartment?"

"Seemed like hours, but I don't really know."

"How did it end?"

"Finally, he cut me loose and threw my clothes at me. He grabbed me by my hair and said I had better keep this to myself or he would kill me."

"What happened next?"

"He threw me outside. I wasn't even dressed. I managed to call a girlfriend; she came and took me home."

"Did you report this to the police?"

"Not at first, but two days later my dad drove me to the police, and I told them what had happened."

"Go on."

"He was arrested, but when it came time for me to testify, I couldn't go through with it."

"Were you afraid of Dan Atwell?"

"Afraid," she said, "and ashamed."

"Why have you agreed to testify now?"

"Following years of counseling and a supportive husband, I know it is the right thing to do. He shouldn't have done what he did and gotten away with it." She then added, almost as an afterthought, "I hope saying this in public will help me sleep at night."

"Ms. Washburn, thank you for coming forward. I know this was painful." I turned to Harbarger. "No more questions, Your Honor."

Tice had no cross. *There was nothing he could do with her testimony.* Once again, we recessed early. Harbarger had some pretrial conferences on other cases.

When Suzelle and I walked out of the courthouse, Duke was talking with Carrie Washburn and a man I assumed was her husband. Carrie saw me and walked over. "Mr. Clearwater, I wanted you to know that I am okay. I could see in your eyes that you hated to put me through that."

"Thank you," I said. "And thank you again for testifying."

Her husband took her arm, and as they walked away, I felt the sting of tears in my eyes.

Duke took off for LAX to pick up Ron Evans.

෭෮෭

Lisa brought two pizzas and a bucket of chicken, along with a large salad to soothe the cholesterol gods. During dinner, we watched the six o'clock news. It was Taylor Hunt time. In some ways, it was our lone link to the outside world's view of the trial. I felt sequestered from the real world. Beyond the courtroom, my only real interactions were with Suzelle, Duke, and Lisa. Bizarre as it seemed, the television news was a way to gauge the trial from a neutral perspective. Taylor Hunt, God help me, was my barometer.

We were the second story of the evening. A fifteen-car pileup in heavy fog just north of town took coveted lead-story status. Once we finished viewing the mangled cars that miraculously resulted in no fatalities, the anchor turned to the trial. "One of the defense lawyers representing Duane Durgeon was accosted by a man the defense has alleged was involved in the Blanco murders. According to an unnamed source within the San Arcadia Sheriff's Office, yesterday evening Suzelle Frost was allegedly confronted and threatened just outside the hotel in which she and the defense team are staying."

"Harbarger is going to blow, now that the cat's out of the bag," Lisa said with glee.

I laughed at her good cheer. "As long as she knows we didn't let it out, so be it."

"Meanwhile," the anchor said, as he turned to Taylor Hunt, "back to the trial itself. Taylor, what does this mean to a trial that has already had a full assortment of twists and turns?"

Hunt took the question and turned to the camera. "If this source is accurate, that someone is attempting to intimidate and harass members of Durgeon's defense team, it is at least some confirmation of Durgeon's lawyers' claim that another individual is perhaps involved in the murders. Keep in mind that Jake Clearwater has alluded to an individual named Dan Atwell as a person of interest."

Right on cue, the anchor prompted, "What is the likelihood the jurors will hear of these attacks?"

Hunt was ready. *Made one think that the catchy back and forth had been rehearsed.* "The judge has already ruled that any testimony involving the alleged attacks will not be admissible. The standard for admissibility of this type of evidence involves a balancing of the probative value of the evidence against any undue prejudice it might have. If true, this evidence could be quite probative in that it may show that someone other than Duane Durgeon might have been involved. However, it takes several leaps to get to the conclusion that Atwell was somehow involved in the attacks on the defense team and that he committed them to dissuade Mr. Clearwater from producing further evidence against him. For instance, what if Atwell was just demonstrating anger at Mr. Clearwater's aggressive cross-examination of his mother? My point is that there is some speculation involved with this testimony, and I think the judge made the correct decision in denying the defense request to admit evidence of the attacks." *Pretty good analysis.*

"So, what happened in trial today?" the anchor asked.

"The defense, over strong objection from the prosecutor, put a woman on the stand who testified that thirteen years ago she was raped by Dan Atwell. Her testimony was compelling. It appears the defense is all in on Dan Atwell. And with today's testimony, he was painted as a violent and sadistic individual."

Following the news, Suzelle insisted on going back to her own room, leaving the bedroom to Lisa and me. Sex, even in my pathetic condition, is a wonderful thing.

CHAPTER 36

RON EVANS

It was still dark the following morning when Lisa left. I climbed
slowly out of bed, pulled on my trunks—my Speedos hadn't
made it up to San Arcadia—and made my way to the Ramada pool.
I left my cane at the edge of the pool and gingerly entered the water
using the steps and handrail. I pushed off into a gentle breaststroke.
My arms and legs were stiff from weeks of inactivity. I reached the
far end and held onto the side, then I pushed off and returned. I
managed four laps, until, gasping, I sat on the second step and let
the ripples from my modest effort rebound off my chest.

I had showered and shaved when Duke brought a reluctant
Ron Evans to our suite at 8:00 a.m. Evans was in his late fifties, with
black hair that glistened with oil. He was dressed in gray polyester
slacks and a white sport shirt. *Right on the cutting edge of fashion.* His
eyes were red-rimmed, his face haggard. He looked like a man who
couldn't decide whether to be angry or nervous. A man waiting for
life to load one more burden on his back.

"Morning, Mr. Evans. Coffee?" I offered, refusing to
acknowledge that he was here against his will. I held out a cup of
coffee. He shook his head. I motioned him to the upholstered chair.

He sat, arms crossed defiantly, jaw clenched. Anger appeared to be winning out. Duke leaned on the wall opposite Evans. Suzelle had not yet joined us.

"When do we get this over with?" His voice was a cross between a bark and a throat clear—a voice that had to be the product of the American tobacco industry. At any minute, I expected him to step to the balcony and spit over the rail. *He was a real charmer.*

He had a pack of unfiltered Camels in his breast pocket. "It's okay to smoke," I said. Even though this was a nonsmoking room, I wanted him to relax. He needed no further invitation, and with an efficiency born of countless repetition, he lighted up and took a comforting intake, held it, and relaxed as the smoke evacuated from both nostrils. I moved to a folding chair and gingerly sat.

"You will testify at nine o'clock this morning," I answered, my voice still conversational. "I want to take a few minutes to let you know what's going to happen."

Evans interrupted me. "I told him," he motioned at Duke, "you make me testify, and I'll point to your guy."

I cut him off. "I know that's what you said. Now let me introduce you to the reality you are about to confront." No longer conversational. "You are going to take an oath this morning to your God to tell the truth. You see, Evans, through some freak accident of being in a particular place at a particular time, you are in the God-like position of helping to determine whether a man lives or dies." He started to speak, but I again cut him off by raising my voice and continuing. "I'm not finished. We are not going to discuss your testimony now. You need time to think, and I'm confident that, despite the years that have passed and despite what you have said in the past, you will do the right thing." *I doubted he would have a come-to-Jesus moment.*

I got up, looking at Duke. "I'm going down to the dining room for breakfast. Please keep Mr. Evans company until we head out." Duke nodded. Evans scowled but said nothing.

ぁぁぁ

Judge Harbarger's gavel sounded. "Let the record reflect the jury and alternate jurors are present, the defendant and his counsel are present, and the prosecution is present. Mr. Clearwater, are you ready to proceed?"

"Yes, Your Honor. The defense calls Ron Evans."

Evans and Duke were seated toward the back of the large courtroom. Heads turned, craning to see Evans as he shuffled across two women to get to the aisle and walk unevenly toward the front. He was clearly aware that all eyes were on him, and he shrunk from the attention. A bailiff held the gate and pointed to the witness stand. Evans was breathing heavily, sucking air into his abused lungs. The color had drained from his face. I hoped he wouldn't have a coronary before he testified. *After that, I didn't much care.* When he reached the witness stand, the clerk stepped to him, holding the Bible. Evans looked momentarily confused, then raised his right hand. "Do you swear to tell the truth, the whole truth, and nothing but the truth, so help you God?" His voice was a hoarse whisper, "I do." If he hadn't been such a shameless coward and liar, I might have felt sorry for him. The clerk motioned for him to take the witness stand.

Harbarger nodded to him. "Mr. Evans, please state your full name and spell your last name."

Another deep breath. "Ronald Dwight Evans, E-V-A-N-S."

I remained seated. It was time to pick up the dice and give them a toss. This was Plan B; Atwell was still Plan A. *I was just trying to raise reasonable doubt; how the jurors got there was of no import.* "Thank you, Judge. Mr. Evans, before we get to the meat and potatoes of your testimony, I think it's important to get a sense of you as a person. Tell us a little about yourself."

"Objection," Tice said. "Your Honor, we do not need to know this man's life history. What is the relevance?"

Harbarger looked at me, her eyebrows arched in question. I slowly worked myself to my feet. "Judge, Mr. Evans's credibility is critical to the ultimate decision these jurors must make. They need to know something of the man if for no other reason than to help gauge whether they can trust his testimony." *Here, however, I wanted the jurors to know what a weasel this guy was.*

"Briefly, counsel."

"Thank you, Judge. Now, Mr. Evans, tell us a little about yourself."

"My wife passed away fifteen years ago."

"Any children?"

"No." He looked down, seeming to reflect briefly on events long past. "No," he said again and started to say something more, then caught himself and sat silent.

"What kind of work do you do, Mr. Evans?"

"I used to be a bus driver here in San Arcadia. For seventeen years."

"I take it from your answer that you are not doing that anymore."

"I retired a while back and moved away."

"Where did you move?"

"I moved back to Cincinnati. That's where my mother lives."

"Do you have a job there?"

"No, my health hasn't been so good. I haven't worked since I left here."

"How do you support yourself?"

"I have a little pension, I get social security."

Without benefit of my cane, I limped behind Tice and Manlow toward the jury and found a spot between the prosecutor's table and the jury box. "Now that we've gotten a little sense of your personal history, I want to go back several years to when you were still living in San Arcadia. Specifically to November 15, 2004. Where were you living at that time?"

"At the Palms Apartments."

"We have heard some testimony about the Palms. Apparently, it was a little run down. Is that right?"

"Yeah."

"You had a steady job; why did you live there?"

Evans threw me a mean look. I think he was trying to figure me out. *Friend or foe?* I patiently repeated, "Why did you live there?"

"I had a drinking problem," he mumbled. Figuring, I guess, that that explained everything. *It probably did.*

"Did you know any of your neighbors?"

"No. Only the Blancos, because they collected the rent. But that was all."

"How about some of the other residents?"

"People were always moving in and out. There wasn't much point in getting friendly with anyone."

"Mr. Evans, I want to turn to the early morning of November 15, 2004. You were home?"

"Yes."

"Tell us what woke you up that morning."

"I heard a woman screaming. At first, I thought I was dreaming. But then I heard it again." He spoke robotically as if he had practiced what he was saying.

"Could you hear what the woman said?"

"She said, 'No, no please.' Something like that."

"Describe her voice."

"It was like she was begging and crying at the same time."

"What happened next?"

"I pulled at the shade and looked out. I saw a woman and some guy with long hair and a beard standing next to her."

"Was she on the ground?"

He nodded. "She was, like, curled up on her side."

"How far were you from the man and the woman?"

"I'd say forty, fifty feet."

"Just to give the jurors a sense of that distance, how far are you and I right now?"

"I say twenty, twenty-five feet."

I hobbled past the prosecution table, through the gate and into the gallery, and stopped. "How about now?"

"Yeah, like that."

"Your Honor, may the record reflect I'm approximately forty to forty-five feet from Mr. Evans?"

"Fair enough," said Harbarger.

"And Mr. Evans," I asked, as I caned my way back to where I had been, "describe the lighting that morning."

"It was sort of dark and foggy."

"Was there any artificial light?"

"The light outside my door."

"Could you see the faces of either the man or the woman?"

Evans sat perfectly still. Seconds crawled in an uneasy silence. Then Evans said, "I never saw her face."

I waited to see if he would continue. He did not. "And the man's?"

He looked down at his lap for several seconds. Then he looked up, and through a set mouth, said, "Yes, I saw him." Lifting his hand, he pointed at Durgeon. "That's him."

Durgeon exploded from his chair. "Mother fuckin' liar!" he screamed as he lunged across counsel table.

Two bailiffs were instantly at Durgeon and sat him forcefully back into his chair. Suzelle had bailed out of her chair and was twenty feet away. The courtroom was a cacophony of excited voices. The pounding from Harbarger's gavel was lost in the din. Harbarger stood and shouted for silence. The courtroom quieted. Harbarger spoke firmly. "We will take a half-hour recess." Then looking at me, "I will see counsel in chambers, again."

Tice and I sat while the judge paced. "I had one miserable trial with your client, Mr. Clearwater; I will not have another." She stopped and looked at me for a response. I did not bite. Whatever I said would be wrong. "I am going to instruct the bailiffs to put the belt on Durgeon." The REACT belt, as it was aptly named, packed a 50,000-watt wallop. If the bailiff activated the remote, Durgeon would be hit with an eight-second blast that would reduce him to a quivering jerking thing, like a freshly caught fish thrashing on the deck.

I nodded, got up, and left. I asked Suzelle to get us coffee. I wanted a minute alone with Durgeon. I went back to the holding cell. He was seated, his face red, drops of perspiration standing below his hairline. He glared at me. "Why the fuck did you put that fucker on the stand?" *The number of permutations of the basic word fuck is amazing.*

"Because he is our best shot at creating reasonable doubt." My voice was impatient and mean. I was in no mood to take any crap.

Durgeon was not put off. "How's that asshole going to help?"

"Because of what he said and did after the murders. And you, dammit, are not helping by throwing a fit. Don't give the jurors any more fuel to hate you." I paused and told him that Harbarger was putting the belt on him.

"Shit," he muttered. He needed no instruction on the belt. I stood and knocked on the door to be let out. As I waited, we held an angry silence. Our truce of convenience appeared to be at an end. I went back to the courtroom. Suzelle, laden with coffee, joined me. We sipped in silence, waiting for the court to reconvene.

Duke sidled up to me and, after looking to make certain no one was in earshot, said, "Our client is a real pip."

"Ain't he though," I answered. "The thing of it is, he may be an innocent pip."

Duke pursed his lips and said, "Innocent being a relative term."

"Dammit Duke, he couldn't have gone off at a worse time. The jurors are getting too much time to think about Evans's ID of him."

Duke surprised me by grinning. "That's why you're getting the big bucks, counselor. Better suck it up." He made me grin. It was nice to have a grounded soul in my corner.

When we had reassembled, I noticed the thick belt around Durgeon's waist. I buried my coffee under the table. Harbarger motioned to me. "Mr. Clearwater, you may continue."

"Thank you, Your Honor." I put my hand on Durgeon's shoulder and hoisted myself up. By touching him, I hoped to dissipate some of the fear and loathing Durgeon had generated among the jurors. If I, as a more or less reasonable man, could touch him without fear or revulsion, maybe he wasn't as bad as he appeared to be. *It was a theory, anyway.*

"You had a good look at the shooter, didn't you, Mr. Evans?" I was leading, but since it was obvious that the witness had gone sideways on me, I had the right to lead. *It was time to put a beating on this guy. I didn't have to worry about losing the white hat; Evans had earned himself a beating.*

"I could see okay," Evans said cautiously, sensing where I was going.

"Big guy, long hair, facial hair?" I asked.

"That's right."

"Mr. Evans, I want to go back to November 16, the day after the murders. A police detective took you into an interrogation room, didn't they?"

"Yes."

"And in that room, there was a man named Anthony Graves, correct?"

"Yeah, that was his name."

"And when you saw Mr. Graves, you told the detective, and I quote, 'That's him. Get me the hell out of here.' Isn't that right?"

"I was nervous. I figured they had the guy who shot her."

"I'm sorry, Mr. Evans, perhaps you didn't understand my question. When you saw Mr. Graves the very next day, you told the detective, 'That's him. Get me the hell out of here.' Isn't that right?"

"That's what I said."

"So your answer is yes?"

"Yes."

"And when you said, 'That's him,' you meant he was the person who shot Doree Blanco, true?"

"Yeah."

"You never said that *might* be him, did you?"

"No."

I let the answer weigh on the jurors before moving to my next question. "Mr. Evans, let's move forward to August of 2005. Nine months after the murders. I believe you were living in Cincinnati at that time, correct?"

"Yeah," he said tentatively.

"An investigator flew back there to visit you, didn't he?"

"Yes."

"That man was Investigator Manlow, the man sitting next to the prosecutor, wasn't it?"

"Yes."

"You and he talked about the upcoming trial of Mr. Durgeon, didn't you?"

"Yeah."

"Investigator Manlow laid out the evidence the prosecution had developed against Durgeon, didn't he?" I was fishing. I was violating one of the cardinal rules: I was asking a question to which I did not know the answer. But my instincts told me that since I knew Manlow had flown to see Evans, and that since Evans was not called by either side at the first trial, Manlow and Tice were confident that Evans, if called, would back off his ID of Graves. Had some kind of a deal been cut? Was Evans threatened? Manlow was tough, and I knew he didn't always play by the rules. Tice was even tougher, and I knew firsthand that to Tice, the rules were sometimes a mere inconvenience.

"Yeah, he told me some stuff," Evans said cautiously. *Outstanding. I had him.*

"Including the fingerprint?"

"Yeah."

"The DA's lead investigator told you about Durgeon's fingerprint found at the scene?"

"That's right."

"And about the gun?"

"He did."

"He told you about the statement Durgeon made about the gun?"

"Yes."

"And during that very same interview," I stepped on *interview*, "Manlow showed you a photograph of Duane Durgeon, didn't he?"

Evans eyes shifted to Manlow then quickly back to me. "Yes."

"And it was when Manlow, this man sitting right here, told you about the fingerprint and the statement and the gun, that you, for the first time in the history of this case, identified Duane Durgeon as the shooter, wasn't it?"

"I guess it was."

"Is that a yes?"

"Yes."

"So it was a full nine months after the murders when you first ID'd Durgeon as the shooter?"

"I guess so, yes."

"This all happened after your conversation with district attorney investigator Manlow. This fellow sitting right here?" I motioned to Manlow, who was writing furiously on a legal pad that he then slid over to Tice. I continued to point at Manlow, until he sensed me and looked up.

"He didn't tell me what to do."

I walked over to counsel table, and Suzelle handed me a one-foot by two-foot blowup of Durgeon's mug shot. "Your Honor, I have a photograph of Duane Durgeon taken after his arrest. May I approach the clerk and have it marked as Defense A for identification?"

"You may."

It was marked and I walked it over to Tice. "Your Honor, may the record reflect I am showing Defense A to opposing counsel?"

"So reflected."

"May I approach the witness with Defense A?"

"You may."

I worked my way up to the witness stand and asked, "Mr. Evans, is this the man, you just told us a few minutes ago, who shot Doree?"

"Yes."

I thumbtacked Durgeon's photograph to corkboard that was to the jurors' right. Suzelle then walked over to me and handed me another photograph, this first one a similarly sized mug shot of Anthony Graves when he was taken into custody. "Your Honor, I have a photograph of Anthony Graves; may I have it marked as Defense B for ID?"

"You may."

"May the record reflect I am showing Defense B to the prosecutor?"

"So reflected." As I approached Tice, he waved me off. Undeterred, I placed it on his table. He could not ignore it, and finally nodded.

"May I approach the witness?"

"You may."

Holding up the photograph of Graves, I asked, "Is this a photograph of the man you identified at the police station as the killer the day after the murders?"

"It is."

"And this is how he looked on that day?"

"Yes," Evans said, with a note of resignation.

I tacked Graves's photograph next to Durgeon's. They were strikingly similar. Both had long unkempt hair and sported full facial hair. Beyond that, they had broad faces; Graves's eyes were set wider apart that Durgeon's.

Suzelle, who had remained up by the witness stand, handed me a third photograph. This was a blowup of the mug shot of Dan Atwell taken when he was arrested in the dope raid along with his mother and Durgeon. As I approached the clerk, I asked to have the photo of Dan Atwell marked as Defense C for ID. The court nodded. I walked over to Tice and carefully laid it out in front of him. With a glance, he took in the photograph and slid back in his chair and stood. Looking at Harbarger, he said, "May we approach?"

Harbarger motioned us up. As we neared the bench, Harbarger covered her microphone. "John?"

"There are limits. I renew my objection to this baseless persecution of Dan Atwell."

Harbarger asked, "I assume this is in reference to the photograph Jake just marked?" *Surprisingly, I had moved to first-name status.*

"Judge," Tice explained, "I understand the role of defense counsel as well as anyone, and I know that there is a line that prevents counsel from dragging in people without sufficient basis and implying they are somehow involved in a heinous crime." Tice's voice was a whispered fury. "Counsel has obliterated that line."

Harbarger looked at me, inviting a response. "Judge, I guess I missed the lecture in law school where I had to clear my case with the prosecutor."

When I did not offer more, Tice started to speak but Harbarger cut him off with her hand held up. "John, we've covered this ground several times already. Counsel has previously indicated a good-faith basis, and on his representation and in light of recent events, I am going to let him proceed."

Tice was exasperated. "I want a hearing outside the presence of the jury to see what evidence he has to validate any good-faith belief."

Harbarger's mouth tightened. In a whispered voice liquid with anger, she said, "Mr. Tice, that is my determination, not yours, and I have made my ruling." Looking over her glasses at Tice, Harbarger dismissed us from the bench.

Returning to counsel table, I picked up the Atwell photograph and, turning to Harbarger, said, "Your Honor, may the record reflect I have shown the photo to the prosecutor?"

"So reflected."

I walked to the board and tacked Atwell's photo next to the other two. *Here's to you, Danny-boy. May you rot in hell.* His photo was a younger version of the other two. There was no gray, but the long hair and facial hair were reasonably similar.

The jurors were studying the three photographs. I gave them some time and then turned back to Evans. "Mr. Evans, how about this last photograph? Have you seen this man before?"

"No," Evans said, as he turned to the board and stared at the photograph of Atwell.

I gave Evans a smile, indicating that of course I knew he would say that. "Mr. Evans, that photo of Dan Atwell was taken about the time of the murders. Would you say that his hair is about the same length as Mr. Durgeon's hair?"

"Pretty close."

"How about the beard, similar?"

"Roughly."

"Mustache?"

"Again, similar."

"Let's see, you were about forty, forty-five feet away?"

"About that."

"And it was still a little dark and foggy?"

"Yeah."

"And you had just come out of a sleep?"

"That's right."

"And you saw a gun?"

"I did."

"And a naked woman, right?"

"Right."

"And it happened very quickly?"

"Yeah, that's right. But I saw—" He cut himself off.

I hesitated. I had intended to stop at this point, but what else was Evans going to say? I worked my way back to my table. I was buying time to calculate where I was and what I might get. Again I rolled the dice. "Mr. Evans, take another look at photo B, Mr. Graves. Could he have been the shooter?"

"No, I don't . . . no, he wasn't."

Then a whole new line of questioning struck me. *I hoped it wouldn't be snake eyes.* "What if I told you that at the time of the murders, Mr. Graves lived just a few houses down from the Palms, and that he was a convicted rapist, and that Anthony Graves told someone that 'Doree was a hot little thing.' Would that change your mind?"

"Objection." Tice was out of his chair. "He is asking the witness to speculate. Mr. Evans said the defendant was the person who shot Doree Blanco."

Without waiting for the judge, I answered Tice's speaking objection. "Your Honor, Investigator Manlow planted the seeds for a misidentification when he tainted Mr. Evans with the incriminating evidence against Mr. Durgeon. I have the right to explore."

Harbarger cut me off. "I will not have this conduct. I alone will decide what evidence is admissible. I will again admonish both of you about speaking objections. Mr. Tice, your objection is overruled." Then turning to Evans, she said, "Mr. Evans, you may answer the question."

Evans looked at the judge. "I don't remember the question."

Harbarger nodded at me. Repeating questions is always useful. They tend to resonate with the jury. "What if, at the time of the murders, you were aware that Graves lived just a couple of houses down from the Palms, and that he was a convicted rapist, and that he told someone that Doree Blanco was a 'hot little thing.' Would that change your mind?"

Evans shook his head and said, "That don't change my mind."

"Let's turn back to Dan Atwell. Could he have been the shooter?"

"He wasn't."

"Okay. What if you knew that Atwell was once Doree's

boyfriend, that he blamed Doree for ruining his football career and getting him kicked out of school, and that his mother is a key witness against Mr. Durgeon. And what if you knew that Atwell walked away from a state prison sentence when his mother agreed to testify against Durgeon. Does this information in any way change your mind as to whether Dan Atwell might have been the shooter?"

Evans was ready. "That don't change my mind either."

"Of course it doesn't, Mr. Evans." I paused, looking at him. "Your Honor, I am finished with this person."

≈≈≈

We broke for lunch. As Suzelle and I made our way from the courtroom, I saw Taylor Hunt talking to Tice. They were oblivious to me and the rest of the world. *Equal time for Tice made sense.* Yet her talking to him irked me. What was that about? Suzelle and I made our way to the courthouse cafeteria, where we had soup and split a sandwich.

"Evans looked really pathetic," Suzelle offered. "But most of all, your insinuation that Manlow manipulated him makes them seem kinda sleazy."

"Manlow knew better than that. It was sleazy. I wonder what they promised Evans to prostitute himself."

After lunch, we settled back into the courtroom. Durgeon was remarkably subdued; the belt was a serious deterrent. I noted Taylor Hunt in her usual third-row seat. Harbarger emerged and ascended and called us back to order. Evans was back on the witness stand as Harbarger beckoned Tice to cross-examine.

Tice went back and cleaned up Evans's testimony, most particularly attempting to explain away the ID of Graves, that it was simply nerves coupled with a general similarity of appearance.

Tice also went to pains to establish that Evans was not manipulated by Manlow.

On redirect, I asked, "What were you promised by Manlow if you backed off your ID of Graves?"

Tice went off. "Objection! He's impugning that character of Investigator Manlow."

"Approach," commanded Harbarger.

"Mr. Clearwater, you are on very thin ice here."

"Your Honor, the facts could not be more clear. Manlow went to Evans to manipulate and alter his story. In my view, that was serious misconduct by the lead investigator in this case."

Tice began but was cut off. Harbarger said, "That was way over the line, and you very well know better. I am holding you in contempt. We will deal with sanctions at the conclusion of trial. This has been a contentious trial from the opening bell. I am ordering both of you experienced trial lawyers to step back and comport yourselves as officers of the court." *I had fired a cheap shot and deserved the rebuke. But I hope the point registered with the jurors.*

I had nothing further for Evans. It was about three o'clock. The judge again had other matters and we adjourned for the day. *Hell, if we got more than four hours a day, I'm afraid Harbarger would pass out from overwork.* My pique at Harbarger wasn't entirely fair; I was being overly harsh. The judge, of course, had other matters on her calendar. I was just anxious to put this trial to bed.

CHAPTER 37

THE PUMP WOULDN'T TALK

A short while later, Suzelle and I joined Durgeon in his holding cell. Suzelle handed him a Dr. Pepper. He thanked her and said to me, "You really punched out Evans." I had obviously won back Durgeon's good graces with my exam of Evans.

"I hope the twelve in the box share your view." I pulled a chair close to the small table where Durgeon remained seated. Suzelle once again took up her spot far from Durgeon.

"I think I was able to establish that Manlow has been playing fast and loose with the evidence. If we can get the jurors to thinking that Tice and Manlow can't be trusted, we've accomplished something."

"I'm with you, counselor," Durgeon said enthusiastically.

"Now if we just had a better idea what happened that night." I was looking Durgeon dead in his eyes.

"I can do a lot better than that," said an upbeat Durgeon. "Put me on the stand, and I'll tell them I wasn't anywhere near that place." Here it was. He wanted to testify. I figured we would be right back here. *Nuts!*

I cut him off with the flick of my hand. "Tice will impeach the shit out of you with the Utah priors." I waited, giving him a chance to speak, but he just sat there. So I went on, "We might have raised reasonable doubt as to whether you were involved. I think we leave well enough alone. We have a fighting chance as things stand now."

He appeared to be weighing my words and slowly shook his head. "I don't know, man. It just feels like I gotta get up there." He paused. "This is my life, man."

"What would you say?"

He shifted into that rocking motion again, psyching himself to begin. If the pump was going to give it up, I did not want to do anything to interrupt the flow. I gave an almost imperceptible nod, hoping it would enhance, not retard. Durgeon collapsed back into his chair as if reconsidering. Behind his narrow eyes, I could almost hear the tumblers rolling. We waited. He gradually began shifting his body out of his slouch until he was on the edge of his chair. Both his arms rested on the table separating us. In a jailhouse voice, honed through years of concern for overheard jailhouse conversations, he spoke. "I'm so fucking pissed at Manlow's shit."

Manlow? Manlow and not Tice, was the focus of his anger. Manlow? In a flash of introspection, it made sense. While Tice and I had been pitted against one another in the courtroom, Manlow and Durgeon were pitted against one another in a more urgent sense, that of hunter and hunted.

"I've been thinking about what you said," Durgeon continued. "Rode's dead, Danny's an asshole, and this is my last shot." He took a deep breath, and still hunkered forward, began. "When Tina and me got back from looking at that apartment . . ." He stopped, shaking his head. "No," he said. "I can't—I just can't do it, man."

CHAPTER 38

THE TEMPTRESS

It was eight o'clock that evening. I was alone and reading the daily transcripts of that day's testimony. Lisa had left an hour ago, Suzelle was in her room, and Duke was wherever Duke was. The Ramada landline phone rang. It was Taylor Hunt.

"Can you talk?" she asked.

Surprised, I answered, "I can."

"I'm down in the hotel bar, can I buy you a drink?" I flashed to Lisa. What was this about? The trial? Or was this about something other than the trial? I had just gotten back in Lisa's good graces. I couldn't envision any positives developing from a drink with Taylor.

"I am buried in trial transcripts right now."

"One drink?"

I hesitated. *Don't waver, Clearwater.* "Taylor, I'm tempted, but I've got to prep for tomorrow."

"Okay . . ." She drew it out as if I was missing out on the opportunity of a lifetime. *Maybe I was.* "See you in court tomorrow."

What was that about? Most likely a reporter looking for some insight on the trial. *Yeah, I'm sure that's what that was.*

I didn't bother watching the eleven o'clock news that night.

CHAPTER 39

MANLOW

The next morning, Harbarger gaveled us to order. "Mr. Clearwater?"

"Your Honor, the defense calls Harley Manlow."

Not surprisingly, Tice was immediately up, and we were once more summoned to the bench. "Here we go again," Tice said, as we reached the bench.

Harbarger looked at me. "Mr. Clearwater?"

"Detective Manlow headed this investigation from day one. It was Manlow who interviewed Christina Atwell, it was Manlow who most likely was instrumental in the deal the Atwells received. It was Manlow who flew back to Cincinnati to 'interview' Ron Evans. I think Manlow has access to Dan Atwell and is deliberately hiding him from my investigator." I looked at Tice. "You bet I want to question him."

Without waiting for Harbarger, Tice said, "I renew my objection to counsel's continued persistence in attacking Dan Atwell. Atwell is not on trial here. Like I have said several times before, this is just a desperate defense lawyer grabbing at straws. He as much as admitted that he is only guessing at what Detective Manlow knows."

Harbarger pursed her lips and pointedly failed to respond to Tice. After a moment, she gave me a nod and said, "Bring him on. Let's find out what he knows."

I started to turn back to my table, but Tice had not moved. "Why are you letting him get away with this?"

Harbarger looked with displeasure at Tice. "When we started this trial, you said that you wanted him"—nodding at me—"to do a competent job so that any conviction would stick. However inartfully you might have phrased your sentiment, you were correct about one thing. Should this trial result in a death conviction, I am not going to be reversed again because defense counsel was denied any marginally plausible area of exploration. While I may agree with you that his pursuit of Dan Atwell is somewhat speculative, he has produced some evidence that suggests Atwell might have been involved. Until he is proven wrong, I am going to give him some leeway." Leaning further into Tice, she said softly, "Don't you ever challenge me like that again."

We retreated, and Manlow was sworn.

"Your Honor, leave to treat Detective Manlow as hostile?" I only wanted to use leading questions.

"You may."

"Detective Manlow, where is Dan Atwell?"

"I don't know." No hesitancy, a hint of defiance.

"Do you have any way of ascertaining his whereabouts?"

"I'm not certain."

"By that, do you mean you know someone who might know of his whereabouts?" Everyone in the courtroom knew Christina Atwell was the someone under discussion.

"Yes."

"And would that someone be Christina Atwell?"

"That's correct."

"Have you at any time during the course of your investigation into the Blanco murders asked Ms. Atwell the whereabouts of her son?"

"I have not."

"Had it occurred to you at any time during your investigation of the murders that Dan Atwell might in any way be involved?"

"I did not believe he was involved during the investigation that culminated in the arrest of Duane Durgeon, and nothing that has happened since has led me to a different conclusion."

"Your Honor, may we approach?" I asked.

Harbarger motioned us up. "What is it?"

"He has just opened the door to Atwell's recent conduct." Harbarger nodded for me to continue. "His comment that 'nothing that has happened since has led me to a different conclusion' will not withstand scrutiny. I want to examine him on the attacks on Ms. Frost and me."

Tice responded, "This is a ploy by counsel to provoke the witness into a particular response and then attempt to exploit that which he provoked. He is trying to backdoor what this court has already ruled inadmissible."

"He is right, Mr. Clearwater," Harbarger said. "My ruling stands. I will have no mention of recent events involving the attacks." *It was a shot. The ruling was correct.*

After we resumed our positions, I asked, "During your investigation, were you aware that Dan Atwell had raped Carrie Washburn just months before the murders?"

"No."

"So you did not know that during Atwell's rape of Ms. Washburn, he tied her up and beat her, correct?"

"I had no way of knowing that."

"Doree was tied up, wasn't she?"

"Yes."

"She was also beaten?"

"That's correct, but she was not raped."

"We don't really know that, do we? The medical examiner's findings were inconclusive, and in fact, Mr. Tice produced testimony that she did suffer some trauma that could be consistent with rape, isn't that so?"

"From what I heard, the medical examiner concluded no rape."

"That's fine, Detective. That's one of the reasons we have juries, to resolve any factual disputes." I nodded agreeably. "It is true that Doree was found naked, isn't it?"

"Yes."

I paused before moving on. "Detective, would it be fair to say that Ron Evans has always been very consistent in describing the shooter as a big man?" *Move around, keep him off balance.*

"Yes."

"And isn't it true that Evans has always been very consistent in describing the shooter as having long hair?"

"Yes."

"And further, Mr. Evans has always been consistent in describing the shooter as having facial hair?"

"That's right."

"Detective, let's turn back to the time of the murders and talk about the physical similarity between Dan Atwell and Duane Durgeon. You did have occasion to see Atwell while he was in custody on the narcotics charges in November 2004, didn't you?"

"I did."

"It would be fair to say that at the time, both men were big?"

"Durgeon was bigger."

I gave him a half grin and repeated, "It would be fair to say both men were big?"

"Yes."

"It would be fair to say both men had long brownish hair?"

"Yes."

"And both had facial hair?"

"Yes."

"At the time you 'interviewed' Ron Evans"—again I emphasized the word "interviewed"—"he had ID'd only one person as the shooter, hadn't he?"

"That's correct."

"And as we all know, that identification was of Anthony Graves, wasn't it?"

"That's right."

"When you had your discussion with Evans months later in Ohio, you told him that Durgeon's fingerprint had been found, didn't you?"

"It wasn't like that at all, counselor." He offered a wry condescending grin. "He made the ID of Graves at a time when he was under the stress of seeing the shooting. I agree with Lieutenant McCoy that that ID was pretty worthless."

"Let me see if I recall correctly, Detective. Immediately on seeing Graves, Mr. Evans said, and I quote, 'That's him, get me the hell out of here.' Is that what you recall?"

"That's what he said then."

"When you told Evans that Durgeon's fingerprint was found, were you concerned in any way that it might influence Ron Evans?"

"No."

I paused and let that answer hang in the air before asking, "When you told Evans that Durgeon had made some incriminating statements, were you concerned in any way that it might influence Evans?"

"I told Evans in general terms about the state of the investigation."

"Returning to my question, when you told Evans about some incriminating statements made by Durgeon, were you concerned in any way that it might influence him?"

"No."

Again, I let that answer settle in before asking, "During that interview, you only showed Mr. Evans one photograph, isn't that right?"

"I think that's right."

"If you are unclear, I can show you your report." *Lock him down.*

"It was one."

"It was Durgeon's photo, wasn't it?"

"Yeah."

"Were you concerned that by showing only Durgeon's photo, that could influence him?"

"In hindsight, that wasn't the best practice," Manlow conceded.

"So back to my question. You were concerned that only showing one photograph might have influenced Mr. Evans?"

"It wasn't the best practice. But given my full investigation, including my overall interview with Mr. Evans, I don't think I influenced him."

I shook my head at his evasiveness. "Okay, let's move forward. You described Evans's ID of Durgeon as tentative?"

"Correct."

"It was not powerful or even conclusive, was it?"

"Like I said, it was tentative. It was only a photograph. When he saw Durgeon in court a few days ago, that's when he made a positive ID."

"Detective, when you began your interview with Mr. Evans, he had only identified Anthony Graves as the shooter, correct?"

"Correct."

"By the time you concluded your interview, he had become settled on Duane Durgeon as the shooter; did I get that right?"

"I guess that's one way of looking at it."

"You were the investigating officer during Mr. Durgeon's first trial, weren't you?"

"Yes, I was."

"Mr. Tice was the trial prosecutor during that trial, wasn't he?"

"Yes."

"Isn't it true that the two of you decided not to call Mr. Evans as a witness during that trial?"

"That was not my decision to make."

"It was Mr. Tice's decision to make, correct?"

"Yes."

"That jury never got the chance to hear from Mr. Evans, did they?"

"He wasn't called as a witness."

"Ron Evans wasn't called as a witness, despite the fact that he was the only eyewitness, true?"

"That's right."

"And during this trial we are in right now, the prosecution did not call Evans, correct?"

"Right."

"Isn't it true that the reason the prosecutor never called the only eyewitness was because his only true and powerful identification was of someone other than Duane Durgeon?"

"Objection, speculation." An angry Tice was standing.

"Sustained."

I nodded, expecting the sustained objection. "Okay, Detective, let's turn back to Dan Atwell. During the course of your investigation, you never uncovered the fact that Durgeon and Atwell knew each other, did you?"

"Atwell was never a suspect. I had no reason to investigate him."

"That is curious to me. You, of course, knew Christina and Duane Durgeon lived together, didn't you?"

"I knew that."

"And you knew that Christina, Durgeon, and Dan were all arrested together on the felony drug charges just days after the murders, correct?"

"I did."

"So you knew that Dan and Durgeon were involved in the same felony drug enterprise, didn't you?"

"True."

"You were aware that Christina bailed herself and Dan out but left Durgeon in jail?"

"I was aware of that."

"You knew that the deal Christina struck with the DA involved reduced charges against her son Dan, correct?"

"Yes."

"And that deal involved lenient treatment for herself and Dan in exchange for incriminating Durgeon?"

"That is my understanding."

"As you reflect back over your investigation, does it concern you that Dan Atwell's mother was the person who first implicated Duane Durgeon?"

He paused and considered before answering. "When you are dealing with these kinds of cases, it's not the upstanding people who usually know anything pertinent to these investigations."

"Let me ask that question again. Does it concern you that Dan Atwell's mother was the person who first implicated Duane Durgeon?"

"No, it doesn't."

"Detective, let's switch gears again. Would it have been

significant to your investigation that Dan Atwell harbored resentment toward Doree?"

"No."

"So the fact that he blamed Doree for getting him kicked off the football team and expelled from school is of no consequence?"

"No, that happened in high school."

"I have one last question. Is it possible that under the intense pressure to arrest someone for these terrible crimes, you latched onto the first likely suspect and channeled your efforts to building a case only against him?"

"Absolutely not."

I gave him an *of course you were going to say that* look and said, "Detective, you have been very helpful to all of us in better understanding your work in this case. Your Honor, I have nothing further for this witness." I walked back to counsel table, moving somewhat better. As I pulled out my chair to resume my place between Durgeon and Suzelle, there was movement from behind and to my left and then a loud explosion.

Someone yelled, "He's got a gun!" The panicked scream triggered an echoed response of shrieks and shouts. Confused and shocked, I saw Durgeon half standing, his back arched, a look of disbelief on his face. My first thought was Dan Atwell. How could he have gotten past security with a gun? Then I looked back into the face of Frank Bennett, Doree's father. His arms were extended, both hands aiming a revolver still pointed at Durgeon. Another shot and Durgeon's body jerked and fell against me, pulling me with him to the ground. Pandemonium reigned as people fought to get out the double doors of the courtroom against several uniforms struggling to get in. My mind worked in slow motion, but my hearing seemed extraordinarily acute. I heard the bailiffs grunting and swearing as they worked to overpower the struggling and screaming Frank

Bennett. Looking over Durgeon's still figure, I saw Suzelle cowering beside the overturned counsel table. I pushed Durgeon off and crawled to her and wrapped my arms around her while she huddled against me.

"Get the paramedics in here!" a voice yelled. Durgeon's face was ashen, and blood covered his upper body. He lay unmoving. Within minutes, he was bundled onto a gurney and wheeled out into the hall. I couldn't tell if he was breathing.

Suzelle and I were ushered hurriedly into the judge's chambers. A suddenly very old Judge Harbarger slumped against her office desk. She motioned us to the couch. Tice was escorted in, yelling orders over his shoulder. A brawny bailiff with a flushed face yelled for him to shut the hell up and remain in the room. Through the closed door, I could hear muffled shouting.

I put my arm around Suzelle. Without looking up, she whispered, "He's dead, isn't he?" Her concern for Durgeon surprised me. She was right about being tough enough for this. *Now if I could convince myself that I was tough enough.* Hell, back when I was a prosecutor, there was hardly ever a gun fired in a courtroom. How in the hell did Bennett get a gun past the metal detectors?

"I don't know," I said softly, "but he's probably okay." I was unwilling to admit that two shots to the torso was very not okay.

In a resigned voice, Harbarger asked, "Is Durgeon dead?"

"I don't know," I answered.

Tice sat on the edge of his chair, his legs apart, his body hunched forward, elbows on his knees. He said nothing.

No one moved. No one spoke. Minutes passed. The noise beyond the door lost its edge. Tice lifted his head toward me. "You sonofabitch!" He stared at me through slitted eyes. "This damn case should never have come back."

Harbarger turned to look at him. "That's enough," she said hoarsely. A heavy silence descended and continued until Sergeant Booker entered the room and said arrangements had been made to take us back to the hotel. And no, he did not know Durgeon's condition.

☙ ☙ ☙

Back at the room, I poured us each a drink, and as I leaned back on the couch, I became aware of a stickiness on my back and peeled off my jacket. A large glob of congealed blood stained my back and right shoulder. Durgeon's blood, and lots of it. I removed my shirt, and Suzelle got a towel, wet it, cleaned me up. Draping a clean towel over my shoulder, I lowered myself back onto the upholstered chair opposite Suzelle and took a long pull of Scotch. Suzelle finished her drink, stretched out on the couch, and was soon asleep. Strange reaction; maybe her system needed to shut down. I called Lisa. I didn't know if she had heard about what happened, but I wanted to let her know we were okay. She did not pick up, so I left a voice message. I closed my eyes and tried to make my mind a blank. The cell jarred me awake. It was Duke.

"Jake, I'm at the hospital." Although he had quit smoking years ago, he still carried the hoarse quality of the chronic smoker.

"And?"

"He was shot twice. One was through and through, and the other in his shoulder. He's out of surgery."

"Sounds like he's going to be okay."

"Looks like it. He's a tough shit."

"Thank God for that."

"Don't go soft on me, Jake. Durgeon's still Durgeon." A sardonic chuckle. "I'll see you in a while."

Suzelle had come alert and was sitting on the edge of the couch, waiting to hear the news. I wondered if she felt what a small part of me felt. If Durgeon had died, this would be over. We could fold our tent and go home. Start living normal lives again. *What a selfish and cowardly thought, Clearwater.*

"He didn't die, did he?" she tentatively asked.

"No, sounds like he's going to make it." *I'm glad she couldn't read my mind.*

"What will happen to Mr. Bennett now?" Her thoughts had switched at adrenaline speed.

"He'll be charged and given a psychiatric exam."

"In some ways, I can't blame him. I mean, if he's not psychiatrically responsible."

"The circumstances and psych exam will go a long way to determining his fate."

I got up and poured us some more Scotch and added some water. Suzelle swirled the Scotch in her glass like a veteran. After a while, she asked, "Jake, how'd he get a gun into the courtroom?"

"I've been thinking about that. Remember the morning after Bennett's wife went off?" I said.

"Yeah, I noticed the next morning, they let him and his family walk around the detector with us."

"At the time, I didn't think much about it. Maybe they kept doing that."

Just then, Lisa hurried through the unlocked door, quickly surveyed both of us for injuries, and then hugged me and sat on the arm of my chair. "Thank God you two are alright. Sounds like you were both really close to getting shot."

"True enough," I said. She took a big swallow of my drink and then went over and made herself a drink.

She asked, "What about Durgeon?"

"Duke called and said he's going to be okay. Surgery was successful."

"Gun in the courtroom?" Lisa asked incredulously.

"I know, we were just discussing that. Our guess is that they let the victim's family members walk around the detector," Suzelle said.

"Those are precisely the people who need to get scanned. What were they thinking of?" Lisa said.

"That is only our theory. I'm certain there'll soon be some terminated bailiffs."

We all thought about that. Suzelle then asked, "What's going to happen now?"

"I guess that depends on Durgeon's condition," I said.

"Will the trial just resume when he's healed? Just pick up where it left off?" Lisa asked.

"If Durgeon's condition permits." I put my unfinished drink down and slowly got up. I felt a hundred and fifty years old. "I'm going to lay down. Lisa?" I gestured to Lisa. She walked to the bedroom with me.

I awoke at five in the afternoon, still exhausted. Lisa was awake. We walked into the living area. Duke was drinking a Corona. Suzelle was still asleep on the couch. The three of us retired to the balcony and Lisa asked, "How close were you and the kid from getting shot?"

"Inches."

"Dammit, Jake," she said, shaking her head.

"Yeah, dammit Jake." Duke said, doubling down.

CHAPTER 40

WAITING FOR DURGEON

The next morning, two detectives came to the suite and interviewed Suzelle and me about the shooting. They were going through the motions. There were probably seventy-five other witnesses, including a judge and several bailiffs. Chances are the basic facts would not be in dispute.

Later that day, Booker drove Suzelle and me to the hospital and then waited in the car. The deputy sheriffs who stood outside Durgeon's room let us in after checking ID in a thorough and deliberately time-consuming way. *They should have been so careful with Frank Bennett.* Durgeon was lying in bed, his head slightly elevated. An ankle cuff protruded from under a blanket at the end of the bed. He was shirtless, and his right arm and shoulder were wrapped. His eyes were closed. His face looked bloodless. We left the room without disturbing him and found the nurse's station. Of course, none of the nurses would tell us his condition. Finally, a Dr. Burge was paged. Fifteen minutes later, Burge appeared and motioned us into a conference room. He explained that Durgeon had been shot twice, once in the right bicep and again in the right shoulder. The bicep wound had punctured the muscle but had not struck bone. The shoulder wound was more serious, as the bullet had cracked the shoulder blade. He said that Durgeon's arm and shoulder would be immobilized for up to eight weeks. He also said that barring complications, Durgeon could be released within a week to ten days.

When we went back to Durgeon's room, his eyes were open and looking at me from the moment we entered.

"That's some goddamned security system they got in that courthouse," he said, through a smirk.

"No question about that."

"Humph."

"How you feeling?"

"Just fuckin' great."

"Much pain?"

"They got me pretty loaded."

"Anything I can get you?"

"Yeah, I want to know what happened. Was it Danny? Nobody tells me shit."

"It was Doree's father, Frank Bennett. Somehow he got a gun in there."

"Did they shoot him?" *Interesting question.*

"No."

"Too bad," he grunted. After a short pause he added, "Probably give him a medal."

It was my turn to grunt.

"Anybody else shot?" Durgeon wanted answers. *Can't blame him.*

"Only you."

"Pretty goddamn lucky for you counselors. You two were right next to me."

"We're real lucky folk."

"Fuck you," he said, and managed a slight grin. "What's going to happen now?" That seemed to be the burning question.

"My best guess is that Harbarger will put everything on ice until you're ready to go."

"You talk to the doc?"

I nodded.

"What's he say about that? Even he won't talk to me."

"He's saying you'll be up in a week or so."

I slapped my hand on the foot of the bed preparing to leave. "Take it easy. We'll be back Monday after I meet with the judge and catch you up on things."

His eyes closed but he managed, "Watch your back, counselor."

❧❧❧

On Monday, three days post shooting, all the principals, save Durgeon, were gathered in Harbarger's chambers. Harbarger had Dr. Burge on the speakerphone. Burge's estimate regarding Durgeon's recovery and release from the hospital had not changed. Harbarger thanked him and disconnected.

"Suggestions?" Harbarger said as she looked around the room.

Of course, the ever-reticent Tice had suggestions. "It's imperative that we get this trial resumed as quickly as possible. I'm worried about losing jurors. If Dr. Burge says Friday, then let's do Friday, no more."

"Mr. Clearwater?" Harbarger looked at me.

"I suggest we push it to next Monday. I want Mr. Durgeon fully functional. Particularly, off drugs."

Harbarger nodded agreement. "I'll order everyone back Monday, a week from today, at which time we will again confer with Mr. Durgeon's physician. Now let's talk about time estimates for finishing the guilt phase. Mr. Clearwater, you've just finished with Detective Manlow. John, any cross?" *It was back to last names for me. Tice was still John.*

"Very briefly," Tice answered.

"Fair enough. Will there be any more witnesses for the defense?"

"I don't know yet," I answered.

"Can you be more forthcoming?" Harbarger arched an eyebrow.

"Our investigation is continuing. If something fruitful develops, I may have more witnesses."

Harbarger persisted. "Would it be fair to say you don't anticipate any further witnesses at this time?"

"That is fair. Subject, however, to further investigation."

Harbarger dismissed us. "One week from today."

☙ ☙ ☙

Tuesday, Booker drove Suzelle and me to the hospital. Durgeon was alone and looking a bit stronger. He looked at Suzelle and said, "I'm glad you're okay. That was a hell of a thing."

"Thanks, Duane. I'm glad you're going to be okay."

We pulled up some chairs, and I caught him up on Harbarger's timeline. As I stood to leave, he said, in his don't-mess-with-me voice, "I'm going to testify."

I mentally rolled my eyes. "We have had this discussion. It's still a bad idea."

"I ain't discussin'. I'm going to do it."

I flopped back in my chair and sighed. "You testify, like I have said a number of times, Tice will slice and dice you. We've got a fighting chance with things the way they are."

"That ain't good enough."

"Better than no chance." We sat staring at each other without speaking.

I relented first. "What would you say?"

"I'm going to give them Danny-boy."

"We've backdoored that theory. There's enough there already. We do not need to run the risk of things unraveling with your testimony."

"*We* ain't running any risk. *I'm* running the risk. It's my ass. It's my call."

I stared at him. "You've heard my opinion."

"Heard it and don't give a damn."

I swallowed my frustration and anger. I could feel the wheels falling off. "I will not be party to your suicide."

"My ass, my call." He pushed the control declining his bed and closed his eyes as his head descended.

CHAPTER 41

A DUMB-ASS MISTAKE

The next morning, I had just dripped my way into the hotel room after my morning swim when my cell alerted. Judge Harbarger's secretary informed us that we were to be at the hospital outside Durgeon's room at 2:00 p.m. that afternoon. She did not elaborate.

When we arrived, Harbarger, Tice, and Harbarger's clerk, court reporter, and bailiff were all waiting in the hall. Harbarger nodded at me, turned to the court reporter, and said, "Let's get this all on the record. Late yesterday afternoon, Mr. Durgeon contacted my office and requested that I terminate defense counsels' representation of him and appoint a new lawyer. Mr. Clearwater, were you aware this was in the offing?"

I exhaled slowly. "Judge, if we are going to have a hearing on whether Mr. Durgeon gets a new lawyer, I believe it is appropriate to do it outside the presence of the prosecutor."

"I am well aware of the procedure. My inquiry was whether you were aware that your client was going to make such a motion."

"I'll be happy to discuss what I know once Mr. Tice has been dismissed from the discussion." Tice stood by impassively. He knew the procedure, even if Harbarger acted like it was foreign to her experience.

"Very well," Harbarger said for the record. "At this time, the court, my clerk, my bailiff, my court reporter, and defense counsel will adjourn to Mr. Durgeon's private hospital room for a hearing brought by Mr. Durgeon to terminate his defense counsel."

Tice turned and unhurriedly walked down the hall. The rest of us entered Durgeon's room. We stood in a crowded semicircle at the foot of his bed. The court reporter took a chair and set up her machine. Durgeon was silent, his eyes on me.

Harbarger began. "Mr. Durgeon, I understand that you are claiming that you and your lawyers have irreconcilable differences, and because of that, they can no longer provide you with adequate representation."

"That's right." Durgeon's tone was uncharacteristically respectful and subdued. "I'm gonna testify, and he don't want me to."

Harbarger shot me a look. "That's it?"

I nodded.

Harbarger turned to Durgeon with a pained look. "This basic philosophical problem is encountered time and again between the accused and their lawyer. The appellate courts have been very clear that the decision ultimately resides with the accused."

"If he testifies, it is without me," I said.

Harbarger jerked back to me. "That is not how it works." Her finger jabbed the air in my direction. "I am not relieving you."

"I will not participate if Durgeon testifies," I said flatly.

"Counsel, you will do what you are bound to do."

"With all due respect, Judge, I will not be a part of any action that increases Mr. Durgeon's chances of being convicted and perhaps executed."

"I will hear no more of this," Harbarger said. "Mr. Durgeon, your motion is denied. I find there is no basis for relieving counsel. You and your counsel are simply disagreeing on a tactical decision which is for you and counsel to work out."

"We ain't working it out," Durgeon persisted.

"Can you point to any reason other than the disagreement concerning your testimony?"

"That's enough." Durgeon's voice was getting louder, and his civility was fraying.

"No, Mr. Durgeon, it's not. Motion denied."

"Motion denied, my ass." Durgeon leaned forward to better confront the judge. The effort caused his face to contort in pain. "He's gone. I won't have him." This was the Durgeon we all had learned to dislike. The bailiff moved forward between Durgeon and the judge. *Apparently, the ankle-cuffed, bandaged, and medicated Durgeon represented a threat to Harbarger's well-being. Maybe they should strap the REACT belt back on him.*

Harbarger did take a step back and said, "He's the only lawyer you are going to get."

"Fuck you and fuck him!" Durgeon yelled. *Bloodied and bandaged, Durgeon was still Durgeon.*

Harbarger turned and slowly walked to the window. No one else moved. Still facing out the window, she said, "Mr. Clearwater, any suggestions?"

"Fresh out, Judge."

"You are being extremely helpful, counsel."

I had enough sense to let it pass. Harbarger walked back to the foot of the bed. "I am not appointing you a new lawyer. I am obligated, however, to advise you that you have a constitutional right to represent yourself. It is a terrible idea, especially in this type of case, but nevertheless it is your right. Is that what you want?"

Durgeon slowly shook his head and looked at me. Speaking to me, he finally said, "She's forcing my hand."

"I am not forcing anything," Harbarger said. "Do you want to continue with Mr. Clearwater and Ms. Frost or represent yourself?"

"If that's it, I'll go it alone."

"So be it. This trial is going to resume when your doctor says you are fit. I will not allow your foolish decision to delay these proceedings." She turned to me. "Mr. Clearwater, you and Ms. Frost are relieved as counsel. However, I am appointing you advisory counsel. In that capacity, should Mr. Durgeon have questions, he may consult you at his instance. You are forbidden from any communications with him except at his express request. In your role as advisory counsel, you will be present at every court proceeding. You are not to sit at counsel table, but rather behind counsel table. Get all your case files to Mr. Durgeon before noon tomorrow." Looking from me to Durgeon, Harbarger added, "Will there be anything else?" Without acknowledging our noes, she left the room, her adjutants following. *The judge's ruling was absolutely correct, pursuant to a Supreme Court decision of years past.*

Without looking at Durgeon, I walked from the room, diverse thoughts flashing through my mind like streaks during a meteor shower. It had all been for nothing. Durgeon would be convicted and once again thrust back onto death row. Tice would get his victory. Danny Atwell would never come to justice. Damn it all, I sincerely believed Durgeon didn't do it. For once in his miserable life, he was innocent.

ॐॐॐ

We packed up the files. They filled four boxes. I had Sergeant Booker drive them to Durgeon's hospital room.

"It's time for you to go home," I told Suzelle when we were done.

"No," she shook her head stubbornly. "I'm seeing this through to the end."

I grinned at her, appreciating her loyalty. "Well, at least go home for a few days until we crank it up again. I am."

"In that case, I will. I'll go see my parents."

"Good. I'll be back Sunday evening for the Monday hearing," I said.

"Okay, Jake," she said. "What do you expect to happen?"

"He will testify without anyone asking him questions, Tice will beat him up, and he will be convicted. As for the penalty phase, I can't envision a favorable outcome."

૱૱૱

Duke called that afternoon from Texas, where he was trying to round up penalty-phase witnesses.

"We've been fired," I began.

"I hate when that happens." No real surprise in his voice.

"He is bound and determined to testify."

"Dumb shit."

"That is pretty much my thought on the matter."

"I suppose my ongoing joyride through Texas is called off?"

"The funds have now run dry. Get on back. By the way, any luck with the Durgeon clan?"

"Not much. Most would rather have already forgotten him. Looks like mom and a younger brother will come out for the penalty phase. They'll both testify about Durgeon's dad and the bruising formative years."

"Good enough. I'm driving back home for a few days. Call me tomorrow when you get in. You'll need to let Durgeon know about who he can expect from Texas."

"Jake?"

"Yeah?"

"You gave it a good run. You had a shot."

CHAPTER 42

HOME COOKING

Lisa spent that night with me at the Ramada, and I invited her to come to Malibu for a couple of days. She couldn't. Work. On my drive home, I called Tony. "Let's have dinner tonight. I could use your company."

"Barbecue in the courtyard?"

"That works."

Instead of barbecue, Tony's wife Eve had a much better idea—chicken Parmesan focaccia sandwiches, a Greek pasta salad with Feta cheese, kalamata olives, red onion, and peppers in a light vinaigrette, two bottles of pinot grigio, and fresh raspberries with crème fraiche. We ate on the deck, with the rolling surf supplying the soundtrack.

Eve asked about my recovery. I told her, "My body's doing okay. I'm off the pain meds and onto Advil."

"You look worn out. I'm still worried about you."

"I'm fine." I gave her my healthiest smile to show her how fine I was.

It was good to be home, if only for a few days. We waited until after dinner to discuss the trial. That was at my request. They were surprised when I told them I believed it was Dan Atwell who had attacked and beaten me. They still labored under the impression that Lisa's ex might have been the culprit. I cleared that up and announced that Lisa and I were very much together. Once we worked through the attack on Suzelle and then Bennett's shooting of Durgeon, it seemed somewhat anticlimactic when I told them I had been fired.

"So your job, if I understand it correctly, is to sit, watch, and be at Durgeon's beck and call?" Tony asked, after being filled in.

"That is the nub of it."

"That seems ridiculous," Eve commented. *Well said.*

❧ ❧ ❧

During my brief hiatus, I indulged. I slept in on Saturday and took my ocean swim, reveling in the pleasure of the late-morning sunlight on the sea, the stretching of rejuvenated muscles, the good kind of tiredness as I climbed from the surf and laid on the sand. My limp was all but gone, as were the bruises and the lingering soreness I had been living with. However, even through the swim, the dread of returning to trial twisted and turned and hurt. If I could forgo returning, I would.

Suzelle had already arrived at the Ramada when I stepped into the suite Sunday evening. It was probably my imagination, but she looked different; more aware, more mature, and perhaps not so trusting. *I guess a death-penalty trial could do that to anyone.*

CHAPTER 43

WALKING INTO THE GRINDER

Monday morning we were again assembled, but this time we were back in the courtroom. The jury and public were excluded. Suzelle, Duke, and I were seated in the chairs just behind defense table. Durgeon sat alone. The bandages on his arm and shoulder were bulky and showed white beneath his dress shirt. I assumed, even though he had been shot, that the REACT belt was back in place.

"We are here to evaluate the condition of the defendant, Duane Durgeon, and determine when trial shall resume." Judge Harbarger was careful to make a thorough record. She knew her actions would be heavily scrutinized, should Durgeon be convicted.

Dr. Burge stepped to the witness stand and was sworn in. Harbarger asked him to briefly summarize his professional background. Harbarger then asked, "Dr. Burge, please give us your assessment of Mr. Durgeon's fitness to resume his trial."

"As you can see, Mr. Durgeon is ambulatory. He is on two milligrams of Vicodin two times a day for pain. It is my opinion that he is fit for trial."

"Thank you, Dr. Burge. Mr. Tice, do you have any questions of the doctor?"

"No."

"Mr. Durgeon?"

"Let's get it on," Durgeon replied. *The rush to doom. What a jackass.*

"Very well. Tomorrow morning at nine o'clock." Harbarger banged her gavel and was gone.

෨ ෨ ෨

That evening, Lisa, Suzelle, and I were in our Ramada home. We had ventured to a Thai restaurant and were now settled in to watch the eleven o'clock news. Ten minutes into the telecast, the anchor turned to Taylor Hunt. "Well, Taylor," he said, flashing his flawless teeth, "could there possibly be any more twists than we've already had in the Durgeon trial?" Without waiting for an answer, he added, "Explain, please, how a lawyer can be fired this late into a trial? Does this happen often?"

"Taking your second question first, it is rare when a lawyer is fired during trial," Hunt said. "As you can imagine, it could be and usually is very disruptive. However, the Supreme Court has held that an accused has a constitutional right to represent themselves, as long as it is a knowing and intelligent decision."

The anchor, with a smirk: "Was it intelligent for Duane Durgeon to fire his lawyers during his death-penalty trial?"

"Intelligent only in the sense that he understands the potential downside of his actions. That is quite different from asking if this was a wise thing for him to do."

"I see," said the anchor, with a trace of a smile. "So, Taylor, what can we expect to happen, now that the trial is set to resume?"

"That's hard to say, since we have yet to hear Mr. Durgeon speak. He's on his own now, with no lawyer, and events will probably be even more difficult to anticipate. The significant issue remaining is whether Durgeon will testify. It is my speculation that that decision may have led to the rift between him and his lawyers. It seems that we will have to wait and see, along with everyone else."

"We look forward to your report tomorrow evening with the latest."

Suzelle turned off the television and asked me, "What do you suppose he's going to say?"

"He told me he's going to implicate Dan Atwell."

"Well, isn't that good, to a point?" Lisa chimed in.

"Yes and no. It won't do him any good to implicate Atwell unless he absolves himself. And I see no way he can point a finger at Atwell unless he was there. If he testifies that they were both there, he may well screw himself. He is walking into a minefield. Our case was much better off raising possibilities of another shooter and then praying reasonable doubt would carry us over the line."

"But he has got to realize that, doesn't he?" Lisa asked.

"I believe he thinks that if the jury believes Atwell was the actual killer, they will look more kindly on him as just the other guy who just happened to be there. That might keep him off death row. But what if all he does is place himself in that apartment?"

"I don't think he sees that," Suzelle surmised.

"Doesn't or won't, I'm not sure which," I said.

⤟⤟⤟

Tuesday morning, I swam for forty minutes in the pool, ate a light breakfast, and rode back to the courthouse with Suzelle and Booker. Booker radioed our arrival and pulled his Crown Vic to the curb. As usual, a uniform emerged from the courthouse to escort us through the crush. Not surprisingly, media interest had grown beyond the local radius; several of the Los Angeles outlets were now in attendance. A courthouse shooting and other acts of mayhem are always media magnets. Television and radio vans lined the red curbs surrounding the courthouse. Several news people were talking into microphones, the courthouse framed behind them. As we neared the doors and were guided through the crowd, we could see that the line to pass through the metal screening extended back at least a hundred people. We were walked around the detector and delivered directly to the rapidly filling courtroom.

Suzelle and I drew celebrity stares as we made our way forward. We took the two chairs behind Durgeon, who sat at the defense table. Security inside the courtroom had been seriously amped up. Three deputies stood at the rail separating the participants from the public. These were in addition to the original bailiffs.

Durgeon seemed oblivious to the throng and the low buzz behind him as he was bent over a legal pad, scribbling away. He did not look up when we sat. Tice and Manlow occupied their table, looking loose and eager. They had to know that I was out because Durgeon and I disagreed over whether he would testify. It was the only conclusion to draw. There was nothing between them and an isolated and defenseless Durgeon. He was like an unsuspecting herd animal that had drifted too far from the safety of his brethren, and Tice was crouching in the tall weeds, ready to pounce and devour. After twenty long minutes, Judge Harbarger stepped to the bench, brought court to order, and ordered the jury in.

"Members of the jury, welcome back. It's only been a week and a half, but it seems much longer. There are a couple of things I need to discuss. It would be foolish of me to ask you to banish from your minds what you saw and heard the last day we were in trial. That will probably be with all of us for the rest of our lives. However, it is important that you all understand that those events have nothing to do with the job you have all taken an oath to do. You will also notice that Mr. Durgeon sits alone, and that Mr. Clearwater and Ms. Frost are seated behind him." Sixteen sets of eyes turned to us, along with every eye in the gallery. "Mr. Durgeon has decided that it is in his best interests to represent himself for the reminder of the trial. That is his constitutional right, and I have honored his request. It is important that none of you speculate as to Mr. Durgeon's reasons. Again, that is not central to the task before you. With that said, let's pick up where we left off. Mr. Tice, I believe it was your opportunity to examine Mr. Manlow."

Tice stood and said, "Your Honor, I have no questions of Detective Manlow." *Why waste time cleaning up after Manlow when the main feast was at hand?*

"Very well. Mr. Durgeon, does the defense have any more witnesses?"

"I'm going to testify."

There was an outburst from the courtroom. Harbarger banged her gavel, and the room quieted instantly. "At this time, I am going to ask the jurors to step back into the deliberation room." Harbarger waited while the bailiffs escorted the jurors out of the courtroom. She then instructed the bailiffs to leave on the REACT belt, which was tucked beneath Durgeon's shirt, but remove the shackles from his ankles. Restraints are considered prejudicial in that they signal the person is dangerous. Of course, that's a decision these jurors had most likely reached long ago.

Harbarger said to Durgeon, "I need your cooperation."

"You got it, Judge."

My stomach knotted.

When the bailiffs finished removing the ankle restraints and installed Durgeon in the witness box, the jurors were brought in. "Mr. Durgeon, since you are self-represented, I am going to allow you to give your testimony in a narrative. However, Mr. Tice is free to object, should he feel it is necessary. Is that understood?"

"Yeah." Durgeon nodded enthusiastically. *The stupid sonofabitch was looking forward to this. I felt I was on a giant roller coaster just at the crest before the ungodly descent.*

CHAPTER 44

THE DESCENT

Durgeon took the oath and fixed himself in the witness chair. He took several swipes at the rail with his left hand then turned his attention to the jurors. "Tina was right about one thing. It started the day me and her went to that apartment where they lived."

"Are you talking about the Blanco apartment?" Harbarger felt obliged to clarify.

"Yeah," Durgeon said, nodding. "Afterwards, Tina told Danny that she had seen Doree Bennett. Danny was pissed just hearing her name."

Harbarger interrupted. "Are you referring to Dan Atwell?"

"Yeah, Dan Atwell. Anyways, later on when Danny wasn't around, Tina told me it was Doree's fault for getting Danny kicked off the football team and school. Tina and Danny thought Danny had a shot at big-time football. I don't know about that. Anyways, Danny's a hothead. He's always going off on shit. Anyways, a week or so later, me and Rode meet up with Danny to shoot some pool."

"Excuse me, Mr. Durgeon. What is Rode's full name?" Harbarger again.

"Todd Rode," he said dismissively, anxious to get on with his story. "We was drinking and shooting pool, and Danny says he knows where we can score some easy cash. Says he knows people at some apartments, and they keep money in the house. So what the hell, pretty soon we're driving in Rode's car."

Harbarger: "All three of you in the car?"

"Right. We drove up, and I seen it was where me and Tina was at before." Durgeon swept the rail with his hand. "Dumb shit that I am, I should have known something was up." He rubbed his bandaged bicep. "Anyways, we knock, and he opened the door a crack."

"Are you referring to Robert Blanco?" Harbarger asked.

"Yeah, him. I said I wanted to talk to him about the apartment. He said it was too late, I should come back later. Then Danny pushes in front of me and slams into the door and the guy goes down. Danny pulls a gun and is on him before he can get up. I'm pretty sure it was Tina's gun from the house. The girl comes running out of the bathroom screaming. I grabbed her and clamped a hand over her mouth to shut her up. Danny gets off the guy and tells him to get up. Danny looks at the girl and then back to the guy and says like, 'You coulda had a real man.' The guy starts at him and Danny steps into him and smashes his face with the gun. The guy is laid out and bleeding. I let go of her and she runs to him and Danny grabs the back of her nightgown and it rips right off. She's only wearing panties. She starts touching the guy's face like she's trying to stop the bleeding. Then a baby starts up." Durgeon again rubs his bicep. "Anyways, me and Rode are just standing there. It was weird. I grab Danny and tell him, 'This ain't about no money.' He shakes me off and says, 'No shit.' He grabs Doree by the hair and pulls her up. She's screaming and crying, her tits have got baby milk dribbling out of 'em. I seen that me and Rode had been had. I tell Danny, 'I don't want no part of this.' He starts in with shit about how I was such a big man, a tough guy. I let it go, and me and Rode go out the door. When we left, they was alive."

Harbarger waited to see if he was finished and then said. "Does that conclude your testimony?"

Durgeon turned full around and looked at the judge. "I guess I should tell where I went then."

"That's up to you."

"Me and Rode took off in Rode's car and went to his place. Me and Tina weren't getting on. Anyways, Rode's girlfriend wasn't there, so I crashed at his place. I didn't kill 'em. They were alive when me and Rode left."

Harbarger again waited, then asked, "Are you through?"

"That's what I had to say."

I let out my breath. I hadn't even noticed that I was holding it. I scanned the jurors; they were sitting bolt upright. It seemed everyone in the courtroom was assessing what they had just heard. His story made some kind of sense. If true, it explained a lot of things. But it didn't explain what most needed explaining: why Durgeon had covered up for Dan Atwell for all these years. It certainly had nothing to do with any sense of loyalty to Christina. That relationship was over well before the first trial. I could only figure his aversion to ratting out Dan had finally worn thin. Was he believable? It has often been said that cross-exam is the crucible for ferreting out the truth. *Tice could ferret.*

CHAPTER 45

THE GRINDER

"Mr. Tice?" Harbarger said. It was all I could do to keep from leaving the courtroom. *God, this was going to get ugly.*

Tice took his time coming to his feet. It was clear to me that he was savoring the moment. He eyed Durgeon like a matador ready to drive the final sword into a mortally wounded bull. "Thank you, Judge." Never taking his eyes off Durgeon, he slowly made his way around counsel table to the lectern.

He began in a low voice. "You were living with Christina Atwell at the time of the murders, weren't you?"

"Yeah."

"Since your release from prison in Utah, you had spent every single night with Ms. Atwell, correct?"

"Yeah."

"In fact, according to your story, the first and only time you didn't sleep in her bed was the very night of the murders, true?" Tice had moved to the side of the lectern. His questions were statements.

"I told you, I was at Rode's."

"In fact, you didn't return home until an hour or so after Doree was shot, isn't that true?"

"I told you, I crashed at Rode's."

"That is what you said," Tice snapped.

Harbarger stepped in. "Mr. Tice. Your observations are neither necessary nor proper."

Tice nodded to the judge, then turned back to Durgeon. "Robert and Doree were murdered years ago, and yet this is the first time you have told us your version of those events, right?"

"Yeah." Durgeon reply was sullen.

"According to you . . . ," he lingered on the phrase, "there were five adults there that night?"

Durgeon thought for a moment, then agreed.

"Doree Blanco, one of the five, is dead, isn't she?"

"Yeah."

"We will never have the benefit of her telling us what happened, will we?"

"Course not."

"Robert Blanco, another of the five, is also dead, true? We will never have the benefit of him telling us the truth, will we?"

"He's dead."

"That's right. And Todd Rode, another of the five, is also dead, isn't he?" *Clearly, they had chased down the Todd Rode angle, as had we.*

"He died in prison."

"Likewise, he can't tell us what happened either, can he?"

"No."

"You claim that Dan Atwell was one of the five, right?"

"Danny was there."

"But we have not heard from Dan Atwell."

"I'm sure Tina knows where he's at."

"You haven't spoken to Christina in years, have you?"

"I still know about her."

"You don't know anything about her current life, do you?"

"I know she and Dan were always close."

"Of the five adults you claim were there that night, you are the only one that is not dead or missing, isn't that right?"

Durgeon shrugged. Harbarger told him to answer aloud.

"That's right," Durgeon answered, maintaining eye contact with Tice.

"In order for the jury to believe you left before Robert and Doree were murdered, they have only your word, don't they?"

"That's the way it looks."

"In other words, for them to believe you, they would have to believe you can be trusted to tell the truth." *How many times is Harbarger going to let Tice make the same point?*

"I fucking told you what happened."

Harbarger: "Mr. Durgeon, this is the only warning you are going to get. Now answer the question."

Durgeon pondered the judge's warning before saying, "Guess so." Then he added, "I'm telling the truth."

"I understand what you want the jury to believe. Would you agree that one of the things they can consider in assessing your credibility is your past conduct?"

"What do you mean?"

"I'll explain," Tice said, ever so patiently. God, he was loving this. It's not often a prosecutor gets to go after a defendant with so many vulnerabilities. "Let's begin with your criminal background. You have been arrested before, right?"

"You know I have."

Without raising or quickening his voice, Tice asked again, "You have been arrested before?"

"Yes." Durgeon was tight, his jaw clenched.

"In fact, you have been convicted on a number of occasions, haven't you?"

"Yes." Durgeon's hand began brushing the rail.

"Let's not dwell on the number of convictions; let's zero in on one in particular. Eighteen years ago, you were convicted in Utah, correct?"

"Yeah."

"That was for kidnapping and robbery, wasn't it?"

"Uh huh."

"You did not plead guilty, did you?"

"No."

"Yet when you were arrested, the police rescued a young woman who was bound and gagged in the back seat of your car, isn't that true?"

"It was complicated."

"Of course it was, Mr. Durgeon. Nonetheless, you fought those charges, didn't you?"

"I went to trial."

"That's right. You denied that you had done anything wrong."

"I pled not guilty."

"Returning to my question, you denied that you kidnapped and robbed, didn't you?"

"That's right."

"And you testified at that trial, correct?"

"Yeah."

"You told those jurors that you did not kidnap that woman, didn't you?"

"Damn right I did."

"You also testified under oath that you didn't rob anyone, correct?"

"That's right."

"Those jurors did not believe you, did they?"

"No."

"In fact, they felt you lied?"

"I was convicted."

"That's right, they disregarded your testimony under oath and convicted you of both charges, didn't they?"

Durgeon stared at Tice.

Finally, Harbarger said, "You must answer, Mr. Durgeon."

"Why? He already knows the answer."

"Mr. Durgeon, please answer the question."

"They said I was guilty."

"They felt you lied, didn't they?"

"I guess."

"Let's talk about your story this time. You were the first one to speak to Robert?"

"Yeah."

"You actually went into their apartment that night?"

"After Danny knocked the door in."

"At the time you entered the apartment, you knew it was against the will of Robert and Doree, didn't you?"

"What do you mean?"

"You were not invited in, were you?"

"Probably not."

"At the very moment of entry, it was your intent to steal money from them?"

"Yeah, Danny said they collected the rent, and it would be an easy rip-off."

"I am curious, Mr. Durgeon. You and the others were not wearing masks or any other concealing devices, were you?"

"I wasn't worried about them folks fingering me. I have that effect on people."

"You mean you intimidate them?"

"Like I said, I have that effect on people."

"Could it be that since Robert and Doree would be murdered, there was no need to disguise yourselves?"

"No, I had no intent to kill anyone. Like I said, people don't testify against me, because I scare them."

"So, if I understand you, it is your story that you could force your way into a stranger's house, and using force, take their possessions without any consequences?"

"Pretty much."

Tice let that sit a while. I looked over at juror number four, an elderly man. He was looking down, holding his head.

"Let's change gears." Tice cranked it up again. "You are aware that your fingerprint was found on the tape used to bind Doree, weren't you?"

"That's what you said."

"But—and help me here—according to you, she was not taped at the wrist when you left?"

"That's right. There was packing stuff all over the place."

"Can you explain how your fingerprint got on the tape that bound her?" Tice's voice demanded an answer.

"I already answered that."

"Of course you have."

"Mr. Tice, I do not want to admonish you again," Harbarger warned.

"My apologies," Tice said, with all the sincerity of a used-car salesman working solely on commission. He walked back to counsel table and picked up and looked at his legal pad. Nodded his head, as if reminded of a crucial point. "You told Christina, 'Just lose that fuckin' gun,' didn't you?"

"No, I never said that. She's lying, and you bought her bullshit story."

Ignoring Durgeon's denial, he asked, "After Christina told you she had thrown the gun into the ocean, you told her, 'That was good,' right?"

"Never said that," Durgeon answered, shaking his head.

"You had access to that gun?"

"I knew she had some guns."

"And you knew right where she kept them?"

"I knew they were in the house."

"You knew precisely where in the house they were kept, right?"

"Yeah, and so did Danny."

"Would you say you are a violent man?" Another quick shift to keep Durgeon off balance.

"I've had some troubles."

"I see. When you robbed that woman in Utah, you used a gun, didn't you?"

"I didn't rob."

"That's right, you are still denying that, aren't you?" Tice cocked his head. "The police found this woman, who you claimed you didn't rob, bound at the wrists and ankles in the back of the car you were driving, isn't that right?"

"Like I said before, it was complicated."

"Yet you were convicted of both robbery and kidnapping?"

"That's right."

"You stabbed another inmate while you were in prison in Utah, didn't you?" Tice was using Durgeon's own statement from the first trial.

Durgeon looked at Harbarger. "Do I have to answer that?"

"Yes, you do."

"Yeah."

"Just so there is no confusion, you used a knife and stabbed another person?"

"Yeah."

"You have killed before, haven't you?"

"That guy didn't die."

"How about the gay man you killed 'just because'—and I'm quoting you—'it was the right thing to do?'"

"Man, I was just blowing smoke." Durgeon collapsed back against his chair, his arms flopping at his sides.

"Are you telling us you lied under oath when you confessed to that killing?"

Durgeon shook his head. "Like I said, I was talking to make a point."

"Well, when you were just talking to make a point about killing a man, you were under oath, weren't you?" Tice stayed right on point. Nothing wasted.

"Yeah."

"Is it your testimony now, as you sit under oath, that you were lying while under oath?"

"Call it what you want."

"I call it lying under oath."

Harbarger finally stepped up. "If you have a question, Mr. Tice, ask it."

Tice kept his eyes on Durgeon, and then, shaking his head with disdain said, "I have nothing further for this defendant."

Harbarger looked at Durgeon. "Mr. Durgeon, you have the right to offer additional testimony at this time, should you so desire."

As Harbarger was speaking, Durgeon stood and faced the jury. "I've said what needed saying. You folks gonna believe me or not."

Harbarger shrugged off the lack of protocol. "That is your decision. Do you have any further witnesses, Mr. Durgeon?"

Durgeon looked confused and stared at Harbarger. Harbarger did not speak. Durgeon looked at me and motioned me over.

Harbarger asked Durgeon if he would like a brief recess to confer with Mr. Clearwater.

"Yes, Your Honor," I said for him.

The jurors were once again banished to the deliberation room, and Durgeon, Suzelle, and I were moved to the holding cell. Without preamble, Durgeon asked, "Is Danny still in the wind?"

"Yes."

"Shit." Durgeon pounded his fist on the table. "Sonofabitch." He sat and closed his eyes. When he looked up at me, he asked, "Tice hurt me bad?"

"Yes."

Durgeon took it in. It was not a revelation. He knew. "If you were still calling the shots, what would you do?"

"I'd have rested before the last witness."

Durgeon shook his head ever so slightly. "Well, that bridge's already been jumped off of." He spit the words out bitterly.

"It was a high bridge."

Durgeon flashed again. "I heard ya, so now what?"

"No more witnesses. Rest your case," I said.

"Thanks, counselor," he said sarcastically, "for all your advice." He looked at Suzelle. "How about you, missy?"

"Like Jake said, rest."

I motioned for the bailiff. When court reconvened, Durgeon rested. Tice had no further witnesses. Harbarger set closing arguments for 9:00 a.m.

CHAPTER 46

END GAME

Normally on the eve of closing arguments, I have trouble sleeping. The adrenaline rush even hours before the argument is intense. But tonight, I was pretty relaxed; there was no argument to make. It was Durgeon's time to further seal his fate. So instead of writing and rewriting my close, I took the whole team out to dinner at Casa Nostra. Lisa knew the owner and claimed it was the premier Italian in the city. She was right. After we made a toast to Durgeon, we moved on to other things. Lisa had an upcoming show. Suzelle had an application in with the Los Angeles public defender' office; Duke had several clients begging for his time. And I would do nothing for the remainder of the summer and then resume classes in the fall. I had called the dean and told him I would not need the semester off. I slept soundly.

In the morning, I swam and felt near normal, my body just about whole again. I had a light breakfast, and Suzelle and I took our last drive to the courthouse, courtesy of Booker. Once again, the media was out in full force. Taylor Hunt caught us as we were walking up the courthouse steps. "Well, Jake, how does it feel to be on the sidelines?"

"Helpless."

"Anything to add?"

"No, except Duane Durgeon did not kill the Blancos." I kept walking, not wanting to say anything I might later regret. Maybe I had already said too much.

As we took our seats, Durgeon was already at his table, as were Tice and Manlow at theirs. Tice turned to me and gave me an absolutely blank look. I wondered what he was thinking, seeing me out of the picture. Maybe he had regrets about not being able to match wits with me during closing arguments. I had no idea.

We waited for Harbarger, who finally entered and surveyed the capacity crowd. The Blanco and Bennett families were well represented, with the exception of Doree's mom and dad, their exits the stuff of local legends. Harbarger briefly pre-instructed the jury and nodded to Tice. "Mr. Tice, you may make your closing argument."

He stood at his table, and without preamble, began. "The defendant is a vicious, cold-blooded predator." He slowly moved to the lectern and settled in. He was resplendent as ever in his tailored black suit, French cuffs, and gold cufflinks. He looked and sounded confident. A master of his universe. Why not; he had a lot of arrows in his quiver. "That man"—he pointed at Durgeon—"is an evil predator who derives a perverse, cruel pleasure in inflicting pain, torture, and death. There are some among us who present a clear and present danger to every human being who crosses their path. The victim could be a convenience-store clerk working the wrong shift at the wrong time, a pizza delivery boy called to the wrong house, or a young couple just getting their start in life, who happened to show an apartment to the wrong man. Thank God these predators number but a few. Thank God there was only one Charles Manson. One Ted Bundy. And thank God there is only one Duane Durgeon.

But for Robert and Doree, who through terrible fate were placed before that predator"—he again pointed at Durgeon—"there was no escape. We take comfort that Robert and Doree are in a better place. A place where they are safe from the monsters of this world. A place the Mansons and the Bundys and the Durgeons of this world will never see." He paused to give his opening grab an opportunity to resonate. And from the upright postures and focused faces of the jurors, it appeared it was resonating.

"Yet, with that said, it remains for the families and friends left behind to seek some kind of comfort by dealing with the individual responsible for their great loss." He turned and took several steps toward the victims' families, studying them. Several were silently crying. He stood there with his head bowed for several seconds. Then turning back to the jurors and moving back to the lectern, he continued. "It is toward that small comfort that we have directed this trial. We have given the defendant every opportunity to show that we are wrong in thinking he is the predator. He has had his chance. We have heard his story. You've had an opportunity to evaluate his ability to be truthful. We can now turn to the task of evaluating his story in light of the overwhelming evidence we have heard. It is all we can do. Let us begin." *Damn, he was good.*

Tice again pushed away from the lectern and walked to the counsel table and picked up a file and flipped it open. He glanced at the papers, closed the file and said, "Judge Harbarger, who has been a tower of strength and a model of tolerance throughout this ordeal, will give you the rest of the law you are to follow. She told you that the state must prove guilt beyond any reasonable doubt. This is a burden we willingly accept. You will notice the standard is not beyond all doubt or beyond a shadow of a doubt, but rather beyond a reasonable doubt. There is a reason for this. Any doubt, no matter how unlikely or even bizarre it may be, is not good enough. If that were the case, any cock-and-bull story would excuse any crime. No, the burden is, and through common sense must be, reasonable doubt. Reasonable doubt. Not imaginary doubt. Not fanciful doubt. But reasonable doubt." *Tice knew that jurors often confused the prosecutor's burden incorrectly, and he did an expert job of clearing up any misconceptions.*

"Judge Harbarger also instructed you on the definition of murder. Murder is the unlawful killing of another. In this trial, with this defendant, we must talk about murder in the first degree. There are two ways that we can get to first-degree murder. One is if the murder was premediated. In other words, did the killer think about the consequences of taking the life of another before he killed? Did he reflect beforehand or plan the killing? The other way we can find first-degree murder is if the killing occurred during an inherently dangerous felony. Felonies like robbery, kidnapping, rape, and burglary are all inherently dangerous. If we find that a person is killed during the commission of one of the inherently dangerous crimes, then the murder is also first degree.

"Another critical piece of law you were instructed on concerns people acting together when they commit their crimes. For instance, is the person who actually fired the fatal shot treated differently from his partner who participated in the crime but did not fire the fatal shot?" He paused. "No, all participants in the felony are equally guilty for any and all deaths that occur during that felony."

"There is one other critical piece of law we need to touch on. The law of special circumstances. As all of you know, California is a death-penalty state. The people of this state think it is a just and proper punishment to execute someone under certain circumstances. For instance, killing more than one person is a special circumstance that will qualify a person for the death penalty. Another special circumstance involves killing someone during the course of a violent felony such as robbery or burglary. There are a number of special circumstances, but for our purposes we need go no further.

"Now I want to make one thing very clear. When you go back and begin your deliberations, you are not determining whether the defendant should be executed. We are not yet at that stage. Remember, this is a two-part trial. First you must decide the defendant's guilt or innocence, and if you find him guilty, you must then determine if he was engaged in either of the special circumstances I just outlined. If you determine him guilty and find either or both of the special circumstances to be true, then we will proceed to the second phase of this trial, and at that time you will be asked to decide whether the defendant should be executed or sentenced to life in prison."

"Before we turn our attention to all the evidence we've heard, I need to comment on the particular testimony we heard from the defendant yesterday. As you may have already figured out from the law of felony-murder and from the law of acting in concert that I just discussed, the defendant has admitted his own guilt." Tice paused, stepped away from the lectern and moved to the jury rail. He slowly surveyed the jurors. "Let me repeat that. The defendant by his own testimony has admitted his guilt. The felony of burglary of the Blanco residence was complete at the very point when the defendant entered their home with the intent to steal or commit any felony. Didn't he admit that he was there to rip off the Blancos?" The elderly gent in the back row of the jury box gave Tice a nod of agreement. In my experience, there is no better feeling than receiving confirmation from a juror during closing. *Even though jurors are precluded from audibly responding, there is significant communication occurring during closing arguments.*

"Think about why the defendant was there. That was no social call. So you might be asking yourselves, if that is the case, then why would the defendant incriminate himself by admitting he was there? It could only be for one of two reasons. The first reason could be that he did not know the law and simply blundered into incriminating himself. But could that be the reason? As we all know, he was represented by Mr. Clearwater pretty much throughout this trial. Now, I may have some issues with Mr. Clearwater"—he gestured in my direction—"but I know he is a smart and resourceful criminal defense attorney, and I'm certain the two of them discussed his testimony." Tice shook his head dismissively. "That testimony, ladies and gentlemen, was not the product of ignorance."

I could not help myself. I stood, and addressing the judge, said, "May we approach?"

"Sit down, Mr. Clearwater. You have no standing here. One more word from you and you will see the inside of one of my cells."

I sat, frustrated and helpless. With no one there to object, Tice was running roughshod over Durgeon.

Tice had remained impassive throughout my brief exchange with Harbarger. He waited a few beats and then nodded for Detective Manlow. Manlow pushed a button on a remote control and a PowerPoint image was illuminated on a screen beside the witness stand. It read **Preemptive Strike—Avoiding the Death Penalty**. Tice gestured at the screen and continued. "I've suggested that there were but two possibilities for the defendant's testimony. We've eliminated the first one; now let's turn to what is really going on. The defendant realized that the evidence of guilt is overwhelming and that you will indeed find him guilty. However, he wants you to find him guilty under his terms. Specifically, he wants you to find that he was merely a participant in the burglary and the robbery but not the actual killer. That he was gone before anyone was killed. He is hoping that you will buy his version of events and find him guilty of felony-murder but not of being the actual killer, so that you will not feel that he deserves the death penalty. Even though you are not making that life-or-death decision now, the defense has cleverly concocted this version of events so that even though you find him guilty, you will ultimately spare his life."

Tice stepped to the counsel table and poured himself some water. As he lifted the glass, he paused, turned, looked directly at me, and imperceptibly lifted his chin. *Got you Jake, you sonofabitch.* I held his look without acknowledging his gesture. He drank to his unspoken toast and turned back to the jury. "Now that we understand the context and reasons for the defendant's testimony, we can relegate his story to the trash heap and consider the overwhelming evidence that the defendant, this predator, this killer of innocent and God-fearing people, snuffed out those two lives. I am not going to belabor the evidence, but rather, I'll list the evidence of defendant's guilt."

He motioned at Manlow, and a new PowerPoint was projected. It read **#1—Previous Visit—Motive**. Tice motioned to the screen. "Why was the defendant there? Remember, he had been there just days before. He knew Robert and Doree collected the rent. There certainly must be money there. In a down-and-out place like the Palms, the rent was most likely paid in cash, not checks or credit cards. The motive is timeless and clear."

Tice motioned for Manlow. A new image read **#2—Incriminating Statements to Christina**. Pointing to Durgeon, Tice said, "Recall the actual words from his mouth. 'Just lose that fucking gun.' Those statements from the mouth of the predator were damning. Do they tell us a lot?" That same elderly juror gave a nod.

Manlow flashed a new slide, **#3—The Gun**. Tice offered a tight, mirthless grin and said, "There was a good reason he wanted that gun to disappear. Remember the urgency he expressed about the gun? He knew if that gun was in the hands of the police and that he had had access to it, he was in trouble. He did everything in his power to make it disappear. That gun cripples him."

Manlow then put up the next slide, **#4—The Bullets**. "The bullets recovered from Doree were consistent with bullets fired from that gun. You heard the testimony; the only thing that precluded an exact match were Durgeon's efforts to suppress this critical evidence. When he told Christina to destroy that gun, he as good as confessed."

The next image was **#5—Absence From Home**. "The defendant and Christina had been living together for months, sleeping in the same bed. Isn't it curious that the only night he is not with Christina is the very night of the murders? There is nobody to verify his pathetic alibi. Isn't it amazing that, according to his story, all the other adults there that night are either dead or missing?"

Manlow illuminated the next image, **#6—The Fingerprint**. "That fingerprint changed everything," Tice continued relentlessly. "With that fingerprint, Durgeon couldn't deny being there. Rather, he was now reduced to explaining his presence, as we heard in his strained, contrived story. Yet even his bizarre story cannot account for his fingerprint found on the very tape binding Doree." He then said again, "The very tape that bound Doree's hands. That fingerprint, and especially the location of that fingerprint, cannot be explained, even with all the creative resources of the defense."

A new image appeared, **#7—Eyewitness Identification**. "In addition to all the circumstantial evidence, we have the rarest of evidence: an actual eyewitness to the shooting of Doree. I have worked on a lot of difficult cases involving cruel facts, but the image of a young mother stripped naked, huddling her body protectively around her baby as she is executed, will forever be the cruelest act I know." Tice pushed off from the lectern and walked behind his counsel table and then behind the defense table. He stopped directly behind Durgeon and just in front of me and Suzelle. Durgeon did not move; his shoulders were hunched forward, and he was staring down at a legal pad. "This man"—he gestured—"was actually seen doing his vicious act. The predator was caught in the act. Now, his lawyer went to great lengths to attack that eyewitness. He had to. He had to, precisely because the eyewitness's testimony is so completely damning. He really went after Ron Evans. But the witness never backed off; he simply told us what he saw. And what he saw was this man"—again Tice leaned forward at Durgeon—"putting a .22 caliber revolver to the head of a pleading woman clutching her newborn and murdering her in cold blood.

"Detective Manlow, new slide please." Tice continued holding his position behind Durgeon as **#8—History of Violence** appeared. "This man is no stranger to violence. He had been a predator before, and he was a predator that terrible night and early morning. He had been out of prison for only a short while for kidnapping and robbery when he killed Robert and Doree. This man will continue to kidnap, rob, and kill if left in society. Even in prison he is a threat." Durgeon, who had not moved, dropped his pen, pushed away his legal pad, straightened his back, and slowly turned until both arms rested on the right side of his chair. His eyes were fully on Tice. Durgeon's face was flushed, his eyes slits. Neither man gave. I leaned back away from the confrontation.

Harbarger finally broke the impasse. "Mr. Tice, perhaps we would all be better served if you were to return to the lectern." Without being aware of what I was doing, I had put my arm across Suzelle's shoulders. Tice held Durgeon's look for another count and then slowly moved away. *What was that about? Was Tice trying to bait Durgeon into attacking him, thus again displaying to the jury Durgeon's violent nature? Or was he displaying, for his audience as their elected DA, how fearless he was? Or was he conjuring the image of Durgeon standing over Doree?*

Positioned back at the lectern, Tice said to Manlow, "Detective, please put up the final slide." It was **#9—His Own Testimony**.

"We've already discussed why the defendant would put himself at the scene, but we have not really gotten into why his testimony is so hurtful to himself. He testified the way he did because he knows the evidence boxes him in. He was trying to squirm out of a very tight place. He was fighting for his life. You see his argument? I was there alright. But it was no big deal, just me and a couple of my buddies going to do a home-invasion robbery. Nothing real serious. But then the damnedest thing happened—some folks got killed. But it wasn't me that killed them. It wasn't my fault. I just went there to burgle and rob." Tice paused, looking at the jurors, waiting for them to see the lie. "Some logic, that. First of all, we know from his 'get rid of the gun' comment that Durgeon was the shooter. But what is interesting about Durgeon's story is that even if you believe him, he is still guilty of first-degree murder. As one of the robbers, he is equally responsible for all that happened. Like I cautioned earlier, the defense figures that if you don't think he is the shooter, you will still find him guilty of murder, but perhaps at the penalty phase you will spare his life, thinking he was not the actual killer." Tice left the lectern once again and this time walked to the front of Durgeon's table. Pointing at Durgeon, he said, "He wants you to spare his life. This brave man who killed a helpless woman and her bound husband. This man who kidnaps, robs, and murders."

Durgeon suddenly jerked himself to his feet and overturned the table into Tice. Tice deftly dodged and stepped back. Durgeon hurled himself over the table at Tice, screaming, "You mealy mouth cocksucker!" Then, Durgeon's whole body convulsed and jerked backward. Some guttural sounds emitted from his mouth. He fell to his right and hit his head against a leg of the upended table. His body thrashed and writhed. We watched in horror and fascination as the 50,000 volts played with his hapless body.

Several bailiffs had positioned themselves around Durgeon,

nightsticks drawn. Harbarger yelled for one of the bailiffs to get the jurors back into the deliberation room. Then she came off the bench and stood looking down at Durgeon, whose body finally lay still. She ordered another bailiff to call for the paramedics. A third bailiff stepped to the still-unconscious Durgeon and felt for a pulse. There was spittle on Durgeon's chin. He was rolled onto his back and a jacket was propped up under his head. Blood had seeped through his jacket at the shoulder where he had been shot. The paramedics arrived quickly and took the now-semiconscious Durgeon away on a stretcher.

Harbarger motioned Tice, Suzelle, and me back to chambers. Harbarger silently paced and then sat with one haunch on her desk before speaking. "For obvious reasons, I am revoking Durgeon's self-representation, and I am confining him in a holding cell for the duration. He will be provided an audio feed of the trial. Meanwhile, Jake,"—*Aha, back to first names. I was a necessary entity now that Durgeon had played himself out of the trial*— "you are back in." Her look did not invite discussion. "Once we get a report on when Durgeon is able to proceed, we will resume closing arguments. Thank you. Dismissed."

CHAPTER 47

BACK IN THE GAME

Two hours later, Suzelle and I were back in Durgeon's holding cell. He had been bandaged and looked only slightly worse for the 50,000 volts. He was seated, sucking on a Dr. Pepper Suzelle had provided.

He gave me an ironic grin. "Well, I gotta tell you, that'll wake you up and straighten your dick."

"Are you alright?" Suzelle asked.

"Better than ever." Then looking at me, "I worked 'em, man."

"What do you mean, you worked them?"

"That testifying part didn't work out so good, but anyways, you're going to make one hell of a closing argument."

"It was an act?" I was incredulous. "Pushing over the table, ranting at Tice?"

"Only way to get you back for the closing argument."

Suzelle and I sat stunned. Finally she ventured, "You could have just tried the judge," as she slumped against a wall.

"Come on, get real. No way the judge was going to go for that."

After another slow beat, I nodded. Apparently, he had been waiting for an opportunity, the right moment. And then he was willing to pay the 50,000-watt price. I had vastly underestimated Duane Durgeon. I realized I was dealing with a sly cunning that, spurred on by self-preservation, was determined to have its way.

"Come on, Jake. I had to testify, and you wasn't going for it."

"Dammit," I muttered mostly to myself. It was not so much an epithet of anger but more a cry of admiration. Even though I felt like a mere accessory in a master manipulator's toolbox, I couldn't blame him for not trusting the "system." The system had not done him right so far. It was the last desperate play at the end of an improbable game. He figured me for closing argument all the while.

As I stood, he said, "Give 'em hell, Jake."

"Yeah." I called for the bailiff to let us out. "Incidentally, Harbarger has kicked you out of the courtroom."

"Had to. She didn't have no choice," he said, as we left the cell.

When court reconvened, all eyes were on Team Durgeon, as Suzelle and I claimed our previous position at counsel table. Harbarger explained the new arrangement to the jury and invited Tice to finish his close.

Without missing a beat, Tice did just that. "I was just about to finish when this latest outburst occurred. Let me leave you with this. At some point during your deliberations, I ask you to think about the last eight hours in the young lives of Robert and Doree Blanco. From ten o'clock on that Wednesday night until five o'clock the next morning, those kids were trapped in that little apartment, stripped of their clothing, subjected to God knows what, and finally murdered. You think about those eight hours. And those good people. And then I want you to think about the defendant. We have learned a good deal about him these past weeks. I am confident that you know and understand what he is, what he did, and what you need to do. Thank you, ladies and gentlemen." Tice held their attention for a count before taking his seat.

Harbarger: "Mr. Clearwater?"

I stood, puzzled. She couldn't expect me to go right then. "Approach?" She nodded.

"You're not giving me any time?" I asked, as Tice and I stood at the bench.

Harbarger stared at me. "How about we recess, and you go at one thirty?"

"How about we recess, and I go tomorrow?"

Harbarger brushed us back, reached for her gavel, struck it once, and said, "We are in recess until one thirty, at which time the defense will have the opportunity to make their closing argument." Harbarger was a judge on the edge. It was not difficult to appreciate her frustration and anger. Durgeon had been a nightmare at his first trial and had proven to be even more of a problem this time around—although somewhat in his defense, some of the events this time around were beyond his control.

༄༄༄

Suzelle sat quietly with me at counsel table as I jotted notes on a legal pad. I didn't have time to retire elsewhere to work. Duke had just returned with coffee and handed us cups. There would be no lunch today. Even if there were time, my stomach would have rebelled. I was tight. I had to fight down a sense of panic. The almost-primal urge to walk away gripped me. I kept telling myself I knew this case, I'd be okay. My plan was to put together a broad outline and then talk through the evidence. I had some specific points in mind that had occurred to me during the days of testimony. Hopefully, I could pull them together in a coherent way. One thing I knew for certain: Very shortly, I would be standing before those same jurors who had just experienced Tice's brilliant closing, and it was my burden to counterpunch. One way or another, it would all be over this afternoon.

The bailiffs were huddled near the witness stand. Many in the audience had remained through the recess for fear they would lose their seats. There was a low hum of conversation.

"Jake, Suzelle." I looked up; it was Lisa, standing at the rail. "I heard you were going to make the closing argument. I thought you were off the case."

I looked into that beautiful face and relaxed. I stood and hugged her over the rail. "Durgeon went off, got booted from the courtroom, and the judge has ordered me to make the closing."

"Can she do that?"

"She is the judge, and this is her courtroom."

She reached back over the rail and kissed me. "Jake, I've seen how good you are at this. You will be brilliant. I know you didn't want me here, but would you mind if I stayed?"

"Please stay. I just hope I don't embarrass myself."

"That will not happen. I'll sit down and let you work." She smiled an encouraging smile, winked, turned, and took a seat next to Duke.

࿇࿇࿇

At 1:32, Judge Harbarger brought court to order and looked at me.

"Thank you, Your Honor," I said, as I rose and looked at the jurors. They were focused, and why not? They had been in the front row of this spectacle. This was the place to be. I stood at my table and began. "There is no way I can accurately describe how I feel as I stand before you today. To say that I am terrified that I am not up to this daunting task does not do the fear justice, but it's probably as close as I can get. I'm terrified that my inadequacy will be reflected in you good folks making the terrible mistake of convicting Duane Durgeon of murders he did not commit."

"Objection." Tice stood. "Counsel injecting personal opinion."

"Sustained. Mr. Clearwater, make your argument."

Damn it anyway. There is a protocol at closing argument that counsel do not object unless the argument is way over the line. I was over, but not enough to draw an objection. I was fighting for a man's life against a hometown judge and perhaps a compromised, if not corrupted, prosecutor. I'll give them an argument. I walked to the lectern, picked it up, put it aside, and faced the jury. "You bet I will make my argument." I looked defiantly at Harbarger. Nerves had been supplanted by anger.

"In law school, I learned from my trial advocacy professor that if you don't have the facts, argue the law. And if you don't have the law, argue the facts. And if you don't have either the law or the facts, then appeal to the jury's sympathy, their emotion." I paused. "Perhaps my teacher was just being cynical. That advice did not originate with him; it has been with us as long as advocates have been trying to persuade jurors. It is a lesson we just saw practiced by the prosecutor."

There were several skeptical looks from the jury box, especially from juror four, the elderly gent in the back row. "I see some of your looks. Bear with me for a few minutes. Let's go back to the prosecutor's conclusion. 'Remember those last eight hours,' he said. That was not law-based, that was not fact-based, that was designed to appeal directly to your emotions. Of course, it's a powerful argument because we all feel for those kids, and for their families and their friends. What happened to them was a tragedy of the worst kind. And if we let our emotions take control, it must cloud our reason and our ability to analyze the evidence in a fair and dispassionate way." Juror number four was not moved; his face remained skeptical. Closing argument is not about making a speech to a group but rather about engaging in twelve one-on-one dialogues. He was my first, and so far, I was oh for one.

I shifted to juror number five, a college-educated woman who was very focused. I said to her, "You will recall during jury selection I asked each of you if you could put aside your emotions, your sympathies, and render your decision only on the law and the evidence. And every one of you looked me in the eye and told me you could. Here we are; it's time." She gave me a slight nod. I nodded back. "I know it is an awesome task. But that is the task you are all bound to do." I moved slightly to my left and squared up with juror number one, a retired high school teacher. "It is unfortunate when we have an officer of the court, in this case the DA himself, pleading with you to make decisions grounded in sympathy and pity rather than logic and reason. It is no accident that he"—I stopped and pointed at Tice—"began his argument and finished his argument appealing to your emotions, and then between those appeals, engaged in only the most superficial review of the evidence."

I walked back to counsel table and rested my hands on the chair where Durgeon had been sitting. "There is another vital aspect of this trial we need to talk about and then dismiss. It is the dislike that everyone in this courtroom feels for Duane Durgeon." I paused. "Isn't that right?" Number one gave a slight cock of her head. "Let's face it, he is an awful man. He has lived an awful life, and he has behaved awfully during this trial. And if we were to convict him because he is awful, you twelve could reach a unanimous verdict in seconds." I nodded my head at jurors eleven, an engineer, and twelve, a self-described homemaker, and received a slight nod from number twelve. "But Duane Durgeon is not charged with being an awful man. Our job is to somehow get around those monumental emotional issues—our sympathy for Robert and Doree and our disdain for Duane Durgeon—and view the evidence fairly and dispassionately."

I moved back toward the right side of the jury box. "We need to begin with this concept of reasonable doubt. The DA gave you an odd notion of what that means."

"Objection, counsel is suggesting that I misstated the law," Tice said.

Harbarger looked at me expectantly. "Mr. Clearwater?"

"It's closing argument. I feel it necessary to clear up a misconception from the prosecutor's argument," I countered.

Harbarger turned to the jury. "At the conclusion of the closing arguments I will again instruct you on the law you are to follow. However, during closing arguments, it is fair for both sides, within limits, to comment on the law. Mr. Clearwater, you may proceed; the objection is overruled."

"Thank you, Your Honor." I nodded my agreement and turned to the jury, and in particular to juror number ten, the attractive Latina who worked at Walmart. I felt that she had been with me since jury selection. "As I suggested, we need to begin with reasonable doubt. Now, that is a phrase we have heard throughout our adult lifetimes, and I suspect many of us have never had to come to grips with the full concept behind that phrase. But right here, right now, it becomes the most important law in this trial. It is no longer a phrase pulled from old history books or just words used for dramatic effect on television or in films. In our efforts to form a more perfect union, we have always required that before we can convict anyone, that person's guilt must be so overwhelming that we are certain of that guilt beyond any reasonable doubt. We must be very certain." Number ten was with me. "There is no greater burden placed on the prosecution in any country in the world. That is not an accident. That is because in this country, we will not convict unless we are very certain. If, at any time during your deliberations, you hesitate or pause or think to yourself 'what if,' then you have found that doubt, that reasonable doubt."

I motioned to Judge Harbarger. "Her Honor is going to finish giving you the complete law in a few minutes—not just the few pieces the prosecutor selected, but the complete law." I moved on to juror eight, a dentist who in my view had been too eager to be on the jury. I hoped that he didn't have some kind of agenda. But, since I had run out of challenges, here he was. He was also worrisome; because of his profession, he could very well be the foreperson. "One of those pieces of law is going to be a particularly helpful tool for you to use as you go through the evidence. It states that if, in reviewing circumstantial evidence, you find that there are two reasonable explanations for any piece of evidence, one pointing to the defendant's guilt and another pointing to the defendant's innocence, then as a matter of law you must adopt the interpretation that favors the defendant's innocence. Let's think about that law, that tool, and how it can be helpful in evaluating the facts that we have heard.

"Suppose we hear a fact, and you find it completely consistent with the prosecutor's theory of the case—is our job done?" I locked up with juror number three, a Metro worker. He would not acknowledge that I had spoken to him, his face impassive. "No. No it's not. You must look again at that piece of evidence and ask yourself if there is another reasonable explanation for that evidence. Could it have happened in the way the defense suggested? And if you find that there is another reasonable explanation, you are required by your oaths to adopt the interpretation that favors the defendant. So why don't we do just that? Together, let's go back through the points the prosecutor has discussed and look at them through the lens of reasonable doubt."

I looked at Detective Manlow, sitting at the prosecution table. "Detective, would you mind illuminating point number one again?"

Manlow looked startled and confused. He did not move. Tice was up. "Objection, Your Honor."

Harbarger asked, "What is the basis?"

"Withdrawn." Tice took his seat. There was no basis. He had jumped up instinctively and now had to swallow hard, as he realized I had every right to use his slides.

I looked at Manlow again. "Detective, number one, please."

Manlow looked at Tice, who hesitated and then reluctantly nodded for him to put up the slide. Manlow picked up the controller and pushed the button. **#1—Previous Visit—Motive** appeared on the screen. "We heard the prosecutor offer his assessment of why Mr. Durgeon went to the Blancos' that night. And you know what? He could be right. It just could be that he went alone to rob them of the rent monies. Given what we have heard, that is a reasonable interpretation of the evidence. But your job doesn't stop there. You must take a second look at this evidence and ask, could the defendant's explanation—that he went there with Atwell and Rode, and together they entered the apartment—be true? Could this have started off with three men intending to rob and then turned into one man's personal grudge? Could it be that Dan Atwell manipulated circumstances to settle an old score, to exact some perverse vengeance for what he felt was some wrong? Could somebody actually do that? We know Dan Atwell was up to it." I zeroed in on number two, a convenience-store clerk. "You remember that ugly testimony from Carrie Washburn?" She nodded, she remembered. "Once Durgeon and Rode realized they had been had by Atwell, they broke it off and left. Their part in the burglary and robbery was over. And for that, you should convict Durgeon, but his role in what happened hours later had ended. That second look is critical."

I looked back at Manlow and said, "Second slide please, Detective." Manlow grudgingly activated the remote to reveal **#2— Incriminating Statements to Christina.** "I am certain some of you noticed the same thing I did about those 'incriminating statements.' The statements that are actually incriminating came only from the mouth of Ms. Atwell."

I moved over in front of juror number six and asked, "Did you notice that? We do not have any tape recordings of those statements, no third-party corroboration, nothing but Christina's word." Juror number six gave me an appraising look. "The only 'incriminating' statement that is independent of Christina is, in fact, not incriminating. Remember the lone recorded statement from Durgeon, 'That was good,' in response to her throwing the gun away? Is that the kind and quality of evidence we need in a case like this? Could there be some other explanation? Think about that. Christina Atwell. Think about that deal your DA cut with her for both herself and her son. No prison, not even any jail. Those were serious felonies, and she and Danny-boy walked clean away. We talked about her at opening statement. About how she is the centerpiece of the prosecutor's case. Let's be very clear about this. The case the DA has put together is absolutely dependent on this woman. Their case will rise or fall depending on your willingness to trust her one hundred percent." I tapped the rail to punctuate my words. "Hook, line, and sinker. And folks, you can't pick and choose what parts of her testimony you are going to accept and what you are going to reject. To convict, you must buy her testimony right down the line.

"Detective Manlow?" I looked at him and then thanked him as **#3—The Gun** appeared. "Let's see. The logic according to the prosecutor is that because Durgeon told Christina to get rid of the gun, that, of course, means he must have been the gunman." I locked up with juror number seven, a slight African American man retired from the postal service. "Any flaws in that logic?" He cocked an eyebrow. I nodded at him. "Only one—Christina Atwell. The alleged statement came only from Christina. It is not tape recorded, it's not written down, and nobody else heard it. Our only source for that evidence was Dan Atwell's mom. The other interesting point about that gun is that Dan Atwell also had access to it." I paused, gauging number seven's reaction. He raised his eyebrows and cocked his head, signaling that he would think about that. "Dan Atwell knew about that gun. Knew where it was."

"Next slide, please," which was **#4—The Bullets**. "Same problem as the gun. It's all about the absolute reliance by the prosecution on Christina, and about Dan's access."

I walked over toward Tice and stopped just off to his left. "It is an interesting irony that Christina Atwell is the prosecution's case. This man," I gestured at Tice, who was a study in nonchalance, his head turned away from me, "has made a career out of prosecuting people like Christina. From his days as a lowly deputy district attorney rookie, John Tice has gone after the Christina Atwells of this county with a vengeance. And now, Mr. Tice is vouching for her credibility. In fact, he is the champion of her virtue. This woman, who has been a lawbreaker for years. This woman, who was virtually a one-person pipeline of drugs into this county. Mr. Tice and Detective Manlow have a stranglehold on her. They say jump, she jumps." I slowly shook my head. "Strange teammates. Gross irony. It is sickening and disgusting what these two"—again gesturing at Tice and adding Manlow—"have done in this case."

"I object to this personal attack!" Tice's face was drained of color as he turned to me. "How dare you attack me!?"

"That's enough!" Harbarger demanded silence. "Approach." As we stood at the bench like chastened schoolboys before an irate principal, Harbarger cupped the microphone and said, "Mr. Clearwater, you are in contempt of court for that personal attack. The appropriate sanctions will be meted out at the conclusion of trial." *I was way over the top and deserved the sanction. My passion had gotten the better of me.* Then, taking Tice in as well, Harbarger continued, "Since both of you see fit to continue to engage in unnecessary and unprofessional tactics, I'm warning both of you that I am prepared to do whatever is necessary to preclude any further behavior I deem inappropriate.

"Mr. Clearwater, I'm instructing you to finish your argument and refrain from any further inappropriate behavior."

As I made my way back toward the jury box, I saw Manlow leaving the courtroom. *What was that about?* Once again, I took in the jurors. "Folks, I just did what I warned you not to do: let emotion, instead of reason and logic, carry the day. I engaged in an emotional attack on Mr. Tice. That was wrong." Turning to Tice, "Mr. Tice, I apologize; I got carried away at your expense." Tice looked at me and gave the slightest nod. "I admit that I am emotionally invested in this case, but that doesn't excuse my harsh words directed at the DA."

I paused and took in the jurors. "Where was I?" I looked back at Suzelle, who held up her hand, signaling five. "Thanks, Ms. Frost. Let's turn to number five." Tice just sat there, making no effort to access the PowerPoint. There was an uncomfortable silence before Suzelle left the defense table, walked behind Tice, picked up the controller, and activated **#5—Absence From Home**. I smiled my approval to her. "Is it just possible Mr. Durgeon and Christina were experiencing difficulties in their relationship? Why did they go apartment hunting in the first place?" I looked at juror number nine, a middle-aged woman who sold high-end cars. "You heard the testimony that their relationship was at an end. Once again, is there another way to look at this piece of evidence?" Number nine cocked an eyebrow, waiting for my answer. "Because Durgeon doesn't come home to their peaceful and tranquil abode, are we to infer he is out committing murder? When held up against reasonable doubt, does this point register at any level?" Number nine gave me a noncommittal look.

I slid back over to juror number seven, the African American retiree. "There is another point that occurs to me. In addition to receiving her stay-out-of-prison card, you think Christina might have some additional reason to testify against Durgeon?" I stayed with juror number seven. "You think Christina might be a woman scorned? Remember her testimony, 'I don't care if he sleeps around'? Is that the way it works? She began writing him while he was still in prison. When he was released, who was there to pick him up? In whose house did he live? In whose bed did he sleep? You think she might have been jealous and angry at him?" Number seven nodded as if considering. "Is it just possible that in addition to cutting that sweetheart deal that keeps her and her son out of prison, she was just flat-out mad at Durgeon?"

I looked at Suzelle, who had taken a chair behind Tice. "Ms. Frost, next slide please." She gave me a subdued grin. **#6—The Fingerprint** appeared on the screen. "There is something compelling and even comforting about having a fingerprint. It represents a solid, irrefutable piece of evidence that we can have confidence in. It doesn't require us to determine who is truthful and who is lying. It transcends all that. It makes your jobs as jurors easier. Right?" With open hands, I gestured to number ten, the attractive and attentive Latina. "Well, I hope we have all learned something about fingerprint identification during the testimony of the state's fingerprint expert. Is it an exact science? Are there ever mistakes? Remember that testimony about false positives? Shoot, the state's expert told us there can even be disagreement about whether individual points are similar. Against this backdrop of uncertainty, he found only five points of similarity. Five."

I moved in front of number six on the far right in the back row. She was an older Asian American woman. "Remember we heard that Scotland Yard requires sixteen points of similarity before they are convinced. We had five. Is that good enough?" She offered no response. Isn't it troubling that the state even put that guy up to testify? He knew"—I pointed at Tice—"it was not good enough. He knew it and put that evidence before you anyway." *Careful, Jake. No personal attacks.* "I am sure the thought was, put on enough witnesses and evidence, regardless of the quality, tell the jurors what a dreadful man Durgeon is, and get a conviction.

"The second point about the partial print—perhaps it should have been my first point, I hope you'll excuse my lack of organization—anyway, the other point about that fingerprint is that it was found on packing tape. Is there another reasonable explanation for that print?" I cocked my head. "An explanation that favors the defense? We all know that Durgeon was in that apartment twice before the murders, and both times the Blancos were packing; packing stuff was all over that apartment. Another explanation? Do we have some hesitation, some pause as to that print?

"Ms. Frost, we are ready for number seven." **#7—Eyewitness Identification** appeared. "Ron Evans." I shook my head and gave a brief smile and turned back to juror number eight, the dentist. "Perhaps the most important safeguard in the American criminal justice system is the jury's opportunity to actually watch and listen to the witnesses. Thank God all of you had that opportunity with Ron Evans. I leave his ID of Duane Durgeon to your common sense." Staying on the dentist, who I believed could end up being the foreperson, I continued, "Let me tell you why I put Evans on the witness stand. First, there is Anthony Graves. He was a convicted rapist who lived near the Blancos and had said some worrisome things about Doree, though no further evidence has been found in the investigation of Mr. Graves that would implicate him in the murders. Second, I put Evans up there to show the twelve of you how adamant he was that it was somebody other than Durgeon who fired those shots. And folks, he told us in the strongest language. But the primary reason I put Evans on that stand was for you to understand the lengths this prosecutor"—I looked at Tice—"and his investigator have gone to manipulate the evidence. I hope you were surprised and even outraged at how Detective Manlow suggested fact after fact selectively designed to get Evans into thinking it was Durgeon. I'm not going to belabor the details; you heard it from his own mouth." I took a breath and worked my way to the front and center of the jury box. "Members of the jury, it's got to be about truth and justice. That may sound corny, but that is our job here. And frankly, that should have been on Detective Manlow's mind when he was jerking and manipulating Ron Evans to suit his purposes."

"Let's turn to the next 'compelling' point on the DA's list. Ms. Frost?" She activated **#8—History of Violence**. "No question, Duane Durgeon is a bad man. A violent man. But we need more than that. When a prosecutor is reduced to arguing past conduct, it is a telltale sign that his case is lacking in the essential facts." I spoke directly to number nine, the woman who sold luxury cars. She was my second guess at being the foreperson. Make no mistake about it, Mr. Tice needs you to dislike and fear Mr. Durgeon and, if necessary, convict him because he is a bad man with a bad history.

"Ms. Frost, please put up number nine." **#9—His Own Testimony** appeared on the screen. "The prosecutor has taken an interesting view of Duane's testimony. He suggests that even if Durgeon's testimony concerning Dan Atwell is true, you must find Durgeon guilty of first-degree murder. I have two things to say about that. One, this is a multiple-choice approach. First, we believe Durgeon was the shooter, but if you have a problem with that theory, then try this one: he wasn't the shooter, but he is guilty anyway under the rules of felony-murder. It doesn't work like that—we do not play guess-em in criminal trials, especially in death-penalty murder trials. And two, to find Durgeon guilty under this theory of felony-murder, you must believe that the deaths of Robert and Doree were in the perpetration of the felony of burglary or robbery. Let's assume when the three men entered, they intended to steal. That makes them all guilty of burglary. But if the killings happened long after Durgeon and Rode left, those killings were no longer in the perpetration of the burglary. When Dan Atwell went off half-cocked, he was on his own, and he alone is responsible for those deaths."

I stepped back and surveyed the faces in the box. They were listening, they were focused. "That's the state's case. He"—nodding at Tice—"is hoping you'll be impressed that he has nine points that he says incriminate Durgeon. But the truth cannot be obscured by numbers and phrases illuminated by PowerPoint. We needed to do what we just did: look behind the facade and examine the substance. The law requires us to hold each of those points up and examine them for some other reasonable explanation." I returned to number four, the skeptical older gentleman, and asked, "Did we find some areas that made us pause and think, 'Well, I'm just not sure?' If so, then you are doing your job. You are being critical of the evidence set before you. You are asking the hard questions. Could there be some other reasonable explanation?" Number four was still a tough sell; I got no reaction from him.

I stopped and walked back to counsel table and poured some

water. My legs were tired and sore. I slowly sipped and then turned back to the jurors. "We, as defense counsel, weren't content to sit back and critically analyze the prosecution's case. We went beyond that. We were not required to, but we did. Through digging, prying, and hard work, we offered up what the police and prosecution failed to find. When it started to emerge that Dan Atwell was involved, I kept asking myself, my investigator, and Ms. Frost, 'Why didn't the police investigate him?' They are smart professionals. Why didn't they see what by now should be clear? The case has Dan Atwell all over it. How could DA Tice and Detective Manlow miss that?

"I've spent some time thinking about that question. And I think the answer goes something like this: In the weeks following the murders, we know there had to have been intense pressure to produce the killer. This was described by the media as one of the most horrific murder cases in county history. The early leads did not pan out. They had nothing. Absolutely nothing. But when Christina Atwell came forward, everything changed. She gave them a viable candidate. And they"—I motioned at Tice and at Manlow's empty chair—"did precisely what they should not have done. They didn't let the facts fit Durgeon; they made Durgeon fit the facts. They were hell-bent to be done with this thing, and Durgeon fit the bill. If something didn't fit Durgeon, ignore it. If evidence pointed elsewhere, bury it. They had their man."

I picked up several skeptical looks from the jury. "I see some of you giving me that 'prove it' look. Okay, let's talk specifics. Let's talk about Evans's first ID. He was certain it was another man. Now let's think back to how the prosecution team handled Evans." I locked up with number eleven, the engineer. "Did they own up to his ID? Did they even call him to the witness stand and then explain how the investigation played out?" I gave him a questioning look. "First they tried to turn him, and then they tried to hide him. That meeting

Manlow had with Evans, where he laid out the case against Durgeon and then had him look at only Durgeon's photo, violates common sense and police procedure. That, folks, is base manipulation. Make Durgeon fit the facts." The engineer put his hands over his mouth and looked at me over his glasses. I thought he might be with me.

"What about Dan Atwell? We've got a police investigation that failed to consider perhaps the key character in this horrible tragedy. How in heaven's name do we get to the bottom of this case without dealing with Atwell? He fit Evans's description. He had access to the gun and the bullets. He had a violent history. Will any of us ever forget the testimony of Carrie Washburn? Not only does Dan Atwell have a violent history, but he also likes to tie up women and hurt them. Did he tie up Doree? He also had a motive. He blamed Doree for his failures. He had an opportunity. He was there with a gun. And now he is in the wind. He is out there somewhere. Have we heard any testimony about any kind of police investigation of him? What do we do with all of that? Do we ignore him, like they did?"

I stepped back from the rail, walked over to Suzelle, who had moved back to our counsel table, and stood at her shoulder. "Ms. Frost and I want to thank you for your indulgence. This has been a hard trial. Certainly the hardest and most difficult I've ever been involved in. In addition to the tragic facts involving the deaths of Robert and Doree, we've had a shooting. Lots of disruptions. High emotions. Yet somehow, we expect you twelve people to keep your balance, to follow your oaths and your common sense, and to emerge with a verdict that is just." I pushed off and slowly began making my way back to the jurors. "We are asking a lot of you. But I've been watching you for all these days. I've watched you in the morning when the listening is easy, and I've watched you in the late afternoons when it's not so easy. I know you are up to the job. You have hung in there. You have battled through this thing, and now we are at the end. I feel good that justice is in your hands. I know you will do the right thing."

❧ ❧ ❧

Tice's rebuttal was a disconnected blur in my mind, and I struggled to focus on his words. I was spent. I didn't know whether Tice went after me personally or was content to pummel my argument. When he finished, Harbarger instructed the jury and sent them off to deliberate. It was just past four o'clock. Harbarger put everyone on call and adjourned until we had word from the jurors.

CHAPTER 48

THE FINALE

Suzelle pushed my suddenly clumsy hands aside and began stuffing everything in our briefcases. A bailiff told me that Durgeon wanted to see me. I thanked him but said no. Let Durgeon stew. I was sick of him.

Duke held the gate for us, and Lisa gave me a hug. Together the four of us proceeded through the crush in the hall and out onto the steps. Taylor Hunt was there with her cameras, beckoning me.

Duke asked, "You wanna talk to her?"

"No." Then I reconsidered. "Okay. What the hell, no harm could come of it."

As we approached her, several other TV crews converged on us. I ignored the other crews and focused on Taylor. She held her microphone to her mouth. "Mr. Clearwater, how did you feel about the closing arguments?" She held the microphone to me, where it was joined by three others.

"The prosecutor is pretty polished." I gave a slow grin.

Taylor smirked and asked, "How did you feel about your closing argument?"

"The jurors were focused and paying attention. I felt connected with them."

Another reporter asked, "In light of events, did you expect to be making the argument?"

"No, I figured I was on the sidelines." I then added, "Frankly, I would have liked more time to prepare, but the judge felt otherwise." *Harbarger would not like hearing that. Tough.*

"Did the latest outburst from Mr. Durgeon surprise you?"

"Sure, it did. Courtrooms are serious and solemn places where we expect important decisions to be made with care and deliberation. When something like that happens, it's unsettling." I paused, then continued. "Let me say this, though. Duane Durgeon didn't kill those two kids, and yet he has spent years on death row and now faces the real possibility of returning to San Quentin and once again facing execution. Perhaps when his actions are viewed in that light, his frustrations are better understood."

"What is Mr. Durgeon's condition?" one of the other reporters asked.

"For a man who has been shot twice and then electrocuted, he seems to be holding up."

"What's your guess, will the jury be out long?" Reporter number three.

"Hope so." The old adage was long deliberations favor the defense.

As I began to move away, Taylor asked, "What are you going to do tonight, now that the trial is over?"

"Good Scotch and a soft mattress."

Duke broke off from us as we headed for Booker and the car. "Unfinished business," he explained.

Once in the car with Suzelle in front and Lisa and me in the back, Booker broke the silence and told us the sheriff's department would now pull protection.

"I figured that," I told him. Booker pulled the car away from the curb and entered the traffic flow. He looked at me in the mirror. "I gotta tell ya, I didn't want this assignment. I didn't want anything to do with Durgeon and his lawyers. But listening to you today, I'm almost convinced that he didn't do it. For what it's worth, they need to take a real hard look at Dan Atwell."

Lisa squeezed my knee.

I studied Booker's face in the rearview mirror, hoping I had planted some level of doubt with the twelve in the box. "Thanks, Sergeant. I know this hasn't been good duty for you. We all appreciate your professionalism and courtesies."

Against the backdrop of street noises, I heard an engine rev behind us, and it reminded me of my seat belt. For some reason, fastening my seat belt still did not come second nature, and I was usually working on it after the car was moving. Suddenly, Booker yelled out and swerved hard to the right. The car behind us had drawn even and banged into the front left of our Crown Vic. In the narrow street, we were driven into a car parked at the curb. The impact slammed me into the back of Booker's seat. *Funny how seat belts only worked when buckled.* I bounced back and looked at Lisa who, good citizen that she was, was belted in and unhurt. Booker, however, was not moving. Suzelle seemed okay, buried in an airbag. I pulled myself forward. The driver's-side airbag laid limp in Booker's lap and there was a nasty gash across his forehead. He appeared to be unconscious. I felt for a pulse in his neck. It was fast and strong. I looked out the left side window at the car that had struck us. It was pinned against my door. It was an old primered gray Charger. The lone occupant, the top of his bald head catching the light, lay slumped across the front seat. Another seat belt scoffer. He wasn't moving.

I turned back to Lisa and Suzelle. "You okay? You're not hurt?" They nodded assurances. Suzelle was trying to rouse Booker.

I motioned toward Lisa's door. "We need to get out. Gotta check on the other driver." I anxiously motioned with my hand. She unbuckled and pushed at her door. Together we got it opened sufficiently to climb out.

"Call 911," I instructed, "while I check on the other car."

As she pulled her cell from her bag, I could hear Booker grunting. I ran around to the driver's side of the Charger and opened the driver's door. The driver was groaning but still slumped on the seat. I pulled open the door, reached in, and holding him by the shoulders, pulled him upright. Still groggy, his head rolled toward me. Then I saw the revolver on the passenger seat. I jerked back. Gun. Big. Bald. Dan Atwell? His eyes cleared and fixed on me. He let out a fierce yell and turned to find the gun. I dove into the car across his body, driving my elbow into his face. His hand was still grappling for the revolver. I managed to pin his right arm, which had just grabbed the gun. My right arm lit up in pain. The sonofabitch was biting me. I heard the back door of the Charger jerk open and Booker yell, "Don't move!" The man froze as Booker's revolver was at his temple. "Get out of there, Jake," Booker ordered. I scrambled back over the man, resisting the temptation to elbow him again. The welcome sound of sirens converged on us. Spectators were gathering on the sidewalk. Booker dragged the man from the car and slammed him down on the asphalt, his knee on the man's back.

❧ ❧ ❧

Forty-five minutes later, as we stepped into the Ramada's elevator, Duke ran to catch the door and climbed in. He saw my rolled-up sleeve and the bandage on my arm where Atwell had bitten me. "What the hell happened? An accident?"

"No," Suzelle said, "an attack—it was Dan Atwell—he

rammed our car and was going to shoot us." Her words came out in a rush.

Duke's eyes were back at me for confirmation and clarification.

"It was Dan Atwell, alright. The dumb sonofabitch had his wallet with his ID. No doubt about it. He rammed our car. He had a gun," I confirmed.

"Shit, you guys okay?" I had never seen Duke worked up before. I looked down at his gray-fringed head. It seemed that his hair had receded further from his brow just since the trial began. *Every day, a little more face to wash.*

Lisa and Suzelle nodded their assurances. Suzelle had quickly snuggled next to Duke.

"He in custody?"

"Yeah, thank God for Booker."

We got into the room, and I collapsed onto the sofa.

"You folks need a drink." Duke was taking charge. He fixed drinks all around. I felt fragile, breakable. The Scotch helped. "I'd like to be in the interrogation room with that crazy asshole. What was his point? What was he trying to accomplish?" Duke wondered out loud. Getting no response because no one had any answers, he went on. "I didn't get the chance to tell you, but your close was terrific. Turning Tice's list on him was genius."

Suzelle chimed in, "When we were doing our lunch-break prep, you didn't mention using Tice's list."

"That just hit me in the moment. Otherwise, there was no way I could remember what I needed to cover."

Lisa joined in. "Jake, you had the jurors, just like you had the jurors in Suzelle's father's case. You were magnificent."

I wearily held up my glass and tipped it to my support group.

No one even mentioned watching the eleven o'clock news. We had all had enough for the day.

ลิ๋ลิ๋ลิ๋

The following morning, I was up before dawn and drove the three miles to the nearest beach. I figured the ocean water would help heal my bite wound. More importantly, I needed some exercise. I swam beyond the small breakers and then parallel to the shore. There was a strong current against me, so when I climbed out a half-hour later, I didn't have a long walk back to my car. My lats and pecs had that warm tightness. I picked up coffees at a Winchell's and returned to the hotel. Lisa had gone to work. Suzelle was working through the two local newspapers. The attack made the front page in both papers. Speculation was rampant as to Atwell's motives and whether he had been involved in the Blanco murders. As for the trial itself, the print media had given my closing argument high marks. The *San Arcadia Breeze* praised me for my "direct, no-nonsense style that disarmed a jury that most likely wanted his client guilty." Another account called me "a worthy adversary for the legendary John Tice."

The comments were flattering but meaningless. There were only twelve critics that mattered, and they were excluded from any reports on the trial. And, of course, they were ignorant of all the out-of-court developments. With two hours of deliberations yesterday and nearly an hour already this morning, the jurors were likely to be past the preliminaries and into a serious discussion. I vaguely mused about who they had selected as their foreperson: the dentist, or the luxury car salesperson. During the close, I intuited that the salesperson might have overtaken the dentist as the stronger personality.

ลิ๋ลิ๋ลิ๋

While the jury worked, we waited. I tried to concentrate on the latest Michael Connelly but spent more time staring out the hotel window.

Suzelle paced. And paced. I bit my tongue to keep from telling her to light somewhere. She finally went out to the pool. Duke was off somewhere. I suspect another job had cropped up. I hoped so. At four o'clock, Suzelle called the clerk for an update. "Nothing doing; we'll call you when there's some word."

At five, Duke walked in with a smug, knowing look. Danny-boy had been getting trial updates from Christina, who in turn had been getting updates from Manlow.

"How'd you find that out?" Suzelle asked. I had long since quit questioning Duke on his sources.

"I still know a few people around these parts."

"Maybe Manlow felt he needed to leak to Christina to keep her in the fold," I speculated. "When you think about it, Christina's deal was to help the police through the first trial. I got a feeling when she was testifying that she was balking at doing it all over again." Duke and Suzelle took that in without comment. I went on. "Another thing occurs. If Durgeon was only one of three that night, the lone remaining one is ripe for prosecution. Let's take it step by step. First, there is no statute of limitations on murder, so even years later, a murder case can be brought. Second, using accomplice and co-conspirator theories, they can now go after Atwell."

Duke thought that over and agreed. "At the first trial, Dan's possible involvement wasn't raised by anyone. Christina could put the hurt on Durgeon, and Tice would do the rest. But this time around, our nosing around ruffled some feathers. For the first time, Dan's name surfaced. Keep in mind, you were first attacked after we made a point that we were looking at Dan."

తతత

At six o'clock that evening, the clerk called and said the jurors were calling it a day. Lisa brought some Chinese, and we watched a mindless movie. Lisa and I retired to the bedroom at ten. Duke and Suzelle were determined to watch the eleven o'clock news.

Morning came, and I swam again. Later, Suzelle and I were walking to Subway for lunch when the clerk called us on Suzelle's cell. No verdict, but the jury had a question. Judge Harbarger wanted everyone in chambers at one thirty. We arrived at the same time as Tice. Harbarger, sans robe, sat behind her cherrywood desk. She did not stand when we entered but motioned us to chairs. Without preamble, she said, "I received this note from the foreperson, juror number nine, at eleven thirty this morning." The car salesperson had beat out the dentist. *Good. I think.*

Looking over her glasses, she read, "We need some clarification on felony-murder." Tice's face tightened. Suzelle's eyebrows arched. Seemed someone was at least considering Durgeon's version. But I had long ago realized that reading the tea leaves was crap. Harbarger placed the note on her desk and tapped it with her finger. "It is my intent to read them the felony-murder instruction again. I do not want to get into a lot of discussion on this topic that might get us in trouble with the appellate court." She looked first at Tice and then at me.

Tice spoke first. "I agree."

"What if they want more?" I asked.

"I will read the instruction and send them back to continue deliberations." Harbarger's course was clear.

"Judge, before we go back, I need to raise a point," I said. Everyone remained seated. "As I am sure you are aware, and as I am certain Mr. Tice is aware, we were attacked again. This time the man was arrested, and it was Dan Atwell." From the judge's lack of reaction, it was clear she was aware. "This substantiates our position that Dan Atwell was present the night of the murders and was quite possibly the murderer."

"This is conjecture—" Tice began, only to be cut off by the judge.

"This latest incident, though very unfortunate, occurred after the jury began deliberations. I have no authority to terminate deliberations, reopen the trial, and take new testimony, or whatever course of action you might propose. That would be unprecedented."

"This jury is completely ignorant of three separate attacks on the defense in deliberate efforts to dissuade defense counsel from producing credible evidence of Dan Atwell's involvement." I took a breath. "There are times when extraordinary measures should be undertaken for the sake of justice. Judge, I am formally moving that the trial be reopened and testimony relating to these attacks and Dan Atwell's involvement be taken."

Tice again interjected, only to be once again cut off by Harbarger. "Mr. Clearwater, your motion has been made, considered, and denied." *Yet another appellate issue.*

When we moved to the courtroom, it was obvious that the word had spread that court was reconvening. The seats filled in minutes. The excited throng was ready for the next act. Harbarger stepped to the bench and called for the jury. As they moved into the box, they were animated. Juror number nine made a point of looking at me. Coming from the foreperson, how was I to read that?

Once they were settled, Harbarger said, "Good afternoon, members of the jury. I have conferred with counsel as to your request. They agree that I reread those instructions regarding felony-murder. It is our belief that this further reading will provide the answer to your question."

You could hear and feel the energy evacuate the courtroom. The assembled masses had expected a verdict. Instead, they got a delay.

Harbarger read the instructions and excused the jurors to resume their deliberations.

The prevailing wisdom, as I already noted, is that the longer the jury deliberates, the better the defendant's chances. The fact that we were in the third day, coupled with the request for the felony-murder instructions, was cause for mild, but very cautious, optimism. *It was hard not to read the damn tea leaves.*

∾∾∾

Deliberations continued Friday with no result, then onto Saturday, when the jury reported that they were deadlocked. A disgusted Harbarger brought court to order at four thirty and had the jurors brought in. Despite the day and the hour, most of the seats were filled. "Madam Foreperson," Harbarger inquired, "you have indicated that the jury is deadlocked, is that correct?"

"I'm afraid so, Judge Harbarger," the foreperson replied, defeat and disappointment in her voice.

Harbarger cast a quelling look at the jurors and addressed them sternly. "You twelve are under a solemn oath to deliberate faithfully and truly. You are to listen to your fellow jurors and have them listen to you. There will never be a better opportunity for any jury to be in a more advantageous position to render a fair verdict on these charges." Harbarger leaned back, her tone now more conciliatory. "I am going to send you back to continue your deliberations, and I want each of you to dig deep within yourself to make the efforts of everyone involved in this trial fruitful. I have confidence that you can do the job." She then instructed the bailiffs to lead the jurors back to their deliberations. "We are adjourned until further notice."

As I stepped from counsel table, Tice called, "Got a minute?"

I turned to Suzelle. "Give me a few minutes."

Tice motioned to the attorney conference room. Although there was a table and several chairs, we stood.

"Durgeon pleads to the murders, I drop the death penalty."

I took a step back. Tice's offer was stunning. This guy never gave on anything. Equally stunning was the thought that Durgeon may walk away from this. As I think back now on that brief meeting with Tice, the incredible idea that Tice was willing to settle for less than Durgeon's ears had not even occurred to me. Despite my quickened pulse and heightened blood pressure, I maintained a neutral demeanor.

"I'll run it by Durgeon and get back to you." It was a cold, detached, professional exchange that barely managed to paper over our mutual contempt.

༺༺༺

I filled Suzelle in as we walked to Durgeon's cell. She was speechless. Durgeon did not get up when we entered the holding cell. I hadn't seen him since he'd been banished. His look was appraising and noncommittal when Suzelle handed him a Dr. Pepper. The cell reeked of body odor. Maybe shower privileges had been suspended. I pulled a chair away from the table and sat. Suzelle assumed her position at the far wall. "Tice has an offer."

He cocked his head in surprise. I think he had been ready to launch into a tirade about his absentee lawyer, but my announcement superseded all else. "No shit!"

"Plead to the murders, he'll drop the death penalty." I laid the cards out without editorial comment. As he had told me, it was his ass. I was merely the messenger.

He slowly stood, turned from me, and clasped the bars of the holding cell in both hands. He stretched his head back and forth and then rotated it slowly left and then right. Without turning, he asked, "They been talking for four days. How do you make that?"

"Long is good," I said. "Sometimes."

He grunted. "What else you got for me?"

"Just passing along Tice's offer. It keeps you off death row."

"What about that felony-murder business?"

"At least one of the jurors is or was considering your story." I was careful to purge any emotion from my voice. Not that I for a minute believed my opinions were persuasive on Durgeon. He was simply soliciting input. He alone would determine its weight.

"That's how I seen it," he said, as he began pacing the eight feet of the cell. "What about the other stuff the judge said?"

"Harbarger's instruction was standard. She's trying to break the logjam."

He nodded absentmindedly, still pacing, still thinking. He laughed softly under his breath and said, "Didn't expect no offer from that little ferret." I crossed my legs and waited. "Hell, if they're fucked up on this guilt part, I figure I'm good on penalty." He offered this as a supposition inviting my comment.

I did not bite.

"Nothing to say, counselor?"

"Like you said, it's your ass."

He stopped pacing and leaned into me. "That's right, it's my ass. Tell Tice to shove it up his."

I remained seated. "Are you certain? They still have the power to execute you."

"Fuck 'em."

I stood without another word and we left. *There were gambles and there were gambles.*

Tice was waiting in the courtroom. The room was empty but for the three of us and a bailiff reading the sports section. I moved out of earshot of the bailiff, who was much too involved in the paper to actually be reading. "No deal," I said.

Tice's impassive face nodded acceptance. "I assume you told him that he's playing with fire." It was a statement.

"I passed along your offer." My voice was conversational but far from conciliatory.

"I guess we wait some more." He turned and began walking away.

"Hold on a minute," I said. Tice stopped and turned. "How did Dan Atwell know I requested his rap sheet?"

Tice again turned and started to walk away.

"Way I see it, I have an obligation to talk to the attorney general's office and have them investigate possible illegal conduct by the local prosecutor and his investigator."

That got his attention. He stopped and once again turned to me. "You would, wouldn't you?" He gave a dismissive head wave. "Manlow has been placed on leave pending criminal investigation."

"Who's doing the investigating?"

"San Arcadia Police."

"Sounds too cozy."

"Clearwater, you do what you got to do."

We returned to Durgeon's cell.

"How'd Tice take it?"

"He said you were playing with fire."

Durgeon grunted and rattled a brief cackle. "Yeah, that's what I'm doing." He was up and pacing again. "This waiting is driving me fuckin' nuts. It's hard to know what they're doing. Talk to me."

"This waiting is getting to everybody. I could use a Coke. How about the two of you?" I asked.

"I could handle another Pepper," Durgeon said.

"How about you, Suzelle?" I asked, as I got up to do the fetching.

Suzelle said, "I'll get them." She gave me a pointed look. Stupid me—no way she was going to be in the cell alone with Durgeon. She left to get our drinks.

"You want my opinion?" I asked.

"Lay it on me."

"I think Tice is afraid of a hung jury. This case would be a nightmare for him to try again. His offer is a way out for him. He knows he will take some body blows for cutting you any kind of deal, but I think he knows that if this jury does not convict you now and recommend the death penalty, the chances of that happening in the future are dicey."

"I like what I'm hearing." Durgeon stood and paced the four steps the cell permitted. "But if that fuckin' jury is hung, he can do it again, right?"

"Yep. But the chances for conviction lessen with each trial. As time gets you further and further from the crime, witnesses become more problematic, they die, move from the area, remember things differently. Or just plain forget. In this case, Tice would have the added problem of Dan Atwell. They can't hide him anymore. We've raised enough concerns about Atwell that he would have to rule him out through an investigation. This would be a very difficult case for Tice to put on again."

"Wait a minute. What do you mean they can't hide Atwell no more?"

I'd forgotten that Durgeon had no access to news. He had missed all the excitement. I told him that Atwell had ambushed us after the closing and that he was in custody, looking at a pile of felonies.

"No shit. What happened?"

Suzelle had just returned with drinks and I asked her to catch Durgeon up on developments. She gave him the CliffsNotes version.

"No fuckin' way." *The man had a way with the language.*

Durgeon sat and thought about that.

We sat and watched him think.

"Am I doing the right thing, telling Tice to fuck off?"

"I am not going to offer an opinion on whether to take the deal."

"But you think I'm right?" he persisted.

"I very carefully didn't say that."

"So what the fuck are you saying?"

"As long as this jury is out, they have the power to convict. Right now, because of the questions they've asked and the time they have been out, you have some leverage. One option is to use that leverage and make your own offer."

"Shit!" He pounded the table. Frustration. Life was simpler without options. Options can be debilitating as well as empowering. Again he was up and pacing, his fingers kneading his eyes and forehead. "What? What offer?"

"Offer to plead to one count of murder two. Everything else dropped. You do eighteen to twenty-five. You've got a lot of that done already. You would get credit for that time."

Durgeon stopped pacing. "Shit." He shook his head, trying to absorb and factor in the ramifications, his knuckles rearranging his forehead. "That could be another twenty years."

"Probably would be. The parole board is not likely to cut you any time."

"Fuckin' A," he agreed.

"That's just an offer. Nothing says Tice will accept it."

"I hear ya," he said. "But the jury could hang up like you said, and it'd be hard for him to do again."

"Hard, but not impossible," I cautioned.

Durgeon sat and pulled himself close to the table. "Gimme your best guess. What is the jury gonna do?"

"I think they're going to convict you. It's been a while since the judge sent them back with their marching orders to reach a verdict. If they hadn't moved off the dime, we would have heard by now."

"So make an offer?"

"That's my best guess. But it's just a guess."

He turned to Suzelle, "What do you think?"

"I'm just a rookie, no experience in all this."

"Yeah, but you've been here the whole time. I've watched you starin' at them jurors. What does your gut tell you?"

She took a deep breath. "They can't stand you. I think they want to convict."

He gave her a flicker of a smile, closed his eyes, rubbed his forehead, and with his head down, and in a voice just above a whisper, said, "Okay. Do it. Make the offer." He kept rubbing his eyes. "It ain't right. I didn't kill those kids. It just ain't right."

❧ ❧ ❧

Tice walked into the attorney conference room ten minutes after I called. He nodded coldly. "Ms. Frost, Jake, what can I do for you?"

"He pleads to murder two, does eighteen to twenty-five."

"Both counts?"

"One count."

Tice considered. "I've got two bodies."

I shrugged. "Jury's been out a while. Durgeon is not the only one playing with fire."

"I can't have him plead to just Robert or just Doree. I would get crucified. I have got to account for both of them."

"That is a problem," I acknowledged.

"He pleads murder two to both victims. The sentences to run concurrently, eighteen to twenty-five."

It was my turn to consider. *No additional time. What difference could it make, pleading to a second murder after you've already pled to one? It's not as if I had been trying to save his reputation or that he was likely to run for political office.* "Let us run it by him."

We shuttled back to the cell. The air quality had not improved. He looked at me expectantly. "You plead murder two to both murders and the times will run concurrent. You would not do any more time than if you just pled to one."

"Is he fuckin' with me?"

"I don't think so. He raised a legitimate concern. If there was just a plea to one, what about the other victim? Do we just forget that other person?" I shrugged. "Anyway, that is his thinking."

"Hell, I don't give a damn. What I care about is the time. That don't change from our offer?"

"No, time's the same."

"Do it."

જ જ જ

"We have a negotiated disposition," Tice said to Harbarger.

Harbarger stared at Tice. "You're going to settle this case?" Surprise mixed with question in her voice.

"That's right, Your Honor," Tice said.

Harbarger's office phone rang. She picked up, listened without speaking, and returned the receiver to its cradle. "They have a verdict." She looked over her reading glasses, gauging our reactions as we all calculated what this could mean and how it played out when held up to our pending agreement.

Tice stood and said, "Excuse me, Your Honor." Without waiting for a response, he left. Suzelle and I followed.

Talk about bad timing. A verdict in a criminal case is almost always a conviction. Defense verdicts, O. J. notwithstanding, are rare creatures. *Shit!*

Word had already spread, and the bailiffs were preparing to open the doors. Tice entered the courtroom from a side door and motioned us back to chambers. The hair bristled at the back of my neck. I felt there were circles within circles, and I was not in any of them. Tice led the way back to the judge's office. Harbarger was pulling on a robe. Tice said, "Judge, in light of the fact that the jury has reached a verdict, there will be no disposition."

"Oh no," I countered, "we reached a disposition prior to the verdict. I mean to hold the state to its bargain."

"Wrong," Tice rejoined. "There is no disposition until the court agrees to it. We hadn't even talked specifics."

"Your Honor, we confirmed with you that there was a disposition before we received word of a verdict."

"Mr. Tice is correct, there is no disposition until and if I approve it," Harbarger said. "They have a verdict. Let's find out what they have decided."

They were right, of course. "Give us some time. We need to talk with our client. He thinks we have a disposition."

"Ten minutes."

When we reached the holding cell, Durgeon had already heard that the jury had reached a verdict. "We got a deal, right?"

"We were too late. The judge received notice of the verdict before we could run the deal by her. It's too late."

"Well fuck that," he retorted angrily, slamming his hands on the bars.

"There's nothing we can do about it now." I waved for the bailiff to let us out, then paused and said, "We'll come back after the verdict."

"That would be fuckin' great."

᜕᜕᜕

Suzelle and I stepped into a full courtroom. The air seemed to shimmer with excitement. Spectators who couldn't find a seat were lined on the side and back walls. The bailiffs made no effort to move them. Tice, at his table, appeared to be oblivious to everything as he stared straight ahead.

A bailiff commanded, "All rise, court is in session, the Honorable Alise Harbarger presiding." We stood as Harbarger entered the courtroom and took her seat. She instructed that the jury be brought in. The twelve were solemn as they filed into their seats. Not one of them made eye contact with me. But I noticed that none of them made eye contact with Tice, either. There would be no early tip-off. I felt my heart thumping. I could not imagine what Durgeon was experiencing, alone in his cell. When the jurors were seated, Harbarger said, "Madam Foreperson, has the jury reached a verdict?"

"We have, Your Honor."

"Please pass your verdict forms to the bailiff."

The bailiff handed Harbarger the folded sheets. Harbarger unfolded them and read, her face a perfectly inscrutable mask.

She handed the sheets back to the bailiff, who relayed them back to the foreperson.

"What say you to count 1, the murder of Robert Blanco?" Harbarger's question was followed by a perfect quiet. Suzelle clutched my arm.

The foreperson looked down and read, "We, the jury, find the defendant, Duane Felix Durgeon, not guilty of the murder of Robert Blanco." There was a stunned silence, then an explosion of sound, a cacophony of dismay and surprise. My brain had to format the words. Like everyone else, I had thought only in terms of conviction. Conviction had been the only option. Suzelle's fingers dug into my arm. I stared at the foreperson. Her eyes never left the verdict sheet. Harbarger repeatedly banged for the room to come to order. Bailiffs removed two men who were shoving each other. Control was quickly reestablished.

Harbarger, her face grim, turned to the foreperson. "What say you as to count 2, the murder of Doree Blanco?"

"You Honor, we, the jury, find the defendant not guilty of the murder of Doree Blanco."

The crowd had recovered its equilibrium, and only a low murmuring greeted this verdict. Harbarger gaveled for silence. She turned back to the foreperson. "What say you to count 3?"

"We, the jury, find the defendant guilty of burglary of the home of Robert and Doree Blanco."

They had believed Durgeon. He was there but left before the murders.

"And Madam Foreperson," Harbarger continued, "what say you to count 4?"

Still reading without looking up, she said, "We, the jury, find the defendant not guilty of robbery."

Harbarger looked first at Tice, then at me. "Counsel, do either of you care to have the jury polled?"

Tice stood. "Yes, I do."

"Very well. Madam Clerk?"

The clerk repeated the first verdict and asked each juror in turn if that was their verdict. They each acknowledged that it was. The process was repeated as to the other three verdicts. Each juror recited their verdict stoically. Harbarger thanked the jurors for their service and excused them to return to their lives.

Harbarger went on as if nothing extraordinary had just happened. She was all about business, form, and protocol. She set sentencing on the burglary conviction for four weeks hence and adjourned. The courtroom exploded at her departure. Two people turned pushing into a fistfight. The bailiffs were busy. Duke made his way to us and gave me and then Suzelle a bear hug.

The three of us crossed to the door leading to Durgeon's holding cell. We could hear him whooping; even his whooping had variations of "fuck." The bailiff let us through and then into his cell. I got a full body bear hug, and surprisingly, Suzelle let Durgeon hug her as well. Duke got a handshake.

"Dammit, Jake, you did it. You fuckin' did it." Durgeon's eyes were watering. "God, I would've loved to seen Manlow's face, the lying sonofabitch." Durgeon pulled a deep stabilizing breath. "So, what happens now?"

"In a month, the judge will sentence you on the burglary, and you will most likely get time served on that. Then I suspect Utah will revoke your parole because of the burglary and you'll do four or five more years there."

"I can do that standing on my fuckin' head." He hugged me again. "You gave me my life back." He paused and then said something completely out of character. "Maybe I'll quit being such a hard-ass. Maybe when I get out, I'll do something worthwhile." I nodded, speechless. *Maybe years of death row had that effect on everyone.*

࿓࿓࿓

On our way back to the Ramada, I called Lisa and filled her in. It was her turn to be speechless. She would meet us at the hotel. When we arrived, the news crews and Taylor Hunt were waiting. With her microphone thrust out and her cameraman at her back, she asked, "Your reaction to the verdict?"

"The jurors got it right. I am continually amazed that twelve folks in the box, sworn to do the right thing, mostly get it right."

"Were you surprised?"

"I was, to the extent that the crime was so heinous and Durgeon was so unlikeable. But my surprise is tempered because the prosecutor left some holes in his case and failed to undertake a thorough and complete investigation." *I hope when Tice runs for reelection that his opponent uses that line. Maybe I'm not such a good winner.*

Just then, Lisa walked through the throng. I went to her and we embraced and walked arm in arm into the Ramada lobby, with Suzelle and Duke clearing the way.

ABOUT THE AUTHOR

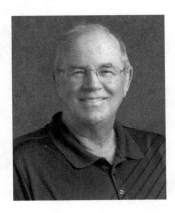

HARRY CALDWELL is a law professor at Pepperdine/Caruso School of Law. He teaches criminal procedure and trial advocacy. Professor Caldwell routinely represents death row inmates appealing their convictions before the California Supreme Court. He has co-authored several trial advocates textbooks as well as the critically acclaimed *Ladies and Gentlemen of the Jury* series of books. He resides in Southern California.

CPSIA information can be obtained
at www.ICGtesting.com
Printed in the USA
BVHW030904041021
618091BV00014B/301/J